Holiday Mishaps

Samantha Baca

A Steamy Collection of Holiday Novellas

Contains The Following Books:

Holidays Hijinks
Snow Place To Go
A Christmas Wish
A Very Merry Kissmas

Holiday Hijinks
Samantha Baca

One
Holly

"It's so beautiful up here," I said dreamily as I pressed my nose against the window to get a better look at the snow-covered forest surrounding us. "It's going to be such a romantic weekend."

I glanced over my shoulder at Henry, batting my eyes at him playfully, but his attention was laser-focused on the road in front of us, so he hadn't noticed.

Not that it was odd for him. He was always so uptight about everything; I rarely saw him relaxed and enjoying himself these days. I knew that he must be stressed with putting together such an elaborate plan to finally pop the question to me after five long years, so I was cutting him some slack— even if it felt like he was pulling further away by the day.

I was a city girl—born and raised—and rarely took the time to go on adventures in the mountains. When Henry suggested that we come up to his family's cabin for the weekend, I couldn't say no. I'd even gone to great lengths to google what one should pack for a *wilderness retreat*. It was disappointing when I got a handful of results leading me to sites full of flannel and long johns. How the hell was I supposed to make *that* look sexy?

"It's going to be cold," he replied, ignoring my comment about it being a romantic weekend.

Okay, okay, I like the secrecy bit. I'll just continue to pretend like I don't know he's going to ask me to marry him and make me the happiest—and richest—woman alive!

"Yeah, but the cabin has a heater, so we'll be fine."

I lifted my shoulders and let them fall. The loose neck of the ivory cowl neck sweater I was wearing slid to the side, exposing my shoulder. I had picked this one to wear on our drive out, along with my skinny jeans tucked neatly into the sexy knee-high boots I bought at the last minute. Henry shook his head when he saw my outfit, and I knew he must've been frustrated to have to wait that long before ripping it off of me.

When he didn't answer, I felt a slight tingle of dread creep down my spine.

"There is a heater, right?" I asked, turning to face him.

He glanced briefly at me before turning his attention back to the road.

"There's a fireplace."

My eyebrows shot up.

"And a heater. RIGHT?"

He rubbed his lips together the way he always did when he didn't want to tell me something.

"Henry Aaron Smith—you're taking me to a secluded cabin in the middle of the woods, and it doesn't even have a heater?!"

"I told you that it was a little *outdated*."

"Yeah, and I thought maybe that meant that your mom had some hideous curtains hung from the seventies or beat-up wood floors. You never said anything about there not being proper heat in the damn place." I turned and folded my arms over my chest, more frustrated with myself for not asking more questions before packing for this damn trip.

"You'll be fine, Holly. My dad grew up in this cabin. His parents did before that. It's not as bad as you're making it sound."

His tone was snappy, as if he was angry with me.

"Why haven't you guys fixed it up? I mean, you have the money to…"

I felt rude for asking, but it wasn't like Henry didn't constantly remind people of his family's empire and the wealth he'd been born into. I didn't know many of the details of how they came to be so well off, but I knew it had something to do with his grandparents, Texas, and a lot of oil. Like A LOT of oil.

"Why fix something that's not broken?" His hand gripped the steering wheel tighter as he slowly turned down another dirt road.

We were literally in the middle of nowhere with snowbanks at least ten feet tall on either side of the SUV. Even if I wanted to turn and run back to the city, I couldn't. I was officially stuck here with him—in a heatless cabin—until Monday.

We kept driving until the road curved, and he stopped in front of a log-looking cabin. He frowned when he noticed the other car parked in front of the garage.

"What's wrong?" I asked.

"My parents are here."

"What?" My head whipped around in panic, looking for them. "Did you invite them?"

He shook his head and grabbed his cell phone from the cupholder in the middle console.

"No, Holly, I didn't invite them. Apparently, they had the same idea as us."

I swallowed hard, nervous about seeing his parents. I'd met them a few times, but they never seemed to like me. We lived in Los Angeles, while they had a massive mansion in Beverly Hills. Needless to say, the holidays were usually spent with them at their house because they didn't like to *slum it* at mine. They never said that, but they didn't have to. Margaret, Henry's mom, had no problem wearing her emotions on her face, which usually gave way to what she was thinking.

"We better get inside before we freeze to death out here," Henry said sternly, climbing out before giving me a chance to process his words.

<u>Two</u>
Holly

We walked through the door, and I felt my stomach knot harder. His parents weren't in the living room, so Henry called out to let them know we were there. The last thing any of us needed right now was surprises that could traumatize us.

I lingered by the door, wrapping my arms around myself to try to get warm. It was freaking cold in here, and they hadn't even bothered to start a fire yet. Maybe they hadn't been there that long, or perhaps they didn't get as cold as I did.

I looked around, taking in the floor-to-ceiling windows that spanned around the small living room. Two leather couches sat in the middle, facing the TV mounted above the fireplace that wasn't lit. Was I bitter about it? Maybe.

Part of me wanted to take a tour through the rest of the cabin, but I stayed put until I knew where Margaret and Stan were. Henry was already looking for them, so I didn't need to.

I was busy browsing through the collection of books lining the bookshelf that was part of the entertainment center when Henry walked in with his parents in tow behind him.

"Mom, dad, you remember Holly," he said, though it sounded a bit forced. He raked a hand through his hair and forced a smile.

"Yes," Margaret said coldly, giving me a judgmental once over before turning to her husband. "Stan, why don't you and Henry go unload the vehicles? It's obvious none of us are getting back down the mountain before this storm hits, so we'll all have to figure out how to share this space *together*." She looked down her nose at me.

"I can help," I volunteered to Henry, not wanting to be left alone with his mom.

I knew that if he were going to propose, he probably wouldn't do so now with them hovering around us. It was a small cabin which meant we were all going to be on top of each other for the next few days.

"In those boots?" His mother rolled her eyes in Stan's direction, not bothering to hide it from me. "You'll fall and break your leg before you even get one bag out of the car. It's fine; I'll help them. You can just stay inside, where it's safe."

I felt my cheeks flame with embarrassment. At least the heat spreading through my body worked to warm me up for a few minutes before it passed.

The three of them went to the car and started unpacking. I was curious why they hadn't just pulled into the garage, where it was dry and not covered with snow, but what did I know? I was just a silly girl from the city who knew nothing about the wilderness.

It was over seven hours to drive to Hope Valley from Los Angeles, and now I was ready to pack up and head home. This was not how I wanted to spend the weekend—cooped up with people who couldn't stand me and a boyfriend who seemed more preoccupied with something he wouldn't talk to me about. I could be enjoying the weather in LA or working on getting new auditions. Lord knew I needed some if I was ever going to achieve my dream of being a movie star.

A few minutes later, the front door flew open, gaining speed as a gust of wind whipped past. Henry pushed inside, setting our luggage behind the couch before helping his mother. Her perfectly manicured nails struggled to keep hold of the bags in her hands before he grabbed them and relieved her of them.

Stan came in right as Henry slipped back outside to grab the rest. Aside from our suitcases, I had a few duffle bags that contained my makeup and bathroom stuff, and Henry had brought a few boxes full of groceries. I had offered to help, but he declined and said he would get things that would last—whatever that meant.

"Um, what room would you like us to take?" I asked as nicely as possible while Margaret lifted the handle to their hard-shell luggage and started pulling.

"Well, we haven't talked about that. We hadn't expected any guests, so I was planning to use the other bedroom for my craft stuff. I guess you guys can take the other room. It's through the kitchen."

She turned on her heel and took off down the hallway.

I muffled the groan that wanted to escape my lips and grabbed my luggage. There were only two doors in the kitchen, so I tried the first one, which ended up being a rather decently stocked pantry of canned goods and gallons of bottled water that lined the floor. I closed it and then opened the other door, gasping when I saw the *room* she was talking about.

It wasn't a room at all. It was the garage that someone had once started to convert to a bedroom but never finished. There were no windows, so I fumbled around, trying to find the light switch when I slipped off the step down that I hadn't seen.

My hands flew in the air as I landed hard on my ass. I let out a slew of curse words as my ass ached from the fall. There was no padding beneath me, just hard concrete.

I bit the inside of my cheek to keep from crying, but it didn't help. The pain was intense and radiated throughout my body. I took a deep, steadying breath and tried to stand up, only to realize that the heel of my boot had broken off in the process.

That was the final straw that broke the camel's back.

I let my head fall forward and covered my face with my hands as the tears started streaming down my face.

"What's wrong?" Henry asked, coming up behind me. He reached in and flicked on the lights.

I held the broken piece of my shoe in the air and kept crying.

"Yeah, well, I could have told you those were the wrong shoes to wear out here," he said before brushing past me and setting the rest of our luggage beside a rickety-looking futon.

I couldn't stop crying to tell him about the fall. It wasn't even just that; it was a combination of things that kept building. The way his mother acted toward me. The fact that his father hadn't said a single word to me. The way Henry had been the entire drive up. The crappy room we would be spending the next few days in when he'd promised me a romantic getaway at his family's cabin. Okay, so maybe he hadn't promised me any romance, but he also didn't forewarn me about what a shitshow this would be.

"The futon is kinda old, so we can decide who's going to sleep on it and who wants to take the couch," he offered, completely dismissing the fact that I was still sitting there crying. He finally looked down at me and then pointed to a small couch in the corner of the room that looked like it had seen better days.

I took one look at it and then cried harder.

"I don't know what you expected, Holly. It's not like we were planning a stay at some fancy resort or something."

I threw my hands in the air and let out a whoosh of air.

"I don't know what I expected either, *Henry*. You've been so distant and aloof with me that I have no idea what's going on. Don't sit there and act like I'm some princess who's throwing a fit about not staying in a five-star establishment. I was fine coming to the cabin with you. In fact, I was excited about it! But now that we're here—with *your parents*—I'm not feeling anything but irritated with how everyone is treating me!"

I knew that I was yelling and his parents could probably hear me, but I didn't care.

It was like something snapped inside him, and the grumpy Henry left.

"I'm sorry," he said softly, coming over and wrapping his arms around me. "I've been super stressed out with stuff at work this week, and it just caught up to me. I was hoping that this weekend would be the break that I needed to reset before the holidays. I didn't mean for it to start off this way, and I honestly had no idea that my parents would be here. Usually, they go to the ranch in Texas and spend the holidays there. I know that it sucks having to sleep in here, but we can try to make the best of it. If not, I can rearrange the living room, and we can sleep up there. It'll be much warmer since we can keep the fire going at night."

The corners of my lips turned up into a smile as I allowed my body to melt against his.

"That sounds like a plan, but what happens when I want to take advantage of you? We can't do *that* in the living room," I whispered playfully.

"No, we can't," he laughed. "But we can come in here for quickies, then go back to the living room."

"Deal," I giggled as he tickled my sides.

His hands slowly caressed my back and then dipped lower, hovering right above my ass when I winced in pain.

"What's wrong?" His eyebrows pulled together in concern.

"I fell and landed on my ass. That's how my heel broke." I held up the piece again to show him.

"Ouch, are you okay?"

"It hurts pretty bad. Definitely going to have a bruise."

"Let me see."

"What?" I pulled back and laughed at him. "I'm not going to show you my ass."

"Why not? I see it every time we have sex."

"Yeah, but that's different." I felt the blush creeping up my neck under the thickness of the sweater.

"You're so weird," he laughed but didn't push further. He let go and walked back to our luggage, opening his suitcase and pulling out the hoodie on top.

"So, how many bathrooms are there?" I asked, chewing my bottom lip as I prayed that he would say at least two.

"Just one."

I frowned. That sucked. I really wanted to soak in a long, hot bath, but I couldn't easily tie up the only bathroom for a few hours. That wouldn't be fair.

"I'm going to go see what my parents need help with and get the groceries unpacked."

He walked out and left me standing there, *nice Henry* gone just as quickly as he appeared.

HOLIDAY HIJINKS

<u>Three</u>
Holly

The fire crackled and roared as I curled up on the couch, tucking my feet beneath me. There was no need to wear shoes, but it was still too cold to go without socks. Now I understood why so many of those websites had thick, non-slip socks for sale. Easy to keep you warm without the risk of slipping and falling on hardwood floors because very few cabins would have carpet, given how much snow people would trek in from outside. Not that they had gone into that much detail, but Margaret had when she lectured me about the boots I had been wearing earlier.

We were all holed up in the small space in the living room, with Henry and me sharing the small loveseat while Margaret and Stan spread out on the oversized couch that had recliners. I already knew where I was sleeping tonight.

The conversation had been dull and pretty much one-sided at that. The sun was starting to set, casting a warm reddish-orange glow on the trees outside. My stomach growled, reminding me I hadn't eaten since the breakfast burrito I bought this morning.

"I'm going to go make dinner," I announced, getting up and not bothering to wait for anyone to object.

I wasn't a terrible cook, but I wasn't an award-winning chef, either.

When Henry and I first started dating, he did most of the cooking, and I simply enjoyed it. I was barely eighteen and had just moved out of my parent's house, while he was twenty-three and had just graduated from college. We were as different as different could be, but that was what I always thought pulled us together. You know, opposites attract and all that.

After three months of dating, Henry asked me to move in with him. It was definitely quicker than I had imagined us moving, but I was also in between roommates and needed to find more stable housing. Living with Henry was easy, and he turned out to be one of the best roommates I'd had. Everything since then seemed to fall naturally in place until recently.

I rummaged through the fridge, looking for something to cook but unsure of what Henry had brought and what was his parents. Deciding that I would use this weekend to get in his parents' good graces, I wanted to make dinner for all of us. I was going to be their future daughter-in-law, so it wouldn't hurt to start trying to impress them now.

I preheated the oven and then began prepping the ingredients. It was a dish I'd made for Henry plenty of times, and if he liked it, surely his parents would too. Granted, it was no filet mignon, but it wasn't inedible either. Whether or not I could ever live up to their expectations was still beyond me.

The oven beeped, letting me know it was ready. I slid the foil-covered casserole dish in and closed the door. There wasn't much else that needed to be done, but I still wasn't ready to go back into the living room and sit with them. It was awkward, and I had difficulty getting comfortable on the couch without room to spread out. Not only that, but I had to sit in a way that put a lot of pressure on my hips and ass, which were still sore.

Suddenly remembering I had brought wine, I headed into the garage and rummaged through my bags until I found the bottles I had packed. There were a few that I thought Henry and I would drink with dinner, a few that were planned for our romantic late-night lovemaking, and a bottle of champagne that I added, just in case Henry forgot to bring one to celebrate our engagement with.

I loaded my arms with the bottles and then made my way back into the kitchen.

No one had bothered to ask if they could help with anything, which honestly didn't upset me. I preferred solitude right now, anyway.

I took the liberty of putting the bottles in the fridge to let them chill while I set the table for dinner.

I knew that it shouldn't matter to me that much whether his parents liked me or not, but I literally had nothing else to do with my time than try to get them to. Leisurely, I looked around the kitchen, gathering the things that I needed. I wiped down the table and then found a pile of linens in the pantry that were tucked inside a box.

Choosing to make dinner more to their liking, I grabbed a deep maroon-colored tablecloth and then draped a lace table runner on top of it. It was an odd shape that was narrow at one end and flared out at the other, but I tucked in it and made it work the best I could.

Then I grabbed some wine glasses from the cabinet, as well as some glasses for ice water, and washed the dust off of them. There weren't many dishes to choose from, so I picked the solid white set since it looked less breakable than the fine China sitting next to it.

Once the table was set, I grabbed the loaf of French bread I found on the counter and began cutting it. Dinner already smelled amazing and I couldn't wait to sit down and eat.

I debated which wine to open for dinner but decided to go with a pinot grigio since it would pair well with the chicken. I filled a glass for each person and then went to the freezer to get ice for the water. I frowned when I pushed the button and nothing came out. I opened the door and peeked inside, looking to see if I could find an ice bin instead.

The bin was empty, and I realized that the water line probably wasn't set up for it. I found a small bag of ice cubes and hoped they would work. Once the glasses had enough ice, I grabbed one of the gallon jugs of water out of the pantry and filled them.

I stepped back, impressed with the beautiful display, given there were limited supplies.

The timer on the oven dinged, so I grabbed some potholders and pulled the casserole out, setting it on a trivet in the middle of the table. Next to it, I set down the cutting board with the French bread and a bottle of balsamic oil.

My nerves were at an all-time high as sweat dotted my forehead.

"Dinner's ready," I announced as I walked into the living room and held my hands in front of me.

Stan faked enthusiasm as he plastered on a smile and stood up while Margaret didn't bother to try. She followed her husband into the kitchen, leaving me alone with Henry for a few seconds before we joined them.

"It smells delicious," he whispered, walking behind me as he led me in with his hands on my shoulders.

"They're going to hate it," I muttered right before we went through the door.

<u>Four</u>
Holly

"This is…. Lovely." Margaret stared at the display in front of her, not bothering to serve herself.

"Thank you," I said nervously and took my seat. "It's this chicken and rice casserole that Henry loves." I reached over and squeezed his hand, hoping he would jump in and talk it up.

"Chicken?" his mother asked, her eyebrow attempting to lift but permanently frozen in place from the constant supply of Botox.

I nodded slowly, unsure of what the problem was.

She gave me a cold smile and looked at Henry with a look that only a mother could give their child. It was the *what the hell were you thinking* look that my own mother had given me several times in my life.

Henry winced and closed his eyes.

"My mom is a vegetarian."

My eyes widened in horror as I stared at the dish. Not only had I shredded the chicken and spread it throughout, but I also cooked it in chicken broth and then used cream of chicken soup for the casserole mixture.

"I'm so sorry, I didn't know."

She lifted her glass of wine and lifted it to her lips.

"It's fine. Just as I'm sure you didn't know that Stan is twenty-seven years sober and doesn't drink."

I felt my heart sink and looked at the glass of wine in front of him.

"Don't worry, dear; I'll relieve you of that. It looks like I'll be drinking my calories tonight instead." Margaret reached over, took the glass from him, and then set it in front of her as she took another large drink from hers.

"I really am sorry," I apologized, looking between them. "I had no idea."

I turned my attention back to Margaret, feeling bad that I'd ruined dinner, and now she had nothing to eat unless she cooked something herself.

"There's bread if you want to start with that. I can check to see what else there is and make you something," I offered.

"I don't eat bread," she spat out as if I had somehow insulted her—which I probably did.

Henry said nothing as he served himself and then passed the dish to his father. Both of them took heaping portions while his mom sat there drinking her wine and staring at the tablecloth.

"Where did you get all of this?" she asked, pointing to the table runner.

"Oh, I, um, found it in a box in the pantry with a few other linens. I hope you don't mind."

I was in the middle of dishing some of the casserole out onto my plate when she spoke.

"Absolutely I mind," she scoffed, reaching out to run her fingers over the delicate lace fabric. "This isn't a table runner; it was my mother's wedding veil."

The metal serving spoon slipped out of my hand, dropping the chicken casserole onto my plate and sending a spatter of food onto the wedding veil.

"I had no idea," I whispered, covering my mouth with my hand. This was turning into a total and utter disaster.

"Here, I can take it off real quick," I offered, standing up and bumping my glass of wine. I watched in horror as it tipped to the side before Henry's hand reached out and grabbed it.

"Oh, for the love of God, I've had enough." Margaret grabbed both glasses of wine and pushed away from the table before leaving the kitchen.

I covered my face with my hands in embarrassment while the guys continued eating as if nothing had happened. My world was ending before me, and they were stuffing their faces.

I heard a chair scraping against the floor and opened my eyes. Stan's plate still had food, but his water glass was empty. I knew he was heading to the sink to refill it, so I stood up to stop him.

"Here, let me refill that for you," I offered, trying my best to smile despite everything that had happened.

With curious eyes, he handed me his glass and watched as I slid past Henry to open the fridge. I grabbed the gallon of water and started to refill it when I heard a quiet gasp escape Henry's lips.

I spun around and looked between them, trying to figure out what I had done wrong now.

"Where did you get that?" Henry asked quietly.

The words were stuck in my throat, so I pointed behind them to the pantry.

Henry set his fork down, closed his eyes, and took a deep breath.

"What?" I asked worriedly. "What did I do wrong this time?"

"That's our emergency stash. When the weather gets terrible, it can be hard to get into town for supplies," Stan explained.

"Of course," I sighed and handed him the glass of emergency water. "I'm so sorry. Again, I didn't know."

He pulled his lips into a thin line that was supposed to be a smile but wasn't. After that, we all ate in silence. Henry insisted that he would handle the dishes, which was probably the best idea at this point.

Deciding that I couldn't face his parents right now, I retreated to the cold garage and added a few more layers of clothing to keep from losing a limb to frostbite.

It was going to be a long weekend.

Five
Holly

"Are you going to hide in here all night?" Henry asked, leaning against the doorframe but not bothering to come into the freezing cold garage.

I wrapped my arms tighter around myself and felt my teeth chattering.

"It's not like anyone misses me," I snorted and rolled my eyes.

"That's not true. I do."

I pinned him with a look that called him on his bullshit.

He crossed the room and sat down on the futon beside me.

"I'm sorry that today was so rough and eventful. I should have been in the kitchen helping you make dinner. I just didn't trust my parents not to come in and harass you while you were cooking, so I thought I was keeping the calm by keeping them out of your way. I let you down so much today, and I hate that."

"It's okay," I said softly as he reached over and pulled me closer to him.

I yelped in pain, and he immediately let go and looked down at my ass.

"You should go soak in a hot bath," he offered, his eyes softening as he looked up at me.

"Thanks, but I don't think so," I laughed. "There's no way I'm tying up the only bathroom for a few hours. I'll *never* live that down, along with everything else that happened today."

"Don't be so hard on yourself; they were honest mistakes."

"I'm sure your parents don't think so. I tried to feed your mom meat, gave your dad alcohol, and dropped chicken casserole on your grandmother's wedding veil. Why was that in the pantry anyway?"

He tilted his head back and laughed.

"I have no idea. But I'll go talk to them and let them know you're going to soak for a bit. Grab some of your bath stuff, and I'll meet you in the bathroom."

I was reluctant to take him up on the offer, but the way my body was aching, I didn't have much of a choice.

He headed back inside while I rummaged through my duffle bags and collected the items I wanted.

When I found him in the living room, he was talking to his parents, who got up the moment they saw me. They walked past without saying a word and closed their bedroom door.

"They're going to retire to their room early tonight," he explained though I could read the words he didn't say all over his face. *They hate you. They wish you weren't here. You're inconveniencing them.*

"Okay," I whispered, feeling my throat tighten with emotion.

"Let me show you how to work the tub."

I was going to object and tell him that I knew how to use one, but when I followed him into the bathroom, I realized that this wasn't an ordinary bathtub. It was a large soaking one with jets and different settings with an LED touch-screen to control them.

He turned on the water and explained the different features, but all I could think about at that moment was how badly I had to pee. I had gotten so caught up with everything earlier that I didn't realize I hadn't gone since the gas station we stopped at right before we got to the cabin.

I squeezed my thighs together and squirmed, hoping he would leave me alone so I could pee. As if sensing my discomfort, he glanced at me doing the potty dance and nodded.

"Just call me if you need help with the settings. I've already programmed it with what I think you'll like, but I can come back if you want to change anything."

"Okay, thanks."

Once he was gone, I closed the door and locked it before rushing to the toilet.

After what felt like the longest pee in the world, I dipped my hand into the running water to test the temperature. Henry had set it perfectly where it was hot enough to melt my troubles away but not hot enough to burn me.

I opened the bag of coconut Epsom salts, sprinkled some in, and then set out the loofah and bottle of body wash I had just bought for the trip. There were towels hanging by the tub, but I didn't trust that they weren't special or reserved for the Queen or something, so I opened the large cabinets on the far end of the wall and grabbed a basic-looking towel from the pile. Odds were it was a safe bet if it was mixed with the others.

Slowly I climbed into the oversized tub and sank into the water, closing my eyes as it warmed the chill I hadn't been able to shake since we got here.

I grabbed my phone and turned on one of the audiobooks I had been listening to while resting my head against the pillow Henry had set up for me. The water felt amazing and was just what the doctor ordered.

I didn't know how long I had my eyes closed, but suddenly, the room was silent as my audiobook ended. I swiped my finger and checked the text notifications that had come in from Henry. Usually, I heard them, but I must have been so relaxed and out of it that I completely missed them. I checked the time and noticed they were sent half an hour ago.

Henry: Hey, how much longer do you think you'll be? My mom needs to use the restroom.

Henry: Sorry, I don't want to rush you, but my mom really needs to go. I told them to go before you got in, but they didn't listen for whatever reason.

Henry: Don't worry about it. She went outside. Enjoy your bath.

I read the last one again and cringed. Not only had I cooked a meal she couldn't eat, but I also used mother's veil as a table runner, and now I'd forced her to pop a squat in the woods. This wasn't going to be good.

Trying to move as quickly as possible, I grabbed the towel

and wrapped it around my body before stepping out of the tub. I looked down for a plug to pull and couldn't find anything. Then I looked at the control panel and assumed it was on there, but now wasn't the time to break their fancy tub by button mashing. I'd just leave it for Henry to take care of so I didn't screw anything else up.

I looked around for the pajamas I'd picked out but frowned when I remembered that I had left them on the futon. Not having any other options, I quickly put on the clothes I was wearing earlier and hung the towel on the rack mounted to the back of the door.

I hoped to sneak out without running into his parents, but luck didn't seem to be in my favor today. As soon as I opened the door, his mother came out of their room and glared at me.

My mouth opened to say something but snapped shut when I realized I didn't know what to say.

Henry came around the corner at that moment and seemed startled to see me.

"Hey, I was just coming to check on you," he said happily, avoiding the look his mom was giving him.

"Sorry, I didn't hear my phone and lost track of time."

"No worries, it's fine. I'm going to use the restroom real quick."

"Oh, do you mind draining the tub? I wasn't sure how to do it and didn't want to break something," I said quietly, tucking my chin to my chest.

"Sure, I'll take care of it. I'll be done in a few minutes, mom."

"Don't rush on my account. I'll be waiting for the hot water to return."

She turned on her heel and shut the bedroom door on us.

Henry tried to smile, but neither of us felt it. I left him to his business and went to the garage to take care of mine.

Just as I expected, the pajamas I picked earlier were still sitting on top of my suitcase. I felt silly now for wearing them, but when I packed, I had expected it to be just Henry and me. I also thought I would be happily engaged by now, so I didn't bother to pack warm or comfy—I packed sexy.

I picked up the black lace lingerie and matching robe and held it up. There was absolutely no way I was going to wear that. I hadn't even paid attention to it when I pulled it out earlier; I was just too excited about the bath that I didn't think about anything else.

I opened my suitcase and looked around for something decent to wear. His parents had already deemed me to be incompetent, and the last thing I wanted was to prove them right.

There weren't many options, given it was a short weekend trip. I had a few pairs of jeans, some bulky sweaters, a couple of tank tops to wear underneath them, and then sexy lingerie. It wasn't going to be comfortable sleeping in jeans, but then again, it would be much less comfortable if his parents spotted me in the crotchless underwear I brought to seduce their son.

I sighed and got dressed, tucking the lingerie into the bottom of the suitcase, so I didn't accidentally pull it out again.

Henry was sitting on the larger couch when I went to the living room. I looked around for his parents, but they were nowhere to be found. Thankfully.

He patted the spot beside him, so I gently sat down, making sure not to put too much pressure on my swollen backside.

"Did the bath help any?" he asked, brushing a strand of blonde hair from my face.

"It did," I smiled. "But I feel terrible for taking so long in there. I completely lost track of time."

He kissed my forehead, then looked back at the TV and flipped through the channels with the remote in his other hand.

"Don't worry about it. It's not a big deal."

"Tell that to your mother," I bit out sarcastically. "She had to pee in the woods, and then I used all the hot water."

"It comes with the territory. She knows that."

"Yeah, but if I weren't here, she wouldn't have to worry about either."

He didn't respond, which was probably for the better. The last thing I wanted to do was keep obsessing over how much Margaret didn't like me.

We watched some sports channel for a bit until Henry yawned and lifted his arm from around my shoulders.

"I think I'm going to call it a night," he announced.

"Okay." I started to get up but stopped when he frowned at me.

"What are you doing?" he asked.

"Getting up so you can go to bed."

I looked at the couch I was sitting on, wondering if he had changed his mind about sleeping in there. I really, really hoped he didn't. I couldn't stand the thought of sleeping on the hard futon in the freezing-cold garage.

"You're fine," he laughed. "I'll sleep on the other couch."

"But it's way too small. You won't fit comfortably. I can take that one, and you can sleep on this one."

He walked over to the other couch, removed the cushions, and then pulled a cloth handle that released a pull-out bed. It was small and definitely wouldn't fit both of us, but it was decent-sized for him.

"Oh," I laughed. "I didn't expect that to be in there."

"I used to sleep on this couch a lot as a kid. It's pretty comfy, actually."

I smiled and looked at the couch I was sitting on, wondering what the most comfortable position would be. I figured we could both use one of the recliners and sleep there, but now that I had the entire couch to myself, it looked comfier to lie across it.

 Henry grabbed us some blankets and found a pillow for me to use. I knew that once he was ready for bed, that was it. So, I said goodnight to him, then got situated on the couch with one of the books I'd decided to try from the bookshelf. There were a lot of non-fiction ones about success and building your empire, but there were also a few older romance-looking ones tucked into the corner.

The fire put out a surprising amount of heat but started to die down right before I fell asleep. Not wanting us to get cold, I grabbed a few logs from the wooden basket next to the fireplace and tossed them in, just as I had seen Henry do earlier.

Satisfied and proud of doing something right for once, I got comfortable on the couch and drifted asleep.

I woke up to the sound of someone clearing their throat and blinked a few times to clear the sleep from my eyes.

Standing across from me was Stan. Beat red, looking more uncomfortable than I'd ever seen anyone before, Stan.

I struggled to sit up and felt the chill on my skin when the blanket slid down. At some point, I must've gotten too hot last night and taken my sweater off. It was tossed on the floor in front of me.

I was about to say something, but then I heard Henry shift on his bed. He sat up, rubbed the sleep from his eyes, and then his jaw dropped in disbelief.

I followed where his eyes dropped and found that my left tit had popped out of my tank top and was hanging freely for everyone to see.

Lovely. Just freaking lovely.

<u>Six</u>
Holly

I spent the majority of the morning hiding out in the garage as I tried to avoid seeing Henry's parents after the whole tit-gate scandal this morning. I was mortified the moment I realized what had happened and fled the room before anyone could say anything.

An hour had passed, and Henry hadn't bothered to come check on me yet. He sent a few text messages, but other than that—nothing.

I couldn't blame him; I mean, I flashed his very prim and proper father my breast as if I were some girl trying to get beads at Mardi Gras. I had already embarrassed him more than once, but this time it took the cake.

There was the sound of voices outside, and I sighed a breath of relief that they were all gone for now. I pulled on my only other pair of shoes—also knee-high boots with stiletto heels, but in brown leather instead of black—and headed to the kitchen.

I was starving but I wasn't about to cook for everyone again. Hell, I wasn't even going to cook for myself. I rummaged through the bags of nonperishable groceries Henry had brought but didn't unpack and found a box of organic energy bars he loved.

Knowing he wouldn't miss one, I took it out of the wrapper and quickly scarfed it down. I looked around for a coffee pot but not finding anything. Before I could look further, I heard the front door open, and voices floated through. I finished chewing my bite quickly, cursing when I accidentally bit the inside of my cheek, and then swallowed.

I rounded the corner to the living room at the same time Stan was heading toward the bathroom. I stepped to the side, moving out of his way, my face blushing red when I remembered the unfortunate incident from earlier. I didn't have to ask whether Margaret had heard about it, given the daggers she was shooting at me at the moment.

Henry sat down on the small couch he slept on last night and motioned for me to join him. Before I sat down, I noticed the fire was dwindling.

"Do you want me to add another log to the fire?" I offered, feeling the heat of his mother's glare on the back of my head.

"I can do it," he said, getting up.

"I know how to do it," I said flatly, blowing out a breath of frustration. "I did it last night after you fell asleep and nothing terrible happened."

I heard his mom clear her throat and ignored it.

"Okay, sure."

I smiled and turned around, ignoring the way my fingers

trembled as I reached into the basket to grab another log.

Henry jumped forward, holding his hand out to stop me.

"What are you doing?!"

I pulled back in surprise and looked at him. *Had we not just talked about this?*

"I'm adding a log to the fire…" I said slowly, just in case he was having trouble processing things this morning without coffee.

He pinched the bridge of his nose and closed his eyes.

"Please tell me you didn't use those logs for the fire last night."

I looked at them and then at the other pile stacked tightly and piled high in a hole in the wall beside the fireplace.

I could feel my heart hammering in my chest.

"Holly," he pressed. Standing up to join me in front of the fire. "Which logs did you use last night?"

I discreetly pointed in the direction of the logs in the basket.

"What did I do wrong?" I whispered, not wanting to draw his mother's attention any more than I had already.

She stood up behind me and pointed at the logs.

"Those aren't for the fire. They're logs that have had names and special dates carved into them from many generations." She smugly looked down into the basket and shook her head. "At least they *were*."

She left the room, and I let out the shaky breath I'd been holding.

"Henry, I'm—"

He lifted his hand to stop me.

I pressed my lips together and closed my eyes. When I opened them again, Henry was gone.

Twenty minutes passed without anyone returning to the living room, so I grabbed Henry's car keys and went outside to get some fresh air. If anything, I could sit in the SUV and listen to music. At least I wouldn't be in anyone's way, and there was nothing I could destroy.

I stepped outside and gasped at the bitter cold that nipped at my nose. I definitely didn't pack enough warm clothes for this weather. Thankfully we were spending our time inside, warm by the fire that was burning the precious memories that had been engraved onto the logs I had so absentmindedly thrown into the fire.

I walked around, enjoying the way the snow crunched beneath my heels, but reminded myself to be careful that I didn't slip and fall. The last thing I needed right now was broken bones or a trip to a hospital, given that I couldn't imagine one was close by. I scanned the area around me and felt an eerie chill when I realized that there was *nothing* close by. Not even another cabin if we needed help.

While I had taken the time to google what to wear in the wilderness, I hadn't bothered looking up what kind of animals to expect. There were large prints in the snow on the side of the house that seemed to go deep into the woods. Whatever it was, I was pretty sure I didn't want to meet it up close and personal.

Deciding that I'd already roamed too far, I turned to head back inside when I heard voices on the other side of the house. I stepped lightly and watched my footing until I was close enough to listen to what they were saying.

"What are you even doing with her, son?" Stan asked, his words sending knives straight to my heart. "I know you've been with her for a while, but you can't honestly tell me that you see yourself settling down and starting a life with her."

"I don't know," Henry answered. "Things have been rough for a few months now, and I thought that if I brought her up here for a weekend away that it might be the reset that we needed."

Reset? What in the world was he talking about?

I stepped closer, pulling down branches of the tree in front of me so I could hear better.

"I think you need more than a weekend."

"I know. I just didn't want to give up on us so easily, you know? It's been five years, dad. How did I not see that it wasn't working for me before now?"

A tear slid down my cheek and froze before it could make it all the way down.

"You've been busy with work and setting up your future. Sure, Holly has been fun, and I'm sure it's been nice having her at your house for some companionship, but she's not wife material. Just look at all the blunders she's made in the twenty-four hours she's been here. You can do better, I hate to say it."

"Yeah, I know." Henry exhaled heavily. "I actually met someone at work. I've been trying not to act on the chemistry between us, but it's hard not to when I don't feel the same heat between Holly and me anymore. It's like whatever we had when we first started dating has just fizzled and died. We've been together so long, but I can't imagine spending the rest of my life like this—with someone who will never live up to our family's standards."

"We have a reputation to uphold," Stan agreed firmly. "It would suit you well to find someone more within our class, so to speak."

"I don't know how I'm going to end it with Holly without her losing her mind. I guess maybe I brought her up here to buy some time. Give her one last weekend together before I break up with her."

"Is she going home for Christmas?"

"I doubt it. She doesn't talk to her family anymore, which has made it harder for me to do this. I know how much she clings to me and what she thinks we have together. It's like she's a frail person who can't function independently without someone holding their hand."

"Well, I can't help with that. But my recommendation is to rip the band-aid off now. Do it before you get back to the city. Then you can come spend Christmas with your mom and me in Texas on the ranch."

"I didn't even get her a gift yet," Henry said with a lack of emotion. "I know she's had her shopping done for months, but I haven't bothered looking for her. Maybe I knew all along that we wouldn't be together for Christmas?"

My body trembled as I stood there and listened. In an instant, the world around me started to crumble.

Here I had thought that he was bringing me up for a romantic weekend getaway so he could propose to me when in reality, he brought me here to see if there was anything worth trying to save before he broke up with me.

I turned to leave, having heard enough when I tripped over a low tree branch and snapped it. The sound was loud enough to get Henry and Stan's attention as they whipped around and caught me.

"Holly—" Henry said, his face turning red with embarrassment.

"Don't." I held my hand up. "If you want to break up with me, fine. I'm gone. I deserve better than this, anyway. Maybe you'll actually be able to satisfy the girl at work because you sure as hell haven't been hitting the mark with me."

I knew it was a low blow, but I didn't care at that point. It wasn't like he'd tried to spare my feelings, even though he didn't know I was listening.

He took a few steps toward me, but I shook my head and stormed off. There was nothing left to say—he'd already said it all; he just didn't know I had heard him.

What was I going to do anyway? Beg him to reconsider? Ask him to love me again when apparently he had already fallen out of love with me? He'd admitted that he had already met someone who gave him something I didn't—a spark. Chemistry. There was nothing left to try to save, and we both knew it.

I still had Henry's keys to his SUV in my pocket, so I dug them out, unlocked it, and climbed inside. I didn't give it a second thought as I started the engine and put it in drive.

The window was covered with snow and ice, which made it hard to see anything in front of me. But I didn't have time to stop and worry about scraping the ice off. The last thing

I wanted right now was to see Henry or his parents. I drove slowly, praying that I didn't hit anything as I cranked the heater up to full blast and turned the defrosters on.

Things were going okay as I gripped the wheel tightly and shivered against the cold leather seat. I didn't want to turn the seat warmers on until after I could get the windows cleared, so that meant I was going to freeze my ass off for a few minutes.

Thankfully I was in the middle of the woods and didn't have to worry about other vehicles right now. Soon a small patch of the window was clear at the bottom, so I leaned down and kept driving now that I could see what was in front of me.

I don't know how far I'd gotten before more than half of the window was clear, but I was happy that I could see and that there was no sign of Henry coming after me. Not that he had any reason to—this was what he wanted, after all.

My stomach turned, and I started crying again, trying to wipe the tears away as quickly as possible so they didn't blur my vision. I needed to focus on driving so I could get the hell out of there.

I was finally gaining some confidence in handling the SUV in the terrible weather, even with the snow falling faster than I could clear it with the wiper blades. I held my breath and kept my foot over the brake in case I needed it. Suddenly, a large animal darted out in front of me, and instead of hitting the brake, my foot tapped the gas. Realizing my mistake, I quickly reached over and slammed on the brakes, not remembering that I was technically driving on a sheet of ice.

There was no traction as the SUV spun wildly out of

control. I pulled the wheel in every direction I could to keep the vehicle on the road but watched in horror as it plummeted down the side of a hill and straight into a tree.

<u>Seven</u>
Blake

I was busy splitting logs for firewood when I heard the sound of metal crunching in the distance. Luna's head whipped up, and I knew she heard it too.

"Let's go check it out." I set my ax down on the stump and started walking with her leading the way.

We walked a few miles with the snow whipping around me. I pulled the beanie down lower on my head and adjusted the insulated face covering I had on. I followed the sound of the horn blaring and discovered an expensive SUV stuck headfirst into a large pine tree.

I circled around to the driver's side and found a mess of blonde hair covering the steering wheel.

I knocked on the window, hoping they weren't dead. I really didn't feel like dealing with that today.

A few seconds passed, and nothing.

I pulled my glove off and knocked louder.

Suddenly the head lifted, and a very dazed looking—yet beautiful—woman looked up at me.

I used my finger to motion for her to roll the window down.

Once it was at least halfway, I leaned in and spoke loudly to try to be heard over the horn.

"Do you think you can lean back so the horn will stop blaring?" I yelled, startling Luna beside me.

She seemed a bit dazed and confused but did as I asked.

I shook my head, trying to get my ears to stop ringing. Not wanting to scare her, I reached up and pulled the face mask off so she could see that I wasn't some creepy killer from one of those horror flicks everyone obsessed over.

"Are you okay?" I asked, pulling her attention back to me.

"You look like a lumbersnack," she whispered, her brown eyes dancing with delight.

"I'm sorry, a what?"

"A lumbersnack."

"What's that?" I asked though I wasn't sure I wanted to know.

"It's like a lumberjack that you want to eat. You know, like a gingerbread man. But yummier."

I raised an eyebrow, wondering how bad of a concussion she had.

"Do you think you can turn off the car?" I asked, ignoring her lumbersnack comments.

"Huh?"

"Turn off the car." I held my hand up and made the motion for her. I would've climbed in on the passenger side and done it myself if the whole front end wasn't crunched up like an accordion. It was going to be a big enough challenge getting her out of the vehicle.

She reached over and turned the ignition off and then leaned back against the seat again.

"Can you unlock the doors?"

She seemed to be a little more aware than a few minutes ago and did what I asked without any additional demonstration from me.

I grabbed the handle and tried to pull but didn't have any luck. The frame was completely bent, and the doors had been jammed.

"I'm not going to be able to get you out through the door, so you're going to have to climb out of the window. Okay?"

Her eyes widened as she stared at the small opening.

"You should be able to roll it down the rest of the way," I added. "I'll help you out."

"Okay," she said nervously and finished rolling it down.

"Are you hurt at all?" I asked, not trusting that she would really know whether or not she was. If anything, she would be in shock, and injuries wouldn't make themselves obvious until later.

"I don't know. I don't think so."

"Do you think you can lift yourself enough to get your upper body out? I can pull you through."

She looked down at her feet and wiggled them free.

"I think so."

I waited for her to get situated and then stepped to the side as she stuck her head through the window. She seemed uncertain as she reached for my shoulders and allowed me to hold her waist as I gently pulled her through.

Once she was out, I kept my grip on her until she could stand on her own. She smiled a nervous smile and stepped away, her knees instantly buckling beneath her.

I reached out and grabbed her, looking down to find the culprit for her falling.

"Son of a bitch," she grumbled, looking down at the bottom of her boot that was missing the heel. "Not another one."

I eyed her suspiciously, wondering why anyone in their right mind would be wearing boots like that in this kind of weather.

"I take it this has happened before?" I asked, my arm still wrapped around her small waist.

"Unfortunately, yes. Guess I won't be buying that brand again," she scoffed. "Someone is going to get a bad review when I get home."

"Okay," I said, ready to change the subject. "Do you have anything in the car that you need before we go?"

She shook her head no.

"Where are we going?" she asked.

"Back to my place."

She held a hand up and placed it firmly on my chest.

"What? I'm not going back to your place with you."

I frowned.

"Why not?"

"Because I'm not that kind of girl, you asshole."

I sighed heavily and shifted my weight. It was getting colder as the temperatures dipped with the heavy snow that was falling.

"I don't care what kind of girl you think you are, but you're about to be a frozen dead girl if we don't get moving."

I let go of her, making sure she was steady on her feet for a few minutes as I put my face mask back on. She wasn't dressed for this weather, and it was at least a few miles away from my cabin. Carrying her back would be enough of a workout to keep me warm, so I shrugged out of my flannel coat and held it out to her.

She was shivering and looked terrified as she took it.

"Look, we don't have time to stand here and talk about this. That storm is moving in quickly, and if we don't get back to my cabin, neither of us are going to survive the night. So, we need to get going now."

"But I don't know you," she whispered.

"Then I guess it's either trust me not to kill you or risk surviving out here."

Luna chose that moment to howl in the distance, striking fear in the woman's eyes.

"Alright, fine. I guess I have no choice," she said stubbornly.

"Put the coat on. It'll keep you warm."

"I'll be okay, thank you."

I worked my jaw back and forth in frustration.

"Just put the damn thing on," I growled.

Her eyes widened, and I thought maybe my tone had gotten to her. But then I followed where she was looking and spotted Luna.

"There's a wolf," she hissed without moving her mouth.

Luna moved forward, her eyes fixated on the woman. She let out a low snarl and showed her teeth.

"Sit, Luna."

I kept my eyes on the woman, knowing that Luna would immediately obey me.

"That was amazing," she whispered. "How did you do that."

"Basic dog commands. We need to get going."

"That's not a dog," she stuttered, looking down at Luna, who was still sitting.

"I'm going to carry you back," I said, ignoring her rambling about how huge Luna was. "We don't have much time—"

"I can walk," she interrupted.

I looked down at her shoes and then met her eyes.

"Fine," she sighed and looked away.

I debated on the easiest way to get her back without causing either of us too much strain.

"Ready?" I asked.

"As ready as I'm ever going to be."

I nodded, then lifted her over my shoulder and commanded
Luna to follow me.

 It was a long trek back, but I kept my pace and adjusted
her a few times as needed. Once we got within a few yards,
I set her on her feet and slowed down so she could keep up.
The storm had already dropped at least six inches while I
was gone, and it was just the beginning.

50

Eight
Holly

"How's your head feel?" he asked, holding out a bottle of water and two Tylenol.

"Like I whacked it on a steering wheel," I joked, taking them from him. I took a sip and tossed back the pills, hoping they would numb something—anything would work at this point.

He sat on the arm of the leather chair across from where I was sitting on the couch, studying me carefully.

"So, what happened out there?"

I closed my eyes and willed myself not to cry. He was a stranger who was stuck with an injured crazy woman he didn't even know their name.

"I was trying to leave."

"Leave? Where?"

"I don't know. Anywhere but where I was."

"Why?"

I sucked in a deep breath and exhaled slowly through my nose.

"I was spending the weekend with my boyfriend at his family's cabin, and everything that could go wrong did. And now I'm stuck in some stranger's cabin with a possible concussion and no way to get home."

"I'm Blake."

"Holly."

He stood up and walked into the kitchen, which was part of the living room. The cabin appeared to be close to the same size as Henry's family's but felt larger, with the two rooms combined as one instead of separated. There were wood floors, though these ones were more scuffed up, and the rugs appeared to be used and not just decorative.

Large windows framed the room with minimal decoration on the walls. It was obvious that he lived here and wasn't caught up in the appearance of his living space but in the functionality.

I leaned back against the cushion and pulled my feet under me to warm up. He'd helped me out of my boots as soon as we got in and left them on the mat by the door to dry, though he said I wouldn't be going anywhere any time soon with the storm that was rolling in.

The snow fell heavily around us in a blanket so thick that you couldn't see the trees through it. It would be a beautiful image if I weren't stranded and inconveniencing the lumbersnack who had to carry me for miles back to his cabin. If I wasn't making life hard for Henry and his family, then I was apparently destined to do it to Blake.

He returned a few minutes later with a coffee mug and extended it to me.

I carefully grabbed it, making sure not to spill as I sat up.

"It's hot chocolate," he announced as he watched me stare into the cup.

"You made me hot chocolate." I chewed the inside of my cheek to keep from crying.

"Yeah…"

He lifted his mug to his lips and took a drink.

He didn't strike me as the kind of guy who drank hot chocolate. Maybe it was the way he sat on the arm of the chair again like he was too manly to sit down and get comfortable. Or perhaps it was the way his hand wrapped tightly around the mug with little effort, showing the strength in his hands. It could've been his rugged good looks or his strong jawline that was covered in a neatly trimmed beard. Either way, it was his dark eyes that studied me under his thick brows that made me nervous. He had yet to take his beanie off his head, but I would be willing to bet that he had unruly hair that begged to be touched.

I shook my head to clear my thoughts and took a sip.

"Thank you for the hot chocolate," I said, holding it between both hands as I let it warm me up.

He gave me a curt nod but said nothing before tossing the rest of his back and emptying the cup.

I raised my eyebrows in surprise, wondering how in the hell he didn't burn himself.

"I'm going to go get more wood for the fire."

He got up and took his cup to the kitchen sink before snapping his fingers down by his side.

The dog that had startled me in the woods got up from the rug she was lying on and followed him out the door before he pulled it shut behind them.

Once I was alone, I tried to relax and let everything that had happened in the last forty-eight hours process through my mind. It was still boggling to me that I had left for the trip so excited to go home an engaged woman, and now I was stranded with a stranger and unofficially single.

The headache that started a while ago was getting worse, and I began to feel nauseous. I knew it was likely because I hadn't eaten anything since the protein bar I'd stolen from Henry this morning, but I wasn't about to make myself at home and go rummaging through his cabinets.

I pulled my phone out of my pocket and tried to get a signal so I could get a ride back to LA. Not that I had a place to stay once I got there, but that was a problem to solve another day.

The door opened and brought in a gush of cold air. Blake pushed it closed with his heavy boot and dropped an armful of wood into the basket on the floor next to the fireplace.

"There's no internet here," he said curtly, nodding to my phone.

"Oh." I frowned and pouted my lips. "I was hoping to get an Uber back to LA."

He was bent over, arranging the firewood before tossing a few into the fire and then closing the screen.

"You're not going to find an Uber out here. Even if there were internet, getting to LA would cost you a fortune. Plus, that storm isn't letting up anytime soon, so you might as well get comfortable. You'll be staying a few days at minimum."

"I can't do that," I said, standing up and immediately felt the pain radiate up my leg and back. When I'd crashed the SUV, the impact of it not only broke the heel of my boot but also left my ankle sore and achy.

He reached out a hand and steadied me.

"Can you stand on your foot?" he asked, ignoring my objection.

"I think so."

"Let me see."

He was still holding onto me as he waited for me to put weight on it.

I rolled my eyes and let go of him as I tried. Slowly I pushed down, swallowing the cries of pain that wanted to escape.

"Sit down," he commanded, pointing to the couch as he helped me over.

I did as he asked and knew it was worse than I thought.

He sat on the edge of the wooden coffee table, gently brought my foot up, and placed it on his thigh.

"Can I take a look?" he asked, his fingers hovering over the bottom of my jeans.

"I don't think you'll be able to see much. My jeans are pretty tight."

He nodded and slowly pulled them up as far as they would go. Then he gently grabbed the top of my ankle sock and pulled it down, exposing my foot which was already shades of blue and purple.

"You definitely sprained it, but you might have a fracture or small break."

"Great," I mumbled. "What am I supposed to do now?"

"First, change out of the tight clothes you're wearing. Then you'll need to rest it and keep any weight off of it."

"I don't have anything to wear. Everything I had is back at my boyfr—*ex-boyfriend's* cabin." Not like I had packed anything loose to wear there either, but the point was that I literally had nothing but the clothes on my back.

"You can borrow something of mine."

I eyed him suspiciously, knowing that anything he had would fall right off of me, given his large frame and muscular body.

"Trust me. You'll be fine."

He got up, went to his bedroom, and returned a few minutes later with a stack of folded clothes.

"I can help you to the bathroom so you can change," he offered.

I nodded and accepted his hand as I stood up. He wrapped one arm around my waist and assisted me the short distance down the hall.

"Do you need help with the rest?" he asked, seeming slightly uncomfortable.

"No, thank you. I think I can manage."

He gave me another nod and pulled the door closed.

I exhaled heavily and tried to focus on the task at hand and not the way my body felt when he touched me.

I sat on the edge of the bathtub and slid my jeans off, being mindful of both my ankle and the bruising that still hurt from the fall in the garage. At first, I'd felt uneasy about wearing his clothes, but when I pulled on the black sweatpants, I felt so comfortable that nothing else mattered. I stripped off the sweater I was wearing, as well as the tank top underneath, and pulled the hoodie over my head.

I immediately felt more comfortable and warmer than I'd been all weekend. I wasn't trying to impress him, so to speak, but that didn't stop me from stopping in front of the bathroom mirror to fix my hair and try to freshen up.

A gasp escaped my lips when I noticed the red gash on my forehead from where I'd hit my head on the steering wheel. There were streaks of blood that had been wiped into my blond hair and a bruise almost as dark as my eyes.

No wonder he was taking pity on me—I looked like the trainwreck that I was.

A few seconds later, there was a knock on the door.

"Everything okay in there?" he asked.

I hopped slightly, keeping my weight off my foot while holding onto the wall. I opened the door and stepped to the side.

"Yeah, just peachy." I tried to smile, but it was pointless.

His eyes searched my face, and I noticed little golden flecks in the dark brown I hadn't seen before. They were pretty. I tilted my head and kept staring, feeling transfixed on them.

"Let's get you off of your feet." He wrapped his arm around my waist and pulled mine up over his shoulder as he guided me back to the couch.

Once I got settled, he handed me the throw blanket from the back of the couch, lifted my foot, and rested it on a stack of pillows. An ice pack was planted on top and then covered with a towel wrapped around it to keep it in place.

"You didn't need to go through all of this trouble," I said, feeling bad that he had to take care of me. "Thank you."

"Not a problem," he mumbled as he walked into the kitchen. "Do you eat meat?"

I turned and looked at him.

"I'm sorry, what?"

"Meat," he repeated, standing with the fridge wide open as he stared at me. "Do you eat it?"

"Yeah…"

He nodded his signature nod and then went about his business in the kitchen while I sat on the couch and watched some movie that was on the TV.

An hour later, my stomach growled as a heavenly aroma floated in from the kitchen. Blake came in from the kitchen, carrying two plates of food that he set down on the coffee table before helping me adjust so I could eat.

"Thank you so much for dinner," I said, excited to dive in.

"It's nothing fancy."

I smiled and took the time to check him out as he shuffled about around me. I let him move my foot and noted the gentle way he'd set it on the pillow he'd placed on the floor for me to rest it on.

He wasn't wearing the beanie anymore, and I was right about his unruly hair. It was long, but not long enough to put in a man bun, though he didn't strike me as the kind of guy who would wear one even if he could. It was the perfect length to run my fingers through, and fell in his eyes as he leaned down to adjust the pillow.

Having him kneel in front of me while his hands gently touched my body was electrifying, and I wondered what it would feel like if he were doing something other than tending to my injured foot.

Before I was ready for the daydream to end, he pulled away and sat beside me on the couch. I was ready to lean forward to eat but was surprised when he lifted the top and it extended into a table so we didn't have to.

"Wow, that's a fancy table you've got there," I said, offering him the first genuine smile I'd had all day. "Where did you get it?"

Now that I was going to be starting over, it wouldn't hurt to get some functional furniture for wherever I ended up next.

"I made it," he said, glancing at me and then turning back to his food.

My jaw dropped as I turned fully to look at him.

"You *made* this? It's amazing!"

"Thank you."

He was constantly short with me, and I realized that it wasn't anything I'd done wrong; it was just his personality. I didn't continue to bug him about the table since he seemed a little uncomfortable with my praise.

I lifted my fork and pierced a piece of potato. It was a simple meal of steak and potatoes, but it was amazing. I hadn't realized how quickly I was devouring it until I felt his eyes on me.

"Sorry," I said, covering my mouth to hide the bite I was still chewing. "This is delicious."

"I'm glad you like it."

"I was starving," I laughed, setting my fork down on the now empty plate.

He finished his last bite, set his down too, and turned to face me.

"You should have said something. There's plenty of food."

I felt my face redden with embarrassment and looked away.

"Look," he said with a sigh, pushing the top of the table down. "We're going to be together for a few days, maybe a week or longer. You're going to have to get comfortable helping yourself to whatever you want around here. I don't mind cooking, but you need to tell me when you're hungry."

"It's not a big deal, really."

"No," he said more aggressively. "It is. There is no reason to sit here and be hungry when there's plenty to eat. Consider this place your home until the weather clears and you can go home. You don't need to tiptoe around and act like you're an inconvenience."

"But I am!" I blurted out, shocked by my own outburst. "I can't remember the last time I didn't feel like I was inconveniencing someone in the past forty-eight hours."

He leaned back against the couch and relaxed for the first time I'd seen since I got there.

"Come on. It couldn't have been that bad."

I shifted as much as possible, got comfortable, and then recounted the events that had happened once I set foot inside Henry's family's cabin.

He winced when I told him about the fall in the garage, cringed when he heard about me using the dead grandmother's wedding veil as a table runner, and burst out laughing when I got to the part about my boob falling out of my tank top and flashing Henry's father.

"Okay, that's bad," he admitted, a smile still teasing his lips.

He had a great smile, and I wanted to see more of it.

"So see, I don't want to cause any more trouble. I just want to get out of here and get back to LA as soon as possible, so I'm not in anyone's hair."

"What are you going to do once you get back?" he asked.

"I honestly don't know," I admitted sadly.

I had also told him about Henry's confession to his father about breaking up with me and being interested in someone that he works with. Talking to Blake felt different. Liberating. And suddenly, I found myself not in a hurry to get back to LA anytime soon.

Nine
Blake

As the evening progressed, I noticed that Holly seemed to be more uncomfortable and achier, even though she wouldn't say anything. I'd kept up on giving her Tylenol and Ibuprofen to help with the swelling in her ankle but didn't know about her other fall until she told me at dinner. To say she'd had a rough few days was an understatement.

I cleaned up after dinner and then decided to run a hot bath for her. I didn't bother asking first because I knew she would fight me on it.

Once it was ready, I went into the living room and held out my hand for her.

"What are you doing?" she asked, lifting hers to mine.

I gently pulled her up, making sure to keep her weight off of her foot.

"I ran you a bath so you can soak."

"What?" She pulled her head back in disbelief. "You didn't have to do that."

"I know. I wanted to."

"But what if you need to use the bathroom?"

I frowned and looked down at her.

"I'll go outside."

She hesitated for a moment, not letting me move her toward the hallway.

"But it's cold out. It's snowing. I mean, it's practically a blizzard out there."

I nodded, still not understanding what the problem was.

"I'm not going to tie up your bathroom and force you to pee in the woods during a blizzard, Blake."

She tried to plant her hand on her hip but lost her balance and fell into my chest.

I caught a whiff of the shampoo she used in her hair and tried not to focus on the light citrus smell.

"I hate to break it to you, but I've peed outside in worse. Trust me, I'll be fine."

"But—"

"Holly, it's fine."

She snapped her cute little mouth shut and allowed me to help her to the bathroom.

Once we got in there, I debated how to get her into the tub without her putting weight on her foot. I wasn't sure that it was broken, but I also wasn't sure that it wasn't. At this point, I wanted to err on the side of caution since it would be hell to try to get her to a hospital in town with the storm raging outside.

"Thank you, I appreciate you doing this for me," she said softly.

"No problem," I mumbled as I shuffled around her to get into a better position. "Umm, if you want to get undressed, I can look away and then help you in once you're ready."

Her cheeks flushed pink as she looked at the tub and then back up at me.

She pulled her lower lip between her teeth while she debated.

"Okay."

I made sure she was steady and wasn't going to fall before I turned and faced the wall to give her some privacy. A few minutes later, I heard her clothes drop to the floor and tried not to focus on her being naked.

"Alright, I'm ready." There was a hesitancy in her voice.

I kept my eyes on hers as I wrapped my arm around her waist and held onto her with both hands as she did her best to climb in. I guided her the best I could and then bent down and lowered her into the water.

I had taken the time to add some Epsom salts to the water as well as some bubble bath my sister had left behind the last time she was here, which I was thankful for as she sank beneath the bubbles.

"Is the temperature okay?" I asked, hoping it hadn't gotten cold in the time it took from when I started it to when she got in.

"It's perfect, thank you."

"Alright," I said, clearing my throat. The way she looked at me as her naked body hid from my view made me think things I shouldn't. "Just yell for me when you're ready, and

I'll come help you out."

"Okay."

She smiled, and that was my cue to get the hell out of there.

An hour later, I heard her soft voice calling my name and went to the bathroom to help her out of the tub.

She was still sitting in the water, only this time, there were no bubbles to hide her naked body. I immediately looked away, trying not to be disrespectful. I grabbed the clean towel I had set out for her earlier and tucked it under my arm.

"You ready?" I asked, unsure of where to look.

"Yes, please."

I struggled to figure out how to get her out of the damn tub without seeing her body, but it didn't seem like it would be possible. I shuffled the towel from one hand to the other before finally giving up and setting it down on the toilet.

"Blake?"

"Yeah," I stuttered, staring at the wall.

"It's fine. It's just a body. If you can lean down some, I can try to push myself out of the water."

I swallowed hard, knowing she was right. It was just a body. I had done this before, and I could do it again.

Okay, so maybe I'd never done *this,* but I'd done other stuff that was similar, and that's what mattered.

I bent down and braced the sides of the tub as she wrapped her arms around my neck. Once she had a good hold, I wrapped one arm around her while I used the other to push us up. She was tiny, to begin with, but felt even smaller as I held her against me and pulled her wet body out of the water.

Once she was out and standing safely on the rug, I let out the breath I had been holding. It had been a while since I'd been responsible for helping someone, so I was worried I would screw up and hurt her more.

She was breathing heavily as her breasts heaved against my chest. I could feel the hardening of her nipples as they brushed against the material of my t-shirt. My arms stayed wrapped tightly around her waist while she didn't bother to remove hers from my neck. A heat spread through me, quickly sending a rush of blood straight to my cock, which was pressed tightly against my jeans.

I noticed the small gasp that pressed through her lips, knowing that she felt how hard I was for her.

My body reacted to hers in a way I hadn't ever felt with anyone before. This raw attraction made me want to rub my hands all over her before plunging inside and claiming her pussy as mine.

I wanted to tilt my neck and kiss the inside of hers, but then I felt her weight shift and remembered that I was supposed to be helping her out of the tub, not fucking her.

"I'm going to get the towel so you can get dried off, okay?" I asked, my voice strained.

She nodded.

I pulled one hand away from her and quickly reached for it. I wrapped it around her body the best I could without touching her. She giggled and took the ends from me as she secured it to her body.

She lowered her eyes and tucked a strand of hair behind her ear.

"I'll, um, leave and give you some privacy."

I spun to leave, but her voice stopped me.

"Do you think you can help me get dressed?"

I froze in place, unsure of what to do. There was something about the way she said it and how her voice changed that made me think there was something more to what she was asking.

"Please."

My heart hammered in my chest as my cock stirred at the thought of seeing her body again.

"Sure."

<u>Ten</u>

Holly

What the hell was I doing?!

I had never been braver in my life than I was when I asked Blake to help me get dressed. Could I do it on my own? Probably. Would it be easy? Not likely. Was it an excuse to get him to touch my naked body again? Absolutely.

I stood there, allowing him to hold me up while he debated his answer. I knew it was a gamble asking him to help me, but I also couldn't deny feeling something a few minutes ago when he was holding me. I mean, I *literally* felt it against my thigh.

Maybe I was just desperate and imagined that there was chemistry between us. Maybe his stunned silence was because I revolted him so much that he couldn't stand the thought of seeing or touching me again. Or maybe it was because he knew I was fresh off of a relationship that barely ended a few hours ago. It could be that I was just crazy and imagining Blake was interested in me, just like I thought Henry and I were on the path to getting engaged.

But then again, he was really, really hard when I brushed

my nipples against this chest.

He swallowed hard, his Adam's apple bobbing up and down as he grabbed the clothes I'd dropped on the floor earlier. He set them neatly on the toilet and then turned to face me. We locked eyes, and I could see the struggle warring in his eyes.

Without saying a word, I unhooked the towel, spread it open, and then let it fall beside me.

I licked my lips, enjoying the liberating feeling that was washing over me. I'd never been this sexually open, but suddenly, I didn't care about Blake seeing me. In fact, I wanted him to want me the way I wanted him right now.

Maybe this was exactly what I needed to get over Henry. Another man to make me feel alive for a bit. A distraction while I was stranded in the mountains with a frightening blizzard outside.

I tried to focus on the empowerment I felt instead of the nerves that were pulsing through me.

His eyes darkened as they roamed over my body and then suddenly widened when they landed on my bruised hip.

Before I could say anything, he whipped around faster than one of those Cullen kids in *Twilight* and was bent down looking at it.

"You didn't tell me it was that bad, Holly."

"Honestly, I don't know how bad it is," I laughed. "I haven't really been in a position where I could see my own ass."

"It's bad."

I frowned and pouted my lips. Maybe I hadn't paid much attention to it because Henry hadn't made a big deal out of it either. I didn't want to be a crybaby, and it wasn't like there was anything anyone could do about it. It just needed time to heal.

"Well, that's not very nice. I've always been told I have a nice ass. Other guys seem to like it."

He ignored my joke and gently brushed his fingers across my skin, tracing the outline of where I was bruised to give me an idea of how big it was.

God, his touch was addictive. It was light and feathery to not hurt me, but even pressure to let me know he was there. And dear Lord, my body knew he was there.

Instinctively, I stepped to the side some on my good foot, allowing my legs to part. I could feel the heat of his breath against my thigh and trembled, imagining his face between my thighs. He was so close that I could almost feel it happening.

He looked up, and I knew he could see the desire etched on my face. Not only that, but my nipples were also hard again, and there was an aching in my core.

Not sure if he was getting the message about what I wanted, I reached down and gently grabbed his hand as his fingers trailed over my skin. Then, I slowly moved it over my hip and hissed out a breath as I skimmed it over my pussy.

He groaned as he pressed kisses to my leg as his finger trailed the inside of my lips. I wanted to open for him and let him know I was ready, but I couldn't stand on both feet. As if reading my mind, he picked me up, backed me against the wall, and then sunk to his knees again.

Without asking, he lifted my injured leg over his knee and then leaned in to lick my pussy as he held my body in place on the wall. *Henry had never done anything like this with me before. While he'd gone down on me a few times, it was always in bed with me on my back, and it never lasted more than a few minutes. I couldn't even remember the last time he made me come from oral sex. Hell, I couldn't remember the last time he made me come, period.*

I cried out as he licked again, spreading my folds with his tongue as it dipped inside and tasted me.

"Yes!" I panted, grabbing a handful of his hair and yanking as he pushed his face deeper into my pussy. I knew it would feel good between my fingers. He officially had sex hair because it was the perfect length to hold onto as I rode his face.

He reached up and pulled my other leg over his shoulder, holding my ass in place as I slid a little down the wall. He was still eating me, his tongue working its magic against my clit, when he slipped two fingers inside my folds.

I was close to the edge with the friction he was giving me and wanted to come right then and there. Suddenly, he curved his fingers inside, hitting a spot I never knew I had, and I could swear I saw stars. I bit down on my lip to keep from screaming as I rode his face during climax.

A few seconds later, I was still panting as he slowly removed his fingers and sat me down on the floor.

"That was amazing," I said breathlessly.

My head was spinning, trying to focus on what had just happened. I wasn't the kind of girl to just jump into bed with a guy she didn't know—or be pinned against the wall, for that matter. But something about this didn't feel wrong. It didn't feel dirty. It felt good, and I wanted more of it.

For once, I didn't want to stop and think about what I was doing. I wanted to act on impulse and see where it took me. Again, it wasn't like Henry was out looking for me.

He nodded, breathing heavily himself.

"I want more."

His eyes widened and then roamed over my body again.

I glanced down and found that same bulge in his jeans that I had seen earlier.

"Just a fling, Blake. It doesn't have to mean anything other than two people who are horny and stuck together for a few days." I don't know who I was trying to convince more—him or me.

He licked his lips, and I prayed he was about to say yes.

My chest was still heaving as the blood flowed back through the rest of my body.

"I know you're hard," I said quietly. "Let me take care of you the way you just took care of me."

He shook his head and then got up and left.

I sat there for a few moments, trying not to cry as I processed his rejection. But then he returned a few minutes later with a stack of condoms in his hand, and I knew I was in for a good time.

He extended a hand and helped me up before setting me down on the vanity.

"Are you sure this is what you want?" he asked as he unzipped his jeans and started stroking his cock.

He wasn't wearing any underwear.

I nodded and chewed my lower lip.

Within seconds, he tore the condom open, slid it onto his penis, and then lined up his head at my entrance.

I spread my legs for him, showing him how wet he'd made me just a few minutes before. He rubbed my slit with his thumb and then pushed inside.

My head fell back as I moaned. He gripped my hips, pulled me further to the edge of the counter, and began thrusting.

He was big—freaking huge—as my pussy wrapped tightly against him. I wanted to take it in my mouth and suck him off, but this was just as good. I gasped when he leaned in and pulled a nipple into his mouth, nipping lightly before clamping down and sucking.

The friction felt so good as he rubbed against my clit while he fucked me, but combined with the nipple stimulation, I was ready to come again. I dug my nails into his hair and pulled tightly as we came undone together.

This was a high I had never been on before, and I wasn't ready to come down anytime soon.

Eleven
Blake

My mind was racing a mile a minute while my body hummed with satisfaction after being inside of Holly. I had no idea where in the world that came from, but I wasn't complaining.

That also didn't mean I wasn't sitting there next to her on the couch, wondering if I should have tried harder to say no. Not that I didn't find her attractive or that I didn't want to do it, but I wasn't the kind of guy who jumped a girl's bones less than twenty-four hours after her breaking up with someone. I had more class and respect than that, though I guess that wasn't really showing right now, was it?

An old black-and-white movie played on the TV, but neither of us was really watching it. I could see Holly's mind racing as she nervously chewed her nails. Her foot was propped up on my lap with another ice pack to reduce the swelling, and it took everything I had in me not to let my fingers trail up her leg and caress it.

She was wearing my sweats and hoodie again, and I had to admit—I kinda liked it.

It was getting late and we had yet to talk about sleeping

arrangements. Once I saw how bad the storm was getting, I knew she would be staying with me for at least a few days, probably longer. There weren't any other options, even if she wanted to go back to her asshat of an ex-boyfriend's cabin—there was no way to get her there safely.

My cabin wasn't huge, but it was big enough for me. There was the guestroom that my sister stayed in when she came to visit, but the bed was old and needed to be replaced. I didn't want Holly to be in any more pain than she was already in, so I decided she'd sleep in my room, and I'd take the crappy bed.

When she yawned, that was my cue to get her settled.

"Ready to call it a night?" I asked, noticing the way her body was sinking into the couch as she relaxed.

"Yeah, I don't think I could stay awake right now if I tried," she laughed. "Is it okay if I sleep on the couch?"

"No." I frowned and shook my head.

Her head tilted to the side in confusion.

"You'll sleep in my bed, Holly. I'm not letting you sleep on the couch."

"Oh, no," she rushed out. "I couldn't do that. I'm fine on the couch, really."

I pinned her with a look that got her to snap her mouth close before she said anything more.

"You're not sleeping on the couch."

"I did at Henry's family's cabin, and it was actually comfortable."

"Well, I'm not Henry, and this isn't his pretentious family's cabin. You're sleeping in the bed."

She swallowed hard and started chewing her nails again.

"Um, where will you sleep?"

In bed beside you so I can roll over and make love to you throughout the night.

"There's a guest bedroom." I cleared my throat, pushing the dirty thoughts aside.

"Oh, why don't I take that room, so I don't put you out?"

I shook my head again.

"Why not?"

"Because, Holly, that bed sucks, and your body is seven shades of black and blue right now. You need to rest and let your body heal. You will sleep in my bed, which is the most comfortable option in the cabin."

I gently lifted her foot and then set it on a pillow as I got up and walked away, effectively ending the conversation.

I hurried to get the room set up for her and made sure I took what I needed to the guest room. There was only one pillow that I slept with; the rest were all brand new and never used. I tried to arrange them for Holly on the bed without looking like I was trying too hard. Not sure if she got cold easily, I grabbed an extra blanket from the closet and added it to the edge of the bed so she could use it if she wanted to.

I tossed the pillow onto the bed and grabbed an extra blanket. It wasn't a large room, but it had everything I needed, including a nightstand with a phone charger and a TV mounted on the wall in case sleep eluded me again tonight.

When I walked back into the living room, I found Holly asleep on the couch. I hadn't been gone that long, but she looked exhausted. I didn't want to wake her, but I knew she would be stiff and sore tomorrow if I let her sleep in that position, so I bent down, picked her up, and carried her to my bed.

Once she was settled and covered under the blankets, I grabbed her phone from the living room and put it on the charger beside her bed. I wanted to reach down and kiss her goodnight, but that felt really out of line, so I pushed that thought aside, closed her door, and pretended that I wasn't already starting to feel something for someone who was still a stranger.

The next morning, I was up before Holly. Probably because I had slept like shit the night before and didn't fall asleep until around two. I padded around the kitchen, starting a pot of coffee while I watched the snow falling outside.

It was going to be a brutally cold day. Thankfully I had planned ahead and brought in enough firewood to last a few days. Aside from taking Luna outside, there was no reason either of us would need to brave the storm.

I'd lived in Hope Valley for ten years and had never seen a storm this bad. Sure, we got plenty of snow each year, which brought in many skiers, but this was enough snow to shut down the slopes for a few days.

I was standing at the kitchen sink, drinking my coffee when I heard Holly coming down the hallway. I set it down and rushed to help her, so she didn't hurt herself.

"Hey, you should've called for me. I would have come and

helped you."

"It's okay," she said softly. "My foot actually feels a lot better this morning. It doesn't hurt to walk on it."

I nodded and led her to the couch. She sat down and I arranged a pillow for her to put her foot on.

"Do you mind if I look at it?" I asked, my fingers reaching to pull off her sock.

She nodded.

Slowly I pulled it down and cradled her foot in my other hand while I examined it. There was still some bruising, but overall the swelling had gone down. I turned it and looked at the other side, not noticing anything worrisome.

"I think it was a bad sprain," I said, continuing to check it out. "It doesn't look like anything is broken, and since you can walk on it without pain, I'd say it's a safe bet. However, sprains can be painful for a few days, so it's best to stay off your feet today and rest. I'll grab you some Ibuprofen and an ice pack."

"You don't have to keep taking care of me," she insisted, pulling her foot back after I set it down.

"I don't mind. But I'm serious—stay off of your foot. Unless you need to use the bathroom, there's no need to be on it."

"You sure seem to know a lot about it. Are you a doctor or something?"

I avoided looking at her as I got up and grabbed the first-aid kit from the kitchen.

"I was a medic in the Army."

"Army?"

I nodded and pulled out a roll of elastic bandage. I'd debated whether or not to wrap her foot last night but decided against it because of the amount of swelling she had. Now that the swelling had gone down, I wanted to make sure we kept some compression on it.

"Eight years. I got out ten years ago and moved to Hope Valley."

"Why did you leave?"

"My mother was sick, and I couldn't stand the thought of her dying while I was stuck somewhere overseas."

"I'm so sorry."

"Don't be. I got to spend the last few years of her life with her. Took care of her. After that, I realized that life is too short to spend doing something you don't want to."

I felt her eyes on me and looked up to find emotions flashing across her face.

"Being a medic was fine. I loved helping people. But at the end of the day, a career in the Army wasn't for me. I wanted to be on my own. Do what I wanted. Come and go as I pleased."

"So what do you do now? Are you like a real lumberjack?"

I chuckled and sighed.

"You mean *lumbersnack*?" I teased, looking up to meet her eyes.

Her brow furrowed in confusion.

"When I found you yesterday, the first thing you told me was that I looked like a lumbersnack. Kinda like a gingerbread man—"

"Oh my god!" She lifted her hands and covered her face with embarrassment. "I thought I dreamt that!"

"Nope. It really happened."

"I'm so sorry," she apologized with a laugh. "I guess I hit my head harder than I thought."

"No need to be sorry. Though you are the first person to call me that."

"Well, I mean, you kinda looked like one with the beard and the flannel." She paused and looked down at Luna, who was sleeping on the rug by the fireplace. "And the pet wolf."

My cheeks split into a grin that I couldn't stop.

"You're half right about that. Luna is a Siberian Husky and wolf mix, though she's more husky than wolf."

"She's beautiful, but I'm not going to lie—I was sure I was going to shit my pants yesterday when I saw her."

I laughed and finished wrapping her foot.

"What do you feel like for breakfast?" I asked as I went to the kitchen and put the first-aid kit back where it belonged.

"You don't have to feed me," she insisted.

"I know I don't have to. Now, what do you want to eat?" I stood in front of her, arms folded over my chest.

She giggled and pulled the sleeves of my hoodie up to hide her mouth.

"What are my options?"

"Eggs, bacon, sausage, frozen hash browns, toast, and possibly a Pop-Tart. I need to check the stash of those, though."

I didn't eat Pop-Tarts, but my sister did, and I couldn't remember if there were any left after the last time she visited a few months ago.

"What are you going to eat?"

Her question was innocent enough, but that didn't stop my eyes from wandering hungrily to between her thighs, remembering the way she tasted last night when I ate her out against the bathroom wall.

Her brown eyes darkened, and her legs shifted slightly as if she was inviting me in for another taste.

"That depends on what *my* options are."

The tension palpitated between us as our eyes locked onto each other.

"You can have whatever you want."

"Whatever?" I confirmed, my voice deep and husky.

She nodded, her chest rising and falling rapidly as I approached her.

"In that case, I think I want to eat you again."

A small gasp escaped her full lips before she licked them and nodded as I leaned down to pull her sweats off.

I gently removed them, making sure not to hurt her, and then tossed them across the room. I snapped and pointed to my room, knowing that Luna would follow my command

and leave. Next, I slowly pulled her panties off, taking my time teasing her as she wiggled anxiously beneath me.

Her legs fell open and welcomed me as I laid in front of her and got myself situated. I lifted her injured foot, rested it on my shoulder, and then added the other.

She giggled and tried to squirm, but I pinned her down with my body.

"You need to keep your foot elevated. Basic first-aid," I teased before dipping my head between her thighs and licking her lips.

She gasped and arched her back as her fingers grabbed my hair and pulled. God, I loved when she did that. I didn't usually keep my hair this long, but I was going to if she kept doing that.

I held her thighs in place while I teased her with my tongue, circling her clit before flicking it rapidly. She was already wet for me, and that made my dick achingly hard. I wanted to be inside her again, but I also couldn't get enough of this. I could eat her for every meal for the rest of my life.

She panted as I slid my tongue between her folds and fucked her with it. Keeping her injured foot braced on my shoulder, I lowered my other hand between her thighs and started to rub her clit while I continued thrusting two fingers deep inside.

"Fuck me," she cried out, her thighs squeezing my face as she came.

I sucked every last drop of wetness from her pussy and then came up for air.

"I plan to," I assured her with a wink.

I set her leg down gently, then ran off to grab a condom. I stripped down in the bedroom and rolled it on as I headed back to the living room.

She was still lying in the same position, looking completely sated and satisfied.

"You ready?" I asked, stroking my cock for her.

She nodded and licked her lips again.

"I want to taste you," she whispered. "I want that huge dick in my mouth."

I climbed on top of her, lining myself up at her entrance.

"It's a good thing we're snowed in with nothing else to do."

Before she could say anything, I pushed inside, closing my eyes as I went slowly to let her adjust to my size.

She was so fucking tight that it made me want to shoot my load that much quicker.

"Fuck me, Blake. Now," she urged.

Not needing any more encouragement, I pulled out and then slammed into her, groaning as she moaned my name.

Her pussy greedily clenched around my cock, milking every last drop of cum while I rubbed her clit with each thrust, making sure she came again too.

Her orgasms weren't quiet—which I loved. They were loud and sensual, and I couldn't get enough of them. I loved the way she scratched my back and clawed at my skin as if she needed it as much as I did.

Before pulling out, I gently cupped the side of her face and lowered my lips to her. We had fucked twice, and I knew what her pussy tasted like, but I had yet to kiss her. Once I did, I knew I would never want to stop again.

Twelve
Holly

The next few days were uneventful as the snow continued to fall, blanketing us inside the cabin. My foot had recovered enough to where I could put weight on it for short bouts of time, but Blake was adamant about keeping me off of it when he could. While sometimes that meant he was doing the cooking or cleaning for us, most of the time, it was an excuse for him to be between my legs—not that I was complaining.

I was only twenty-three, but Blake showed me more in the bedroom in three days than Henry had ever shown me in five years. He was my first, so it wasn't like I'd had anyone else to compare him to until now.

When we weren't busy humping like bunnies, we found different ways to kill time while cooped up inside. Which, honestly, wasn't that bad. While I loved life in LA and the constantly rushing around to auditions, I was actually enjoying my downtime with Blake.

He had a small collection of board games that we played when we needed a break from watching TV, which happened more frequently after I suggested a few rounds of strip Monopoly. Turned out Blake didn't mind making me homeless after I had to sell off all of my properties and beg him for a place to stay while I was naked and riding his cock.

It was four days until Christmas, and I was starting to stress about not getting back to LA. I hadn't mentioned it to Blake yet, but I felt bad that I was keeping him from whatever plans he might've had. While I had nothing going on back home for me, that didn't mean he didn't have a family he wanted to spend it with, without some strange woman intruding.

I sat on the couch and watched him throw a stick for Luna as she ran through the snow to fetch it. He was bundled up in a thick coat that made him look twice as large, and I wondered how easily he could move inside. It was bitterly cold out there, so I couldn't imagine they would be out there for long.

I was flipping through the channels, looking for something to watch, when the door opened, and Luna came rushing in, covered in snow. Blake came in behind her and shut the door before the heat escaped.

Luna shook in front of the fireplace, sending chunks of snow my way, before plopping down in front of the fireplace.

I squealed and held up the blanket to shield myself.

"Sorry, she loves the snow," Blake laughed, pulling off his beanie.

"I can see that," I laughed along with him.

Luna had grown on me during the time I'd spent with them, and she no longer came across as the scary giant wolf dog I initially thought she was. She was incredibly sweet, and an amazing dog that followed every command Blake gave her.

"What are you up to?" he asked as if there were that many options available.

"Nothing, just browsing through the channels."

"Do you want to help me outside?"

I turned the TV off and set the remote on the coffee table before pushing the blanket off of me and standing up.

"Sure." It didn't matter what he needed my help with; I was ready to do it.

"You're going to need some warmer clothes. I'll be right back."

He returned a few minutes later with a thick flannel coat that he helped me into, as well as a scarf, some gloves, and a face mask like the one he was wearing. Then he grabbed a pair of boots that were easily three times too big for me and helped me into them after adding a few pairs of socks to pad them so they wouldn't pull off.

"You ready?" He looked me up and down, answering for himself. "Let's go."

"Show me the way."

We stepped out into the cold, and Blake pulled the door closed behind us. I shivered and wrapped my arms around myself, wondering what in the world he could need help with out here. He'd already come out this morning to bring in more firewood.

"Don't worry, it'll be worth it," he shouted through the thick fabric covering his face as he tried to be louder than the wind whipping past us.

"Okay," I yelled back, following him into a small clearing beside the house.

He led the way, checking behind him every few feet to make sure I was still there. Finally, we were far enough away from the cabin that I couldn't see it anymore. I started to panic that we would get lost or stranded until I remembered Blake had lived here long enough to know which way was home.

Finally, he pulled me to the side and looked at the trees in front of us.

"Which one do you like?"

I tilted my head in confusion.

"You brought me out here to pick a favorite tree?"

The wind was quieter here because of the thick trees surrounding us, blocking it out.

"I brought you out here to help me pick a Christmas tree."

I tilted my head up and grinned at him, though he couldn't see it through my face covering. That certainly explained the ax I saw him bring with us. At first, I thought it was for protection in case we ran into a wild animal. Now it made much more sense.

"We're going to cut down a Christmas tree?!" I couldn't contain the excitement in my voice if I tried.

"Yup. Just pick one, and it shall be yours."

I looked around, trying to find the perfect one, touching each of the branches as I passed by. Suddenly I stopped. Standing before me was the *perfect* tree.

"That one," I said, pointing at it.

"Yeah?"

I stepped back and watched in awe as he got started. Luna waited patiently at my side, giving him the space he needed as the tree fell onto the ground on the other side.

I clapped excitedly when he was done and then helped him carry it back to the cabin. Thankfully it wasn't a huge tree and didn't need to be cut again once we got it inside. Blake grabbed the tree stand and got it secured while I held the tree in place.

He stood up and nodded for me to let go.

My heart raced wildly like a little girl in a toy store for the first time as I stared at the beautiful tree. It was tucked into the corner between two windows, making it the most gorgeous image I'd ever seen with the snow still falling outside.

"It's incredible," I whispered, continuing to stare in awe. "I could look at this every day."

The words escaped my lips before I could think about them.

"It's quite the beautiful sight, isn't it?"

The butterflies swarmed in my stomach when I noticed that he was looking at me, not the tree.

HOLIDAY HIJINKS

Thirteen
Blake

I'd never been one to put up a tree for Christmas. I just never saw the point since I spent the holiday alone. My sister was a traveling doctor and was usually somewhere international this time of year, so we stopped celebrating it together around the time my mother died. My dad was never in the picture, which left me with no other family to spend it with.

But seeing how Holly lit up seeing the tree made me want to do all of the things my mother used to do with us when we were little. Back when Christmas was a magical time of year. I'd tucked those feelings away for so long now that it felt weird letting them rise to the surface again. But as far as Holly was concerned, something was constantly growing around her. Usually my cock.

I went out and rummaged through the shed until I found the boxes marked *Christmas* in the back and brought them in. There were tangled messes of lights that we sorted together and then hung on the tree. Holly seemed to enjoy herself, so I didn't stop her from hanging them above the windows or throughout the rest of the cabin.

I was nervous about going through the box of ornaments with her, but we also needed to decorate the tree, so I sucked it up and plopped down on the floor beside her.

Her foot was ten times better than it was a few days ago, and I was glad to see that she wasn't in much pain from her fall, either. A little bit of rest and TLC seemed to be helping her.

"Did you want to go through them first?" Holly asked, sitting with her hands in her lap as I opened the lid to the box.

"Honestly, it's been so long since I've packed these away that I don't even remember what's inside." I shrugged.

"I don't want to intrude on something personal."

"I appreciate that. It's okay, let's go through them together."

She nodded and smiled softly as if she knew this might be hard for me.

The truth was that most of these were from my childhood and I'd packed them up and brought them home after clearing out my mom's stuff when she died. I had a great childhood, but I regretted the years I'd been away for Christmas, and she was left to decorate the tree and spend it alone.

My sister and I had tried to convince her not to go through all of the efforts of putting the tree up if it was just her, but she insisted that she enjoyed looking at it and that it reminded her of beautiful memories.

When I pulled the first ornament out, I felt a pain in my heart and knew exactly what she meant.

The fragile angel hung on a gold hook with frayed threads that looked like they would break at any moment. I continued to stare at it for a few minutes until I felt Holly's eyes on mine.

"My mom got this ornament when I was five, and my sister was two. My dad had just left, and she didn't have money to buy us gifts. One day while she was on her break at work, a man approached her. She was crying, upset that she couldn't get us anything, and he sat down and talked to her. It turned out that he owned a toy store a few blocks away and needed help with the holiday rush. My mom was working as a waitress at a diner and was stuck working the graveyard shift. She took the job he offered her, and he was so thankful for the help that he let her pick a toy for each of us, free of charge. When she'd finally chosen what she wanted, he added this ornament to her bag and told her it was her guardian angel. As long as she had it, she would never lose her way."

Her eyes welled up with tears as she listened to the story, reaching her fingers up to brush them away.

"He passed a few days later, but not before he promoted her to manager. His son took over the store and kept my mom there until she got too sick to work. It was the best thing that ever happened to her. I'd forgotten about this angel until now. My mom used to say that it was magical and would help those who had it find their way."

My throat burned as I fought back the tears.

"That's a beautiful story," she said, her face still wet.

I stood up and looked for a spot on the tree to hang it, making sure it wouldn't fall off and break if Luna bumped it.

We spent the next hour going through the ornaments and decorating the tree as we laughed and shared stories of our memories from Christmases growing up.

Once we were finished, we stepped back and looked at our masterpiece. It was beautiful, but not only that, it brought back a feeling that I thought had died inside. The only problem was that it wasn't the tree that made me feel alive again. It was Holly.

I made dinner while she flipped through my stack of DVDs, picking something for us to watch. It was weird how quickly we'd fallen into a routine with each other after only a few days, but everything with Holly felt right and oddly comfortable. It wasn't forced, and neither of us seemed to pretend to be something we weren't.

Holly devoured her bowl of fettuccini and then went for seconds while I sat on the couch and digested. While she was in the kitchen, her phone vibrated on the coffee table. I tried not to be nosey but seeing her ex-boyfriend's name on the screen made my stomach drop.

Why was Henry calling her? Was he just now getting around to checking on her? As far as I knew, this was the first time he'd bothered to reach out since she confronted him at his family's cabin after overhearing his plans to break up with her.

When she returned, her phone dinged to alert her to the new voicemail. I kept my eyes glued to the TV and acted like I hadn't seen anything.

Her brow furrowed as she pressed it to her ear and listened to the message.

"Everything okay?" I asked, still refusing to look at her or acknowledge I knew who had called.

She paused for a moment before setting her phone down

and twirling her fork around her noodles.

"Yup."

We went to bed that night, both of us ignoring the new elephant in the room. I had hoped that she would tell me about Henry calling but I felt uneasy when she didn't bother to mention it. Was she planning to call him back when I wasn't around? What had he said in the message? My mind was spinning a mile a minute as I struggled with one dreadful thought—what if she goes back to him?

The next morning I woke up to the sun shining through the sheer curtains in my bedroom. We'd given up on sleeping in separate rooms after we kept banging nonstop, but last night I couldn't sleep knowing that she'd kept Henry's call from me.

Holly had been with me for almost a week, and we still hadn't talked about what would happen once the storm passed and the roads were clear enough for her to get back to LA. Maybe that was what the call was about. Had Henry offered to take her home? Was she going to take him up on it? There were so many unanswered questions that we needed to discuss, but I didn't know how without overstepping.

I was in the kitchen making breakfast when Holly came in after taking a shower. She hopped up onto the counter beside me, wearing another one of my hoodies and a new pair of sweats she found in my dresser. I'd told her to help herself to whatever she wanted but was glad she'd decided to forgo underwear since she only had one pair, and I conveniently kept forgetting to do laundry. Even though she was flirty and in a good mood, I couldn't shake the feeling that something was off. It was like I was just waiting for the other shoe to drop.

"Breakfast smells good," she said, smiling at me as I turned the sausage link in the pan.

"Thanks. It should be ready in a few minutes."

She frowned a little, obviously aware that something was off with me but not knowing what.

She got down and made herself busy with fixing our coffee for us. I joined her at the table a few minutes later and set her plate down in front of her.

I took a bite of my toast while she ate her scrambled eggs and looked out the window behind me.

"I can't believe the sun is finally shining," she commented with a huge smile.

"Yeah, they should have the roads clear soon." I didn't bother to turn around to see what she was talking about. It didn't matter how bright it was outside; it did nothing to ease the darkness that was seeping into my heart.

There was no use in beating around the bush. It wasn't like I could pretend she was still stranded and force her to stay with me if she didn't want to. For all I knew, she had a family waiting for her in LA that she needed to spend the holiday with. *Or Henry.* Christmas was only three days away, yet she hadn't mentioned what her plans were.

"Oh. Wow, that quickly?"

I couldn't tell if she was genuinely surprised or if I detected a hint of disappointment in her voice.

"They're pretty good at clearing it as soon as the storm passes."

I lifted my coffee to my lips and took a sip.

"I can drive you if you need me to."

She was mid-bite when she stopped, a panicked look on her face.

"Unless you wanted someone to come get you. It doesn't matter to me." I didn't bother to mention Henry's name, but the look that flashed across her face told me I was right about him.

I got up and took my plate to the sink before it could get any more awkward.

"I'm going to take a shower and clean up."

I felt like a dick for leaving her to finish eating by herself, but I didn't have a choice. I was already in too deep. I needed to separate myself from her as soon as possible. I was too old for her, and she was still in love with another man.

This was the reason I distanced myself from people and stayed to myself in the middle of nowhere, deep in the woods. Because allowing yourself to get close to someone meant that it hurt like hell when they walked away and left.

Fourteen

Holly

What the hell just happened?

I sat at the table by myself, trying to pick my jaw up off of the floor after Blake abruptly left. He'd been acting strange since last night, but today was even worse. It was like he'd gone back to the grumpy, cold Blake that I first met a few days ago.

I knew he had probably seen my phone last night when Henry called, but he didn't say anything. I wasn't sure whether to bring it up or not, but after seeing the way he worked his jaw while I listened to the voicemail, I decided not to.

It wasn't like Blake was a child who needed to be coddled—he was thirty-six and had probably been through his fair share of relationships and breakups. Granted, I was barely twenty-three, but I didn't feel like I was too young to know how to handle this one. Just because Henry called and asked me to call him back didn't mean I was going to. He hadn't bothered to check on me since I left, so as far as I was concerned, he could go kick rocks.

But I wasn't sure that it was just the call from Henry that was under his skin. When I mentioned that the weather had cleared, he seemed almost anxious to get me out of his cabin and back on my way to LA. Maybe I was hallucinating again and imagined that things were going better with Blake because *I* wanted them to be that good.

I wasn't going to beg anyone to want to have me around—not Henry, and sure as hell not Blake. If he didn't want me here, fine. I would find a way back to LA.

While he was in the shower—the longest one he'd taken since I'd been there—I searched for rides back to the city. I knew it would cost a fortune, and unless I maxed out every single one of my credit cards, I couldn't afford to do that.

Renting a car would be somewhat easier, but I still had to find a ride to the lot, which meant that I would have to find an Uber or ask Blake to take me. I really didn't want to inconvenience him, and then I read the fine print about there being a *young renter fee* for renters under twenty-five. That was going to get expensive as well.

There was only one option, and I hated to use it. Henry's voicemail said that he was catching a ride home with his parents today since I had taken his SUV and that he wanted to make sure I'd gotten home alright with the storm. He went on and on about being worried sick about me—*not so worried that he called before now*—and asked that I at least let him know that I was okay.

I groaned and then lifted my phone to my ear and pressed send.

Luna watched me from the rug in front of the fireplace, and I swear I could hear her snarling under her breath as if she knew what I was about to do.

"Holly," Henry breathed out as if it pained him not to hear from me.

"I need a ride. Your SUV is totaled and stuck in a tree."

"Okay. Okay, sure. Just tell me where you're at."

I sucked in a deep breath and pinched the bridge of my nose. I hated that I was going to have to ask Blake for his address so I could give it to my dumb ex-boyfriend.

When I opened my eyes, Blake was standing in front of me, drying his hair with just a towel wrapped around his waist.

"Holly?" Henry asked.

"Yeah. I'm still here."

"Okay, what's the address?"

I kept my eye's on Blake's and felt the knot in my stomach grow larger by the second.

"Ummm. I don't have it. Hold—"

Before I could say anything else, Blake reached out and snatched my phone from me.

He must've heard me ask for a ride and knew I didn't know his address.

He walked into the living room and faced the window as he rattled off directions. When he was done, he ended the call, and his fingers flew across the screen before he headed back to where I was sitting and handed it to me.

"He'll be here in thirty."

My heart beat wildly in my chest as my blood pressure

rose. He walked off, closing his bedroom door behind him.

I looked at my phone and found the directions to his cabin sent in a text message to Henry.

I closed my eyes and tried to force the tears away.

Twenty minutes later, I had cleaned up the mess in the kitchen and put the extra food in the fridge. I didn't have any belongings other than the clothes I'd been wearing the day Blake found me. I also didn't have time to wash everything I'd been borrowing, so I left a note thanking Blake for his generosity and tossed everything into the washing machine.

It felt weird to wear the same thing Henry had seen me in when I fled from the cabin. It was even more embarrassing that I was wearing another pair of knee-high boots that had a broken heel—just like the ones his mother judged me for the first day we'd arrived.

Blake had been outside with Luna, avoiding me while I waited for Henry and his parents to arrive. The tension between us was so uncomfortable that I didn't blame him, though I also hated ending things this way.

I was pacing by the window, ignoring the beautifully decorated Christmas tree I had picked out and Blake had chopped down, when I saw a black Ford truck pull up in front of the cabin. I swallowed my nerves and my pride and walked outside. Blake was nowhere to be found, which might've been better since I wasn't sure I could handle saying goodbye to him.

Fifteen
Blake

Luna whimpered as the truck drove away, knowing that Holly was with them. She was gone, and I wasn't even man enough to say goodbye.

But honestly, I didn't trust myself not to get down on my knees and beg her to stay. Holly did something to me that I didn't understand. It was like she put a spell on me and had me willing to do anything and everything she asked just to see her happy.

Now she was on her way back to LA with her dumb-ass ex-boyfriend, who didn't deserve her, and his parents, who were probably judging her for breathing too loud in the backseat.

I took Luna inside, having had enough of the bitter cold. Even though the sun was shining, it was still hovering in the negative digits, and nothing was going to thaw this frozen heart of mine.

I tossed a few logs into the fire and headed to the laundry room to start a load since I'd been slacking on chores the past few days with Holly here. I set the hamper down and went to open the washer when I found a note on top.

Blake,

Thanks for saving me, in more ways than one.

XoXo

Holly

I held the paper in my hands and stared at it, wondering what in the world had changed her mind so quickly. I felt like things were going fine between us until she got the call from Henry, but maybe I was wrong. Maybe I just wanted to think that things were good between us because I was tired of being lonely.

In the end, it didn't matter. Holly chose to leave. She chose to go with Henry. I couldn't have changed any of that if I had tried.

I tossed the note in the trash and started the laundry.

By midday, I was going crazy being cooped up in the house. Every little thing reminded me of Holly, and I couldn't get her off my mind. There wasn't a safe space in the cabin that was free of thoughts of Holly.

Finally, I gave in and headed into town, knowing the roads were already cleared.

Shopping proved to be just as difficult as staying home when everything I saw made me think of her. From the plush bathrobe, I could picture her wearing after soaking for hours in my tub to the cute hoodie that would look adorable on her, it all pulled on my heartstrings so much that I found myself adding stuff to the cart that I had no intention of buying.

But apparently, I had taken crazy pills today because not

only did I buy stuff for Holly, but I also grabbed wrapping paper and tape so I could have gifts under the tree for someone who wouldn't be there to open them. I also picked up a few things for Luna and a bottle of whiskey for me since this was turning into the most depressing, pathetic Christmas I'd ever had in my life.

When I returned home, I was disappointed that Holly wasn't there. It wasn't like she was going to turn around and come running back to me—even though I desperately wanted her to.

Unfortunately, life just didn't work out that way.

Sixteen
Holly

I pretended to sleep the entire drive back to LA, which was longer than the drive to Hope Valley.

Henry tried to apologize when he got out of the truck to help me in, but I brushed him off and climbed inside without saying a word to his parents. I didn't owe them any pleasantries and was only taking Henry up on his offer for a ride back to LA because I had no other options that I could afford. In all fairness, this was the least he could do.

I had no idea what I was going to do once I got back to LA other than pack up my stuff and start looking for a new place. I had a few friends that I could reach out to, but it would only be temporary. I needed to figure out a plan for my life and didn't have any time to waste.

Once we got back, I went into the house without bothering to help Henry bring his stuff in. I knew that he would want to sit down and talk about things between us, but I didn't have the energy for it right now. I was drained—mentally, physically, and most of all—emotionally.

Leaving Blake felt harder than it should have, especially

since I had only known him for a few days. But there was something about him that made me feel like I had known him my entire life. I was more comfortable around him than I had been with anyone else, even my own parents. He got me in a way no one ever had, which felt special. That was until he was ready to kick me out of his cabin and send me on my way.

I still had no idea what had happened and why there were so many mixed signals. He was a complicated man, but I thought I was finally starting to figure him out.

I heard Henry say goodbye to his parents and then closed the door. Needing my space from him, I brushed past him in the open foyer and headed toward the master bathroom.

"Holly, can we talk for a minute?"

"I'm going to soak."

I didn't wait for him to respond before I closed the door and locked it. I sat on the edge of the tub and let my fingers feel the trickle of water as I waited for it to get hot. Even though our house wasn't as big or as expensive as his parent's, I was going to miss this tub. It wasn't as fancy as the one at their cabin, but it was deep, and the water got the perfect temperature to soothe my achy body.

I added some bath salts and a squirt of my favorite bubble bath, then let it finish filling while I undressed and grabbed a clean towel from the linen closet.

As I passed the full-length mirror on the wall, I spotted the bruise on my hip and stopped.

It was big, just like Blake had said, but luckily it had started to fade. I trailed my fingers over it the same way he had.

My eyes fluttered closed as I tried to remember his touch on my skin and the fire that had spread beneath.

My phone dinged with a new text message and snapped me out of my trance. I dropped the towel to the floor by the tub and climbed in before checking it. Part of me hoped it was Blake, texting to make sure I got home okay, but then I remembered that he didn't have my number. Aside from directions to his cabin, I didn't have any other way to get in touch with him.

I responded to my friend and told him I could get my stuff moved over tomorrow since he was off and had a truck. I didn't want to spend Christmas here with Henry and didn't want to inconvenience anyone any more than I had to with it being so close to the holiday.

Disappointed with how things ended between Blake and me, I sank into the water and tried to wash my heartache away.

By the time I got out of the tub, my skin was wrinkly, and I felt somewhat better about things. That was until I walked down the hall and found Henry waiting for me on the couch.

"Holly, please," he said as he stood up and tried to stop me from walking past him. "I know that I messed up."

I yanked my arm out of his grip and glared at him.

"You think?"

"I'm sorry, Holly. Just tell me what to do, and I'll fix this."

"Fix what?" I asked with my hands on my hips.

"This—between us. Come on; we've been together for five years. We have a house together. We can't just walk away from that."

"You were literally just telling your dad about how you planned to break up with me and how you were interested in someone you work with. And now you want to *fix* this? Henry, you didn't even bother to call and check on me after I left. You waited days and only called to ask about your car so you could get home."

He sighed and hung his head.

"The only thing that needs to be fixed is you, Henry. You're so concerned with what people think about you that you don't bother to figure out what you want for yourself. I'm not interested in being a part of that anymore. I know you want to try to make this work, but you can't fix what's been broken for so long. We got comfortable, and that's okay. But now that we know that neither of us is in love anymore, it's time to set each other free, so we can both be happy."

It felt good to say the words I'd been thinking in the tub out loud. I wasn't sure how I was going to handle things with Henry, but I trusted that I would figure it out when the time was right. Apparently, now was the time.

"I'm going to stay with Isaac for a while. He's helping me move tomorrow, but you don't have to be here."

He nodded and rubbed his lips together.

"I'll probably head into the office and give you some space."

"Thank you. I'll only take what's mine. You can keep anything we bought together."

"Holly, you don't have to do that."

"None of that matters to me. You know that. I'm a simple girl, Henry. I don't need money to make me happy."

It felt weird to say that because up until a few days ago, I was pretty sure that money did make me happy. But then I spent time with Blake and realized that it wasn't that at all. I didn't need material things to be happy, I was just used to associating them with my happiness because Henry spent so much time trying to buy mine. Blake, on the other hand, gave me his time and attention, which was all I needed.

"Okay," he sighed. "But if you see something you want, you don't have to ask."

I nodded and headed down the other hall and to the guest room. It wasn't my house anymore, so I had no desire to sleep in the master bedroom with a man I barely knew anymore.

Seventeen
Holly

"What are we doing here?" I groaned as Isaac pulled me down another aisle, searching for the *perfect gift*. I had no clue who it was for, given that he had already finished all of his holiday shopping and it was already Christmas Eve.

"Shopping."

"For who?"

"Shhhh...."

He held up a finger and shook it at me, then pulled my hand and stopped in front of a cologne display. It was too early in the morning for this, and I definitely hadn't had enough coffee.

I tried to take a deep breath and calm the frustration that was building inside, but all I really wanted to do was go home—well, to Isaac's house, grab a pint of ice cream, a bottle of wine, a fluffy blanket, and crawl into bed.

My depression was in full swing, and I was the least jolly person around. But seriously, what was I supposed to be happy about? Tomorrow was Christmas, and I was single, homeless, and officially unemployed. I had absolutely nothing to look forward to.

Isaac talked with the woman who sprayed some of the cologne onto a small piece of paper, then waved it in the air and handed it to him. They talked about the scent and how it had hints of this and that, but I got bored and wandered off.

He was dating a new guy and wanted to impress his parents—even though I told him not to get his hopes up too high—which meant we were on the hunt for more gifts for him to shower them with when he met them for the first time on Christmas day. Talk about a lot of pressure.

I strolled down one of the aisles and stood in front of an artificial tree that had a few ornaments left hanging on it. I was about to walk off when I noticed that it looked almost identical to the one Blake had cut down for me. It was just about the same size and color, but this one had specks of white that were supposed to look like snow.

It was uncanny how much this one resembled his. I was about to blow it off and chalk it up to my constantly imagining things when my eyes landed on an ornament in the center of the tree.

I gasped and reached up, gently lifting the angel to my fingers.

A tear slid down my cheek as I continued to stare at it. While it couldn't possibly be the same one that Blake's mom had, it looked almost identical.

When Isaac approached, I was still lost in the moment, holding it in my hands.

"Whatcha got there?"

I looked up at him, my eyes red and tear-stained cheeks.

"What's wrong?"

I took a deep, shuddered breath and told him the story about Blake's mom and the angel she had been given.

"Wow. And it looks just like this one?"

I nodded.

"Well then, it's a sign."

"What is?" I asked, wiping my nose with a tissue as I sniffled.

"That you need to buy it for Blake."

"What?" I asked, pulling my head back in confusion.

"You said his mom thought the other angel was magical and brought people where they needed to be, right?"

"Yeah."

"So then this is your sign that you're meant to be with Blake. You found the only angel ornament in the damn store, which just happens to be hanging on a tree that looks like the one he cut down for you—it's a sign, Holly! This angel is taking you to where you belong."

I shook my head. There was no way he was right. These were just random coincidences.

"I know you don't believe in signs," he continued, nudging me with his elbow. "But if you don't trust that one, what about another one?"

I followed his finger as he pointed across the store where there was a display of custom engraved signs. At the top was one that read *Blake* with two angels beside the name.

No. Freaking. Way.

"Are you doing this?" I demanded, spinning to face him.

His cheeks split into a grin, showing off the dimples I loved.

My stomach fluttered at the thought of fate bringing Blake and me together again.

"So what do I do?"

"Listen and follow your heart. What does your heart want, Holly?"

I felt the corners of my lips turn up. I knew exactly what to do.

Eighteen
Blake

I had dozed off when Luna startled me awake with her barking. I jumped off the couch and spotted a beat-up truck pulling up out front beside mine. Not expecting any visitors, I watched from the window, waiting to see who it was before deciding what action to take.

The passenger door opened, and then Holly appeared. My heart stopped for a second as I blinked quickly, making sure I wasn't dreaming she was there.

When she nervously started heading toward the door, I rushed over and opened it for her.

"Holly, what are you doing here?"

She chewed her lip nervously and then looked over her shoulder. I couldn't tell who was in the truck with her, but I really hoped it wasn't Henry. I'd hate to have to kick his ass on Christmas Eve.

"I was at the store with my friend, Isaac," she said, pointing over her shoulder to the guy who had just gotten out. "And there was this artificial tree on display that looked just like the one we cut down. It made me think of you."

I leaned against the doorframe with my arms folded while Luna stayed at my side. Holly smiled at her and then looked back up at me.

"There weren't many ornaments on the tree, only a few that hadn't been purchased yet. But then this one seemed to appear magically and was hung in the middle, right where I could see it."

She walked closer and pulled something out of her pocket. Once she was in front of me, she pulled back the tissue paper and handed me the ornament.

My eyes widened as I studied it, noticing how it looked exactly like the one my mom had.

"I know this is a far stretch, Blake, and I'm sorry for just showing up uninvited. But I couldn't ignore the signs that I needed to come see you. I mean, they were everywhere. Like literally *everywhere*."

I rubbed my lips together, still staring at the ornament. I wasn't trying to make Holly feel uncomfortable, but I couldn't get my words out. My throat burned from the emotions that were bubbling up inside.

"I'm sorry, I should go. You can keep the ornament if you'd like. Or don't, it doesn't matter."

She turned and started to walk away when I began speaking.

"My mom thought the angel brought her where she needed to be in life. I think she was right, and now it's brought you to where you need to be."

She stopped and froze where she was.

"I don't know what's going on with you and Henry, but I

know my life has been miserable without you, Holly. You deserve so much better. I know I'm not perfect, and I don't have much to offer, but if you give me a chance, I will love you like you need to be loved. I'll cherish and worship you every damn day. I'll—"

"There's no Henry," she interrupted, turning to face me.

"It's over?"

She nodded.

It felt almost too good to be true, but I didn't want to waste another second without having her in my arms. I nodded to her friend, who was grinning from ear to ear as I walked over and pulled her into my arms. She quickly wrapped her arms around my neck and pressed her lips to mine.

"You're the best gift I've ever gotten," I growled as I lifted her to my hips. She wrapped her legs around me and giggled before I captured it with a kiss.

"Does that mean you don't want the ones I bought you?" she giggled once she had her mouth free again.

I chuckled, knowing my mom must have had a hand in this all along. She showed Holly the angel and got me to purchase all of the stuff I got for Holly when I thought I'd never see her again.

After chatting for a few minutes with her friend, Isaac, we said goodbye and then went inside, where it was warm. I was thankful for him bringing Holly up to see me, even if he insisted that it was on his way and not a big deal. It was a huge deal to me.

I was more excited than a kid on Christmas morning,

unable to believe I was spending the holiday with Holly.

This time she planned ahead and brought a small suitcase with her. At first, I thought it was just for an overnight stay and felt disappointed that our time was once again limited. But then she sadly admitted that she didn't take much when she moved out of Henry's house, and that was all she had in general. They had packed up her stuff from the cabin, but she said that when she sat down and looked through everything, she realized that all of the materialistic things didn't matter to her anymore. Plus, she left most of it with Henry as it was stuff he'd boughten her and she didn't want anymore reminders of him.

The thought of Holly officially moving in with me was mind-blowing in the best way possible.

We got her stuff situated, and I made a note to take her into town after Christmas to get the things she needed. I wanted her to feel at home here and not have everything be mine. Even though she only had a small suitcase full of personal belongings, she came with armfuls of gift bags that Isaac helped bring in before he left.

It turned out that they had been shopping this morning, and she decided on a whim to come up here when she found out Isaac was already headed this way to go to his boyfriend's parent's house for Christmas. She sat in the backseat of his truck and wrapped gifts on the drive out here. Thankfully the roads were all cleared so they didn't have too many delays, other than heavy traffic here and there.

I offered to cook dinner, but Holly insisted that we eat a bowl of cereal and call it a night since it was so late. Once I saw her in the new pajamas that she'd bought for tonight, I didn't object one little bit.

Nineteen
Holly

"Is that a candy cane in your stocking, or are you just happy to see me?" I teased, rubbing my butt against the morning wood that was greeting me.

It felt good to wake up in Blake's bed again, but even better to be wrapped in his arms.

"What can I say? Santa has packages to deliver." He nipped my ear and then licked his way down my neck to my shoulder. "Have you been a good girl?"

I moaned as he reached forward and caressed my breast before moving his hand down to my pussy and teasing my lips.

"Nope."

He rolled me off my side onto my back.

"Do you know what Santa does to naughty girls?"

I pulled my bottom lip between my teeth and shook my head.

His eyes danced with excitement as his fingers trailed over my pussy, finally pushing one inside.

"He makes them come."

"Is that so?" I breathed out, closing my eyes as he inserted another finger.

"It is. And he spanks them."

"Mmmmm…."

He pumped his fingers faster, spreading my wetness between my folds.

I was close already, which was quite surprising given how many times I came last night. I didn't know my body was capable of having that many orgasms in such a short time.

Just as I was starting to get close, he pulled out and licked his lips.

"Ready for your punishment, naughty girl?"

I grinned; the damp fabric between my thighs confirmed that I was.

He rolled me over and lifted my waist to get me onto my knees. I loved this position and he knew it.

I spread my legs and lifted my ass, waiting for him to roll a condom on his hard cock. Then I felt the bed dip as he climbed up and spanked my ass, sending a jolt of pleasure and pain through me at once.

"Ahh," I cried out as he did it again. Before I could adjust to the sting of it, he slid inside and began thrusting.

I moved my neck, allowing him to kiss me while I frantically rubbed my clit, desperate for the orgasm that was building so quickly.

A few minutes later, I felt him grab my wrist and stop my hand.

"I make you come," he growled and replaced my fingers with his.

I whimpered as he kept the rhythm and brought me to climax within seconds while he continued to thrust hard before coming in the condom.

"Best. Christmas. Ever." I sighed contentedly and fell onto the pillows after he pulled out.

Once we were both cleaned up and dressed, we went to the living room and sat down on the floor in front of the tree. We'd added my gifts to the pile when I got there yesterday, but I was still shocked that he'd taken the time and energy to buy me gifts when he didn't even know that he would see me again.

He handed me a box wrapped with a gold bow, and I gave him a gift bag that had several wrapped gifts inside. Luna was already busy chewing the bone I got her last night and couldn't be bothered with our festivities.

I opened mine first and pulled out a light pink hoodie and matching leggings, both fleece lined and super warm. I grinned stupidly as I thought about how I would be comfortable here without having to steal any more of his clothes—even though I was still going to just because I liked how he looked at me when I was wearing them.

He opened his gift and smiled when he held up the wooden sign I'd convinced them to sell me from the display. The owner was reluctant until I told him my story, and his wife made him give it to me. It was perfect with his name and the two angels on it—the one his mom originally had and the one we believe she helped me find.

We continued opening gifts, and I was amazed at how thoughtful he was in his gifts for me. Besides warm clothes and bath products, he'd also grabbed me some snacks that he knew I liked, which was going to make today that much more special.

I'd grabbed a few sentimental things for him and then let Isaac shop for some of the other stuff. He was impressed with the insulated gloves Isaac insisted he needed and the new pocketknife. It was fun shopping for each other, but I could only imagine how great it would be once we knew each other better. This was such a whirlwind start, but I wouldn't change a single thing about it.

"So, what did you want to do today?" he asked as I laid against his chest on the couch.

We hadn't bothered to clean up the mess from opening gifts, and I was in no rush to. It felt good to just be with him.

"I didn't have any plans. Maybe watch movies? Play a board game? You?"

"Nothing either. But we're probably stuck inside for a few days. There's another bad storm moving in tonight."

I looked outside and noticed the white clouds hovering above the trees. It seemed like getting snowed in together was our thing now, and I had no problem with it. Memories of making love to him to pass the time flooded through me and spread heat throughout my body.

"Don't worry," I assured. "I know some things we can do inside."

His fingers tickled my sides as I felt him hardening beneath me. It was going to be a good Christmas, indeed.

SNOW PLACE
TO GO

Samantha Baca

<u>One</u>
Tiffany

"Hi, I'm checking in," I said to the woman with curly red hair that was pulled into a ponytail with a ribbon wrapped around it. I would probably think she was a cheerleader if it weren't for the bifocals that she had on. She leaned closer to the computer, typing something on the keyboard before she looked up at me.

"What's the name, dear?" she asked, her voice soft like my grandmother's.

"Tiffany Thompson."

I glanced over at the man who had been standing behind me, who was now being helped by the other receptionist. The only reason I knew it was a man was from his brash phone conversation that took place the entire time I waited in line.

I imagined an older man— someone powerful and aggressive based on how he was speaking to people. Instead, I found that he was actually younger— maybe a few years older than me, and quite attractive. His dress slacks and crisp, white button-down shirt didn't mesh well with the log cabin and lumberjack vibe of the other men who were running around, but it suited him well.

I listened to their conversation shamelessly while the woman in front of me struggled to get her computer to work.

"Your name, sir?"

"Luke Lane."

A few clicks on her keyboard, and she had his reservation pulled up.

She was younger— probably twenty years younger than the woman helping me, and seemed much more comfortable with technology.

"Alright, I show that you'll be staying in cabin 6. It's outside, around the corner, the last cabin on the left."

I let out a soft sigh, wishing this would move faster and that I could be on my way too.

"Okay, dear, I show that you'll be in Cabin 6. Let me get your key."

She turned around and reached for the key at the same time the other girl did. They both pulled back then frowned when they realized that it was the only set of keys left on the pegboard, and there were two separate people checking in.

"That's my key, dear," she said to the other woman, her hand slightly trembling as she reached up for it.

"I don't think so," the other girl replied. "I show cabin six on his reservation, and that's this key."

"Mine shows cabin six as well."

"Mind if I take a look?"

I exchanged glances with the attractive stranger beside me, wondering what in the world was going on. Surely, there had to be some sort of error in their computer system and another key lying around somewhere.

They stood at her computer, confirming the information for my reservation before turning to the other one and checking his. Finally, the younger woman looked at us and held her hands together in a peace offering.

"I'm sorry," she said firmly. "It appears that there's been a mistake, and both of you have been assigned the same cabin."

"That's fine, I'll just take another one," I replied, waving my hand dismissively.

"Unfortunately, there aren't any. We're completely booked with it being five days before Christmas. This is the last cabin that we have available."

I closed my eyes and pinched the bridge of my nose. This was just my luck with everything else I had going on. *Why wouldn't I be able to escape for the holidays and hide away in a cabin in the middle of nowhere?*

"We can add a rollaway bed to the cabin, free of charge for the inconvenience," she added nervously, looking between us for an answer.

"You're suggesting that we *share* the cabin?" Luke said, speaking for the first time since this whole debacle started.

"I would strongly encourage it. There's a storm moving in that will shut down all of the roads to and from the cabin for a few days. There's no way to make it down the mountain safely before it hits." She paused for a moment, letting this news sink in. "Our one bedroom cabins are very spacious and can easily accommodate two guests," she assured.

He let out the breath that I had been holding as we sighed heavily together.

"I'm fine with sleeping on the rollaway bed in the living room if you're okay with sharing the cabin," he offered, turning to face me.

I felt my cheeks blush, feeling his curious dark gray eyes watch me.

"Sure, that works for me," I choked out. "As long as there is a separate bathroom and bedroom, that's fine."

"Perfect," the girl said, holding the key out between the two of us.

He reached forward and took it, giving me a tight smile, before reaching down to grab his luggage.

"The dining hall is open until seven pm and will open again at six tomorrow morning. Your cabin is fully stocked with extra linens, however, you can call the main desk if there's anything else you might need. We're honored to have you stay at Bear Creek and hope you enjoy your stay."

I turned on my heel, pulling my suitcase behind me as I struggled to keep the duffle bag and my purse from sliding off. Luke led the way out, holding the door open for me as we stepped out into a bitter gust of wind. I covered my mouth with my hand, trying to shield myself as it took my breath away. He looked around, his eyes narrowed and focused, before he set off in the direction of our cabin.

It was a short walk but felt longer with the ankle-deep

snow covering the ground. I was thankful that I had packed accordingly. It was a very purposeful plan—rent a cabin in the woods, watch the snow fall while cuddled up under a blanket with a good book, and blame getting snowed in as the reason why I couldn't make it home for Christmas with my family.

It had *nothing* to do with the fact that I was the oldest of my parent's four kids and the only one who was still single and childless. I was reminded of it *every single year* during the holidays when my mom would moan and complain about how she wished I would find someone to settle down with. *You're not a spring chicken anymore, Tiffany. Men don't want women the same when they're in their thirties. The clock is ticking, you better start looking.*

That was a few years ago, right after my thirtieth birthday. Nothing had changed since then other than the number of extra prayers my mom said for my poor eggs that would never be fertilized while I blew out the thirty-two candles on my cake. It felt juvenile to have a cake that was basically *on fire*, but she wanted to make sure that I didn't forget just how old I was or how much harder it was to do things—like blowing out candles—the older that I got.

Once we found our cabin, he fumbled with the key until it finally turned and opened into a cute, rustic-looking room. We walked inside and closed the door, keeping the cold out as he turned on the rest of the lights. It wasn't a huge cabin but had plenty of room for us to move around each other without getting in the way.

The living room and kitchen were all one room, divided by a breakfast bar that extended past the sink. Cream-colored paint covered the walls, making it look more open and homier. I was relieved that it wasn't over the top with log walls like the main area where we had checked in. This was calmer, more relaxing.

I set my luggage down by the couch, out of the way, and walked around, taking in the views from the oversized windows that framed the living room. The room darkening curtains were pulled back with sheer curtains covering the panes. Off to the side of the room was a large, plush chair that would be the perfect spot to sit down and read.

A decent-sized tv hung mounted to the wall above an entertainment center that was fully stocked with board games and DVDs. There were plenty of places to sit with the loveseat and sofa taking up the majority of the space around the dark gray wood coffee table.

I was walking to the back of the cabin to check out the bathroom and bedroom, when there was a knock on the door. Luke nodded and walked over to answer it, while I continued with my tour. The bathroom was spacious, with a double vanity and a large mirror that stretched the width of the counter. There was a walk-in shower that was easily big enough to fit two people, accompanied by one of those fancy shower heads that has twenty-some different water pressure options. Beside it was an inviting tub with an assortment of soaking salts and bath bombs lining the shelf behind it.

The door closed, and I felt the gush of cold air rush in as I went back to the living room. The rollaway bed had been delivered, along with a bottle of wine—compliments of the manager for our inconvenience. The bed in the back was a king and looked plenty big to fit both of us comfortably, but I was too nervous to suggest that. If needed, I could sleep on the other bed until he left—which reminded me that

I didn't know how long we were going to be shacked up together.

"So, I checked the closet in the bedroom, and it's pretty big if you wanted to share it," I said awkwardly, unsure of what else to say.

"Thanks, I don't think I'll have much use for it. I won't be here that long."

"Oh?" I blurted out, feeling the heat of embarrassment wash over me.

"I'm only here through Christmas. I'll be checking out the day after."

Of course, he is.

"I'm leaving the same day."

It felt like a stupid thing to say since he hadn't bothered to ask.

"Well, I'll take the rollaway bed. You can have the bedroom and the closet."

"I don't mind—"

"I insist," he interrupted firmly. Just like that, it was the same cold, harsh tone that I had heard earlier when he was on the phone.

"Okay, thank you," I mumbled, walking over to grab my suitcase.

I went to the bedroom and closed the door, needing some space from the mysterious man on the other side of the wall.

<u>Two</u>

Luke

There were plenty of things in life that I didn't like, and surprises were one of them. When they informed me that there was a mix-up with their system, I would have normally raised my voice and demanded that they fix it— immediately. But the beautiful blonde-haired woman next to me with the sparkling green eyes had me agreeing to share a cabin with her, just so I could see her again.

I didn't even care that I had spent my entire holiday bonus to rent a cabin up here at the last minute and was now stuck sleeping on a rickety rollaway bed instead of the comfortable king bed with the plush pillow-top mattress. It was worth the sacrifice, as I watched her move around the space, her curiosity about me as high as mine was about her.

When she offered to sleep in the living room on the crappy bed, I scoffed and tried to decline as politely as I could. That didn't mean that it didn't come out gruff—just that I tried. There was no way in hell that I was going to let it happen. I was raised better than that, even if I was currently avoiding any and *all* interaction with my family right now.

She had been in the bedroom for over an hour before the door opened, and she walked out, wearing a thick wool coat and a beanie.

"I'm heading over to the main hall to grab dinner. Did you want to join me?"

I realized that it was already after six, and if I wanted to eat tonight, this was probably my last chance.

"Sure, let me grab my coat."

I had taken the opportunity to change while she was in the bedroom and traded my work attire for a pair of jeans and a ribbed fitted sweater. I pulled on my coat and then grabbed the key from the table before heading out into the cold with her.

The dining hall was surprisingly busy with other guests milling around, chatting as they added food to their plates from the buffet. I had assumed that there would be a formal dining experience with a menu and waiters, but apparently, I was wrong.

We checked in with the hostess and took the number that she gave us to an empty table before heading over to the food. I stepped back and let her go first, smiling as I held my hand out in front of me for her to pass. She grabbed a plate and walked down the side, leaning forward to get a better look at the salad options in front of her.

I picked up a plate and wandered over to the meats. The selection didn't look that great, and I assumed it was because they were getting ready to close down soon and weren't planning on making anything fresh. I chose a grilled chicken breast and loaded my plate with a side of mashed potatoes and a cob of corn before returning to the table.

Tiffany was already sitting there, picking at her salad with her fork. I was surprised that she didn't get anything else, but then again, her plate didn't look like it needed anything else. There were so many vibrant colors, from the dark green of the spinach to the orange carrot sticks and deep red tomatoes—it looked like something you would see on one of those fancy cooking shows.

"That's quite the salad," I commented, pulling out the chair across from her and sitting down.

"Thank you. There weren't a ton of options, so I worked with what I had."

"Yeah, I agree. I'm hoping that there's a better selection in the morning."

"I'm sure there will be. It's hard this close to closing time, they don't want to waste food by cooking fresh items when there's still stuff that hasn't been eaten."

I smiled and studied her as I cut into my chicken and took a bite.

"You seem to know a lot about how restaurants work," I noted after I swallowed my bite.

While we were gone, the waitress had come by and left glasses of ice water on the table for us. I took a drink, washing down the somewhat dry chicken.

"I'm a chef," she shrugged as if it were no big deal.

"Oh yeah?" I asked, wiping my face with a napkin and leaning back against the metal seat. "Where at?"

"A little café, just south of the Oregon state line."

"So, what brought you to Bear Creek?"

She paused for a moment, taking a bite before she answered.

"I wanted to spend the holiday snowed in somewhere. If I were snowed in, then I'd have no place to go," she giggled nervously.

"Or *snow* place to go," I joked, smiling when she laughed at my corny attempt to be funny.

"What about you?" she asked. "What brought you to the middle of nowhere, five days before Christmas?"

"Family."

Her eyes widened as she looked around the room.

"Oh, are you joining your family up here for the holiday?"

I was mid-chew when she asked, which caused my food to get stuck in my throat when I tried to swallow. I started choking, reaching for the glass of water before I caused a scene.

"No," I choked in between drinks. "I'm here to avoid seeing my family. As far as they're concerned, I'm working and can't make it home."

"Where's home?"

"Cedar Plank, Nebraska."

"Why don't you want to see your family?"

I felt my hands start sweating from the constant questions, suddenly feeling like I was being interrogated.

"Because they're incredibly judgmental, and I never live up to their expectations," I said gruffly. "Are you here because you want a Hallmark Christmas, or are you here to avoid your family too?"

"You caught me," she laughed, the sound of it sending a warm feeling straight to my heart. She covered her mouth with her hand and continued to giggle.

"I knew it," I teased. "No one wants to willingly get snowed in somewhere."

"That's not true," she objected, pointing her fork in my direction. "I would very much love to get snowed in somewhere. No responsibilities other than relaxing and watching the snow fall—it would be so wonderful."

"Okay, *maybe* if there were no responsibilities. But where I come from, you never get away from them, so it wouldn't be a realistic option for me."

"Well, that's unfortunate," she said, her eyes narrowing as she focused on me. When the light hit them just right, I could see small brown flecks mixed in with the emerald green, and it was hypnotizing.

"That's the same thing my parents always say," I muttered under my breath while poking at my chicken with the fork.

"So, why are you avoiding your family?"

She popped a piece of spinach in her mouth and chewed as she waited for me to answer.

"Because I can't handle *another* holiday of them riding my ass about my life choices."

She pulled her head back, and her jaw dropped open.

"I thought I was the only one with parents like that."

"Nope," I laughed. "I can guarantee that mine are probably *the worst*."

"Okay, let's see," she said, her eyes filled with mischief.

"See what?"

"Whose parents are worse. We'll compare battle stories and then decide."

"I don't think you know what you're getting yourself into," I warned playfully. "Unfortunately, I will always win at this game."

"We'll just see about that," she retorted. "I'll even let you go first."

I pushed my plate to the side and folded my hands in front of me on the table.

"Fine. My parents tell everyone they meet that I'm gay when I'm not."

"What?!" she gasped. "Why would they do that?"

"Because they don't want to believe that I've intentionally stayed single. Plus, I'm a wedding planner in Los Angeles and work with a lot of LGBTQIA clients."

"Wow," she said, nodding in disbelief.

"Your turn."

"Well, my mom tried to marry me off to the new guy in town, right after the Sunday service at church. When she heard that he was a doctor, she made sure to tell him that she thought my eggs were getting too old and dried up and asked if he wouldn't mind taking a look."

I choked on the drink of water I had just taken, embarrassed that it was the second time to happen in under an hour. *What was wrong with me?*

"That's pretty bad, but you still don't win. My mom actually created a profile for me on a men's only dating site. She even attempted to photoshop my driver's license photo to a beach scene she found online. It was a terrible picture. I hurt her feelings even more when I told her that gay men would not be impressed by it and that she was dooming me to stay single."

She tossed her head back and laughed, her blond hair cascading down her back.

"I'm sure that got her even more riled up."

"That it did," I chuckled.

"So because you're a wedding planner, you're automatically gay?" she questioned, leaning forward and resting her elbows on the table.

"It would seem so. I guess it doesn't help that I've *never* taken a woman home to meet my family, and unlike my siblings, I choose to keep my personal details just that— personal."

"How many siblings do you have?"

"I have four sisters. Two older and two younger, which leaves me as the middle child, and of course, the only boy."

"Man, this just keeps getting better," she giggled, covering her mouth.

"See, I told you—I win."

"Not so fast," she countered. "Gay wedding planner isn't that bad. If anything—I would say it's pretty damn good, because I would totally hire you to plan my wedding, knowing that you would have every detail on point, and it would be perfect."

"Oh, so now I'm planning your wedding?" I teased, enjoying the playful banter between us.

"Yeah, once I find someone willing to marry me," she snorted and rolled her eyes. "I have to beat them away with a bat, there's so many lined up."

"I'm sure it's not that bad," I said softly, sensing the hurt in her tone.

"It's not that I want to stay single—even though my mother would say otherwise. I just haven't found *the one*. I'm only thirty-two, why should I settle?"

"I'm thirty-eight and still refuse to settle. I don't think there's a damn thing wrong with you waiting for the right person."

She smiled, but it fell flat before it reached her eyes, the sadness overshadowing it.

"So, what made you decide to be a chef?" I asked, shifting the conversation to something lighter.

"I've always had a love for food—as you can see," she said shyly, extending her arms for me to see her body. "At one point, my mom tried to get me to enlist in the army so I would stay away from food. She said *maybe if you had a job where you were physically active and not constantly around food, then you wouldn't have to worry about your addiction.*"

"Addiction?" I asked, raising an eyebrow. She was curvy and in the best way. Not overweight like her mother seemed to imply.

"She thinks that I'm addicted to food."

I looked down at her salad, wondering if she was eating it because she wanted to or because she held this heavy guilt that her mom loaded onto her.

"I don't see anything wrong with what you're eating," I muttered. "And I don't see a damned thing wrong with your body either—just for the record. Curves are sexy, and I like a woman who wears them proudly."

"Well, thank you, I appreciate your gay insight," she teased with a wink. "But trust me—I like to eat. I'm a meat and potatoes kind of gal. I want savory foods with robust flavors that burst on your tongue. I only got salad tonight because it looked like the safest option out of what was left."

I felt my lips turning up into a smile. It had been a while since I was able to talk to a woman and have it stay this lighthearted and fun. I didn't date much because it was hard to meet women close to my age who weren't talking about ticking biological clocks and pressuring me for a second date before the check came.

"That's impressive," I commented, meaning it. "My job requires me to have a broad palate, and honestly, I enjoy when I get roped into food tastings."

"I bet it's a lot of fun, getting to meet so many new people and plan weddings. I've always wanted to get into catering so that I could network and get out more. Plus, growing up in a large family trained me to know how to cook for large groups."

"Why don't you do it then?"

"Do what?"

"Catering."

"Oh," her face fell. "I don't know. I guess I've just never had the opportunity. Most people want to hire someone with years of experience, so it makes it hard to get your foot in the door."

"What about the place you currently work? Do they do any catering services that you could help out with?"

She paused for a moment, taking a drink of water before she set the glass down on the table with a shaky hand.

"I'm actually in between jobs right now."

"Oh, I'm sorry," I apologized.

"It's okay. I'm taking a few weeks off to rest and recuperate, and then I plan to hit the ground running on January first to find something new. It's a great opportunity to find something that I really want to do and start over."

"Well, here's to new opportunities," I said, raising my glass. She lifted hers, and they clinked in the air.

Three
Tiffany

I didn't know if it was possible to be colder outside when we left the dining hall than it was when we first went over there. It felt like the temperature dropped at least twenty degrees which made the falling snow feel like shards of glass that poked at my face which was already stinging from the gusts of wind that had whipped past us.

Once we got to our cabin, we rushed inside and locked the door. I pulled off my coat and hung it on the back of the kitchen chair, rubbing my hands together to warm myself up. Luke worked on starting the fireplace before taking off his coat and hanging it next to mine. I curled up on the couch and tucked my legs under me, thinking back to dinner.

I had expected Luke to have some sort of comment about my body or how I needed to eat more salad, but he surprised me when he said that he liked a woman who had curves and wore them with confidence. The one thing that I didn't have was confidence, but he hadn't caught onto that yet.

The flames of the fire danced across the walls, making me feel more relaxed. I hadn't thought much about what we would do or how we would share this space. Then, realizing that I was technically in his bedroom, I started to worry that

I should move to my room and give him some space.

I got up and folded the blanket, hanging it over the edge of the couch while he was in the bathroom. I was on my way to the room when the door opened, and we almost collided in the hallway.

"Sorry," I laughed, stepping to the side. "I was just heading to the room so you could have some space."

His dark eyes narrowed at me before he said, "you're fine, I don't need space."

I paused, unsure of where to go. I wasn't ready for bed yet, but I also didn't want him to feel obligated to spend more time with me.

"I saw some board games, did you want to play one?" he asked, lingering beside me.

"Sure, that sounds great." My voice was quieter than usual, straining to come out.

I followed him back to the living room and sat on the couch while he scanned the options.

"We have Battleship, Monopoly, or Clue. The rest I've never heard of unless you have the desire to play Mall Madness."

He arched a brow. I chewed my lower lip and giggled.

"Oh, I totally have the desire to play Mall Madness," I snickered.

He sighed dramatically, letting his head fall to his chest. He ran a hand through his dark hair and then muttered, "I knew I shouldn't have mentioned that one."

"Hey, you're just afraid that I might know more about shopping than a *gay wedding planner*," I teased as he grabbed it from the shelf and brought it over.

"Do you want to play on the couch, or should we move to the floor and use the coffee table?"

"Honestly, if I get down on the floor, you probably won't get me up again," I joked, knowing how much truth there was to it.

"Fair enough, I don't know that my knees could handle it either."

I scooted to the end of the couch and helped him set the game up in the middle between us.

"Do you know how to play this, or should I read the directions?" he asked once everything was out of the box.

"Please, I grew up in the eighties. I don't need no stinkin' directions," I laughed.

Twenty minutes later, we were staring at the board, unsure of what to do next.

"Are you sure that we don't need to read the directions," he teased, smirking at the confused look on my face.

"No, I just need to concentrate."

"On a shopping game for ages nine and up?"

"I need the sound," I whined. "I can't play without hearing where the sales are."

"Okay," he said. "I can fix that."

He jumped up and walked over to the entertainment center,

grabbing the handful of remotes and bringing them back to the couch. A few minutes later, he was swapping batteries and the game came to life.

"There's a sale at the record store," the voice said.

I squealed and clapped my hands excitedly.

"Alright, now it's on," I taunted.

"I thought it was supposed to be on from the moment we started," he countered. "It seems like maybe my internal gay guy does know a thing or two about shopping after all."

I rolled my eyes and took my turn after pressing the button to start the game. I already had three of the six items that I needed to purchase, while Luke had four. I looked at the cash that I still had on hand and knew that I would have to stop by the bank unless I could hit one of the sales on the way to the parking lot.

Luke reached the record store before I could and added another item to his purchases. I was feeling the tension, knowing that he was probably going to win after all. The next sale ended up being at the pet shop, which I was standing right in front of. I smiled as I swiped my card to pay for my purchase, giggling at the gargled sound the game made from years of use and abuse.

We were neck to neck, in the final stretch, both sitting with five purchases and heading toward the parking lot while trying to get the last item on our list.

I tapped my finger nervously against my chin as I waited for my turn. There was a clearance sale at the fashion boutique, but it would force me to move away from the parking lot in order to get to it. I didn't have enough money to purchase anything else along the way.

Luke headed into the store to grab his last purchase and covered his face with his hands when he realized that he didn't have enough money to make it. He was in the same position now, and either had to head back to the ATM to take out cash, or he had to get to the same clearance sale that I was closer to.

He scrunched his face and glared at me as he ended his turn and watched me win the game. I laughed at the sour expression, knowing that he must be a sore loser.

"Wanna go again?" I asked, making my girl dance her way out to the parking lot.

"No way," he laughed. "That was brutal enough."

I leaned against the couch and laughed with him. It had been fun, but I had to admit that I was pleasantly surprised to see how invested he had gotten in the game.

"Well, I guess I shall leave you to dwell on your loss," I teased. "It's getting late, and I'm sure you want to get some rest."

He hesitated for a moment, a look of uncertainty on his face.

"I was thinking about watching a movie if you wanted to join me?"

I noticed how his eyes seemed to beg me to stay even though he didn't say it.

"Sure, that would be nice. I'll see if there's some popcorn in the kitchen."

I got up and walked into the kitchen, wondering who this man really was. The cold, demanding man I had heard on the phone earlier was now replaced with a nice, gentle one who didn't seem to want to be alone.

<u>Four</u>
Luke

I sat next to her on the couch, sharing a giant bowl of popcorn while we watched Top Gun. I had assumed that she would pick a chick flick when I gave her the option, so color me surprised when she went for a classic. It was getting late, and I knew that the movie would be over soon, but I didn't want my time with her to end.

It wasn't like I didn't enjoy being alone—hell, I preferred it over most people's company. But there was something different about her that made me desperate to hang out with her. It was like she was a magnet, and I couldn't escape the pull toward her. Maybe it was because she was the first person I had talked to in a long time that was genuine and cared about what I had to say. She didn't just humor me and listen to my stories. She made eye contact and gave me her undivided attention as if I was the most interesting person she'd ever talked to.

I shifted on the couch, relaxing against the soft leather as I considered sleeping on it instead of the rollaway bed they brought earlier. That thing looked like it had seen better days, and I was pretty confident that I would wake up tomorrow stiff and sore from a poor night's sleep.

The not so gentle sound of snoring escaped from Tiffany's

mouth as her head fell to the side, sound asleep. I fought the urge to pick her up and carry her to the bedroom, knowing how inappropriate that would be given that she barely knew me. Instead, I cleaned up our snacks and carried our glasses to the kitchen before grabbing a blanket and covering her. I gave in and set up the other bed, wincing as it creaked under my weight, afraid that it would wake her up.

I was just getting settled in when I rolled over and saw her eyes flutter open. She sat up and looked around the room, finally finding me in the dark after her eyes adjusted. I had left the light on in the bathroom with the door cracked to give off a small amount of light so she didn't freak out if she woke up in the middle of the night to a pitch-black room that she wasn't familiar with.

"What time is it?" she asked sleepily.

"Just after midnight," I replied, rolling onto my side and propping myself up on my elbow. "You were in a deep sleep, so I didn't want to wake you."

"Was I snoring?"

"Not that I could tell," I lied, not knowing if it would embarrass her if I said yes.

"You're a terrible liar," she laughed. "But I'm going to head to bed and let you get some rest. Are you sure you don't want to switch and take the bedroom?"

"No," I said sternly. "I want you to sleep in the room. I'll be fine out here."

"Okay, thank you. Good night."

"Good night."

Once she was in her room, I waited until I heard the door locked and let out a sigh of relief. As much as I wanted to spend time with her, I was thankful that she was smart enough to protect herself after being forced into this situation. While I didn't have any intentions of doing anything to her, I had four sisters that made me overly protective of all women when it came to their safety.

I rolled over, cringing when the bed creaked again beneath me. Finally, I gave up and moved to the couch. It was already ten times better than the bed, and within minutes, I was fast asleep.

The next morning, I was up first, so I went ahead and took a quick shower, not wanting to tie up the bathroom if she needed it. I dried off and was about to get dressed when I realized that I had left my clothes in the kitchen, on the counter. I had been so distracted making a pot of coffee that I hadn't paid attention before I jumped in the shower.

I wrapped the towel around my waist and opened the door, hoping to grab my clothes before Tiffany got up and saw me. I was looking over my shoulder, feeling relieved that the bedroom door was still closed, when I rounded the corner and ran right into her.

Her hands planted firmly against my chest as she let out a squeal. I lifted my hands defensively to keep from touching her while I was naked, but unfortunately, all of the movement had allowed the towel to loosen its grip around me and fell to the floor.

My hands darted down to cover myself as her eyes widened. Her mouth dropped open as she took a small step back and stared at my naked body in front of her as I scrambled to figure out a way to get my towel back on without showing her my dick.

"I'm sorry," I apologized, feeling the heat flush my cheeks.

"No, I'm sorry," she stuttered. "I didn't hear you coming."

Her face turned crimson as she covered her mouth.

"I mean, I didn't hear you walking down the hallway. Not that you were coming. Or not coming. I um—"

"It's fine," I said quickly, trying to stop this conversation before it got too out of control.

"I wasn't insinuating that you were--."

"Really, Tiffany, it's fine."

She took another step back and tried to keep her gaze from wandering, but I caught her anyway.

"I'm gonna go back to my room," she announced, pulling her shoulders back as she sucked in a deep breath.

I stood there, unable to move as she walked past me. I felt her eyes on me and glanced over my shoulder to find her checking out my naked ass.

Well, things just got awkward.

<u>Five</u>
Tiffany

"It was so huge that he couldn't fully cover it with *both* hands!" I whispered into the phone, covering the mouthpiece even though I was alone in my room.

"What did you do?" Charlie asked, almost squealing. She had been my best friend since we graduated high school.

"I didn't know what to do! I tried not to look, but it was hard."

"Oh, I'm sure it was," she cooed and then giggled.

"Not like that," I laughed, feeling the blush cover my skin again.

"Well, that's too bad. I'm sure that would have been a sight to see."

"If it's as nice as his ass, I bet it would be."

"You checked out his ass?"

"Yeah," I admitted, chewing my nail nervously. "But he turned around and caught me."

"He caught you!! Tiffany! You naughty girl." Her tone changed from shocked to approval within a matter of seconds.

"I don't even know how I'm going to look him in the eye now."

"Well, just imagine him naked," she suggested. "Oh, wait. You've already done that."

She laughed, bringing mine out with hers.

"It's not funny," I said as convincingly as possible. "I'm stuck with him for the next four days—maybe longer, while we're snowed in."

"I really don't see what the problem is. If it were me—I would already be taking advantage of that situation and hiding *all* of the towels in that damn cabin."

"You're so bad," I laughed.

"Yeah, but it would be a fun time. And seriously, Tiffany, with everything you've been through recently, you deserve to have some fun."

I felt the happiness quickly slip away. Part of escaping to a remote cabin in the middle of nowhere was to run away from the problems I left behind in Oregon. I wasn't ready to deal with them then, and I sure as hell wasn't ready to deal with them now.

"So, tell me about this place. What's it like?" she asked, changing the subject when I stayed silent for too long.

"It's so beautiful, Charlie. There's so much snow that I could spend all day curled up under a blanket, drinking coffee, and reading books and not have an ounce of regret."

"Are there a lot of cabins close to you, or is it as secluded as you hoped it would be?"

"Our cabin is at the very end of our row, so we get an unobstructed view of the woods and don't see any other cabins. There are a few rows of cabins, with probably ten or so in each row. There's a main lodge in the middle. It's all surrounded by thick forest."

"That sounds dreamy," she sighed. "We should go together next year."

"That would be nice," I agreed. "We'll probably have to book it early. It seems like they fill up fast."

"Well, we'll make sure we get ours. And I want a room with a dick."

"I think you mean deck," I corrected, laughing.

"You can have your deck, but I want a dick in mine. If you get one, I want one too."

"I didn't get one," I snorted. "It wasn't like it was planned or anything."

"Then I guess I wouldn't mess with fate too much. I mean, if she's lining it up for you that much, you should definitely *jump* on that opportunity."

"Well, on that note, I better get going," I said. "I'll talk to you soon."

We hung up, and I laid back on the bed, debating how long I could avoid seeing Luke. I grabbed my clothes from the bed and made sure I had a towel before I jumped in the shower and tried not to picture him in it not that long ago.

162

<u>Six</u>

Luke

I pressed the button to silence my mother's phone call as Tiffany came down the hall. She had showered and gotten ready, which gave us a little bit of time to avoid each other after the towel incident. I didn't know who was more embarrassed—her or me. I could honestly say that I had never seen that shade of red on a woman before, and I've been with my fair share of them.

I stuffed my phone into my pocket and tried to pose in a way that didn't look like I had been standing around waiting for her. She smiled when she saw me, nervously tucking a strand of hair behind her ear as she avoided looking me in the eyes.

"Did you want to head over to the dining hall and see what the breakfast options are?" I asked, fastening my watch on my wrist.

"Sure, that sounds great."

I grabbed my coat from the back of the chair, then handed her hers. We walked in silence, trying to keep our balance in the knee-deep snow before we reached the portion that had been cleared by the maintenance crew. Soon, we were inside where it was warm and free of dangerous hazards.

"Luke!"

I froze at the sound of my name, the shrill sound of her voice sending chills through my body. There was *no fucking way* that she was here right now. I swallowed hard, forcing down the nausea that was rising, and turned around stiffly.

Making her way toward me with the speed of a cheetah closing in on a gazelle, there was no way to run and pretend that I hadn't seen her. Her heels clicked annoyingly on the tile floor as she rushed over in her designer suit—oblivious to the weather outside.

"I've been trying to call you," she said, annoyed.

"I've been busy," I muttered, glancing at Tiffany, who was standing beside me, curious as to what was going on.

"I can see," she replied snidely as she looked Tiffany up and down, not bothering to hide the judgment on her face.

"What are you doing here, mom?" I asked, ready to get this over with.

"Well, when you *wouldn't* come home for Christmas, your father and I decided we would come to you. Laney found out that you were staying at this beautiful resort and knew that *this* was the place she wanted to have her wedding!" She pressed her hands together, her face squinched with excitement.

"I'm sure she'll enjoy hearing about it when you get back home. Now, if you'll excuse me, we were on our way to get some breakfast." I placed my hand on Tiffany's lower back and gently pushed to guide her away from my mother.

"Oh, there's no need for that." She waved her hand as if clearing away the absurd thought. "She's here with us. Well, technically, the whole family is. When she decided that she *had* to get married this weekend, everyone jumped at the opportunity to spend Christmas in this magical wonderland. We were so lucky to grab the last few rooms, I heard that they *overbooked,*" she whispered in disbelief.

I rolled my eyes and ran a hand down my face. She had to be kidding me. There was no way in hell that my entire family had all made it down here for a last-minute wedding for my bratty baby sister. Although that explained how they ended up short on rooms by the time I got here to check in.

"Sounds like Laney," I muttered.

"Oh, don't be grumpy, you ol' Grinch." She swatted at my chest playfully before turning her attention back to Tiffany. "And who are you, dear? My son seems to have lost his manners, not bothering to introduce me to his date."

Tiffany looked at me nervously, her mouth slightly open as she was about to speak, when someone from the lodge walked over and interrupted before she could.

"Mr. Lane, I apologize for interrupting, however, we needed to confirm whose credit card you wanted to keep on file for the cabin you're sharing."

I watched as my mom's eyes widened with surprise as she listened in, checking for Tiffany's reaction.

"Please use my card," I confirmed, holding my mom's gaze, willing her not to say anything and make a scene.

"Yes, sir. If there is anything we can do to make your stay more comfortable, please let us know. We hope you and

Ms. Thompson enjoy your visit," her voice was pleasant yet heavy with forced sincerity.

She turned and walked away, leaving the air thick with tension.

"Well, now I see why you *couldn't* come home for Christmas," she scoffed.

Before I could say anything, my sister came rushing over, tears running down her face.

"Everything is falling apart," she cried, throwing herself into my mom's arms.

"Oh, honey, what happened?"

"I spoke with the manager and asked about having the wedding here on Christmas Eve. They said that they couldn't cater the reception with that short of notice because they didn't have anyone equipped to handle the large party. What am I supposed to do now?" Laney whined, not bothering to look up to see me standing there.

"Well then, I guess it's a good thing that your brother—the *wedding planner*—is here. Surely he'll know what to do."

My sister whipped around, rubbing her tears away with the back of her hand.

"Luke! Can you help me?"

"I don't know," I sighed, not wanting to be part of this drama but also feeling a little intrigued by the idea of proving to them once and for all that my job wasn't the joke they made it out to be. If I could pull this off and give my sister the wedding of her dreams on three days' notice—I would go down in the wedding planner hall of fame. Not that we had one—but I would be sure to start one.

"Please, Luke," she begged, standing as close to me as possible with her hands pressed together in prayer. She hadn't bothered to notice Tiffany yet because she was too focused on getting what she wanted.

I turned toward Tiffany, a devious smirk on my face.

"What do you say, baby? Do you think you're up for catering this wedding?"

She narrowed her eyes at me in confusion and searched for the answer to the question she didn't have to speak. I knew what she was thinking—*what in the hell is he doing!*

"Um, sure?" she replied with far too much uncertainty.

"Great! I'll talk to Julianna and get everything arranged," I said smugly to my mom and sister, my hand still pressed firmly against Tiffany's back. It wasn't necessary, given I had managed to shock her into a state of being paralyzed, but it made me feel better that I would at least feel the moment that she tried to run.

"Well, it looks like we'll finally get to see you in action as you put together your baby sister's *wedding of her dreams*."

I didn't miss the snide tone as my mother spoke. Thankfully, it just fueled the fire that was now raging inside me to prove that she didn't know me or what I was capable of.

"Laney, I'll need you to come by the cabin in an hour so we can discuss details. Don't be late. Your wedding is on the line."

She nodded but didn't say anything as she finally noticed Tiffany.

"Now, if you'll excuse us, we're heading to breakfast." I turned and guided her in the other direction, my hand gently sliding down her back and grazing her ass as my mom and sister watched. I didn't have to turn around to know that they had seen it because I could feel their eyes burning holes in the back of my head.

Once we were in the dining hall, Tiffany turned on me, shoving me up against a wall. Her emerald green eyes flashed with anger as her jaw tightened.

"What the hell was that?!" she demanded, making sure she kept her voice low enough not to draw attention to us.

"I'm sorry," I blew out, the adrenaline starting to wear off. "I didn't know what else to do. I panicked, and since my mom was already assuming that you are my girlfriend, I just went with it."

"You volunteered me to cater a wedding! I've never catered anything in my life! And then you throw a wedding at me with no warning whatsoever?"

"I know," I apologized, gently reaching out to hold her shoulders. "I should have asked you first and again, I'm sorry. I guess I just saw an opportunity, so I went for it."

"Because it made *you* look good. What happens when I mess everything up and ruin your sister's wedding?"

"You're not going to mess it up."

"How do you know that? You don't even know me."

"Fair enough," I shrugged. "I guess we'll have plenty of time getting to know each other over the next few days."

"This was supposed to be a *relaxing* week off," she

muttered, her shoulders dropping.

"How about we make a deal?" I offered, pulling my hands away before it started to feel awkward.

She looked at me and waited, still looking as stressed as I was starting to feel.

"I'm starting to get a Pretty Woman vibe from this," she joked. "But, I'm listening."

"Well, for starters, if you do the catering for this wedding, I'll make sure that you're paid accordingly and that you are recognized as the caterer. Then after the wedding, I'll pay for you to stay in the cabin through New Years so you can soak in the giant tub and watch the snow fall. What do you say? Your first paid catering job and a week's stay paid for at this beautiful lodge?"

"I'll do the job," she sighed heavily. "But I'm not accepting your offer to stay another week at your expense. Thank you, but I can't do that."

"Why not?" It didn't make sense to me why she wouldn't want to stay another week and not have to pay for it.

"Because I'm not looking to take advantage of you or to have you spend your money on me. You're doing me a favor by getting me this job. I've been looking for a way to get my foot in the door, and now I have one."

I stared at her in disbelief. I had never met a woman who wasn't jumping at the opportunity to get something from me. Whether it be a girl that I was dating or my own family—someone always wanted something. Yet with Tiffany, all she wanted was a chance to do something on her own.

We went through the buffet and grabbed breakfast, neither of us bothering to say much as our minds raced with the details of what we needed to do to pull this wedding off. An hour later, we were back at our cabin, talking to Laney and Jake about the extravagant wedding that she insisted on having.

Seven
Tiffany

My head felt like it was going to explode from the enormous amount of information that had been shoved into it since this morning. I kind of missed when my only problem was looking Luke in the eye after seeing him naked. Now, I was responsible for catering his sister's *small* wedding of a hundred and fifty people.

My palms had been sweating all day as my nerves ran wild. I tried to remind myself that I didn't have to worry about the small details of what Laney wanted because that was Luke's job. So what if she wanted hibiscus flowers lining the walkway to the altar or demanded that they have a live band perform at the reception. I snorted when she insisted that she wanted to have one dozen doves released when they said "I do," earning a dirty look from her.

We were on our way to meet with Julianna, and even I was impressed with how well Luke did his job as a wedding planner. The confident and direct man I had heard on the phone yesterday was in full charge today. We walked to the main hall and waited at the front desk as the receptionist called to let her know we were there. A few minutes later, we were led down a long hall to a large office with a beautiful view of the snow-capped mountains.

"Luke," she said evenly, shaking his hand when we walked in. "I wasn't expecting to work with you again before the end of the year."

"Yeah, I wasn't expecting it either," he laughed. "But my baby sister threw me one hell of a curveball, so here we are."

"Well, I'm happy to help however I can."

Luke introduced me before we all sat down, and I pulled out the notepad and pen that I had swiped from the room before we left. I had no idea what notes I would take, but I wanted to feel prepared.

"As I've told your sister, we simply don't have the staff to cater the wedding," Julianna said, leaning back in the tall leather chair. She looked to be close to his age with soft wrinkles around her amber eyes. Her features were soft, but she carried her attitude well. I couldn't imagine that she got to the position she was in as the executive director of the lodge by letting anyone walk all over her.

"Yes, she's told me. However, I have a solution to your problem," Luke said, grinning at me before looking back to Julianna. "Tiffany can cater the wedding. If you can provide the ingredients, the kitchen and waitstaff, then she can handle organizing and running the kitchen to make sure everything runs smoothly."

She turned in her chair and studied me for a moment.

"What events have you catered in the past?"

"None," I admitted nervously.

"She has the experience that you need," Luke assured her.

She pursed her lips as she thought about it.

"If you want this wedding to happen here, you need her a lot more than she needs you," he added.

"Fine. But I'll need to check references," she said dryly. She picked up her pen and pulled a notepad over to write on. "What culinary references do you have?"

"I've only had one, but I would rather that you don't call them."

I knew that this would be what kept her from hiring me and chewed the inside of my cheek.

"Why not?"

"Because," I looked sheepishly at Luke, who was waiting for an explanation as well. "I didn't leave on good terms."

I swallowed down the panic that was threatening to rise.

She didn't say anything, just looked at Luke and raised an eyebrow that confirmed her *you've got to be kidding me* look that was plastered across her face.

"What happened?" Luke asked softly, ignoring Julianna.

I sucked in a deep breath and lowered my head. My hands trembled in my lap as I fought to find the courage to speak. Charlie was the only person I had told what happened, and she was still begging me to let her handle things for me.

"I was promised a position as an executive chef, however, I didn't find out until it was too late that the owner wanted something in exchange for that title. When I refused to sleep with him, he fired me and tried to force himself on me anyway."

My leg shook as my emotions flooded through me.

"What did you do?" Julianna asked, setting her pen on the desk and leaning back casually in her chair.

"I kneed him in the balls and left. Then, when he tried to reach for me again, I grabbed the cast iron skillet from the counter and hit him with it. It knocked him out long enough for me to get away."

"Wow," Luke said quietly, reaching over to rest his hand on my knee. "I'm so sorry that you had to go through that."

"Thank you," I let out the breath that I had been holding. "It's still pretty fresh, and I honestly don't know what I'm going to do when I go home. I have a chance to start over, but I don't know where to begin."

"Any woman who can handle a jerk like that can sure as hell handle the men in my kitchen. The catering job is yours," she said with a smile. "And I'm trusting Luke's recommendation that you're qualified to handle the position."

"Thank you," I replied, trying to contain my excitement.

"I'll take you to the kitchen so you can meet the staff and start working on the planning and preparations. Do you have a menu in mind that you wanted to make? We may or may not have the supplies you need, so you might have to get creative."

"Um, well, no," I laughed nervously. "I haven't had time to think about a menu, but I can put one together rather quickly once I know what my options are."

"Perfect," Julianna said, standing up. "There will be a food tasting tomorrow afternoon, so please make sure you have everything you need before then. If the food is approved at the tasting, then you can proceed with setting everything up for the wedding."

"And if you don't approve?" I asked, knowing that I would regret it.

"Then the bride will be rather disappointed that her guests will be visiting our buffet that night with the rest of the guests."

I felt the air whoosh through me as my head started spinning. There was no pressure *whatsoever.*

Eight

Luke

I stood back and watched Tiffany take control of the kitchen as if she naturally belonged there. Julianna had been kind enough to do the introduction, but after that, Tiffany wasted no time setting the tone with the kitchen and waitstaff. She talked with the executive chef and discussed menu options, before checking out the inventory.

"That's all there is?" she asked, panicked, as she came out of the walk-in freezer.

"Unfortunately, yes. Our next shipment of meat won't be in until after the wedding."

"Okay," she exhaled, tapping her fingers together as her beautiful mind worked. "Since the steaks are thick, let's cut them into smaller portions, and that will double what we have. We can also add a vegetarian dish to save on meat, and I'm thinking we can have pizza for the kids. We'll use half of the salmon, half of the chicken, and three-quarters of the steak for the wedding, while the rest of it can be used for the buffet."

"That can work," he agreed, making a note on the worn-out paper in his hand. "We already have the Christmas day meal planned with the ham and turkey, so we don't have to worry about meat that day. We'll get our new shipment the next morning."

"Perfect. I think that will handle the food. I'll put together the menu, and then we can sit down again and make sure we have everything that we'll need."

She finished writing her notes and looked around to find me. I pushed off of the wall and walked over to where she was standing as the kitchen started to fill with noise while the staff got back to work.

"How'd it go?" I asked, even though I knew because I had been standing there the whole time.

"Good. I think we might be able to pull this off after all," she laughed, walking with me toward the door. "I just need to figure out *what* to cook and then hope that Julianna likes it when I make it for her tomorrow."

"Um, about that," I said nervously, pulling out my phone to show her the email that had just come through. "It won't be just her."

"What are you talking about?" she asked, leaning forward to read the email. A few seconds later, her head whipped up as she pinned me with a look.

"I'm cooking dinner for your family tomorrow, as well as the upper management of the lodge?"

"Yeah," I said slowly, worried that she was about to find a cast-iron skillet and whop me with it like she did that dirtbag at her last job.

"How many people?" she asked with her eyes closed and shoulders tense.

"Twenty-five."

She opened her eyes and glared at me.

"Fine. But you're going to pay for this," she teased.

I chewed my bottom lip, figuring now was as good of a time as any to add the other bad news.

"Also, my mom already told everyone that we're dating, so they're going to expect us to be *together* tomorrow night."

"What is that supposed to mean?"

"It means that I need you to pretend to be my girlfriend for the next few days, at least until my family leaves after the wedding."

She rubbed her lips together while shaking her head and resting her hand on her hip.

"You owe me big."

Nine
Tiffany

"I've put together a delectable menu that is sure to please all of your guests," I said nervously as I stood in front of the two round tables in the ballroom where the wedding would take place in two days. I could feel everyone's attention on me as I tried not to pass out.

"The first item," I said as my voice caught in my throat. "Is a steak au poivre, with a side of roasted red potatoes and served with a creamy cognac-based sauce. The second item is chicken francese, which is a pan-fried chicken breast with a buttery lemon sauce, served with a side of savory mashed potatoes. Next is a honey garlic glazed salmon with a side of white rice. All entrees are accompanied by a spinach strawberry salad with a poppy seed dressing. For the children's menu, I've prepared a pepperoni pizza and side salad."

I pulled in a long, steady, deep breath to replace the oxygen that I had just expended getting all of that information out as quickly as possible. Ernesto, the executive chef, had helped me prepare the meal, and the waitstaff had assisted with serving the equally portioned plates that had a small sample of each item I'd mentioned. I hated using potatoes for the side on two dishes, but given the limited ingredients available, there weren't many choices.

"Thank you, Tiffany," Julianna said. "Everything looks and smells wonderful, I can't wait to try what you've prepared for us."

I smiled nervously before sitting down next to Luke, ready for the attention to be off of me. The room started to fill with noise as everyone began eating and talking about the different flavors. So far, the feedback sounded positive, but then again, I could only hear the people around us at our table, which included the upper management. Even if they didn't like it, they were trained to be professional enough not to say so in front of everyone else.

"You did great," Luke whispered as he leaned in close to me.

"Thank you, I was so nervous that I don't know if I even said the right words."

He looked around at the heads that were all hung as they focused on their food.

"I don't see a single person complaining," he laughed. "Now start eating before your food gets cold. It would be a shame to miss the best meal you've had since you've been here."

I giggled, knowing that it was true, and cut into my thin strip of steak. I had to portion everything perfectly to make sure there was enough meat for this meal, as well as for what I needed for the wedding. Ernesto and I agreed to use three of the steaks that were supposed to go to the buffet for today instead and cut them thin enough that we could serve twenty-six people, including myself.

We ate in silence, my stomach thankful for the food, given that I had been too nervous to eat this morning.

When everyone was done, the waitstaff came by to collect our plates before serving coffee and refilling the glasses of water. The tables had turned, and now it was the local baker who was up to present the cake options. I was thankful for the shift in attention but still felt uneasy that they would come back and say that the bride and groom weren't impressed with my food.

I leaned back in my seat and listened as the short, curvy woman in a *You're Baking Me Crazy* apron explained the layers of the cake and the filling options. I felt eyes on me and slowly looked around the room, finding Luke's mom staring at us and not paying any attention to the speaker.

"Your mom is watching us," I whispered without moving my mouth, trying to be as discreet as possible.

Luke didn't say anything, but I noticed how his head slightly turned to the side to confirm. Next, his arm came up and wrapped around my shoulders, resting on the back of the chair. It was meant to make her see that we were a couple, but it was odd that it didn't feel weird to me. I didn't fight the feeling of him suddenly being too close. Instead, I craved it.

I shifted in my seat, resting my back against his side as I reached up and laced my fingers with his. If he wanted to put on a show for his family, I was happy to help him do it. I knew she was still watching when I tilted my head back and whispered something in his ear, letting my breath tickle the stubble that dotted his jawline.

While his mom probably imagined that I was saying dirty things to him, I had really just informed him that there was a sale at the pet store and that I was going to beat him at Mall Madness again when we got back to our cabin.

I felt the vibrations of his chuckle as his chest rumbled with it. He leaned closer and playfully nipped my earlobe before threatening me with a game of Monopoly instead. It was the most basic conversation, but we made it seem like we were two people who were madly in love and couldn't keep our hands off of each other.

Once the baker was finished, we were served samples of cake. I slid a small piece onto my fork and then turned to Luke, licking my lips as I offered him the bite. He slowly wrapped his mouth around the fork, locking eyes with me as his hand reached up and gently held mine. He took the bite and then stole my fork, offering me another one.

We sat there, flirting shamelessly with each other while his mother continued to watch us. Everything was almost wrapped up, and I was ready to get out of there and outside where the cold air could lift this fog I was in. As we were heading out, I heard footsteps quickly approaching behind us. My stomach knotted, knowing that his mom was probably tracking us down to give a lecture about inappropriate behavior. He had already warned me to expect it.

Instead, Julianna called out my name, and we stopped. Her face was lit up with a smile that spread across it.

"You got the job!" she squealed excitedly, pulling me in for a hug. "Everyone *loved* your food and are still talking about it!"

"What?!" I gasped in disbelief. "That's amazing!"

"I won't keep you guys, I just wanted to share the exciting news! Have a wonderful night celebrating, and I'll see you in a few days at the wedding."

She smiled and rushed off to the sound of someone calling her name. I turned to look at Luke, a goofy smile on my face, still not believing it myself.

"Congratulations," he said, his lips turned up in the corners. "I knew you could do it."

He leaned forward and gently grabbed the sides of my face before planting his lips on mine. Everything felt perfect about it, but this time, no one else was watching.

186

Ten

Luke

I couldn't believe that I had kissed her, but when she kissed me back, I knew that I couldn't stop. Once we got back to the cabin, our hands desperately rushed to get clothes off while our mouths devoured each other.

"Are you sure you want to do this?" I asked between kisses as she pulled her sweater over her head and flung it across the room.

"Yes," she panted before wrapping her arms around my neck and kissing me. She was down to just her bra and panties, and I was desperate to see her. My chest heaved as I tried to catch my breath, breaking from the kiss for a second to open the door to the bedroom. I hadn't asked her whether she wanted to go in there, but when she led me down the hallway, I assumed that's where she wanted to take this.

I walked her to the bed, hearing her giggle as she bumped into it before I gently pushed her down on it. I took a moment to look at her beautiful body as she laid on the bed, her blond hair fanned out around her. I knew that her body was curvy and that she was self-conscious about it, but seeing her lay on the bed wearing nothing but her bra and panties, she looked sexy as hell. Her chest moved quickly as her breathing increased with anticipation, making her plump breasts dance on display.

I grabbed a condom from my wallet then tossed my jeans to the floor before stripping off my underwear. She locked eyes with me, reluctant to look down at my cock as it grew thicker by the second. I took my time stroking it while watching the way her breathing changed the more turned on she got. When she looked like she couldn't take it anymore, I took the last few steps to the bed and crawled on top of her, holding myself up on my elbow.

Slowly, I kissed her neck while my free hand caressed her breast through the thin fabric of her bra. I could feel her nipple harden beneath my touch and longed to suck it. I made my way down her neck before reaching behind her and unclasping her bra. Once it was undone, I worked the straps down her arms and flung it across the room.

She smiled and pulled her bottom lip between her teeth when she saw the hungry look on my face. I leaned down and began kissing her breasts, teasing her before I pulled a nipple into my mouth and sucked. She moaned and muttered a string of curse words before digging her fingers into my hair and pressing my head tighter against her.

My dick was throbbing with the need to be inside of her. I kept my mouth focused on sucking her nipples while my hand slid down her stomach and over her pussy. I dipped a finger inside her slit, feeling how wet she was already. She parted her legs, allowing me more access as I pushed another finger in and started fingering her.

She felt so good wrapped around my fingers that I couldn't wait to feel her around my cock. I wanted to make sure that she was ready before that happened, so I took the time to move down her body and teased her clit with my tongue. She moaned even louder this time as her knees fell open. I looked up to find her head back and eyes closed as she caressed her breasts, flicking her thumb over her nipples.

If I kept watching what she was doing to herself, I was going to come before I was even inside of her. I sucked harder as my fingers fucked her fast, drawing her orgasm out of her as she clenched and spasmed around me. I couldn't take it any longer. Once she was finished, I rolled onto my back and rushed to get the condom on.

She was smiling sexily at me as she waited, propping herself up on her elbows as she watched me cover myself. Her eyes shamelessly traveled down to my throbbing cock and took it in. She licked her lips before looking up at me, the desire flashing in her eyes. She laid back down on the bed and spread her legs, waiting for me to slide inside of her.

I got up and stood at the edge of the bed, pulling her hips toward me until her ass was hanging halfway off the bed but supported by my thighs. I loved the perfectly unobstructed view of her wet pussy, knowing that I was the reason she was practically dripping. I kept my eyes locked on hers as I grabbed my cock and guided it inside of her.

My eyes closed as she gasped, her pussy eagerly clenching around me. It was our first time together, and I didn't want to look like some fifteen-year-old boy who couldn't control himself. I grabbed her legs and pushed them together, making sure I was still snug inside of her. Resting them against my chest, I wrapped my arm around them to make sure she stayed in place before I started thrusting. The sound of our bodies slapping against each other was overly stimulating, bringing me closer to the edge as my balls felt the sting of hitting her ass with each hard movement.

"Oh God, yes," she moaned, her hands roaming over her breasts again. "Fuck me harder," she begged.

I did as she asked, pumping as hard as I could while quickening my pace. The harder I fucked her, the louder her moans became. The way she moaned my name had me wishing I could listen to it forever.

Her hand slipped down and started rubbing her clit, and I could feel the way her body was reacting. I looked down and watched as she let her legs fall open to the sides, giving me the perfect view again. My dick looked huge as it pushed through her swollen pink lips that were glistening wet. Her fingers desperately rubbed her clit in circles while her other hand worked her nipples.

Even if she hadn't groaned loudly, I would have still known that she was coming again from how tight her pussy was wrapped around my dick. I felt my orgasm rip through me as I gave her a few more fast, hard pumps as I spilled my load into the condom.

We were both breathless and sweaty as I pulled out of her.

"You're so fucking beautiful," I whispered, leaning down to kiss her.

Eleven
Tiffany

My body was pleasantly sore from the multiple orgasms and the best sex I had ever had. Hands down—the best EVER. I didn't bother getting up from the bed while he went and cleaned up. There was no energy for that. I was totally and completely spent.

A few minutes later, he came back into the room and looked unsure whether he should get dressed or what he should do.

"Come lay with me," I offered, scooting over and patting the bed beside me.

"You sure?" he asked, his voice softer than usual.

I nodded and closed my eyes, hoping that I didn't fall asleep.

The bed dipped as he climbed up next to me and laid down. I rolled onto my side and laid my hand on his chest, trailing small circles through his hair.

He moved closer so I could lay my head on his shoulder as he wrapped his arm under my neck.

"How are you feeling?" he asked, gently rubbing my back.

"Wonderful," I sighed. "That was amazing."

He chuckled and kissed the top of my head.

"What about you?"

"Same."

His answer was short and simple, yet I believed him based on how relaxed his body was next to me.

I didn't know what all of this meant, but for once, I wasn't concerned with trying to figure it out. We laid together, our breathing falling in sync as we drifted asleep on the bed.

At some point in the middle of the night, he must have gotten cold because I woke up to find him still in bed beside me, with a blanket from the living room wrapped around us. I looked at the window and saw that the sun was already up, which meant that we needed to get the day going.

The wedding was tomorrow which meant that there was still a ton left for us to do today, and I likely wouldn't see him most of the day. I would be in the kitchen with Ernesto, preparing the food for tomorrow, as well as for the rehearsal dinner tonight, while Luke would be meeting with everyone else and running at full speed.

I rolled over and gently kissed his lips, hoping it would be a good way to wake him up. He kept his eyes closed as his hand reached behind my head and pulled me closer as he started kissing my neck again. I was close enough to feel the heat coming off of his body and knew not to look beneath the blanket. He was hard and already ready for more.

"We have to get ready, or you're gonna be late this morning," I warned.

"I can be quick," he murmured, his hand roaming down to my breast.

"Alright, Romeo," I laughed and pulled away. "But at least multi-task."

I got up and walked off, winking over my shoulder as he watched me shake my ass for him before making it to the hallway. I went to the bathroom and turned on the shower, giving it a few minutes to warm up while brushing my teeth.

A few minutes later, he joined me with a condom in one hand and his hard dick in the other. We climbed in the shower and wasted no time cleaning each other's bodies before he turned me around and took me from behind as the water rained down my back.

Once we were finished getting ready, we grabbed a quick breakfast in the dining hall before heading our separate ways while I tried to force myself not to think about what had happened between us. I had a job to do and needed to focus on that instead.

I had spent the morning with Ernesto preparing the food for the rehearsal dinner. Thankfully, the groom was more laid back than the bride and had asked for pub food instead of a fancy seated meal. It was the only item that she had compromised on, but I was happy to have a lighter menu of hot wings and mini sliders to prepare instead of two big meals with several dishes. Tonight's dinner would be served buffet style, which meant that I wouldn't be needed after the food was served. I would have time to spend with Luke *if* he wanted to. As far as I knew, we were still supposed to be pretending to date, so I couldn't imagine that I wouldn't attend the rehearsal dinner with him as his date.

Around one o'clock, Ernesto took a lunch break and offered to bring me food on his way back. I declined and worked on cutting the meat for the wedding so we could get that out of the way. I was deep in the zone and hadn't heard anyone walk up behind me when a voice startled me, and the knife I was using went straight through my thumb.

"Son of a bitch!" I yelled, dropping the knife into the sink and moving my hand away from the food as quickly as possible. Red spots splattered the sink as I looked around for something to use to stop the bleeding.

"Oh, dear!" Luke's mom exclaimed, rushing beside me with a clean towel from the counter behind me. "Here, let me see your hand," she demanded, holding her hand out for me.

I eyed her carefully, not sure why she was back here to begin with. I lifted my hand and laid it on the towel, frowning when the blood-soaked it immediately. She wrapped it tightly and put pressure on the cut.

"There, there," she said quietly. "Let's see if we can stop the bleeding. Try to be still and don't move."

I did as she said, still feeling guarded as to why she was here.

"What are you doing back here?" I asked, keeping my tone level.

"Well, I came to talk to you about the menu. The nice young man at the hostess station said I could find you back here. I didn't mean to startle you, though."

"I wasn't expecting anyone," I admitted.

"I can see that," she laughed lightly, gently lifting the towel to check the bleeding. Her brows pulled together when she noticed the bleeding hadn't slowed down yet. Without losing the pressure that she already had on it, she carefully reached behind her and grabbed another towel, wrapping it around the one that was currently soaked with my blood.

I felt my stomach tighten when I wondered why she wanted to talk about the menu. If she was going to demand some last-minute change—I would lose my shit. Everything was falling together nicely, but it was a very delicate balance to keep it that way.

"So, what did you want to talk about?" I asked, ready to just get it over with.

"Well, I just wanted to tell you how much I enjoyed the meal that you prepared last night." She kept her eyes on my hand as she spoke, not bothering to look up. "You and Luke seem to be quite the team."

And there it was.

"He's easy to work with and has done a wonderful job putting this wedding together on such short notice."

"Yes, we're all thankful for that," she said with a hint of sarcasm in her voice that got under my skin. "Just as I'm sure you're thankful for him getting you this job. I think we can all safely say that you haven't been dating long, so I had to wonder what was in it for you."

She studied me closely, trying to gauge my reaction. I kept

my face straight as I pulled my hand away from her and held it close to my chest. I had no idea whether the bleeding had stopped or not, but I didn't want her touching me.

"I'm thankful for everything that Luke does for me," I said sharply, hearing someone approaching. "Like the multiple orgasms he gave me last night and the quickie we had in the shower this morning."

Her jaw dropped open just in time for Luke to walk around the corner. His face confirmed that he heard everything.

She clutched her chest in fake surprise, acting as if I had just told her that he had eight eyes and a cock made of titanium.

"Mother," Luke said coldly, coming to stand beside me. "What are you doing here?"

He looked down at the bloody towel wrapped around my hand and glanced at me, concerned.

"I was just coming to tell Tiffany how much I enjoyed her food last night."

"And to question how I got this job," I bit out sharply.

"She got the job because she's qualified for it. It shows in her food that *you* had no problem devouring last night. And just for the record—it's none of your business how she got the job."

"Oh, please," she muttered. "We all know that this isn't a real relationship, Luke. You can stop pretending and let your sister have the attention she deserves for her wedding."

He turned his back to her and gently reached for my hand,

shaking his head while he ignored her comment.

"What happened?"

"I didn't hear her coming and accidentally cut myself."

"Can I see?"

I nodded, sucking in a deep breath as he slowly pulled the towel away. Thankfully the bleeding had stopped for the most part.

"Do you need to have this looked at?" he asked, turning his head to get a better look.

"I think it'll be fine," I assured him. "It's stopped bleeding, so I shouldn't need stitches. I can ask Ernesto to help with the cutting work while I focus on the other prep."

"Okay, if you need anything, just let me know."

"Thank you."

For a moment, it felt like it was just the two of us until his mom cleared her throat to remind us that she was still there.

"I just stopped by to say hi, but I've gotta get going. I'm meeting with the photographer and the DJ here in a few minutes."

"Okay," I smiled. "Thanks for stopping by, that was a nice surprise."

"I'll see you at the rehearsal dinner." His smile brightened as he said it.

"You're seriously bringing her to your sister's rehearsal dinner?" his mom scoffed.

I watched the anger flash through his eyes before he turned and glared at her.

"Why wouldn't I?"

"I just thought you would have more respect for your family than to bring some floozie that you barely know to your sister's wedding. Like I said, we're all onto your game, and you're not fooling anyone. If you need to try to prove to us that you're not gay, then fine, so be it. But I thought you had more class than this." She tossed a nod in my direction.

I felt the sting of her words as I flinched away from them.

Luke reached down and wrapped a hand around my waist, pulling me closer to him.

"The only one who's been putting on a show is you. If you have a problem with Tiffany being there as my girlfriend, then I'll make it easy for everyone, and *neither* of us will be there. Just be sure to remember who it was that pulled this shit show of a wedding off when *you* couldn't."

She narrowed her eyes at him before turning and storming out of the room.

Once the coast was clear, I turned to him and smiled sadly.

"I'm sorry, I didn't mean to cause problems for you with your family."

"You didn't," he said calmly. "For the first time in a long time, you've helped me to see things clearly when it comes to family."

"How's that?"

"I've always thought that I didn't want to fall in love—I purposely avoided it at all costs. But being with you these past few days has shown me a different view of love and what it could be. You're nothing like my mom and sisters. You don't demand things or expect that everything goes your way. You're funny, and genuine, and caring. You're everything that they're not, and it opened my eyes to what I want in life."

"And what's that?" I asked, reaching up and wrapping my arm around his neck as I searched for the golden flecks in his eyes that I had come to love.

"I want to be snowed in with no place to go while losing to you at Mall Madness and making love to you all night long. I don't care about anything else—I want those moments with you because they make me feel like I'm finally happy, and I look forward to when I get to see you again."

"I feel the same way," I said nervously. "But is it too soon for us to feel this way about each other?"

"I don't think so," he shook his head, gently caressing my cheek with his knuckles. "I think that when you have someone who makes you happy without even trying, that's something worth holding onto. We have a chemistry that's stronger than I've ever felt with anyone else, and that tells me that there's something there. Something that makes me want to do whatever I can to make you happy so I can see that beautiful smile that lights up your entire face."

I felt butterflies in my stomach as his words hit me straight in the heart.

"I really do need to get going," he said, slowly pulling away. "But I'll come pick you up around 6 for the rehearsal dinner if that works for you?"

"Sure, that sounds nice." I smiled, fighting the urge to protest and tell him that I shouldn't go. If *he* wanted me to go with him, then I was going to. His mother was rude and borderline intimidating, but that wasn't going to keep me away from him. Besides, we had already come this far with proving that we were in a relationship, I wasn't going to stop now and give her the satisfaction of knowing that she was right. He deserved better than that.

He turned and left, leaving me with a warm fuzzy feeling that I hoped didn't go away any time soon.

Twelve

Luke

It was 5:45, and I had confirmed that the rehearsal dinner was good to go and that the buffet would be opened promptly at 6:15. Ernesto and his team had taken over with plenty of direction from Tiffany. This meant that the kitchen and waitstaff would handle everything, and Tiffany would be free for the rest of the evening.

I walked back to the cabin and smiled when I found Tiffany inside wearing a pleated black dress that hit just above her knee. Her hair was pinned up nicely on top of her head with a few strands that hung around her face in delicate, soft curls that complimented the light makeup she was wearing. The neckline was flattering and high enough not to expose any cleavage, but the rose gold pendant that hung from the thin chain around her neck dipped right at the top, reminding me of her beautiful breasts that I couldn't wait to get my hands on again.

"Are you ready?" she asked, pulling her black peacoat on and smoothing down the front of her dress.

"You look incredible," I said, unable to think straight. "You're so beautiful."

"Thank you." She smiled and tucked a curl behind her ear.

"I couldn't decide what to wear. Everything else was too casual, and I didn't want to stick out like a sore thumb more than I already do. This was the only dress that I brought with me."

"It's perfect. Although I will admit one thing," I teased. "You look so good that I'm thinking that we should skip the rehearsal dinner and stay here instead."

"You're so bad," she teased, smacking my chest lightly with the clutch in her hand. "Let's go before we're late."

I followed her out of the door, taking the opportunity to check out her ass in the dress and the way her heels made her legs look longer.

The snow had started to fall again, making it hard for her to walk through it without soaking her feet. I watched as she studied the area around her and tried to figure out the best path to take. Instead, I reached over and picked her up, carrying her in my arms.

"What are you doing?" she giggled, reaching down to make sure her dress was covering her butt.

"Making sure your shoes don't get wet, and you don't lose a toe to frostbite."

"I'll be fine," she laughed. The sound of it felt wonderful against my chest.

"Okay, so maybe I just wanted to hold you before we got there, and I had to keep my hands off of you."

"Is that why your hand keeps grabbing my ass?"

"Nope, not at all. That's for your safety, to make sure that you're secure and not going to fall."

"Mmhmm."

I laughed, feeling the joy radiating through me. I wanted the moment to last as long as possible before we got into the ballroom, and it was ruined by my family.

A few minutes later, we were heading toward the entrance and had reached dry land. I carefully set her down, making sure she was steady before letting go of her. I reached down to hold her hand when I remembered her injury. It was bandaged nicely with plenty of gauze, but I still wondered whether she needed stitches after all when I saw that it had been bleeding again.

I was so focused on her hand that I hadn't noticed anyone heading our way, until I heard my name.

"Luke!" Laney shrieked, rushing over with her arms extended. She ran into my arms and wrapped me in a hug. "Everything is perfect and beautiful, thank you so much!"

"You deserve the best," I said, planting a quick kiss on the top of her head.

"I appreciate all of it," she replied, pulling back. She looked at Tiffany and smiled. "And thank you for helping with the catering. My brother told me everything you've done for us, and it means so much to me. You're an amazing chef!"

"Thank you," Tiffany said, her cheeks blushing at the compliment. "It's been my pleasure."

"Well, I'm going to go grab my phone before dinner starts. I'll see you guys in there," Laney said, smiling as she rushed off and left us behind.

"Are you ready to do this?" I asked, noticing how nervous Tiffany seemed.

"Yes. Let's go practice eating dinner," she joked, laughing nervously.

I placed my hand on her lower back and led her into the room that was already filled with the majority of my family and some of Laney's friends. I didn't have to scan the tables to know where we were sitting since I was the one who had organized everything. Much to my mother's dismay, I had seated Tiffany and myself at another table, away from her and my sisters. When asked about why I had done it, I pretended that there wasn't enough room for us to all sit together, so obviously, we should sit at another table to make room for everyone.

I walked her over to our seats and held her chair out for her. Julianna was already seated next to Tiffany and smiled when we joined her and the few other staff members. It made sense that we would sit at this table, given that I was now the *hired* wedding planner and Tiffany was the caterer. My mom liked to make a big show of how much money they spent on things, and I made sure she had plenty to brag about with how much this wedding was going to cost my parents. I didn't go overboard but made sure that Tiffany received a fifteen percent bonus for the last-minute job.

"Luke, everything looks wonderful," Julianna cooed. "I think you've outdone yourself."

"Thank you," I said coolly, adjusting my tie and unbuttoning my jacket as I sat down. "In all fairness, we've only done a few weddings here, and they were in the summer at the stables."

"Well, I think we've got a new venue to look at for your winter weddings if you're interested. Maybe a new caterer too?"

"We'll discuss options after this one is over. Let's make sure everything goes off without a hitch first," I chuckled.

I spotted my mom from across the room, glowering at us and making no effort to hide the disgusted look on her face. I smiled smugly and lifted my glass of wine in the air to her, raising my eyebrows. That pissed her off even more as she grabbed my aunt Jolene by the arm and rushed her off to the side to talk about me.

I took a sip, allowing the merlot to calm some of the nerves I was starting to feel. Tiffany and Julianna talked about the plans for tomorrow and discussed options for getting someone else to help when she noticed Tiffany's hand. I was impressed with how well she handled herself, and not once had I seen her look intimated or unsure of herself after being thrown into the middle of all of this. She handled everything with grace and looked like a total pro, which made me proud to have her on my arm tonight as my date, as well as the incredible chef that everyone was starting to rave about again as they got their food.

We ate and talked, enjoying the company of those around us. It felt nice to have genuine conversation without feeling constantly judged. Tiffany was a hit and had everyone's attention as she tossed her head back, laughing, telling a story about a time when she accidentally caught her sleeve on fire and set off the sprinklers in the kitchen at work. Her mother—who was almost as bad as mine—didn't bother asking if she was okay after suffering a burn. Instead, she lectured her about not getting the hot firefighter's phone number.

Once we were finished, we made our way around the room, saying hello to my family and mingling for a few minutes, before it was deemed an appropriate amount of time to excuse ourselves without being rude. I could care less about visiting with everyone, I just wanted to get back to the cabin and have some alone time with Tiffany.

We were wrapping up when I turned to head out the door. My jaw dropped when I saw who had just walked in. Tiffany was completely oblivious to the drama that was about to unfold right in front of her.

"Hey there, handsome," she said seductively, running a freshly manicured fingernail down the length of my tie. I reached out and grabbed her wrist before she got any lower, our hands hovering over my belt buckle. "Such a tease," she winked.

"What are you doing here?" I asked, my voice low and angry.

"Laney invited me."

"She shouldn't have."

"Aww, is that really how you want to treat me?" She stuck out her bottom lip and fake pouted. Her raven black hair was pulled back into a slick ponytail that swished down her bare back from the dress that dipped down so far it barely covered her ass. The front didn't cover much more than the back with a plunging neckline that barely contained her breasts. I looked at her and then at Tiffany, noticing the apparent differences between them.

Tiffany looked between us, an awkward smile on her face as she tried to figure out what was going on.

"This is June," I said tightly, shoving my hands into my

pockets. The soft silk of the fabric reminded me that we were in a public place where I couldn't make a scene.

"Oh, are you Luke's family?" Tiffany asked innocently.

"No," June hissed, eyeing Tiffany callously. "I'm his wife."

Thirteen
Tiffany

"I don't want to hear it!" I screamed, slamming the bedroom door behind me. My feet were frozen after I took off my heels to trek through the snow without falling. I was too angry to be anywhere near Luke and didn't want his family to see us fighting. I held out as long as possible, plastering the smile on my face as I met *his wife*.

His WIFE. How the hell did he not tell me that he was married? After our conversation earlier about finding that special someone that makes you happy and not having to work hard at a relationship that comes so easily--- well, apparently that was a bunch of bullshit.

I stepped out of the dress, laying it on the bed as I grabbed my sweats and put them on. I couldn't tell if I was shivering because I was still cold or if it was because I was so livid with him. I had finally given in and let my walls down long enough to let him in, and it bit me in the ass. How had I been so stupid to believe his lies? I blamed it on reading too many romance novels. It was the perfect setting for a book—stranded in a winter wonderland with an attractive stranger who just happens to be your soulmate while surrounded by the freshly fallen snow and some Christmas magic. There's always some sort of Christmas magic in those books.

But the problem was that this wasn't a book. It was my life, and it was going to hell in a handbag faster than a sinking ship. I pulled my phone out of my clutch and dialed Charlie's number, desperate to talk to her. I glanced at the time, not sure if it was too late, then remembered that she was usually up at all hours of the night anyway, doing things I only dreamed of.

"Hey," she said breathlessly. "What's up?"

"Are you doing what I think you're doing?" I asked, feeling slightly annoyed that she was having sex while I was in the middle of a meltdown—not that she knew I was.

"No," she laughed. "I just got home from the grocery store, and I didn't want to make two trips, so I lugged all of the bags upstairs at once, and now I'm out of breath."

I rolled my eyes and felt the smile tugging at my lips. It was good to talk to her, and she was already starting to calm my nerves some.

"So, what's up? Aren't you supposed to be at the rehearsal dinner tonight then having more hot sex?" she asked.

"Yeah, well, that's over," I huffed.

"Why? What happened?"

"He's married."

I heard her gasp and waited.

"Like *married* married?"

"Like I just met his wife fifteen minutes ago married."

"I don't understand. I thought you said that he was single?"

"Yeah, I thought he was too. He never mentioned anything about a wife. I guess it's my fault for not asking before we had sex."

I sighed and reached up to pull the bobby pins out of my hair. I was already starting to get a headache and didn't need the tension in my head to make it worse.

"Ugh," I groaned. "Everything happened *so fast*. Why didn't you talk me out of this when I first told you?"

I knew it wasn't her fault, but it made me feel better to think that someone else shared some of the blame in this.

"You mean when you were drooling over his monstrous one-eyed beast?" She laughed harder, and I found myself getting the giggles.

"Okay, well still. It should have ended there. I should never have allowed myself to—." I stopped talking, realizing what I was about to admit to someone other than myself.

"You fell for him," she said quietly, the laughter coming to a halt. "Oh, honey."

"It's fine," I lied. "Really. It's only been a few days. It's not like I'm in *love* with him. It's just the infatuation and excitement of something new. It'll pass as quickly as it came."

"Does he feel the same way?" she asked, ignoring my attempt to dismiss what had happened.

"He said he did earlier. I asked if it was too soon about us feeling this way about each other, and he assured me that when you know something is right, you don't fight it—or some shit like that."

My mind was swirling with thoughts of everything that had happened today: Luke admitting that he had feelings for me; him confessing how I was so different from his family; his mom insinuating that I was a slut and slept with him to get the job (if only she knew that I slept with him *after* I got the job!). Then, there was the bombshell of meeting his wife.

"How did he act when you met his wife?"

"He was pissed that she was there and wasn't friendly to her at all. He even asked her *why* she was there. She said that his sister invited him."

"Do you think she would do that?"

"I don't know, honestly. I barely know him or his family. But his sister seems nice, so it doesn't seem like she would do it to piss him off—especially since he's responsible for making sure her wedding is perfect tomorrow. If anyone was that malicious, it's his mom."

"Maybe that's who invited her?"

"Who knows. She doesn't like me, but there hasn't been much time for her to sit around plotting this either. Unless she had it planned—."

I stopped what I was saying when it finally clicked.

"What? What did she have planned?"

"I bet you she planned to invite his wife all along. That's why she was so mad that he was there with me."

"That would make sense," Charlie agreed.

I heard a knock on my door and knew that I needed to talk to Luke at some point.

"Luke's at my door," I explained quietly in case he could hear me on the other side.

"Okay, text me later and let me know what happens."

I hung up and set my phone on the nightstand before checking myself in the mirror as I walked over to answer the door.

I pulled it open and found him on the other side, changed out of his dress attire and wearing a plain white t-shirt and gray sweats.

"I know that you're mad at me—and you have every reason to be, but can I please talk to you and explain what happened?"

"Luke, you don't need to," I sighed, leaning against the doorframe. "I wish you would have told me that you're married before anything happened between us, but we're past that now. So let's just move on and forget that anything even happened."

He closed his eyes and pulled his lips together in frustration.

"I'm not the kind of girl who gets involved with married men. It's my fault for not asking if you were married before anything happened, but I can guarantee that nothing will happen again."

I grabbed the door and started to close it when he stuck his hand out and held it open.

"Tiffany, I'm not married. We're separated and have been

for five years. The only reason that we're not divorced is because she refuses to sign the papers."

"Why?"

"I don't have any freaking idea," he mumbled, running a hand through his hair. "She and my mom stayed friends after we split up, and I'm sure my mom has been the one convincing her not to sign, hoping that I'll give in and move back to Cedar Plank. She would love nothing more than to have me move back home and try to control my life like she does my sisters."

"Do you think that it was your mom that invited her to the wedding?"

"I can almost guarantee it."

I nodded and processed what he was saying. It made sense, and I wanted to believe him, but part of me felt like I needed to slap a handful of Band-Aids on my heart and get that wall up again before I ended up getting hurt.

"I'm sorry that I didn't tell you about her and that you had to find out the way that you did. June isn't someone that I like to talk about, and seeing her tonight just reminded me why I left home, to begin with."

"I didn't like finding out that way either," I replied bitterly. "But thank you for being honest with me and telling me what happened."

"You deserve to know the truth, and I'm sorry that I hurt you."

He turned and walked down the hall to the living room. I debated whether or not to chase after him. My heart begged my feet to start moving, but my head screamed for me to stop.

Fourteen
Tiffany

I stood there in awe, checking out the room where the ceremony would take place this afternoon. There were white folding chairs lined up in rows with an aisle down the middle that had a deep plum-colored runner leading to the altar at the front. Behind that was a floor-to-ceiling window that took up most of the wall, showcasing the perfect winter wonderland outside. Fresh snow had fallen, making it look light and fluffy against the dark evergreen trees that lined the back.

The altar had ropes of white Christmas lights strung throughout the wrought iron arched with a heart at the center. White roses were tucked into the structure and added to the soft romantic feeling in the room. Along the aisle were lanterns with tea lights that flickered shadows on the walls of the dimly lit room. I closed my eyes for a second and imagined what it would be like to have a wedding like this someday.

"It's beautiful, isn't it?" Julianna asked, coming to stand next to me.

"Gorgeous. I can't believe this is the same room. It looks so different from when I saw it the first time."

"Wait until you see the ballroom where they're having the

reception. It's just as stunning. Luke does amazing work."

"I can see that," I laughed, feeling butterflies at the mention of his name. "I'd better get going, or we're not going to have a dinner to serve tonight," I joked, winking as I headed out.

I passed a few staff members on my way to the kitchen, saying hi and chatting for a few seconds as I walked. I loved that everyone was so nice and easy to work with. While I had no catering experience, I had expected it to be more of a challenge than it was. Going into someone's kitchen and taking over isn't usually met with the courtesy and respect I had been given from the start.

I spent the day working with Ernesto and his staff, getting ready for the big event. I was more nervous than anyone— probably even the bride. There was so much on the line that my palms had sweat so profusely that I worried I would lose my grip on the knife I was holding.

Just as I was about to cut into a tomato, I felt a hand slide around my waist and startle me. I dropped the knife before I cut my finger.

"Do I need to worry about you with a knife?" Luke asked, his voice low in my ear. His hand stayed on my side, spreading heat throughout me as I remembered the way it felt when it caressed my body this morning. Last night, I went to bed upset about what happened and woke up to him wanting to make it up to me.

"I'm starting to think that maybe I should stay away from them," I laughed, turning to face him. "Aren't you supposed to be getting ready for the wedding?" I asked, checking my watch. "It starts in an hour."

"Yeah, I'm heading that way now, but I wanted to stop in and say hi. I hate that you won't be there with me."

"Well, I would, but then no one would have anything to eat once it was over," I teased, bopping him on the nose with my finger.

"I know what I want to eat," he whispered in my ear with a growl.

I felt the heat spread further throughout my body, a slight ache starting between my thighs.

"If you keep talking like that, we're going to find ourselves in the same position we were in this morning," I giggled as his fingers dug into my sides and tickled.

"Well, I have to admit, it was a nice way to start Christmas Eve. You were the best present I found under the tree."

I hid my face in his neck, turning away as I had a vivid flashback of him going down on me in front of the Christmas tree while I was sprawled out on the plush shag rug. It was hard to believe that it was already Christmas Eve and that I wasn't spending the holiday with my family this year.

Then I thought about how happy I was this morning and how I didn't have to bother getting dressed up and making sure my makeup was perfect. Hell, I hadn't even bothered to put any on this morning, knowing that I would sweat it off in the kitchen. The expectations that usually followed me during the holidays were so far out of reach that I felt liberated for one in my life.

Luke gave me a quick kiss and headed off to the wedding while I tried to get my head straight and focus on the meal. A couple of hours later, the appetizers and side salads were being served, and I felt myself starting to relax, knowing that everything was running smoothly. The waitstaff was on point, delivering meals and grabbing hot plates before we could set them down. Dinner was out in record time with only a few stray plates that went out a few minutes delayed, and those were to the photographer and DJ who hadn't been at their table to eat right away anyway.

After the food was served, I tossed my hat and apron to the side and sat down on an empty crate. My feet hurt, and my back was achy. My job was officially done, and the kitchen would soon be handling the cake, which I had no desire to stick around for.

Just as I was getting cleaned up and changed, I heard Luke's voice in the kitchen. I smiled, knowing that he was waiting for me. When I walked out, I found him talking with Julianna, who was grinning from ear to ear.

"This is UNBELIEVABLE!" she exclaimed. "I can't wait to tell her!"

"Well, there she is," Luke said, nodding to me and smiling.

"What's going on?" I asked, feeling the excitement in the air.

"I was just telling Luke that thanks to Laney's recent posts about the wedding, we are already booked solid for weddings starting next September!"

"That's awesome, congratulations!" I said, not sure what this had to do with me.

"Laney shared pictures of the food that you served for the rehearsal dinner, and her posts have already gone viral!" Julianna added, her eyes wide.

"It was just basic bar food," I laughed, remembering how I tried to make it fancy by adding some garnishment to the buffet at the last minute before Ernesto stopped me.

"Not according to her and her new husband," she gushed. "They absolutely loved how you quote, *turned simple pub food into something extraordinary and worthy of a five-star restaurant.*" She used her fingers to end the quote.

"I don't do much on social media, but I'm guessing this is pretty big? Does she have a couple hundred followers or something?" I asked, completely clueless.

"My sister has a decent following and declined my parent's help paying for the wedding due to how padded her bank account is. They laughed when she told them she was going to be a social media influencer, but the joke is on them."

"Well, thanks to your sister, we are now on the map as the top destination for winter weddings next year. She's called it a Wonderland Wedding, and now everyone wants one!"

"That's great! I'm so happy for you guys."

"That's not the best part," Julianna said with a smirk growing across her face.

I narrowed my eyes and waited.

"The best part is that she gave you a glowing review as the caterer, and you've been personally requested for at least half of the weddings!"

"But I'm not a caterer," I stammered, looking to Luke for help. "I don't have a business set up or any supplies. I wouldn't have any idea how to get started, and honestly, I don't have the money—"

"That's why I would like to offer you a position at Bear Creek as our caterer. Now that we have a booked calendar next year, we need a caterer that we can rely on and that works well with our staff."

"You're offering me a job?" I asked in disbelief. There was no way this was real.

"I am. And I'm hoping that you'll say yes because I have a lot of brides that will be disappointed if you say no."

"But, I don't even live here."

"If you took the job, we would provide housing in the staff cabins. The monthly rent would be included in your salary package. What do you think?"

I looked at Luke, who was grinning with a proud smile.

"I think that I would love to work here. I accept!"

She gave me a quick hug and promised that we'd sit down after Christmas and go over the details. After she left and we were alone, he walked with me down the empty corridor to the reception hall.

"So, how do you feel about it?" he asked.

"Wonderful," I gushed, still feeling the high of it all. "I can't believe that I'm getting my dream job and the chance to start over."

I knew that we hadn't talked about it before now, but I hated that he was going back to LA. Would we even be able to make a long-distance relationship work?

"You deserve it, Tiffany."

"I'll miss you," I blurted out, stopping in my tracks. He reached out and held my hands, bringing them up to his lips to kiss them.

"Then I guess it's a good thing that I accepted her offer to become the exclusive wedding planner for Bear Creek."

I smiled and reached up to kiss him, knowing that he was the best gift I could have ever asked for.

A CHRISTMAS WISH

Samantha Baca

Dedicated to my Nana Barb, who loved Christmas as much as I do. Enjoy your first Christmas in Heaven, I'm sure it's a lot sweeter now that you're reunited with your one true love.

<u>One</u>
Everly

"Can I bring you another glass of wine?" the waiter asked, standing impatiently beside the table.

I glanced down at my phone, confirming that there were no new text messages or missed calls. It appeared I had been stood up. Again.

I searched the room for any sign of hope, spotting an attractive man waiting by the hostess station, a few feet away from me. It would be great if he was my blind date and maybe just hadn't seen me yet, but I already knew that I wouldn't be that lucky. IF my date did show up, I imagined it would either be some overly cocky douchebag who thought a $7.99 steak would get him into my pants or an inexperienced geek who had no idea what a clitoris was.

"I'm fine, thank you," I pushed out anxiously. "I'll wait until my—"

"Date arrives," he finished for me with a hint of snark. He rolled his eyes and trotted off to another table. That was the excuse I had been giving him for not ordering over the thirty minutes that I had been sitting there.

It was two weeks until Christmas, and every restaurant in

Chicago had long wait times. I felt bad for tying up a table and keeping him from waiting on someone else that would order more than a house glass of wine, but, I was desperate to have my date show up. I didn't want to take any chances that they would after I left. I *needed* this more than I wanted to admit.

As I unlocked my phone and opened the text messages to *Brad*, if that was even his name, I heard someone walk over and stand by the table. My arms tingled with goosebumps, my fingers shaking slightly as I set my phone down. The excitement that he had finally shown up was quickly replaced with dread and anxiety when I noticed who was standing there instead.

"Hey, Everly," Tom said with a nod. His arm was wrapped around the rail-thin waist of his new girlfriend, who just so happened to be a model.

"Hey," I muttered, adjusting the linen napkin on my lap. I didn't bother to acknowledge her, just as she hadn't bothered to say anything to me.

"You here on a *date*?" he chuckled as if he couldn't believe it, nodding to the place setting beside me. "With your *boyfriend*?"

I looked around helplessly, praying that Brad would magically show up out of thin air.

"She's not here on a date," Staci said sarcastically. "Otherwise, she wouldn't be sitting here by herself, looking so sad and desperate. *If* she had a boyfriend, don't you think he'd be here by now?"

I bit my tongue, refusing to give her the satisfaction of getting a response to that.

"You're here *alone*? I didn't think you liked to eat by yourself," Tom noted.

"I don't," I bit out through gritted teeth. I wasn't going to let him get to me if I could help it, but *man,* if he didn't know how to push my buttons. I was also regretting telling him that I was dating someone since that lie seemed to be biting me in the ass at the moment.

I hadn't planned to make up such an elaborate story. When I saw him making out with Staci in his office after he emailed me that we needed to talk to, I panicked, and it just came rushing out. It was like the brain cells had magically disappeared and weren't allowing me to come up with actual words to reply with.

"So then you *are* waiting for someone. Did you get stood up?" His eyes lit up when he asked it as if it somehow gave him pleasure to see me so miserable.

"Obviously," Staci laughed, snorting in the process. She covered her mouth with a perfectly manicured hand and pretended to be embarrassed.

I was about to say something, though I had no idea what, when someone suddenly slid past Tom and Staci and stepped beside me.

"Hey, baby, sorry I'm late," he said loudly, bending down to kiss me as his warm hand softly tilted my chin up for my lips to meet his.

My eyes tried to focus on the handsome stranger from the hostess station before they fluttered shut with the kiss. His soft, full lips danced with mine as if they had done this a million times. It wasn't the awkward kind of first-date kiss that I was used to. It was the kind of kiss that sent shivers up my spine and sent heat rushing through my body at the promise of what else he could do with his tongue.

He pulled away and gave a tight smile to Tom and Staci as he sat down and placed the napkin in his lap.

Having noticed that someone else had *finally* sat down, the waiter approached our table, pen ready to start our order.

"I see that the rest of your party has arrived," he said shortly. "What may I get you to drink, sir?"

"Go ahead and bring us a bottle of whatever the lady is drinking."

The waiter nodded and walked off, tucking his notepad into the pocket of his apron.

"Well, I guess we should let you get to your dinner," Tom replied awkwardly, staring at the man next to me uneasily.

I simply nodded, glaring at Staci as her jaw stayed open while she stared in disbelief.

Tom nudged her before placing his hand on her lower back and leading her away from our table and out of the restaurant.

I placed both hands on the table in front of me and slowly released the breath I had been holding. I looked over and found dark hazel eyes locked onto me, studying me with curiosity.

"Thank you," I stammered, unsure of how to start. "I'm sorry about that."

"Don't be," he shrugged, getting situated in his seat. He leaned back as the waiter grabbed the empty glass in front of him, filling it with water, then set it back on the table.

I waited until he left before I spoke again.

"Well, if you have somewhere else you need to be, please don't feel obligated to stay with me." I lifted my wine and took a drink.

"I don't have anywhere that I need to be," he answered with a grin that pulled up the corners of his mouth into a dazzling smile. "But if you'd rather that I go, I can."

I was too quick in my response, nearly knocking over my glass of water as my hand darted out to grab his wrist to keep him from moving. It was as if I was afraid that he would vanish into thin air as quickly as he had appeared.

"No," I said abruptly, my eyes wildly searching his. It felt like I was dreaming, and I wasn't ready to wake up.

"I mean, no, please stay," I added with a somewhat calmer breath. "I would love to treat you to dinner to say thank you for coming to my rescue."

"Thank you, but no," he started before we were interrupted again. He gave me a quick, tight smile before turning his attention away.

The waiter was back, this time with the bottle of wine and a basket of bread. This guy had *the worst* timing ever. He set the bread down and refilled my glass before pouring one for—whoever this guy was. I had kissed someone that I didn't even know his name.

"Are you ready to order?" he asked, pulling his notepad out of his pocket.

Mr. Sexy arched a brow at me, silently asking if I knew what I wanted. I felt my nerves running wild again, knowing that I would end up eating by myself after all. He had already declined my offer but didn't have enough time to get out of there before the waiter returned.

"I'll do the fettuccini with grilled chicken and a side salad," I answered.

"I'll do the same," he replied, sliding the menus back to the waiter. I wondered if maybe he was just being polite to keep from embarrassing me.

The waiter scribbled the information on the paper and grabbed the menus before rushing off.

"Thank you for the offer," he said once we were alone again. "But I will not let you pay for my meal."

I pulled my brows in. Out of the handful of dates that I had been on in the past few weeks, he was the first to object to me offering to pay for the meal. Not that I was in love with the idea of paying for every meal when I went on a date, but it was better than allowing some asshole to think that I owed him something because he paid. While it would be grand to simply split the ticket, I found that most of the *men* I had met weren't that open to the idea either.

"But, if you'll let me, I would love to treat you instead."

I laughed before I could stop myself. If I thought I was in a dream before, I was *definitely* in one now. Things like this *never* happened to girls like me. Hell, I don't think they happened to anyone who wasn't a paid actress in a rom-com movie.

"That's not necessary. Really."

Now it was his turn to frown at me.

"I would imagine that it's not *necessary*," he commented.

"However, it would be my pleasure."

"Why are you being so nice to me?" I blurted out, tilting my head to the side. I was studying him like a foreign creature because that was exactly what it felt like he was.

"Why wouldn't I?"

"Because you don't even know me."

"And that's a reason *not* to be nice to you?"

"I've seen worse," I snorted, knowing it was the truth.

He pulled his lips into a thin smile and nodded.

"I'm Jared," he said, extending his hand to me.

I shook it, surprised by the softness.

"Everly."

"That's a beautiful name."

I tried to force down the butterflies that were fluttering in my stomach, impressed by his charm. There was no way that this was really happening. There had to be a catch. Maybe it was all a game, and I was on some reality TV show, like *Pranked*.

"Thank you," I said cautiously, not ready to let my guard down.

"You don't trust me, do you?" he asked, his grin pushing across his olive-toned skin. Suddenly, his eyes looked more green than brown with the way the light was hitting them. They were easy to get lost in.

"No," I laughed, leaning back in my seat. "I really don't."

"Why not?"

"Because you seem too good to be true."

"How so?" His lips curled up into a bigger smile as he seemed amused by my statement.

I took a few deep, steadying breaths before I answered.

"You popped up out of thin air, rescued me from an embarrassing situation with my ex-boyfriend, and you want to buy me dinner. Things like that don't just happen to me. So either I'm drunk," I glanced at what was left of my second glass of wine. "Or you are simply too good to be true. Maybe a figment of my imagination?"

He laughed, and it sounded like music to my ears. It was a deep laugh that made the tight muscles under his buttoned-up shirt move, drawing my eye as my fingers itched to trace the outline of each ridge.

"I can assure you that I'm real and that I just happened to be in the right place at the right time," he assured me.

"I find that hard to believe," I muttered.

"It's true," he chuckled with a wink. "I was at the hostess station, waiting to put in a to-go order when I overheard the conversation. I wasn't sure if someone else was going to show up, so I took a chance and decided to step in."

I felt my jaw drop open, partly embarrassed that he had heard our conversation and knew how pathetic I was, and somewhat impressed that he had wanted to help.

"No one deserves to be treated that way," he added. "I can't stand guys like that."

"Well, thank you. I don't think I'll ever find enough ways to show my gratitude to you for coming to my rescue."

"As I said, it's my pleasure."

The waiter returned with our plates and set them down in front of us. I took the opportunity to think about what he had said as we started to eat.

"So, you got stood up?" he asked, raising an eyebrow before taking a bite of fettuccine.

I nearly choked on my water, caught off guard by his question. I brought my napkin up and blotted my mouth.

"Yup," I said with a sigh as if I didn't care. The truth was that I did—a lot.

"It's his loss." He shrugged, his broad shoulders pulling tight against the thick fabric of his shirt.

I smiled but said nothing for a moment. I twirled noodles around my fork and then stopped.

"I would like to think so, but this is the third time in a week, so I'm starting to think that maybe it's me."

He set his fork down on his plate and lifted his glass to take a drink of wine.

"Why would you think that?"

"Well, there has to be a reason that I got stood up by three different guys in one week. That just seems like it has to be me. Maybe they walked in, saw me, and decided to leave."

"You had three dates with three different guys this week, and they all stood you up?"

I nodded, taking a bite to occupy my mouth, so I didn't say anything more embarrassing.

"Why so many dates?" he asked without any judgment in his tone.

I waited for the waiter to refill our glasses of water before I told him the depressing truth.

"My work is having a big, fancy holiday party this weekend, and I wanted—no, *needed* to find a date to go with me. I don't have much time to get out and socialize, so I had a few people set me up. This one was a blind date that my mother set up with some lady that goes to her church. She knew a young man who would be perfect for me." I laughed at how stupid everything sounded before I added, "I'm not sure if the guy even exists."

"Where is the party at?" he asked, ignoring everything else.

"Palmer House Hotel," I swallowed. "They've booked a ballroom for the party Saturday night, but they're also paying for a room for each employee. It's a formal event, and everyone is expected to stay the night since there's a mandatory brunch in the morning. I think they're bribing us with the party and beautiful room before they unload all of the work crap on us the next morning," I joked, starting to ramble.

He leaned back in his seat and pushed his plate away. A few seconds passed before he reached down and adjusted his black satin tie.

"I'll go with you," he offered, looking deep into my eyes.

I pulled my head back in surprise.

"You want to go to my holiday party with me?" I questioned.

"Sure," he said softly. "You need a date, and I'm free this weekend."

This all felt too good to be true. Just when I was starting to let my guard down and believe this could be real, I began to question everything all over again.

"There's another thing," I added hesitantly. "I kinda told them that I've been seeing someone. So they're going to expect that…." My voice trailed off, too embarrassed to complete the sentence.

"So, not only will I be your *date, but* I'll also be your…?"

"Boyfriend."

If he was the least bit uncomfortable with hearing any of this, he didn't let on. He stayed perfectly composed as he took a drink and then set his glass down.

"Okay," he said smoothly.

"Are you sure you want to do this?" I asked, ready for him to reconsider.

He laughed and nodded his head.

"Yeah, I'm sure. Besides, I have a favor that I'll need in return."

"Well, you've saved me a few times already, I'd be happy to help you however I can."

"Trust me, you might reconsider that once you know what it is." He laughed, sending a surge of nervousness through me as I wondered what I had just gotten myself into.

242

Two
Jared

The week dragged on, as I waited anxiously to pick Everly up Saturday night. I hadn't talked to her much since our unexpected dinner Tuesday night, but I sure as hell hadn't stopped thinking about her. We had texted a few times to confirm the details for tonight, but my head was distracted with thoughts of her brilliant blue eyes and wavy brown hair that hung right above her ass when she got up to leave.

Not only was I obsessing over seeing her again, but I also couldn't get that kiss out of my head. I had kissed what felt like hundreds of women in my lifetime—hell if I knew the actual number—but no one had ever kissed me like she had. There was this intense spark that ignited between us, and I was reluctant to pull away.

It was almost 6:30, and I was picking her up at 6:45. Maybe it was my excitement to see her, or perhaps I was just naturally an early person, but there I was, sitting outside in my truck, watching the clock on the dashboard, and counting down the minutes until I could see her.

I didn't want to look like a pervert stalking her from the street, so I turned up the radio and played on my phone, hoping to look busy.

A few minutes later, I saw her front door open as she peeked outside. I turned the truck off and climbed out, taking in how beautiful she looked. Her hair was pulled up tightly on her head with a few pieces that curled behind her ear. A long black dress wrapped tightly around her body and loosened enough at the bottom to allow her to walk in the thin black heels that she had on.

"You look beautiful," I stammered, as I walked up to her porch. She smiled nervously and ran a hand down her dress.

"Thank you," she said shyly. "You look very handsome."

I watched as she tried to check me out discreetly, her facial expressions giving her away as her eyes roamed over my body.

My suit was custom-tailored and fit like a glove. I wasn't sure what she would wear, so I stuck with the black one, knowing that I couldn't go wrong with that. My tie was black with shades of grey pinstripes that paired perfectly with the silver necklace that dipped into the cleavage of her strapless dress.

"You ready to go?" I asked, shoving my hands into my pockets to keep from touching her.

"Yeah, let me grab my coat and lock up real quick."

I stepped back, giving her some room as a gust of wind pushed past us, sending a chill through me.

A few minutes later, she was wearing a long, thick black peacoat with a small wallet-looking purse tucked beneath her arm and a small duffle bag on her shoulder. She locked the door and then turned to face me. I could tell that she was nervous as I extended my hand to help her down the few steps to the driveway. When she placed her hand in mine, I felt her skin's warmth and softness, which sent another chill down my spine.

I walked her to the truck, opened her door, and helped her inside before I rushed off to the driver's side to get in. Once the vehicle was started, I cranked up the heater, making sure it didn't blow her hair but kept her warm and toasty.

"Are you excited about tonight?" I asked casually, checking my rearview mirror as I made my way to the hotel.

"I'm not sure that excited is the right word," she laughed nervously.

"Why not?"

"I'm not a social person, so these types of things are not my favorite. And then I'm worried that..."

"That people will know that I'm not your boyfriend?" I finished for her. I needed to know where her head was before the night started so that I didn't make things worse for her.

"Yeah," she sighed. "I already know that they'll take one look at you and think that I paid you to be my date."

"Are you calling me a hooker?" I joked, giving her my best smile as I tried to calm her nerves.

I watched for a brief moment as the corners of her mouth tilted up into a smile.

"That's not what I meant," she giggled.

"Well, it worked out well for Julia Roberts in Pretty Woman," I offered, loving the way her smile pulled tighter across her face, lighting up her blue eyes. Unfortunately, it disappeared as quickly as it had appeared.

She stayed quiet, chewing her nail nervously and watched out the window as we got closer to the hotel. Once we were there, I parked and turned to look at her.

"Nothing bad is going to happen, Everly," I assured her. "I'm here as your date, as your *boyfriend*," I added. "I promise that you will not regret having me come with you and that all of your coworkers will believe that we're together by the end of the night."

She shifted uneasily in her seat, staring at someone ahead of us. I turned my attention to where she was looking and saw the same couple that had been at her table harassing her at the restaurant the other night.

"Umm, there's one more thing that I need to tell you," she said quietly, turning to look at me.

I slightly raised a brow and waited.

"The guy you met the other night—Tom. Well, he's my ex-boyfriend."

"Okay…." There was more to that story, I could just feel it.

"And he's also my boss."

I blew out a heavy breath. Things just got a hell of a lot more complicated really quick.

<u>Three</u>
Everly

I tried to get my legs to stop shaking as I got out of the truck and took Jared's hand. Why did I think it was a good idea to wear six-inch heels tonight? Besides the fact that they were the only shoes that were tall enough to keep my dress from pooling on the ground, I had a brief moment where I had wanted to impress Jared. Now I would be lucky if I could manage to walk in them without tripping and breaking my neck.

We were ushered inside and directed to the ballroom, where people were already mingling inside. I glanced around, trying to find where Tom and Staci had gone. Hopefully, they went up to their rooms to get situated. Of course it's what I should have done, but the thought of taking Jared up to my room sent butterflies through my stomach and made my palms sweat. Instead, I accepted the offer to have the bellhop take my bag up to my room for me.

Once inside the ballroom, I looked around to see if there was assigned seating—which there was. I groaned silently when I found my name on the list next to Tom's. It made sense that they would put each department together at their own table, but I hated the idea of having to sit next to him and spend the evening hearing Staci talk about how hard it was to be so beautiful and thin.

"Did you want something to drink?" Jared asked quietly in my ear as his hand rested lightly on my lower back.

It felt like he could sense how nervous I was. He gently led me over to the bar and kept his hand protectively on me as we ordered our drinks. The bartender was handsome but definitely out of my league as he tilted his head back and laughed at something the busty red-headed waitress said to him. It was hard to concentrate on any words coming out of her mouth when her shirt plunged so low that her breasts almost spilled over as she leaned up against the bar top.

He gave a quick nod to Jared before sliding our glasses over and moving on to the next couple who had walked up. Jared tucked some cash into the tip jar and picked up our drinks as we moved out of the way. He handed me my drink carefully before pulling a sip of beer out of the bottle his strong hand was wrapped around. I took a sip of my martini and let the alcohol kiss my tongue before making its way down my throat, spreading warmth and a sense of calm through me with each drink.

People were scattered around the room as it started to get more packed. There was a dance floor off to the side of the room and a band still setting up on the stage.

"Did you want to find our seats?" Jared suggested, likely seeing the look of dread on my face as I considered having to mingle with everyone.

"Yes, please."

We walked over to the tables and scanned them until we

found table 17. I hoped that at least this part was open seating so we could sit next to anyone other than Tom and Staci.

"It looks like we're right here," Jared said, finding our name cards before I could.

I offered a tight smile when I saw Tom's name next to mine. Jared reached over and swapped our names, putting him next to Tom and me next to Susan, the older woman that I absolutely loved in our department.

We sat down, and I felt somewhat more comfortable than I had before. Soon, people started making their way to the tables, and I felt the dread piling up as Tom sat down next to Jared with an audible grunt of disgust.

Without warning, Jared reached up and wrapped his arms casually around my shoulders as if this was the most natural thing in the world. Instead of wanting to pull away from his touch, I found it so comforting that I wanted to lean closer to him and feel the warmth of his body next to mine.

"You again," Tom stated curtly, turning to look at Jared. Since the table was round, I still had a good view of him and Staci as they sat there, staring in disbelief at Jared sitting next to me.

When Jared didn't respond, Tom leaned forward and caught my eye.

"I thought you were coming by yourself?" he asked sharply.

"I told Gail that I was bringing a date when I RSVP'd for two on the form."

Gail was the director of human resources and was responsible for putting together the holiday party. I had given her my form after my fingers trembled when marking the box for two. I had no idea who I was bringing with me and panicked that I would have to pay for dinner for the date that didn't show up. I was desperate to prove to Tom that I had moved on, even if that meant I had to fake a boyfriend at this stupid party. Especially since I had opened my stupid big mouth and told him that I had one.

"Well, she didn't tell me," he scoffed, unfolding the napkin that was resting on his plate.

"Why would she tell you?" I asked, pulling my brows tightly together as I leaned forward. I felt Jared's fingers lightly caress my skin above my dress and started to relax again.

"Because it's *my* department. I should know who's coming."

"You knew that I was coming. Whether or not I brought a date was none of your damn business."

"What you do is my business, Everly," he bit out. "I worry about you and whoever *this* is."

I felt Jared's body stiffen beside me and knew that Tom had struck a nerve.

"As I said, that is none of your business. So stop acting like it is and worry about your girlfriend flirting with the waiter." I nodded at Staci, who was oblivious to our conversation as she was turned all the way around in her chair, twirling her hair on her finger as she giggled shamelessly with the waiter beside her.

I reached forward and grabbed the heavy glass filled with ice water and brought it to my lips, trying to steady my hand enough to take a drink.

Jared leaned in closer, and I felt his breath hot on my neck as he spoke.

"Do you trust me?" he asked quietly.

I nodded, my blood still boiling from Tom.

He leaned back in his seat and lowered his arm from around my shoulders, resting his hand on my thigh.

I gasped from the touch, nearly spilling my glass of water. Tom's eyes darted over to us; his features pinched in annoyance on his face.

I set the glass down gently and shyly looked away from Susan as she eyed me cautiously to see if I was okay.

I heard a low chuckle from Jared as his hand gently squeezed my thigh. I looked up at him and saw a mischievous smile on his face as he winked.

He was so drop-dead sexy that for a moment, I forgot anyone else was in the room with us. I pulled in a slow, deep breath, remembering the way his lips had felt against mine the other night. I had no idea what to expect tonight with him pretending to be my boyfriend, but part of me desperately hoped that it meant that he would kiss me again. Maybe even more.

It had been a long time—a really, *really* long time—since I had felt a man's hands on my body, even longer since I had someone make love to me and not rush through it. Aside from my vibrator, I couldn't remember when someone else had given me an orgasm. My love life was as depressing and even more pathetic than my social life.

The waitstaff moved around the room quickly, placing baskets of bread and butter on the tables and refilling the glasses of water and tea. Jared leaned back as they refilled his water, adding more ice to the glass in the process.

When no one was looking, he dipped a finger in and pulled out an ice cube before putting it in his mouth. The next thing I knew, he was leaning closer to me, gently running his tongue along my neck as the ice melted around it. I closed my eyes and tilted my head to the side, giving him more access.

My heart was racing from the thrill of it. The cold of the ice paired with the heat from his tongue sent my body into overdrive as my senses were pushed to full alert. I wanted to reach over and grab him, pull him closer to me as we forgot about everyone and everything in this room.

"You make it really easy to pretend to be your boyfriend," he whispered in my ear before gently nipping at my earlobe.

"You're better than any boyfriend I've had before," I muttered, digging my fingers into my thighs as I tried to keep from moaning.

"Then you haven't been with the right guy," he added, slowly pulling away.

His eyes were a darker shade of green than they were a few minutes ago, and I could tell that this had affected him as much as it did me. He sat up straight in his chair and acted like he hadn't just tortured me with his skilled tongue.

Soon they were serving dinner, and we were distracted by our food. I speared a piece of asparagus with my fork and brought it to my lips, pausing when I noticed Jared watching me. My lips were parted, ready to take a bite.

"Lucky asparagus," he muttered with a grin before focusing on his salmon.

I felt the blush pinch my cheeks as I took a bite and tried not to choke on it. He knew all of the right things to say and do to make me feel sexy and seen—something I hadn't had in a long time.

After dinner, they cleared our plates and served dessert and coffee. I was already full, but the molten chocolate cake with vanilla ice cream was calling my name.

"This cake looks as good as you," Jared commented, loud enough to earn an eye roll from Tom. I knew he was doing it on purpose, just to get a rise out of him, but there was something about how he said it that almost had me believing it.

"Thank you," I said, suddenly feeling brave. I dug my spoon in, grabbing a bit of chocolate cake and ice cream, and turned to Jared. "Wanna see how good it tastes?"

I knew my choice of words would send a clear note to Tom that I wasn't talking about the cake. I held the spoon steadily as Jared leaned forward and wrapped his mouth around it, slowly pulling the contents off before licking his lips.

He studied me as he chewed, his eyes never leaving mine. His finger reached up and gently wiped the sides of his mouth before he spoke.

"That cake is delicious," he answered sexily. "But you taste better."

I felt my cheeks burn red with embarrassment. Tom scoffed beside him, tossing his spoon onto his plate and shoving it away. What did he have to be angry about? In the five years we were together, he had maybe gone down on me one or two times, using it as his birthday gift to me when he forgot to purchase a real gift.

"So dear, how long have you two been together?" Susan asked, turning her attention to us. She had obviously missed the dirty part of the conversation.

"Four months," I said at the same time that Jared said, "Six months."

She looked between us, confused by our answers. I laughed nervously, not sure what to say. Jared wrapped his arm around my shoulders again, this time pulling me into his body as he hugged me and planted a kiss on my temple.

"She counts the day that she officially said yes to being my girlfriend. I count the day that I first started chasing her. She put up a hard fight, but in the end, I won her love and made her mine."

Susan held her hand to her heart and looked warmly at us.

"That's so sweet," she sighed. "It's good that you found someone willing to chase after you," she said, giving a dirty look to Tom as she looked past Jared. "You look really happy, dear. I'm glad you found someone who clearly worships you the way you deserve."

"There's not a thing in this world that I wouldn't do for her," Jared replied casually. "Especially knowing how much she's been through already, I'm more than ready to show her what a real man can do for her. And *to* her," he said quietly in my ear.

Tom excused himself and went to the bathroom while Staci ventured off to the dance floor. I was tired and had enough socializing already. I wanted nothing more than to leave and head on up to my room, but I wasn't sure I was ready to say goodbye to Jared. While we had talked a few times since dinner, we hadn't discussed whether he was planning to stay the night with me or attend brunch in the morning. Since I knew my luck was coming to an end soon, I assumed he would leave and go on his way as soon as it was safe to do so. Hell, he probably had another date lined up after with some beautiful woman who would reap the benefits of the things he had been whispering in my ear all night.

An hour later, everyone started making their way to their rooms, and I knew it was time to do the same.

"Everly, I'm so glad you made it," Gail said over my shoulder as she came over to our table. "I'm sorry I didn't get over here earlier to say hi. It's been nonstop from the moment I got here."

"No worries," I replied with a smile.

"I don't think we've met," Gail said to Jared, reaching over to extend her hand to him. "I'm Gail."

"Jared," he replied, shaking her hand.

"It's nice to meet you." She smiled and looked past him as someone called her name. "I look forward to seeing you at brunch in the morning. You two enjoy your stay tonight."

She gently squeezed my shoulder before rushing off to tend to someone else.

I had thought—no, hoped—that Tom had left when I hadn't seen him for a while. So it was an unpleasant surprise when he spoke over my shoulder.

"He's staying the night with you?" he asked bitterly.

Before I could answer, Jared wrapped an arm around my waist and pulled me into him.

"How else am I going to make sure she stays warm tonight?" He gave him a smug smile and started to lead me away.

Then, at the last minute, I turned and looked over my shoulder at Tom, who was still watching us. "Oh, and don't worry if you hear me screaming. That's just what I sound like when I'm not *faking* an orgasm," I said with more confidence than I ever knew I had.

My heart was racing when I spun back around and leaned into Jared as his fingers dug lightly into my side. He chuckled as we walked away, leaving Tom in stunned silence as Staci muttered under her breath about me being a lucky bitch.

<u>Four</u>
Jared

It didn't go unnoticed that Everly's fingers trembled as she tried to stick the card into the key reader.

"Here, let me," I offered, placing my hand over hers and sliding the card away from her. She smiled and stepped out of the way as I reached forward and swiped the card, opening the door.

I held it open as she walked in and looked around. The room was beautiful with a king-sized bed centered in the middle of it. There wasn't much else in the room other than a dresser with a tv sitting on top of it, a small table with two chairs by the window, and two nightstands on each side of the bed.

"Thank you for walking me up," she said nervously. "Please don't feel obligated to stay."

She was still standing in the same spot, fidgeting with her purse as she watched me. There was something about the way that she was looking at me that said that she didn't want me to go.

"Do you want me to leave?" I asked gently, giving her plenty of space so I didn't crowd her.

"Do you want to?" She raised her eyebrows as she waited anxiously.

"No."

Her chest rose and fell as she let out a jagged breath.

"I don't want you to go either."

I watched her as she looked around, unsure of herself and her decision.

"If you change your mind, just let me know. I don't want to make you uncomfortable."

She tipped her head back and laughed. A genuine laugh that made her eyes crinkle in the corners.

"Uncomfortable is the last thing I would use to describe how you make me feel."

My eyebrows shot up, surprised by this revelation. I knew that she had been receptive to my touch earlier, and I had noticed how she blushed with the things that I said, but I wasn't sure how much of it was a show for Tom and how much she was genuinely reacting to me.

I took a few steps toward her, gauging her reaction along the way.

"How do I make you feel?" I asked once I was standing in front of her.

She chewed her bottom lip before answering.

"Sexy. Wanted. Nervous."

I reached up and gently caressed her cheek with my thumb.

"Why do you say it like it's a bad thing?" I chuckled.

Her hand reached up and held onto my hand as she closed her eyes.

"Because," she breathed heavily. "I haven't felt this turned on by a man in years, and you barely touched me. It's embarrassing."

I lifted her chin with my finger and waited for her to open her eyes and look at me.

"There's nothing embarrassing about that, Everly. And anyone who tells you otherwise has no idea what they're talking about. You're a beautiful woman who deserves to be touched in a way that makes you feel sexy and wanted."

Her blue eyes locked onto mine, and I noticed the lust simmering beneath.

"How are you so perfect?" she asked, tilting her head to the side. "You know all of the right things to say to make me feel calm when I would normally be freaking out."

"I'm not perfect," I laughed, letting my hand drop from her face. "I'm far from it. But I would like to think that I'm a fairly observant person. Plus, I'm an expert at body language."

I shrugged cockily, earning a laugh from her.

"You're an expert at body language?" she asked, shifting her weight to the other leg and folding her arms across her chest.

Her body was turned toward me with the slit in her dress pulling tight on the leg closest to me.

"I am," I assured her, noting all of the things she was subconsciously saying.

"Okay, then what is mine saying?" She licked her lips before pulling her bottom one in between her teeth.

I made an effort to study her, looking her up and down painfully slow as she squirmed beneath my stare.

Finally, I said, "that you want me."

She let out a small gasp and sucked in a breath.

"The way that you're standing, with your feet slightly spread in a way that makes the slit pull tighter across your thigh. And the way that you have your arms folded, pressing your breasts up so they're on display for me. Both of those confirm that you want me to see your body. But, aside from those, it's the little things. Like the way your breathing has changed or how your eyes have darkened because you're aroused." I stepped closer to her, our bodies nearly touching each other. "I bet if I were to slip a finger inside, I would find out how wet you are."

Her breath caught in her throat as she listened to the words I said. She was so beautiful, and I couldn't stop thinking about how much I wanted her.

"Make a Christmas wish, and I'll make it come true," I coaxed.

"I don't know what to say," she whispered shakily, looking down at her feet.

"Tell me what you want," I pleaded, as I watched the blush creep up her neck.

She chewed her bottom lip before looking into my eyes.

"You," she breathed.

<u>Five</u>
Everly

I tried to act cool and collected as I stood there, watching Jared's eyes scan my face. I knew that he was overly observant, but I didn't know if he knew just how nervous he made me.

I waited, hoping that he would take me at my word and have his way with me. Even though I was scared shitless of that actually happening, a big part of me wished it would. What I would give to just feel careless and free for one night as I enjoyed whatever pleasures he gave to me.

The longer he stayed quiet, the more I worried about what he would say when he finally spoke. The silence between us was deafening.

Panic started to rise within me, my palms sweating as I shifted, praying that my heels wouldn't choose this moment to give in and break. That would be one hell of a way to go.

"I should get going," he said quietly, a hint of disappointment in his voice.

I felt the air rush out of me, along with the hopes I had been holding onto.

"Oh, okay." I frowned and tried to shake off the feeling of rejection that was sitting so heavily on my shoulders.

I stepped back, allowing him to walk past me as he gently slid his hand across my stomach in the process.

 "Did I do something wrong?" I blurted out. I had faced a lot of rejection lately, so this time I wanted to hear why he was leaving. If there was something that I was doing that was driving men away, I needed to know what it was.

He stopped and looked at me.

"No, Everly. You didn't do anything wrong."

"Then why are you leaving?" I was so confused and had no idea what had caused the sudden change between us.

"Because," he sighed and scrubbed a hand down his face. "When you said that you wanted me, your body language said otherwise."

"I meant what I said," I objected.

He dropped his hand and grabbed mine.

"Your body said otherwise," he explained. "Your words said that was what you wanted, but the way your shoulders tightened and you flinched at them said otherwise. And that's okay, Everly. There's nothing wrong with listening to your instincts."

I was frustrated with myself, and I could see that he knew it. I wanted to tear down the walls I had worked so hard to build up and let him in, but I couldn't. Thanks to Tom, I found it nearly impossible to let anyone in.

"You don't have to go," I said easily. "I mean, obviously, we're not going to do anything, but you can hang out for a bit if you want to."

Even though I knew that nothing more would happen between us, I was reluctant to have him leave. Maybe it was me being selfish, but I didn't want to be alone tonight. The few hours we had spent together had been different than I had expected, and I wasn't ready for it to end. Not only did I feel comfortable around him, I felt safe. Even if I couldn't get myself to jump his bones like I wanted to, I didn't want him to leave.

"Sure," he replied with a smile. "Do you want to watch some tv or find a movie?"

I nodded, feeling somewhat relieved that he wasn't rushing off now that he knew he wasn't going to get any. *That was a change.*

"I need to change real quick," I said, eager to get out of my dress and into something more comfortable. "Sorry, I would offer you something to wear, but I only brought a pair of pajamas and clothes for tomorrow."

"It's okay," he laughed. "I wasn't sure what the plan was, so I went ahead and packed a bag just in case. Go ahead and get changed, and I'll run down and grab it real quick."

"Okay," I agreed. "Go ahead and take the room key so you can let yourself in while I get situated."

He smiled and took it, then he was out the door and gone. I let out a heavy sigh as I tried to process everything that had happened tonight. I grabbed my bag from the floor and went to the bathroom to get changed.

It felt nice to take my hair down. Each bobby pin that I pulled out relieved some of the tension and pressure on my head until they were finally out. I ran my hands through my hair, trying to smooth out the tangles.

My eyes hurt from the makeup I was wearing, and I was desperate to take it off. I rarely wore makeup, and when I did, it usually bothered my eyes. Knowing that I didn't have to impress Jared since we weren't planning to sleep together, I decided to go ahead and wash it off. I dried my face with the hand towel hanging on the bar beside me and then brushed my teeth. Just because we weren't having sex didn't mean that we wouldn't kiss. It was better to be prepared, just in case.

I hung my dress over the rod in the shower, not bothering to go out and search for one in the closet by the door. Unfortunately, I hadn't packed for tonight with the idea that Jared would be hanging out with me. It seemed too good to be true, so I had dismissed the thought and packed to stay by myself. I glanced nervously in the mirror at my booty shorts and cropped sweatshirt. It's what I would wear to bed any other night when I was at home by myself, but it felt slightly sexy and inappropriate now. The only other clothes I had with me were the jeans and sweater I had packed for tomorrow.

Deciding that there weren't any other choices, I sighed and slid my duffle bag under the counter before opening the door and walking into the room. I stopped in my tracks, my jaw dropping open when I saw Jared changing.

Gray sweatpants hung low on his hips, and the muscles in his torso were on full display as he lifted his arms to pull his t-shirt over his head.

There wasn't an ounce of fat on his toned body that looked like it belonged on the cover of a magazine. I tried to swallow, but my throat was suddenly dry. Instead, I just stood there, drinking him in like I was stranded in the desert, and he was the last drop of water.

He finished pulling it over his head and turned toward me once he realized that I was standing there. The shirt slowly fell, covering my perfect view.

"Sorry, I thought I could change before you came out," he apologized.

"Don't be sorry," I stammered, trying to force words out past the dryness in my throat.

"Do you want me to run down and see if they have an ice machine?" he offered.

I tried to focus on what he was asking, but the only thing I could think about was the way he made my skin feel earlier when he trailed his tongue along it with the ice cube in his mouth.

His lips turned up into a sexy smile, and his eyes lit up as he walked closer to me. It was as if he was reading every dirty thought I was having.

"Are you okay?" he asked playfully, lifting my chin with his fingers. My eyes locked onto his, and I felt a pull deep inside that made me want to jump into his arms and ride him into the sunset.

"Yes," I whispered.

"So, do you want me to?"

"Want you to what?"

"Get ice," he said slowly. My eyes drifted down to his lips as he licked them when he spoke.

"Ice," I repeated breathlessly. My chest rose and fell heavily as I stood there, hypnotized by him.

"Ice," he confirmed, lowering his mouth to mine. He kissed me softly as his hands slid down and wrapped around my waist. I moaned at the contact and felt my legs start to give. I knew what my body wanted, even if my head kept getting in the way.

After a few minutes, he pulled away, breaking the kiss. I could feel his erection through his pants and knew that he was as turned on as I was. I was practically panting, wanting more.

"I can go get some ice," he stammered breathlessly. "And some bottles of water."

I rubbed at my lips, missing the feeling of his against mine.

"Okay, thank you."

He pulled away and walked out the door, leaving me there in a confused state of bliss.

Ten minutes later, he was back with a bucket of ice, a few bottles of water, and a random assortment of snacks. I was cuddled in the bed, under the covers, after feeling self-conscious about what I was wearing when he walked in.

"Do you want snacks in bed?" he asked, kicking his shoes off and leaving them under the table by the window. He set the ice bucket down and went to the mini coffee bar by the door to bring over two glasses.

"Sure, thank you." I scooted over, giving him room to

climb in next to me when he was ready.

He handed me a glass filled with ice, then tossed the pile of snacks onto the bed beside me. I was surprised by how comfortable I felt with him there, moving around me as if we had done this a thousand times. Finally, once he had everything situated, he climbed onto the bed and sat beside me on top of the covers.

It was cold, even with the heater on.

"You can get under the covers if you want," I offered, hoping not to sound too desperate.

"I'm good, thanks," he said and turned his attention to the bag of Fritos in his hand.

I wasn't sure how to take it, so I turned my attention to the tv and pretended to look for something to watch.

"What do you want to watch?" I asked.

"I'm fine with whatever you want to watch."

I kept flipping through the channels and finally decided on an old action movie. I tried to get comfortable but couldn't. As I squirmed around, I couldn't help but wonder what he was thinking and why he was being so nice to me.

We sat there quietly, watching the movie and eating snacks for a while before I let out a heavy sigh. He turned to look at me, his head tilted in question.

"Everything okay?" he asked.

"Yeah," I sighed. "I'm fine."

I pulled my lower lip in between my teeth and turned my

attention back to the tv.

"You're a terrible liar," he noted, turning on his side and resting on his elbow as he faced me. "What's wrong?"

"Nothing. Really."

He reached over and grabbed the remote sitting in between us, turning the tv off so I would have to stop pretending to watch it.

"Everly, talk to me."

"There's nothing to talk about," I laughed, trying to make light of the situation.

"Remember what I said earlier about being able to read your body language?"

I took a deep breath and slowly let it out.

After a few minutes, I finally gave in.

"I'm just feeling confused, and it's frustrating."

"What do you mean?" he asked, sitting up and turning all the way to look at me.

"I know that you're here, pretending to be my boyfriend for the party, but I can't help but feel like there's something more going on. Like when we kissed a little bit ago. I felt something, and it *seemed* like maybe you did too. But now it's like nothing happened, and you're staying far away from me like I have cooties or something. I mean, you won't even get under the covers with me, and it's freezing in here."

"The reason that I haven't pushed any further is because

I respect you, Everly. There is nothing—and I mean *nothing*—that I want more than to strip you down and devour every inch of your body. To hear you scream my name over and over as you come undone and climax for everyone to hear. I didn't want to get under the covers with you because I don't trust myself enough to keep my hands to myself. I don't want to risk the temptation."

"But I'm sitting here saying that it's okay. You don't have to avoid the temptation," I insisted, suddenly hating how desperate I sounded.

"Trust me," he sighed, leaning forward to run his thumb along my cheek. "I do. Because if I don't, you'll end up regretting it in the morning, and I can't stand the thought of that. But if you're worried that I don't find you attractive, I can tell you with 100% certainty that I would love nothing more than to be inside of you right now, Everly. That's *my* Christmas wish. But not tonight."

He picked the remote up and turned the tv back on, acting as if nothing had just happened.

270

<u>Six</u>

Jared

The sun peeked through the curtains, spreading a warm glow on the wall behind me. I rolled over and looked at Everly, who was still sound asleep beside me. Her hair was fanned out beneath her in soft waves, making her look like an angel.

I hadn't expected to stay the night with her and couldn't remember what time we had finally fallen asleep. I tried to get up and sneak out of the room after she had started snoring, but she reached out and grabbed my arm, holding me in place. I decided to wait a little longer and then try again, but instead, I fell asleep.

I planned to sneak off last night, go home and get some sleep—after dealing with my massive erection in the shower—then come back and go to brunch with her so she didn't have to go by herself. More so, I didn't want Tom to know that I hadn't stayed the night with her after all.

I rolled out of bed and quietly stood up, stretching to wake myself up. I closed my eyes and reached higher, feeling my shirt pull up in the process as my sweats shifted lower. When I lowered my arms and opened my eyes, I found Everly awake, watching me.

I hated seeing the lust in her eyes and knowing that there was nothing that I could do about it. Not right now, anyway.

"Good morning," I said, smiling at her.

"Good morning," she replied, her eyes moving back up my body to my face. "Did you sleep okay?"

"Yeah, I'm a little sore, but I'm okay." I rubbed a hand along the back of my neck, feeling how stiff it was from sleeping in an odd position.

"I'm sorry," she apologized, propping herself up on her arm. "A hot shower might help," she suggested.

I felt the strain against my briefs and knew that a cold shower would be more appropriate right now.

"No need to be," I assured her. "I didn't plan to stay the night. I think I just got too comfortable and fell asleep."

"We both did," she laughed. "At one point, I woke up to you cuddling my breasts."

I closed my eyes and ran a hand through my hair.

"I'm so sorry," I apologized, embarrassed that I couldn't even keep my hands to myself in my sleep.

"It's okay," she giggled, pulling the sheets up to her chin. "I didn't mind. It helped my dreams get a little more *intense*."

Something flashed across her face that was a mix of embarrassment and lust, all mixed into one.

"Now I wanna know about this dream," I said, crossing my arms over my chest and watching her.

She covered her face with her arms and groaned,

complaining that it was too embarrassing.

"Nope," I said with too much enthusiasm. "I wanna hear about it. Remember, you owe me?"

"That's the favor that you're cashing in on?" she questioned, keeping the sheet pulled up to her chin.

"One of many."

She narrowed her eyes at me and pretended to frown. She was absolutely adorable.

"Now spill it."

She looked away, slipping further under the covers.

"I will come in there and tickle you until you tell me," I warned.

She stopped wiggling and looked at me.

"You wouldn't."

I lifted a brow in response.

"Fine," she sighed and puffed a breath of air up, forcing her hair out of her face. "In my dream, we were *doing stuff.* And then I guess my body started to react to you caressing my breasts and I…. you know…." She trailed off, leaving her sentence to wrap around my mind in the dirtiest of ways.

"You had an orgasm?" I asked, intently focusing on her face as the red crept across it.

She nodded and pulled the covers over her head again.

"Wow," I said, sitting down on the edge of the bed with my back slightly turned toward her.

"I know, I know," she whined. "I'm sorry. It's so embarrassing."

I looked over my shoulder and caught her eye.

"It's fucking hot as hell. I just wish I was awake to see it."

We were both quiet for a few moments before she scooted up and out of bed.

"I should probably get ready. Brunch is in an hour."

I nodded, wanting to volunteer that we take a shower together but kept my mouth shut instead. As she walked to the bathroom, I caught a quick glimpse of her and her ass that was barely covered by her shorts. I groaned as my dick pressed harder against my briefs. Today was going to be a *hard* day.

<u>Seven</u>
Everly

I ran my brush through my hair one last time and tried not to stare at Jared's reflection in the mirror behind me as he stripped down to jump in the shower. While he may not have had any intention of *stripping down,* he had taken his shirt off, and his sweatpants were hanging low enough to provoke dirty thoughts about what I wish would happen next.

I had thrown on my pajamas after I got out of the shower because I couldn't stand the thought of pulling on jeans or a tight sweater when my body was still damp. If I were at home, I would just get ready in my towel until I was completely dry, but I wasn't at home.

Once I heard the bathroom door close and the shower turn on, I took the opportunity to get dressed. I pulled my shirt up and over my head, tossing it onto the bed before hooking my fingers into the waistband of my shorts and pulling them down.

I was bent over, ass in the air, as I stepped out of them when I heard the bathroom door open. I didn't have time to cover up before I whipped around, surprising him with my bare breasts as much as he had surprised me.

His eyes widened as he took me in. I brought a hand up to try to cover my chest while moving my legs awkwardly to try to cover myself. I hadn't thought it was necessary to put underwear on since I wasn't getting dressed yet.

"Sorry," he coughed out as he swallowed hard. "I forgot to grab my clothes." He nodded to the change of clothes he had pulled out of his bag.

I nodded and pinched my eyes closed, hoping that I would disappear.

I heard him move past me, then rush back into the bathroom, closing the door behind him once again.

The air rushed out of my lungs quickly, pushing through my lips that were trembling.

Did that just happen?!

I didn't waste any time getting dressed after that. By the time he was done, I was sitting on the bed—fully clothed—pretending to look at something on my phone. Instead, I was obsessing over the fact that he had seen me naked, and there was nothing I could do about it.

"What time does brunch start?" he asked as he approached the bed, rolling his sleeves up. He looked more casual in a dark buttoned-down shirt and dark jeans.

"At eleven," I confirmed, scooting off the bed. I stood up, feeling awkward that he had seen me naked. "If you've changed your mind, you don't have to go."

He reached over to the table where his stuff was and picked up a black metal watch, clasping it around his wrist as he eyed me suspiciously.

"Do you not want me to go?"

I swallowed hard, trying to get past the dryness in my throat.

"No, it's not that," I whispered, unable to look at him.

He let out a soft whistle and took a few steps until he was right in front of me. Gently he cupped the side of my face, lifting it so I would have to look at him.

"I don't know how many times I have to tell you this, but I'll say it again." His voice was as smooth and velvety as his touch. "You have *nothing* to be embarrassed about. I'm sorry that I accidentally walked in on you, but I'm not sorry about what I saw."

My skin prickled as the heat washed over it, making me suddenly uncomfortable as my heart started beating hard against my chest.

"It took everything that I had to walk back into the bathroom and not rush over to touch you."

"Why didn't you?" I asked, nearly panting.

He chewed his bottom lip for a brief second before saying, "because I respect you. If anything happens between us, I want to make sure that you're fully on board."

I nodded, unable to say anything as I stared into his eyes. It amazed me how much they changed color, and I found myself wanting to get lost in the sea of green that was hypnotizing me.

"We should get going, so we're not late," he said as if he hadn't just melted my insides.

I stepped away from his touch and searched the room,

making sure I had packed up everything I had brought. We made our way down to his truck to drop off our bags before heading to brunch.

Brunch was in the same room as the night before, but this time it was decorated with a more festive theme and not the overly elegant feel it had last night. A giant Christmas tree adorned with colorful lights and ornaments stood in the center of the stage where the band had played. Beneath it were several wrapped gifts, begging to be opened. It was hard to believe that they had transformed the room so quickly.

I smiled and looked around, feeling more comfortable with the over-the-top Christmas decorations than I had last night when everything was elegant and formal. Jared and I found seats at the table in the far corner of the room. Thankfully there wasn't assigned seating this time, and everyone was free to sit wherever they wanted.

The noise grew louder as more people packed in and took their seats. Everyone was a mix of comfy and casual, which made me feel better about wearing jeans and a sweater.

Once everyone was seated, Gail made her way to the front of the room and took the microphone handed to her by one of the hotel employees.

"Good morning! First, I would like to thank all of you for attending, and I hope you had a fun time at the party last night and are well rested this morning! The fun isn't over yet," she warned, shaking her finger at the few people who groaned and hung their heads, their hangovers on full display.

"While we wait for the food to be served, I thought we could play a quick game." She waited and looked around the room, trying to find someone as excited about it as she was. "I mean, personally, I *love* games. But you know what I love even more?" She lowered the microphone and scanned the room. "Prizes."

She looked over her shoulder at the wrapped gifts under the tree.

"You don't *have* to participate in the games that we're going to play today, but I can guarantee you that there are some *fabulous* prizes to be won."

I felt Jared's fingers as they gently squeezed my knee. I looked up at him and received a wink before he nodded to Gail and the pile of presents behind her.

"The first game that we have is Christmas Tie. This will be done with teams of two. You don't need anything but a tie, and if you don't have one, there are a few that were left behind last night that you can use. Come on up, and let's get started." She stepped to the side and waved for everyone to join her.

"Do you wanna go?" Jared asked, low in my ear.

I looked around, unsure about it since I didn't love being the center of attention. I felt eyes on me and scanned the room, finding Tom in the corner, glaring at us.

Pulling my shoulders back and letting out a heavy breath, I turned to Jared and smiled.

"Sure, let's go."

We made our way up to the front of the room with the few other people who had decided to participate. It was an even number of males and females as everyone partnered up with someone of the opposite sex.

"Oh shoot, we don't have a tie," I whispered to Jared.

He smiled and reached into his pocket, pulling the one from last night out.

"I forgot to pack it earlier, so I just tucked it in my pocket. Guess that came in handy," he shrugged.

I smiled back and tried to shake off the nerves of having everyone—including Tom—watching us.

"Okay, so the way this will work is one person will use only one hand to tie their partner's tie. The first one done wins," Gail explained.

I wiggled my fingers, anxious to get started. I had tied my dad's tie for him thousands of times as I grew up so I could do this with my eyes closed.

"Since I imagine that most of these ladies have helped tie a tie before, we're going to switch it up and make it a little harder. These are some awesome prizes up for grabs, so we have to make you guys work for them. The first man who can successfully tie his partner's tie using only one hand will be our winner."

I looked at Jared and noticed a smirk flash across his face.

"Can we use other body parts?" Leroy from accounting asked, his brows pulled together in doubt as he studied the tie in his hand.

"You can use whatever body part you want to—as long as it's not your other hand or anything that will go against our handbook—let's keep it clean," she joked.

We all got into position, lining up in front of her with the women on one side and the men on the other. Gail counted to three and then instructed everyone to begin.

Jared kept his left hand tucked behind his back as he stepped closer and held the tie in his mouth as he used his right hand to brush my hair over my shoulder. I felt my heartbeat start to quicken from the warmth of his body as he gently placed the tie around my neck and pulled it to where he wanted it.

His brows were pinched together as he concentrated, and I found it hard to look away. I studied his features as he worked, noticing the light brown specks that complimented the green in his eyes.

"I'm going to lean in to try to tie this, but you have to stay still and don't squirm," he said, raising an eyebrow as if he didn't trust me.

I nodded and pulled my shoulders down to elongate my neck to give him more room to work. He leaned in and tilted his head to the side, his lips grazing my neck as his teeth bit onto the silk of the tie and pulled it. His breath was hot against my skin as his hand trailed across my collarbone, finding the other end of the fabric.

I felt paralyzed at that moment, afraid to move and lose his touch. My body reacted in ways that I didn't need my coworkers to see, but I couldn't stop it if I tried.

"Are you okay?" he whispered around the piece of fabric in his mouth.

"Yeah," I managed to breathe out, staying completely still.

He tilted his head to the side, and his fingers tickled my

skin as they brushed against it. A few seconds later, he was pulling hard on one end of the fabric before he dropped the other end from his mouth and stepped away.

"Done," he announced, watching me with the same lust in his eyes that I had in mine.

Gail walked over and looked at his work, nodding her head in approval.

"Congratulations," she said, patting him on the back. "You guys are our first winners! Go pick your gift from under the tree."

As everyone shuffled back to their seats and complained about how it wasn't fair that Jared was so good with his mouth, we made our way to the tree and studied the boxes. There were so many different shapes and sizes that I felt too overwhelmed to pick one. While Gail assured us that they were all amazing prizes, I kept envisioning something terrible like the people who get a Zonk on *Let's Make A Deal*.

The employees were wheeling in the serving trays for the buffet while we were still up there studying our options. Gail walked up and joined us, placing a hand on each of our backs.

"I know there are a lot of options, but if I can make a suggestion, I would go for those two." She nodded to two small envelopes on top of the pile of gifts. "They seem to *fit* the chemistry you guys have." She smiled and walked away, guiding the employees to form two lines at the buffet to get everyone served faster.

We grabbed the envelopes and headed back to the table. I

wanted to let everyone get through the line before going up there so we weren't just standing there, waiting.

"You open yours first," Jared said, nodding to the blank white envelope in my hand.

I quickly slid my finger under the flap, opening it. I reached in and pulled out two gift cards and a piece of paper. Clearing my throat, I read it out loud.

"Enjoy a weekend getaway at the luxurious Park Springs Hotel. Two nights stay included, along with dinner and two drinks at the world-famous Range steakhouse."

Jared's brows raised in surprise, knowing how expensive this gift was. I lowered the paper and gift cards to my lap and rested my hands while I waited for him to open his. A few seconds later, his eyes widened, and he gave a nod of approval before showing me the gift card that was in his.

"Relax and melt away the holiday stress with a ninety-minute couple's massage."

"Wow," I said, impressed by both gifts.

"Sounds like a nice way to spend the weekend," he replied, his eyes locked onto mine as they tried to read what I was thinking.

"Very romantic," I commented, feeling him out.

"Might be a great way to spend New Year's Eve," he added cautiously. "If you don't already have other plans."

"You know I don't like big crowds," I whispered.

"Then would you like to be my date to a couple's massage?"

"Only if you will join me for dinner and a two-night stay in a beautiful hotel."

"It's a date," he said with a grin that spread across his face.

My stomach somersaulted as I realized that we weren't pretending this time.

Eight
Jared

My fingers drummed on the steering wheel as I waited to take the turn to Everly's house. I hated that I was heading there to drop her off and found it strange that I wasn't ready to say goodbye to her yet. After the time we'd spent together last night, followed by the fun we had at brunch, I was living on a high that I didn't want to come down from.

"Thank you again for everything this weekend," she said lightly, turning to look at me. "I can't imagine having gone through with the entire thing all on my own."

"You would have been fine," I assured her with a smile as I turned into her driveway. I put the truck in park and shifted to look at her. "But it was my honor to accompany you."

"Well, as I said before, I'm happy to repay the favor. Just let me know if there's ever anything you need my help with."

I chuckled and grinned, knowing this was my chance to get her on board.

"There is something that I need help with," I said coyly, pushing my tongue into the side of my cheek to keep from laughing.

She narrowed her eyes suspiciously and studied me.

"Alright," she said slowly. "I'm listening."

I unbuckled my seatbelt and turned to look at her, making sure I had her full attention. It wasn't that it was something overly complicated that I needed her to focus on. I simply didn't want to miss her reaction when I told her.

"Every year, the community center I grew up with puts on this holiday play. The kids dress up and rehearse for weeks—it's a huge deal. Everyone has a fun time, and we invite some of Chicago's most elite to attend. It's our biggest fundraiser of the year, and that money is put right back into the programs for the kids. Aside from funding the programs, we use some of that money to help those who need it. Things like buying groceries for a family in need or getting new shoes before school for those who can't afford them. We help a lot of families in the community, and in return, they volunteer at the community center to keep it up and running."

"That sounds amazing," she replied softly. "What do you need from me?"

I cleared my throat, forcing the chuckle back down before it slipped out.

"Mrs. Bailey always plays Old Man Grumpus—she's the best, and since her personality is naturally sour, it kinda fits her. But this year, she slipped and broke her hip, so she can't do it."

"Okay," she said, her voice more guarded than a few minutes ago.

"So, if you're up for it, I need you to be our Old Man Grumpus." I put my hands in front of me as I begged and made sure to give her the smile that usually got me what I wanted.

She pulled her head back and covered her mouth as she laughed, a snort escaping in the process.

"You want *me* to play Old Man Grumpus?" she asked, snorting again.

I nodded, too fixated on the way her dimples in her cheeks deepened as her smile stretched tighter across her face.

"I mean, I know I'm not the cheeriest person," she joked.

I laughed and leaned back against the door.

"I know that it's not as glamorous as the Christmas party, but I'm in a bind, and the show is next weekend. If you'd be willing to help me with this, I'll owe you again." I could hear the desperation in my voice and hoped she didn't pick up on it. I wanted her to help me with this because it would mean that we could spend more time together, and I really wanted that. Plus, I did need someone to fill the spot. But I didn't want her to do it out of pity or obligation. I had enough of that growing up.

She sighed and looked dramatically out of the window as she tried to keep the grin off of her face. When she turned to look at me, her blue eyes sparkled, leaving me to feel hopeful.

"Fine," she breathed as if it was the most boring thing she had ever agreed to. "I'll be your Old Man Grumpus."

I felt a quick flutter rush through me at the word *your*. I didn't know if she meant to say it, but if she did, she didn't let on.

"You have no idea how much this means," I assured her. "The kids are going to be so happy that we don't have to cancel it."

She let her smile break through as her features softened.

"Wait a minute," she said, her brow starting to furrow. "Why didn't you just do it yourself?"

"Because I'm the director," I said proudly, puffing my chest out slightly. "And the costume we have is pretty hideous..."

<u>Nine</u>
Everly

"Old Man Grumpus?" Becca snorted as she fell into another fit of laughter. I glared at her sitting on my bed as I pulled up my leggings and tossed my jeans to the floor. "How does he know you so well in such a short period?"

Her cheeks were flushed from laughter, and she was getting way too big of a kick out of this.

"Haha," I said sarcastically, rolling my eyes at the joke.

After I agreed to help out on Sunday, Jared and I swung by the community center to pick up the costume that I would be wearing in front of hundreds of people. Since school was still in session for a few more days, he had decided to wait to start the nightly rehearsals until tonight. The only good part so far was that Mrs. Bailey hated trying to talk into the headset that they gave her, so she always insisted that someone else narrate for her, which meant that I didn't have any lines to memorize. I just had to show up to rehearsal and go where they told me to, which was good since we only had three nights for me to practice before the show on Saturday.

"I invited you over to be helpful," I reminded her with my *mom* look.

"Oh honey, I don't think there's *any* help at this point," she laughed, holding up the tattered green fabric that was thin enough you would be able to see skin through it.

"What am I going to do?" I groaned, plopping down on the bed. "I promised that I would help him, but I don't want to go out there and make a total ass of myself on stage in front of everyone."

"It won't be that bad," she tried to assure me. "Remember when you were the ugly duckling in the school play and cried for two weeks because you thought everyone was really calling you ugly?"

I laughed softly and plopped back on the bed, remembering the play and how embarrassed I had felt back then. Becca was one of the beautiful ducks, and I had been jealous from the start. I had come home and cried to my parents, telling them that I was chosen to be the ugly duck because I was the ugliest girl in the class. They held me as I cried and then sat me down in front of a mirror to repeat positive things about myself, as they said them.

"This is different," I countered. "We're not in second grade anymore."

"No," she agreed. "We're not. But you are still beautiful, and we're going to make this the sexiest, gorgeous-looking Old Man Grumpus that Chicago has ever seen!"

She reached down and grabbed my hands, pulling me up.

"Come on, we have work to do!"

I groaned, thinking about how nice it would be to just sit on the couch and watch tv instead of whatever crazy plan she had in mind. We had both worked a half-day, calling it a hump day miracle when we were able to leave early. She had promised to help me find something to fix the costume, while I had promised to pick up her favorite Chinese food. I had fulfilled my end, and now she was ready to fulfill hers.

Two hours later, we were rushing back into my house with arms full of shopping bags. I kicked the door closed to keep the snow from blowing in with the wind that was whipping past us. I set the bags down on the couch then pulled my gloves and beanie off.

"I think they got the weather wrong on the news," Becca commented, looking out the window to the street. "That's not a light snowstorm by any means."

"Yeah," I muttered, still shivering from the bitter cold. "They said that we wouldn't get the big storm until Christmas Eve, but it looks like it started a few days early."

"What time are you supposed to meet Jared at the community center?" she asked, checking her watch.

I pulled out my phone, checking the time and if there were any new text messages from him.

"In an hour."

"Well, let's get you changed and ready to go so you're not rushing in this weather."

I felt my stomach flip-flop with dread, wondering what he would think when he saw what we did with the costume. It was too late for him to change his mind now.

292

<u>Ten</u>
Jared

I was up front, getting the kids situated as they shuffled in from the cold. Thankfully, they all knew where to go and what to do since we had been doing this for a few weeks. The unfortunate part was that they were overly hyper and excited with today being their last day of school before winter break. It was Wednesday, meaning the weekend would be here soon, as would Christmas, if you were the kind of person who looked forward to that.

I greeted the parents that were able to make it and made note of who had come with someone else's family. It wasn't uncommon for one of the kids to show up with another family since everyone in this community was good about looking out for one another. If a parent had to work one night, they asked another parent to cover for them and would help out another time. It was a beautiful dynamic that benefited the group as a whole.

It was almost six o'clock, and I knew that Everly would be showing up any minute. Or at least, I hoped that she would. It wouldn't surprise me if she changed her mind and backed out on me the second she got home and took a look at the costume that I had given her. We had needed a new one for years, but since this play only happened once a year, we didn't bother throwing any of the money that we raised toward getting a new costume. We could be feeding families instead. Our donors that attended were more interested in watching the kids perform and didn't seem bothered by the outfit that was barely held together by threads at this point.

The door opened, and a gust of wind pushed in, that sent a stack of papers flying off of the desk in the corner of the room. I brought my arm up to cover my face while I tried to catch my breath. As I lowered my arm, I saw Everly standing there, desperately trying to pull the heavy door closed so it would latch shut.

"Here, let me help you," I offered, rushing over to grab the handle. I yanked hard against the wind before it slammed into place and locked.

Her hair was blown across her face as she tried to collect herself.

"Are you alright?" I asked, reaching my hand out to help her.

"I'm good, thank you," she said breathlessly. "That wind is something. I thought I was going to blow through the door," she laughed, brushing a strand of hair out of her face.

"Well, I'm glad that you made it here safely. Sorry for dragging you out in this bad weather."

"Eh, I didn't have anything else to do." She shrugged and set her purse down on the counter before bending over to pick up the papers that had flown off.

I was about to help her when she turned to grab one, her ass swinging in my direction. Lime green leggings were clinging to her toned legs and stretched tightly across her plump globes that begged to be touched. I swallowed hard, trying to force myself to think about something else. *Anything else.*

Quickly, I bent down and picked up the remaining papers before collecting the pile from her and set them back on the counter. She smiled nervously and unzipped her jacket before pulling it off and hanging it over her arm.

I realized that I was staring at her when she raised her brows and smiled, waiting for me to guide her on where to go and what to do.

"Sorry," I said, clearing my throat. "Let me show you where you can put your stuff, and then we'll get started."

She followed me to the back and picked one of the empty lockers to leave her coat and purse. I was talking with Shirley, the director of the community center, while she got situated and hadn't heard her come up behind me. Shirley's eyes lit up as she lifted her hands to her mouth, completely ignoring whatever it was we were talking about as she looked behind me.

I turned around and felt my jaw drop as I looked at Everly. Her brown hair was pulled up and tucked into the mask she was wearing on top of her head so we could still see her face. Her body was covered head to toe in the same lime green color of her leggings, only it wasn't just leggings. It was some sort of full-body latex-looking outfit that had me thinking inappropriate thoughts about what I wanted to do to her. I had to clear my head, or it wasn't going to be my *heart* that was going to grow a few sizes.

"I still need to put this on," she said shyly, holding up the frayed fabric of the costume I had given her. "But I need help, so I don't tear it."

"Oh, honey," Shirley said quickly. "I don't think you need that at all. You look simply stunning! With the mask on and the green covering your whole body, I can't see any reason that you need to wear that old, hairy thing."

I laughed and nodded my head in agreement.

Everly's eyes shot open in surprise as she ran a hand down the smooth fabric.

"Oh, I wasn't trying to get out of wearing the other one," she admitted sheepishly. "It was just a little see-through, and I didn't want to risk lights shining in odd places and giving the donors a show they didn't pay for."

"Yeah, unfortunately, that one is pretty much on its last leg," I said with a heavy sigh. "But like Shirley said, if you're comfortable in that, I think it's perfect. The only other outfit change that you'll have is when we add the Santa suit toward the end."

She looked down self consciously and pulled her bottom lip in between her teeth before looking back up at me.

"Are you sure that it's okay? It's awfully tight."

"It's no different than what we see on tv. Besides, he's naked all the time, it's just that no one pays attention to it because he's so hairy."

"That's true," she laughed. "I just don't want to offend anyone, especially the parents or any of the kids," she whispered as a few came rushing over to us.

"Are you the new Old Man Grumpus?" Susy asked, looking up at Everly.

"I am," she replied nervously, looking from Susy back up

to me.

"Wow!" Everett said, his eyes wide with surprise. "You look just like the one on tv!"

"Thank you," she giggled, her shoulders relaxing some. "I'm excited to do this play with you guys."

"I'm playing Cindy," Susy said proudly as a woman walked up behind her and placed a hand on her shoulder. I heard Everly's gasp before I saw what was happening.

"Hello, Everly," a sharp tone bit out.

I looked up and found the woman from the restaurant staring at us, eyes narrowed with her hand gripping Susy's shoulder possessively.

"This is my aunt, Staci," Susy explained, looking behind her. "My mom had to work, so she brought me, so I didn't have to ride the bus by myself."

"They know who I am," Staci said coldly.

"How do you all know each other?" Shirly asked, looking between us. I glanced at Everly, her face a shade paler than a few minutes ago.

I was about to speak but had no idea what to say; I felt completely blindsided by seeing her there. What were the chances that she would show up now? In all of the weeks that Susy's mom had to miss rehearsal before, this was the first that Staci had been sent to take care of her.

"Well, Everly used to date my boyfriend, Tom." Staci pulled her shoulders back then turned to scowl at me. "And it seems she's moved on to *him*."

I narrowed my eyes at her, wondering what Tom saw in such a bitch of a woman. But then again, he didn't seem that smart to begin with if he left someone like Everly for someone like Staci.

"Oh," Shirley said, taken aback by the news. "I didn't know you were seeing anyone!"

Her face lit up, probably relieved to know that I wasn't some poor, pathetic man who couldn't find a woman to date me. She had been running the community center since I was a little boy and started showing up on my own when my mom was working three jobs to support us. In all of the years that she'd known me, I had never brought a woman around before.

"It's a new relationship," I muttered quietly, still glaring at Staci.

"I thought you said you guys have been together six months?" Staci questioned, releasing her grip on Susy to fold her arms across her chest.

I pinned her with a look and refused to acknowledge it.

"Well, we should get started before the weather gets too bad," I said dismissively, placing a hand on Everly's lower back to guide her out to the stage where everyone else was already waiting.

We all walked in silence as Staci's heels clicked against the floor before she stormed off to take a seat with the other parents. I tried to shift my mindset to focus on the play and get Everly up to speed. The kids were amazing with helping me, and in no time, we were doing a complete run-through of the play. Everly laughed and jumped right in, surprising me with how easily she adjusted to everything. I was worried that she would be too nervous—or worse, upset with seeing Staci, but she didn't seem bothered at all.

After we ran through everything a second time, I decided to wrap everything up for the night before the weather got too bad for everyone's drive home. The kids rushed off to put their costumes away and said goodbye to Everly on their way out. I was used to being the last one to leave and lock up for the night.

Everly was in the back, pulling her coat and purse out of the locker, when I found her.

"Thanks for being such a good sport about everything," I said as I pulled my coat on.

"It was so much fun," she smiled. "The kids are truly amazing."

"They seem to have taken a quick liking to you as well."

She blushed and turned to the side as she tucked the mask into the cubby with the old costume.

"I like the new costume, by the way," I added, letting my eyes roam over her body now that no one else was around.

"Thank you," she said quietly, tucking a strand of hair behind her ear as she turned to face me.

I stepped closer, my fingers itching to touch her.

"I was worried that it was too tight," she whispered as I stood in front of her. I could feel her breath hot against my neck as she spoke.

"I wouldn't mind if it were a little bit tighter," I admitted, swallowing as my throat strained against the words that I shouldn't be saying.

"If it were any tighter, I would practically be naked."

Her words sparked a fire inside that I couldn't put out if I tried. A low growl escaped my lips before they crashed down on hers.

Eleven

Everly

I moaned as he kissed me, his hands eagerly moving down until his fingers were digging into my ass to lift me. My legs spread to welcome him as he held me against the lockers, our mouths working against each other in a frenzy. His hands grazed my body, touching every inch as if he couldn't get enough.

"Oh, god," I moaned, ready to rip off these leggings so I could feel him inside of me. Everything felt on fire as he touched me, and I was eager for more.

My legs wrapped tightly around his waist as he trailed kisses down my neck. I could feel the heat between my legs as his hand gently dipped down to rub me through the thick fabric.

"I need more," I panted in his ear. "Please, Jared. I want you so bad."

I heard another growl from him as he lowered me to my feet. His lips landed on mine again as he worked to get his coat off. I was thankful that I hadn't put mine on yet since it felt like I already had too many layers of clothing on. We continued kissing as we walked aimlessly, our hands roaming over each other's bodies as he stripped off pieces of clothing.

We stopped for a brief second as he lifted my shirt and pulled it up and over my head, leaving me in a white lace bra. The cold air made my skin prickle, a welcomed sensation against the heat that was coursing through it.

We were back to kissing when I felt something behind my foot, causing me to trip. Jared's hands caught me as he steered me to the side, out of the way of the light that was bolted to the floor of the stage. There was no one else in the building except for us, but the thought of having the room filled with people in the seats, watching while we had sex on the stage, sent a rush of electricity through me.

I was full on panting, clawing at his ripped muscles as if my life depended on it. I hadn't been this turned on ever. There was something about him that seemed to awaken this sexual beast that somehow had been lurking inside of me all of these years.

Skillfully, he helped me to the floor before situating himself on top of me. He caressed my cheek with his thumb as he waited for me to open my eyes and look at him.

"You're so beautiful, Everly."

"Thank you," I moaned as I reached my hand down and ran it along the length of his erection that was ready to burst against the tight fabric of his jeans.

He chuckled and nipped my ear while allowing me to rub him while my hips started grinding beneath him.

"Are you sure you want to do this?" he asked, his voice strained as my fingers desperately tried to work his zipper down.

"Yes," I growled. "I can't wait any longer. I want this, and I want it now."

He moaned as I slipped my hand inside and rubbed him through his briefs. Quickly, he pulled away and stripped himself to nothing while grabbing a condom out of his pocket. He laid it to the side while he came back and kneeled in front of me.

I lifted my hips, desperate to get my leggings off. The fabric was thicker than I remembered and was frustratingly hard to get off. My body was on the edge of coming undone, and I needed this release more than I needed my next breath.

"Just tear them," I moaned loudly.

He looked down at me and arched a brow before he hooked his fingers in the top and gently tugged them down until they were at my knees. I had enough room to spread my legs wide enough for him that I didn't care at that point. He quickly rolled the condom on before I grabbed him and eased him inside of me as I pushed my panties to the side.

I gasped as his dick slipped in, gliding effortlessly thanks to how wet I was. I arched my back and swiveled my hips, needing to feel him. He started thrusting, building up the pace as he reached up and pulled the cups of my bra down, exposing my pebbled nipples. I scratched my nails down his back and lifted my hips to meet each thrust as he lowered his head and pulled a nipple into his mouth.

He sucked hard, the sensation sending me nearly over the edge as he pounded harder inside of me. As he continued to take turns on each nipple, he dipped a finger in between us and started rubbing my clit.

I tilted my head back and moaned. Everything felt amazing as he worked every sensitive part of my body. I let my head fall to the side and opened my eyes, visioning the onlookers sitting in the chairs as they watched us. I was chewing my lip as the thoughts consumed and hadn't noticed that he was staring at me.

"Imagining us in front of a crowd?" he asked, his voice low and gruff.

I nodded, too aroused to deny it.

"Do you like being watched?"

"I don't know," I whispered, focusing on a seat in the front row. "I think so."

He turned his head where I was looking and kept fucking me harder.

"Picture a man sitting right there," he nodded. "Right in the front row. Watching as I fuck you. He's got his hard cock in his hand, stroking it as he watches your pussy coat my dick with how wet you are."

"Ahh," I cried out, feeling the tingle of an approaching orgasm.

"Or maybe I spread you out in front of your audience and tie you to a bed so you can't move. They'll all get to see you naked and waiting to be fucked. I'll show them how good your pussy tastes as I eat it. Or maybe I'll have you finger yourself so they can see what you like or how tight that little cunt is."

I pictured everything he said as I closed my eyes and felt my body tremble as the orgasm shot through me. He started slamming into me harder, each thrust sending him that much closer to the edge before he came hard and loud in my ear.

We were both sweaty and spent as he rolled off of me and laid on the cold floor next to me.

"That was fucking amazing," he said with a heavy breath.

"You're telling me," I agreed, glancing down to see my tights still stuck around my knees, leaving me fully exposed. I tried to close my legs, but my body was so deliciously sore that I couldn't move if I wanted to. I made an effort to pull my bra back up, but that was it.

"We should get going before that storm gets worse and we get stuck here." He groaned as he pushed himself up off of the floor and extended his hand to me before noticing my tights. "Ooops," he laughed, bending down to help pull them back up my legs.

I lifted my butt as he pulled the thick fabric over it, his eyes flashing with something as his hand grazed my bare skin.

"There you go," he said quietly, standing back and extending his hand to me.

I took it and pulled myself up, trying to stifle the groan that threatened to come out. Sex on the floor used to be a lot easier when I was younger.

"Thank you," I said, looking around to find my shirt.

Jared grabbed our clothes from the floor and handed it to me before he dressed quickly. I was disappointed when his beautiful body was covered again, but having felt it a few minutes ago was a nice memory to hold onto instead.

Once we gathered the rest of our stuff and got our coats on, we headed outside. I shivered and rubbed my hands together as I waited for him to lock the door. The snow had accumulated quickly while we were inside, blanketing my car in an ice cave that covered the tires.

The locks clicked in place before Jared turned around and frowned, taking in my predicament.

"Where the hell did all of this snow come from?" he grumbled, adjusting his gloves.

"I think they misjudged the storm that was coming for Christmas. It seems it decided to show up a few days early."

"Yeah, like a whole week early," he groaned, letting out a heavy breath.

"I can give you a ride home if you'd like," he offered, shaking his head at the state of my car.

"It's okay, I can try to dig it out." I shivered at the thought of standing here for an hour, trying to free my car, when I knew that I didn't have anything that would be useful. Maybe if I happened to have a *shovel* in my trunk, that would be helpful, but since I wasn't planning to bury any bodies any time soon, it wasn't something that I kept handy.

"I don't want to sound like a dick, especially a week before Christmas," he chuckled. "But you're not going to dig that out."

I gently elbowed him, pretending to be offended even though I knew that it was true.

"Fine," I sighed. "If you can give me a ride, that would be great."

I meant for it to come out sarcastically, but my voice betrayed me when it hitched on the word *ride*. While I hoped that he hadn't heard it, the mischievous smirk curling up the corners of his lips confirmed that he had.

"I would love to give you a ride." He licked his lips, pulling the bottom one in between his teeth before popping it free. "Come on, my truck is over here."

He led the way to the only other vehicle in the parking lot and pressed the button to unlock the doors. I stared in surprise for a few minutes, taking in the massive size of the tires on his truck. It wasn't huge like one of those monster trucks that you see on tv that crush other cars, but they were still a lot bigger and thicker than most trucks. Why hadn't I noticed how big and massive it was when he picked me up for the party? Maybe it was because I was so consumed with anxiety that I wouldn't have noticed if he showed up in a school bus that night.

"That's your truck?" I said, looking over at him to find a proud look on his face.

"It sure is."

"It's huge. I don't remember it being this big," I laughed nervously, feeling embarrassed that I hadn't paid attention to it before now.

His grin pulled tighter across his face as he rocked back on his heels.

I shook my head.

"I meant the truck."

"I'm sure you did," he chuckled, walking around to the passenger side to let me in.

I felt my skin flush with heat when he touched me and wondered if I would ever stop feeling this way with his touch. I tried to think back to when I was dating Tom and wondered if I had ever felt that electricity with him when we first started dating. If I did, it must have fizzled out quickly because it would have been nothing compared to this.

I sat patiently while Jared scraped the thick layer of ice off of his windshield. The heater was on, warming me to where I was nice and comfy. A few minutes later, he jumped in and closed the door, forcing a clump of snow to fall from the roof down the windshield.

"Alright, let's get out of here," he said as he put the truck in reverse and headed to my house.

I looked out the window on the drive home, taking in the beauty of the snow around us. It was so calm and peaceful outside with everyone off of the streets and cuddled up at home. When we got closer to my street, I noticed that the lights were off in almost every house we passed. My stomach knotted when I saw the giant limb that had broken, taking down the power line.

"Great," I muttered, leaning back in my seat.

Jared leaned forward to get a better look.

"That doesn't look good," he observed.

"They were supposed to send someone out to cut the tree back so it wouldn't be so close to the power line, but no one has been out yet."

"You're welcome to come stay with me," he offered, pulling into my driveway and putting the truck in park.

"Oh no," I rushed out. "I don't want to inconvenience you."

"You're not. I insist."

I felt the heat rush through me at the thought of being alone with him another night. This time we wouldn't have to worry about the awkwardness of not having sex, given what happened earlier. But still, it felt weird to take him up so easily on his offer.

"You've done a lot for me already, thank you. I'll be fine." I smiled and tried to force it to reach my eyes.

"If you don't have power, then you don't have heat. I'm not about to leave you in a cold house with no power or heat during the worst storm we've had in God knows how long."

I laughed nervously, trying to put my bravest face on.

"I promise, I'll be okay. I have plenty of warm blankets to cuddle up with and wine to keep me toasty on the inside. Besides, I'll be heading to bed soon anyway, so I won't even need the power."

He ran a hand over his face in frustration before looking at me again.

"Just go get what you need for tonight and tomorrow, and let's get going," he said, raising a brow at me to challenge him. "I don't feel like staying in a cold house with no power, and I'm not about to leave you in one either. So, if you're not willing to come with me to my house, then I have no choice but to stay at yours. Make a good choice, Everly," he teased with a wink.

"Fine," I grumbled and pulled the handle to the door. I rushed inside, wondering if sexy lingerie counted as something that I would *need* tonight. I sure hoped so.

Twelve
Jared

I tossed another log on the fire and watched with satisfaction, the embers floating in the air as it started to burn. Everly was in the bathroom getting changed, while I worked on getting the house warm. Thankfully, I still had power when we got here, and the heater had kept it nice and warm. I didn't really *need* to start a fire, but having her here made me want to.

Just like, I didn't *need* to open a bottle of wine but wanted to share it with her when she said she was going to drink a glass at home. Everything was screaming romance, but for once, it didn't freak me out. Maybe, it was because Everly didn't freak me out.

A few minutes later, I heard the door open and turned to find her wearing a baggy hoodie and another pair of tights, these ones black instead of lime green. Her hair was piled loosely on top of her head, and she looked relaxed and comfortable. It had me itching to get out of my clothes and into sweats.

"I poured you a glass of wine," I said, nodding to the coffee table where I had also set out a plate of cheese and crackers in case she was hungry.

"Thank you," she replied sweetly, smiling as she sat down on the couch and picked up the glass. She brought it to her lips and took a sip, her lips parting slightly to let the liquid in.

I swallowed hard, my dick starting to strain against my jeans.

"I'm going to go get changed, but help yourself to anything you need. I'll be back in a few minutes."

She nodded and reached forward, grabbing a cracker from the plate.

I went to my room and quickly changed, wondering if she had eaten dinner before she went to the community center. I knew I hadn't had time to and was planning to grab something on my way home. I could order a pizza, but the likelihood of anyone delivering in this weather was slim.

I joined her in the living room, relieved to see that she was enjoying the snack I had left out.

"I didn't get a chance to eat before rehearsal, so I was going to cook something real quick. Are you hungry?" I asked, hoping she would say yes so I could cook for her.

She shook her head no and covered her mouth with her hand while she finished chewing her cracker.

"I was planning to eat when I got home," she said after she swallowed her bite.

"Well, how about I make us some dinner then?"

"I can come help you cook," she offered, setting her glass down on the coffee table.

"I've got it but thank you," I said, waving my hand for her to stay sitting on the couch. "I'll bring you some more wine, though, if you'd like?"

"Sure, thank you."

I smiled and grabbed the bottle from the kitchen, refilling her glass before I got started cooking. I loved the layout of my house because it allowed me to be in the kitchen but see everything happening in the living room with its open concept. There was a breakfast bar that separated the two rooms and a small dining table off to the side of the kitchen that I never used. Usually, it was just me, and I always ate by myself on the couch.

Since I hadn't planned on having company tonight, I had no idea what to make. Hell, I couldn't even remember what I had in the fridge because my mind was so distracted from having her here. Excitement coursed through me, and I felt like a teenager again with his first crush. I wanted to do anything and everything to impress her.

Every few minutes, I found myself looking into the living room to find her on the couch, drinking her wine and eating crackers while laughing at the funny videos playing on the tv. It warmed my heart to see her so happy and to know that she felt comfortable here with me.

I cracked a few eggs into the skillet, deciding that omelets would be the quickest and easiest meal to prepare this late at night. I had already cut up some veggies and ham when she turned to look at me, smiling happily.

"That smells delicious, what are you making?"

"Omelets," I replied with a grin. "But, I should have asked if that sounded good before I started them." I laughed nervously, feeling stupid for not asking her before I just started cooking.

"I *love* eggs, and omelets happen to be my favorite."

"Is there anything that you don't like in them?"

"Nope," she shook her head. "I'm not a picky eater. I'll pretty much eat anything."

I nodded and turned my attention back to the stove, flipping the egg before I accidentally burned it. Once the food was ready, I served it and went to the living room, handing her a plate before joining her on the couch.

"My mouth is watering just looking at this," she commented, rubbing her lips together.

I looked away, trying to keep the dirty thoughts out of my head as I focused on the food on my plate. I cut into the omelet and took a bite, hoping it would silence the rumbling in my stomach before she could hear it.

She closed her eyes and let out a soft moan as she chewed. I felt my dick hardening as the sound floated around me and wished that I was the one eliciting that noise from her.

"This is delicious," she said, opening her eyes to find me straining to keep mine on the tv.

"Thank you," I replied, giving her a quick smile before turning away. I didn't need her to see the flush in my skin as my arousal pushed harder against my briefs.

Thankfully, we ate in silence after that, both of us devouring our food as if we hadn't eaten in days. I had no idea how hungry she was, so I doubled everything and made both of us giant omelets that took up the majority of the plate.

We both finished at the same time, leaning forward to set

our empty plates on the coffee table. She leaned back and rested a hand on her stomach, looking completely satisfied.

"Did you get enough?" I asked, waiting to get comfortable until I knew that she didn't need more food.

"I couldn't possibly fit another bite in me," she laughed. "That was wonderful, and I am beyond full."

"Good, I'm glad."

She tilted her head to the side and studied me for a moment.

"What?" I asked softly, suddenly feeling self-conscious. "Do I have egg on my face?"

"No," she giggled. "I just can't figure out why you're still single."

I smiled and let out a laugh, relieved.

"Wait--," she paused, leaning forward, her face suddenly serious. "You *are* single, aren't you? Why didn't I ask that before?"

I laughed harder, feeling uncomfortable with my overly full stomach.

"No, I'm actually seeing someone," I said coyly, enjoying the look of panic on her face.

Her jaw dropped as her eyes bulged out.

"What?! Why didn't you tell me?"

I tried to stop myself but couldn't.

"I thought you knew." I shrugged dismissively and pretended to watch the tv.

She threw her hands up in the air and looked around wildly as if she expected some mysterious woman to appear out of thin air.

"How would I know?!"

Her voice raised another octave, and I felt bad for letting her panic.

"Well, you were there when I agreed to date you. I thought we were in on this together," I joked, turning to give her my full attention.

"You brat!" she scolded, reaching over to punch me playfully. I tried to lean forward and move out of the way, but she was too quick for me.

"You're cute when you're mad," I chuckled, watching the corners of her mouth turn up.

She rolled her eyes and folded her arms over her chest, pretending to be mad still.

"Then again, now I see why you're still single," she joked, raising a brow while pursing her lips.

"Just haven't found the right girl," I admitted, shifting on the couch.

"How is that possible?" she asked, dropping the act of being mad.

I shrugged again. There were a lot of women who I had dated over the years, but I just hadn't found the one that felt different. Something was always missing, but I couldn't put my finger on it.

"I don't know." I pulled my mouth into a sad smile.

"Maybe you're just not looking in the right places," she said, turning to look at me.

"Or maybe the right girl just hasn't found *me*," I suggested.

"Trust me, if she knew you existed, she would be destroying everything in her path to get to you."

I let my head fall back as I laughed.

"I'm serious," she said, poking me in the arm with her finger. "I have never met a man like you."

"Is that a good thing?" I joked.

"Yes, it's a very good thing. You're caring and sensitive but not in a wimpy kind of way. You carry yourself with confidence without being cocky or arrogant. You're genuine and don't pretend to be something that you're not just to impress others around you."

I listened as she spoke but couldn't see the same things she saw.

"You haven't known me long enough to know those things to be true," I admitted, feeling the sting of my words.

"Okay, so maybe I haven't known you that long," she agreed, "but I know what I've seen."

"And what's that?"

"A man who is kindhearted and caring. One who makes a woman wait to have sex to make sure that she's not rushing into something she might later regret."

I felt the blood pulse through me, my anger starting to build up as memories of my mother floated to the surface.

"That doesn't make me anything special, Everly. Every woman should be respected."

"Yeah, but so many guys would have looked the other way and gone for it. They don't care whether or not the woman regrets it later, as long as she says yes in the moment. For them, yes is a green light."

"It shouldn't be," I argued, trying to keep the anger out of my voice. "If you can tell that someone isn't fully certain of their decision, then you should always take that as a no."

I looked away at the tv.

"You're really passionate about this, aren't you?" she asked curiously.

I pulled my lips into a thin line and nodded, still refusing to look at her.

"Can I ask what happened?" Her voice was soft, her words sincere. She wasn't prying because she had heard the rumors that used to float around me when I was a kid.

I let out the ragged breath that I had been holding and turned to look at her. I hated talking about my childhood because people always did one of two things—1. Judge my mom for getting herself into a bad situation or 2. Pity me for having a mom who had to make those kinds of decisions.

"My mom was raped when she was a teenager. No one believed her and called her terrible names. She ended up pregnant with me, and her parents kicked her out of the house and disowned her. She didn't have any family or friends to turn to, so she decided to have me and do the best that she could to raise me on her own."

I watched the sadness flash across Everly's face as she listened.

"She worked three jobs to take care of me and raised me the best she could before she got sick. I spent a lot of time at the community center, and they quickly turned into the only family that we had. My mom knew that she could leave me there for a few hours while she worked and that I wouldn't get into trouble. They kept an eye on me, and she helped out whenever she could."

"That's why you help out and give back to them," she replied as if it all made sense.

I nodded.

"My mom passed when I was sixteen. I had nowhere to go and had no idea what to do. Shirley gave me a job and let me stay with her until I got things figured out. She's been like a second mother to me ever since."

"I'm so sorry," she said, reaching over to place a hand on my arm. "I can't imagine how incredible of a woman your mom was. So strong and brave."

"She was," I agreed, feeling the weight of how much I missed her. "She was given a bad hand in life but did the best that she could with it. There were times that we didn't have more than a box of cereal to eat. No milk. Just cereal. She hated it and was always so embarrassed that she couldn't give me more."

I paused for a moment and let a memory replay in my head.

"I remember when I was ten, I didn't know that my mom had just been laid off from one of her jobs, and I had spent the entire afternoon threading Cheerios onto a roll of yarn that I had found in the closet. I strung it all over the apartment and was so proud that I had decorated for Christmas. We didn't have money for gifts, let alone a tree. But we had Cheerios strung all over the living room, and to me, it looked like Christmas.

I was so proud that I waited at the door, and when she came home, I made her close her eyes before I let her in the door. I set her purse down and turned her, so she had the perfect angle to see what I had done. When I told her to look, she was definitely surprised. Then she started crying, and I couldn't figure out what I had done wrong. She explained that she had lost her job and that she wouldn't be able to buy groceries that week."

Everly gasped quietly and covered her mouth with her hand as her eyes filled with tears.

"I thought I had done a nice thing when really I had just strung up our meals as a decoration for the next few weeks." I laughed, reaching up to wipe away the wetness that lined the corner of my eye. "But she didn't let it bother her. She shook her head and wiped away the tears. With her shoulders pulled back, she walked around the room, touching each strand and admiring it as she told me how much she loved them."

"That's so sweet," Everly said, her voice raspy with sadness.

"It made dinner easy that week. I just picked a strand for each of us, and we sat on the couch and told stories as we ate our Cheerios."

She smiled, and I felt relieved that, for once, I didn't feel the shame that I had felt for so long every time I told this story.

"I'm really sorry that you had a hard childhood," Everly said quietly. "But it made you into an incredible man. Your mom would be so proud of you."

"I wish she was still here. I miss her every single day."

She wiped a tear away and tried to blink away the rest.

"That's why I *always* make sure a woman knows what she wants. That she has control over the situation and has a say in what happens. Because my mom had that ripped away from her, and no woman should ever be forced to make the decisions she had to make."

Everly nodded and took the tissue that I handed to her. She wiped her eyes and blew her nose before turning to look at me.

"Just so you know," she said sternly. "I knew what I wanted earlier, and I don't have a single regret about it. I would do it again in a heartbeat."

I smiled as I reached over and grabbed her, pulling her in to kiss her. We might have been pretending for everyone else, but damn if this didn't feel real when we were by ourselves.

Thirteen
Everly

By Friday, I was a walking, ticking time bomb of nerves about to explode. The show was in one day, and I was terrified that I would mess up and ruin it for everyone. Of course, it didn't help that Staci made a point of showing up to every rehearsal after finding out that I was in the show. I was surprised that she hadn't dragged Tom along with her to make fun of me.

I was shutting off my computer, ready to leave for the day, when Gail walked over to my desk.

"Hey, Everly. Do you have a few minutes?"

I smiled and pushed my keyboard back, turning to give her my full attention. She looked around at the other cubicles, making sure no one else was around before speaking.

"What's up?" I asked, feeling the anxiety I felt whenever I had an unexpected visit with human resources.

"I wanted to talk to you about the senior advisor position that just opened."

She gave me a pointed look, and I knew where she was going.

I pulled in a deep breath and let it out slowly.

"I think you should apply for it," she said softly.

I shifted uncomfortably in my seat and looked past her to Tom's office.

"I don't know if it's the best idea," I replied sheepishly, hating that I felt so insecure.

"You've worked your butt off and deserve the promotion, Everly. If anyone should be moved up to a senior advisor, it's you."

"But what about Tom?"

"What about him?"

It was my turn to give her a pointed look as I crossed my arms over my chest.

"You know that he's not going to be happy about it. And then I'll be working alongside him as a senior advisor, which means we'll be competing against each other."

"Then maybe he needs to focus on doing his job and not worry so much about you doing yours."

I let my head fall back and laughed, knowing that Tom would never stop worrying about what I was doing. It was this obsession that he had from the moment we first started dating. That was before he insisted that I be moved to his team. At the time, he hadn't told Gail that we were dating because he didn't want her to deny the transfer. The first few years worked well, and everyone looked the other way anytime anyone suggested that I would be given special treatment working for my boss. Instead, he made sure that I was denied every opportunity I applied for and kept me right where he wanted me.

"All you need to do is apply for the job and knock their socks off in the interview. I'll deal with Tom," she said, tapping her knuckles against the top of my desk before smiling and turning to leave. "I'll let them know there's another application coming in before they start doing interviews next week."

I returned her smile and leaned back in my chair, wondering what it would be like to finally have the job I had been dreaming about for years. I loved working here and had built so many relationships with my clients that I didn't dare leave after Tom and I broke up. If I got the senior advisor position, I would be able to keep my current clients as well as take on some of the larger clients with more assets.

It was almost 5:15, and I still had thirty minutes before I had to get to the community center for rehearsal. I didn't have time to worry about applying if I wanted to get there on time since the roads were still snow-packed and icy. I grabbed my bag from under my desk and headed outside, hoping that tonight would help calm my anxiety about tomorrow.

When I got there, the backstage area was already swarming with kids in their costumes. I got dressed quickly and pulled my mask on, feeling the comfort of being able to hide my face tomorrow night in front of the hundreds of people who were showing up.

"Hey," Jared said, coming up behind me and sliding his hand across my lower back.

I felt the electricity of it sizzle across my skin and smiled.

"Hi," I replied softly as I turned to face him.

"We'll get started in a few minutes. We're just waiting on Susy."

I nodded, not bothering to mention the likelihood that we were probably really waiting on Staci since she insisted on coming every night. Instead, I talked with the kids, listening to their excitement about Christmas, which was only four days away. I thought about the holiday and how I wanted to spend it with Jared, even though it felt a little weird since we weren't really dating.

When we were here for the rehearsals, we had to keep pretending, thanks to Staci. But I found that even when it was just us by ourselves, it felt real, and I worried that maybe I was the only one who was feeling it.

Finally, Susy showed up, and we were able to get started. I kept myself distracted from thoughts of Jared by focusing on the play. We went through it from start to finish three times before he called it a night. There was one final rehearsal tomorrow before the show, which made me feel a little relieved.

"Are you ready to go?" Jared asked, coming up behind me.

I pulled on my coat and tucked the mask inside the locker for tomorrow, along with the costume. The last thing that I needed was to forget part of it and scramble, trying to remember where I left it at home.

"Yeah," I said, looking past him as Staci headed our way, with Tom right behind her.

Before we could turn to leave, they were in front of us, Tom wearing the same scowl he had when he saw Jared at the

Christmas party.

"Um, who do we speak to about getting tickets for the show tomorrow?" Staci asked Jared, tapping her pointy-toed heel on the floor as she folded her arms and waited.

"That would be Shirley, but she's already gone for the night," he answered. "And last I checked, the show was already close to selling out. I don't know if there are any tickets left."

"Well, we *need* tickets," Staci argued. "Tom wants to invite the rest of the department to watch Everly perform."

I groaned quietly and rolled my eyes. Jared gave me a quick look out of the corner of his eye before tilting his head and raising an eyebrow at Tom.

"Unfortunately, the show sells out fast, and once the tickets are gone, there's nothing we can do."

"Or nothing you *want* to do," she sneered.

"It's not a matter of whether I want to or not. The Fire Marshall decides how many people are allowed in, hence why we use tickets to keep track of attendees," Jared explained with a sharp tone. "I suggest buying tickets in advance next time."

He put his hand on my lower back and guided me to the front, ending the conversation.

Everyone else had already left, making it even more uncomfortable to have Staci and Tom still here. I stepped to the side so Jared could open the door when I felt someone grab my arm.

I turned and looked, finding Tom holding onto it with anger flashing in his eyes as he looked from me to Jared.

"Ow," I winced, feeling the sting as his fingers dug into my skin. I pulled away, jerking my arm hard enough to get Jared's attention without meaning to.

He frowned and immediately stepped beside me, placing a protective arm around my waist as he pulled me into him.

"We need to talk, Everly," Tom snapped, his jaw clenched.

"About what?" I asked impatiently.

"It's private." His teeth were gritted so tightly that I don't know how he got the words out.

"I'm not going anywhere private with you. Whatever you have to say to me, can be said in front of him."

"You've lost your damn mind," he sneered, shaking his head in disgust. "You don't even know this guy, and you're acting like you're in love with him. You need to wake up, Everly. He's just after one thing, and once he gets it, he'll be gone. Just wait and see."

I rubbed my temples and closed my eyes. He was the headache I hadn't been able to get rid of for the past six months since we broke up.

"Like I said, what I do is none of your business," I snapped. "Now, if you don't mind, it's time to go."

"Oh, I do mind," he snorted. "I'm not leaving until I've said what I need to say."

"I think you've said enough," Jared said, stepping in. His fingers slid further around my waist, resting flatly on my stomach for Tom to see.

"Gail told me that she was going to talk to you about

applying for the senior advisor position," Tom said, ignoring Jared and me. "I told her that I thought it was a huge mistake and that if she really cared about your well-being, she wouldn't bother."

I felt my shoulders tense and sag, feeling the weight of the control he liked to keep over me. But suddenly, Jared pulled me tighter to him and gave me a gentle squeeze. I pulled my shoulders back and looked Tom square in the eye.

"I've already applied," I lied.

Not that he needed to know that it was a lie. All he needed to know was that he couldn't control me anymore. I would make sure of it. And if I didn't get this position, I would talk to Gail and see what my options were for transferring to another department. I knew that I would have to leave my clients behind if I moved, but at this point, I knew that I needed to get away from Tom.

"You what?" he scoffed, eyes bulging.

"You heard me."

My body was trembling, but I didn't break eye contact with him. For once in my life, I felt strong enough to stand up to him, and I had Jared to thank for that.

"Well, you just screwed up your future with the company," he bit out. He stepped forward, swinging the door open without saying anything more or checking to see if Staci was behind him. She followed him out and let the door slam shut behind them.

Once it was just the two of us, I closed my eyes and took a deep breath.

"I'm so sorry about that," I apologized, looking up at Jared, who still had his hands wrapped around my waist. I shifted so we were standing face to face so I could see him better.

"You have nothing to be sorry about. He's a dick, and I'm proud of you for standing up to him."

"Thank you."

"Did you really apply for the other job?"

"No," I laughed, shaking my head. "I was on the fence about whether or not I should. But I guess that decision is final now."

"Is it not a job that you want?" he asked.

"Oh no, it's my dream job. It's a promotion that I've wanted for a few years."

"So why haven't you gone for it before?"

"Because Tom has always stood in the way. When we were together, he would tell me how I wasn't ready for it yet or that I needed to have more clients or a longer history with them. It made sense at the time, so I didn't question it. I mean, why would my own boyfriend stand in the way of something that I wanted? It wasn't until we broke up that I realized that he was holding me back because he didn't want to work against me."

"Against you?"

"He's a senior advisor. If I became one too, we would be competing for the same clients. It's a very competitive job, and the senior advisors are given quarterly bonuses based on performance. Tom beats everyone each quarter, and I think he was worried that I would threaten that. A lot of the big clients that he has are because of me. I got those leads and helped him work them."

"Wow," he sighed, shaking his head in disbelief. "I couldn't imagine not wanting the world for you."

I felt my heart skip a beat and wondered if he was starting to feel what I was.

"Thank you," I said warmly.

He smiled and hugged me tightly against his chest, planting a tender kiss on my forehead.

"Should we get going?" he asked.

"Yeah, it's supposed to snow again tonight, and I want to get home before it gets too bad."

"Okay," he said, sounding disappointed.

I tilted my head to the side and pulled my brows together.

"Everything okay?" I asked.

"Yeah, I was just hoping that maybe I could take you to dinner tonight. But I don't want to keep you from getting home."

I felt the corners of my lips tug up in a smile.

"Well," I said, leaning up to kiss him. "What if we picked something up along the way and ate at my place?"

His lips found mine again as he pressed tighter against me.

"Sounds like a date," he answered with a cheesy grin.

It was a date indeed and not a pretend one this time.

Fourteen
Jared

I hadn't planned to stay the night at Everly's house, but when I woke up to the sun shining through the thin curtains in her room, I didn't mind it at all. I was happy when she agreed to have dinner with me and even more excited when she suggested that we pick up food and eat at her place to avoid dealing with the storm that was moving in.

We spent the night cuddled up on the couch watching movies until we both fell asleep. Then, somewhere around midnight, she woke up and asked if I wanted to go lay down in her bed. I thought about being a gentleman and going home, but I was too tired to trust myself to drive in the seven inches of snow that had already fallen.

It was a great night, and we enjoyed each other's company without having sex. That was an odd fucking thing to think about because I couldn't remember the last time I had such a great time with someone without having anything intimate involved. That sounded pretty superficial, but it was the truth.

"Good morning," she said, rolling over to smile at me. Her hair was still pulled up on her head, a little messier than it was last night. She looked gorgeous without makeup as the sun warmed her face.

"*Great* morning," I replied, brushing her cheek with my thumb. "Thank you for letting me stay over last night."

"Of course, you're always welcome here."

We both laid there lazily, neither of us bothering to get out of bed. I reached over and picked up my phone to check the time. It was just after eight, and I already had a few text messages from Shirley about some crazy woman who had found her phone number and called demanding tickets to the play tonight.

I rolled my eyes and set my phone down, knowing that I would have to deal with the Staci problem this morning before it got out of hand. But for now, I wanted to pretend it didn't exist and enjoy my time with Everly.

"Are you hungry?" I asked, turning back on my side to look at her.

She rolled over and smiled at me, something hidden behind it.

"I am," she said seductively. "And you're just what I want for breakfast."

My eyebrows shot up as my dick stirred against my boxer briefs.

"I was thinking that *you* looked like something *I* might want to eat for breakfast," I replied, scooting over and wrapping my arm around her waist to pull her closer to me.

"Is that so?" she purred against my ear as I nuzzled my head in her neck, trailing my tongue over her skin, leaving goosebumps behind.

"Mmhmm," I murmured. "I can't wait to taste you."

She moaned as my hand slipped around to the front and dipped into her panties. Her legs opened slowly, allowing me access as my finger glided across her slit. She was already wet, and I felt my dick press harder against my briefs.

I wanted to go slow and take my time devouring every inch of her body, but I couldn't wait. My dick was getting harder by the minute, my balls aching for a release. I moved down her body, licking my way across her sensitive skin until I was between her legs. She rolled onto her back and spread them further with my shoulders as I lined my mouth up to her opening.

I looked up at her one last time before I leaned forward and ran my tongue along her slit. She gasped at the contact, her fingers digging into the sheets. I licked her over and over, lazily drawing my tongue through her folds as her legs shook beside me. Tasting her was even better than I thought it would be, but the way her body reacted so easily to me was an even bigger turn-on.

She moaned quietly as my tongue worked its magic on her body. I sucked her clit a few times before replacing my tongue with my finger, giving her the pressure she needed as I worked it in small circles while my tongue dipped inside her again.

I could feel her hips bucking off of the bed as I rubbed harder, increasing the pressure the faster I went. She was on the edge and ready to come. Her breaths quickened as she gripped the sheets again, her fingers digging into the fabric as she climaxed hard. I continued to rub her, loving the way her pussy spasmed around my finger as she orgasmed.

Her legs fell limp, and her body relaxed as I pulled my hand away. I sat up and stared at her, amazed by the beautiful woman in front of me.

"You taste delicious," I said, licking my lips. "Just like I thought you would."

"Well, now it's my turn to have breakfast," she teased, sitting up and getting on her knees. She reached up and fixed her ponytail, tightening it, so her hair was out of her face. "Stand up and strip down," she commanded.

I pulled my bottom lip in between my teeth and stood up. Hooking my thumb in the top of my boxer briefs, I slowly pulled them down, letting my erection spring free. She watched intensely, her eyes widening when she saw it. Without saying a word, she called me over to her with her finger.

I stood in front of the bed and grabbed the back collar of my t-shirt, pulling it up and over my head. I was fully naked as her hungry eyes watched me.

Slowly, she reached over and grabbed my dick, wrapping her hand tightly around it. She leaned forward, locking eyes with me as she brought her mouth to me and licked the tip. I wanted to close my eyes and savor the moment, but the way she was looking at me as she slid my cock deep into her mouth was too good to miss.

Her head bobbed back and forth as she sucked me. Her fingers gripped the length that didn't fit in her mouth, sliding up and down in the same motion as her mouth. I felt myself getting closer, desperate to release.

"Everly," I moaned. "I'm so close."

She moved faster, hollowing out her cheeks as she took me further into the back of her throat. I held her head as she let me fuck her mouth.

"I'm gonna come, now," I panted, trying to give her as much warning as I could. Instead of pulling away, she wrapped her mouth tighter around my dick and kept the pace. I closed my eyes and let my head fall back as ropes of cum shot down the back of her throat. I grunted as she continued to suck every last drop out of me.

When I was done, she pulled back and planted a quick kiss on the tip before rolling back onto the bed.

My body was relaxed as I collapsed on the bed beside her.

"Out of all of the things that I'm most thankful for this year," I said lazily, laying on my back. "I'm really glad I was at the restaurant that night."

"Why's that?" she asked with a giggle, rolling onto her side to look at me.

"Because I don't want to think about how it could have been another man who got that blow job."

She let her head fall back as she laughed.

"Well, given that I was getting stood up left and right, I don't think this is something we would have had to worry about."

"None of those losers were worthy of having a chance with you, Everly."

"I'm glad it was you that night, too," she said, something in her voice changing. I rolled onto my side and studied her. "You saved me from a lot of embarrassment. If I would have gone to that party alone, I would never have heard the end of it."

"You don't give yourself enough credit. You're strong, Everly. Look at how you stood up to him yesterday. I'm proud of you for doing that."

"That was because you were there with me. If it were just me by myself, I wouldn't have done that. I wouldn't have had the guts to."

I hated the feeling that was knotting in my stomach, knowing that she was telling the truth. I had noticed how she seemed afraid of him and cowered before she stood up for herself.

"I can't believe that he wanted to invite the entire department to the play tonight," she continued with a sigh. "It's like he gets off on embarrassing me. I'll always be stuck under his thumb if he has any say in it."

"Then don't give him a say," I blurted out.

"It's not that easy," she laughed. "I was with him for five years. If anything, I let him mold me into this pathetic person that I am today. Someone who worries more about his happiness than my own."

"I can understand that," I said gently, trying to keep my personal feelings at bay. "My mother was like that."

"What do you mean?" she asked.

"After she was raped, she stayed working for the bastard. He had convinced her that she owed it to him and that it was her fault because she dressed too provocatively at work. He said that she had asked for it, and when she told him she was pregnant, he told her that she would need to work more hours to afford her maternity leave if she wanted to take any when she had the baby."

"Did she know him well?"

"He was her boss. She worked for him for several years before it happened. He made her believe that she couldn't make it on her own, and that fear kept her right where he wanted her. Finally, she decided that she had enough and quit."

"Wow," Everly breathed. "Good for her, but it sucks that she had to go through all of that. I'm so sorry."

I shrugged and let out a heavy breath.

"It happens more often than people talk about. Women are put in these situations all the time, and most of them don't see they're being used and manipulated until it's too late."

I turned to look at her, hoping that she would pick up on what I was trying to say.

"Like me with Tom." She rolled onto her back and stared at the ceiling. The fun and relaxing morning that we started with turned sour quickly.

After breakfast, I took a few minutes to call Shirley while Everly took a shower. I would have offered to take one with her, but she didn't seem interested in having me touch her after our discussion earlier. I didn't blame her, but I also hated that we even had to talk about it to begin with. It felt like I was living my mom's nightmare all over again by watching Everly struggle to gain control over her life with Tom. It wasn't the exact same situation, but I could see the power that he held over her.

By two o'clock, we headed over to the community center to run through a few rounds of rehearsals before the show started at seven. Everly and I didn't speak to each other much while we were there, and it seemed like everyone noticed. I excused myself to handle things up front while everyone got ready. Really I just wanted to give her some space so she could relax before the show started.

I was up front at the ticket booth with Shirley when I saw Staci and Tom show up. I rolled my eyes and turned my head, letting her know I would handle them before they got to the window. She patted my hand and smiled, familiar enough with what was going on to let me deal with it.

"Hi!" Staci said with fake enthusiasm. "Should we go on in?"

I narrowed my eyes and arched a brow.

"Only ticket holders are allowed in tonight," I explained, a little more aggression in my voice than necessary.

"Oh," her face fell. "Well, then can we get two tickets?"

I shook my head and pulled my lips into a thin line.

"Sorry, the play is sold out."

"You've got to be kidding," she griped. "My *niece* is performing, and I came to see her."

"Well, unfortunately, you'll need a ticket, and we're sold out."

She stomped her foot and crossed her arms over her chest as she clenched her jaw. She looked at Tom and nodded in my direction.

"Just give us a ticket," he demanded, irritation thick in his voice.

"No."
"Excuse me?" he bit out.

"What part of *there are no tickets left* do you two not understand?" I asked, looking between the two of them.

"You're just saying no because you're trying to protect Everly," Staci muttered.

"Protect her from what?" I asked sternly, causing Shirley to flinch beside me. "From you bullying her and making fun of her? Or from you trying to bully her into doing what you want? If that's what you're worried about, rest assured that I will *always* protect her. Not only that, but I will teach her how to stand up for herself, so she never has to bother with you again. But regarding the show, WE. ARE. OUT. OF. TICKETS." My voice boomed in the small booth, causing others nearby to turn and look at us. "If you can't understand the basic concept of what I'm saying, then that's your problem, not mine."

Staci's jaw dropped open as Tom's clenched tighter. Before they could say anything more, I leaned to look past them, calling up the next person to check-in. They moved out of the way, and I watched as they walked off. Tom's fists were balled as Staci tried to hold his hand before he jerked away from her.

Once everyone was seated, and the doors were closed, I took my place backstage and sat on the stool to watch as Shirley thanked everyone for coming. Soon the play had started, and I found myself in awe as I watched Everly move around on the stage, interacting with kids as if she had been doing this for years. She was such a natural that I wondered what she would be like someday as a mother.

When the show was over, everyone piled out of the community center and headed over to the dinner that Shirley was putting on for the kids and their families. It was always something simple that the families helped out with. Tonight it was a spaghetti dinner, and I thought about asking Everly if she wanted to go.

The kids had all left, and she was finishing changing while I waited in the lobby for her. She came out a few minutes later, wearing a pair of skinny jeans tucked into some boots and a cream-colored sweater that stretched tight against her chest. It wasn't what she had on earlier, and I wondered if she had plans.

"Are you ready to go?" I asked, unsure of what to say.

"Yeah," she said, reaching into her pocket for her car keys.

"They're having a spaghetti dinner for the kids and their families tonight. Did you want to go?"

She paused for a moment, guilt flashing across her face.

"I'm sorry, I can't," she said quietly.

"Do you have plans?"

She nodded without saying anything else.

"Is it a date?" I asked, feeling my stomach tighten anxiously. While we had been spending a lot of time together—and sleeping together—we hadn't stopped to label whatever this was between us. Which meant that I didn't know that I had any right to be upset with her if she said yet.

"I wouldn't call it that," she replied nervously, fidgeting with her keys.

"Then what would you call it?"

She lowered her eyes and looked at the floor.

"Look," I said with a sigh. "I know that we haven't talked about whatever this is between us, but if we need to label it to keep you from going, then fine. I like you, Everly. A lot. And if you want me to call you my girlfriend, then that's what you are, my girlfriend. But please, don't go on this date."

"It's not that easy," she countered, tilting her head in frustration.

"Why not?"

"Because it's someone that my mom set me up with."

I narrowed my eyes and read between the lines as she looked away, avoiding eye contact.

"Who?"

"Brad."

The laughter rushed out of me before I could stop it. My eyebrows nearly shot off of my forehead as I processed what she was saying.

"You're going on a date with Brad? The guy your mom tried to set you up with and stood you up the night we met? *That* Brad?"

She nodded and looked away.

"Can't you just say no? Say that you're busy?" I offered.

"I can't do that."

"Why not?" I felt like I was on repeat at this point, not understanding why she was agreeing to do this.

"Because you don't know my mother. It's easier just to go."

I pulled my head back in surprise and looked at her. Suddenly, it felt as if I didn't know the woman standing in front of me. The girl who was so playful and confident when we were by ourselves was replaced with the timid, insecure girl I met that first night.

"Well, you know best." I kept my mouth shut after that, refusing to say any more.

"I'm not trying to upset you," she said softly.

"What does it matter? We were just pretending anyway, right," I bit out, letting my anger get the best of me.

I turned and walked out, leaving Shirley to lock up after Everly left.

Fifteen
Everly

"What's up, Buttercup?" Becca said as she walked through my front door. She stepped to the side and took in my messy bun and sweats before narrowing her eyes. "What's wrong?"

"Nothing," I sighed, pushing the door closed behind her and moping into the living room. I plopped down on the couch and pulled the blanket up to my chin.

"You're lying," she said, sitting in the chair beside me. "Do you need ice cream or Chinese food?"

"Neither," I muttered, pretending to watch tv.

She reached over and picked up the remote, turning it off.

"I was watching that," I lied, not bothering to look away from the blank screen.

"Sure you were."

"I was."

"Okay, let's get it over with. Do I need a baseball bat or a sharp pair of scissors?" she asked, leaning forward and resting her elbows on her knees.

"For what?" I turned my head and looked at her, confused.

"It's obvious that someone hurt you. So it's either Tom or Jared. If it's Jared, then I'm going to take a baseball bat and beat him until he comes to his senses. If it's Tom, then you don't need to know what I'm going to do with the scissors." She paused for a moment before adding, "never mind, it's actually better that you *don't know*. You know, for court purposes and stuff."

"It's neither of them," I muttered, turning to look away again. "I was the idiot this time."

"What did you do?"

I waited for a moment before I answered. When I saw the look on Jared's face last night, I knew that I had made the wrong decision.

"Well," she prodded.

I sighed and pushed myself up to a sitting position on the couch.

"I went on a date last night."

"With who?"

"Brad."

She leaned back in her chair and folded her legs under her as she got comfortable.

"*Brad*?"

"Brad," I confirmed.

"As in…."

"The guy who my mom tried to set me up with the night I met Jared."

"The one who—"

"Stood me up? Yup, that's the one," I said bitterly.

"Okay, so why did you go on a date with him last night?"

That was the question that I had been asking myself over and over from the moment that I left the restaurant last night.

"I didn't feel like I had a choice." I shook my head, the disappointment still weighing heavily on my shoulders.

"Why didn't you have a choice?"

"Because my mom called and told me that she had talked to him personally and informed me that I was going to meet him at Le Blue last night."

"Oh," she sighed. She knew my mother long enough to understand what I was saying without me needing to elaborate further.

A few minutes passed before either of us spoke.

"So, was the date bad?" she asked, trying to figure out why I was so depressed.

"It was just as I had expected. He was boring and talked about himself the entire time. When it came time for them to bring the check, he mentioned how my mother had bragged about how independent I was and that I didn't need a man to pay for things for me."

"So you paid for your own meal?"

"And his."

Her jaw dropped open.

"No!" she gasped. "Everly, why did you do that?"

"Because I'm a stupid, pathetic girl who likes to get screwed over?"

She rolled her eyes and waited for me to continue.

"The waitress didn't know to split the check. He had slid his hand over to my knee, and I knew where he was going with it. I told him that I wasn't feeling well and needed to leave. I was over the date and didn't want to be stuck there with him longer than necessary, so it was easier just to give her my card and have her run the whole thing."

"Wow," Becca laughed. "I don't think I've ever had a date *that* bad before. Did he at least give you a reason for why he stood you up last time?"

"Start going out with me. I'm a magnet for them," I sighed. "And no, he simply *forgot*."

We rolled our eyes at the same time.

"That's not true, and he's an idiot," she said, her tone turning more serious. "You've had great dates with Jared."

I laughed and snorted, not bothering to cover my mouth as I let my head fall back.

"Yeah, I'm really good at pretend dating but can't do the real thing to save my life." I could feel the sadness radiate through me when I thought about how happy I had been when I was with Jared. I wished that it was real because pretending had started to feel so easy. Shouldn't it have been harder if there wasn't anything between us?

"What happened with Jared?" she asked softly.

"Nothing," I shrugged. "We were just pretending."

"But were you?"

I looked at her and felt like my heart was on display. She knew me well enough to see through any excuses that I tried to give her.

"It doesn't matter," I sighed. "He didn't take it well last night when he found out I was going out with Brad."

"What did he say?"

I closed my eyes and tried to remember word for word what he had said. For whatever reason, my brain had shut down and kept it hidden. Maybe it was a defense mechanism to keep me from feeling more heartbroken, or maybe I was just finally sinking to a new level of breakdown where I couldn't process words. Who knew at this point?

"He was upset. Said something about being my boyfriend if I needed to label it."

Her face changed from surprise to sadness as she heard the hurt in my voice.

"He asked me not to go."

She slumped back into her chair, feeling the weight of the depression that surrounded me.

"But you did anyway."

"I did."

"So, what are you going to do now?" she asked, a hint of optimism in her voice.

"What is there to do? He stormed out and left. I haven't heard from him since."

"Have you tried calling him?"

I arched a brow and pulled my lips into a thin line.

"Right," she said. "What a silly thing for me to ask."

"What's that supposed to mean?" I asked, suddenly feeling defensive.

"Nothing," she said, getting up out of her chair. "Just that you are too scared of something good happening to you that you refuse to make an effort to go after it."

My jaw dropped open in disbelief.

"I'm not scared," I countered. "He walked out on *me*."

"Because you basically told him that he wasn't good enough for you to cancel the date. He wasn't good enough for you to say no to your mom. Everly, you had a great thing going. A man who genuinely cared about you and asked you to be his girlfriend. He made it clear how he felt about you when he thought you were going on the date because you didn't know where you stood with him. He's told you that he's interested in being with you, and you're sitting here like you're the victim."

I shook my head and turned away. She was right, and I hated it.

"I'm going to go so I can finish my Christmas shopping," she said dismissively. "Try not to wallow in self-pity for too long. Fix it before it's too late."

She gave me a pointed look before grabbing her purse and walking out the door.

I laid back down on the couch, thinking about what she said. As I was about to turn on the tv, I heard my phone vibrate. My stomach fluttered as I hoped that it was Jared texting me. Instead, it was Susan, asking if I could help her with a problem she was having with a client.

I didn't have the file with me and knew that I wouldn't be able to focus on anything productive, so I texted her back and let her know that I was heading into the office and would work on what she needed. It wasn't the first time that I had gone to work on a Sunday. At least no one else would be there to bother me while I worked.

Sixteen

Jared

I stared at my phone and deleted the seventh text that I had started writing to Everly. I hadn't talked to her since I walked out on her last night, and I felt anxious about it ever since. I was pissed when she told me that she was going on a date with the guy that had initially stood her up, but then I had to keep reminding myself that I didn't have any right to be mad.

The day was dragging on at an incredibly slow pace, and I knew that I wasn't going to be able to relax until after I cleared the air with Everly. I needed to talk to her but didn't know whether she wanted to speak to me. Last night, I asked her to be my girlfriend, and she still decided to go out with another guy.

My head was a mess wondering whether she had been into things as much as I was or if she had really just been pretending. It wasn't like we had been dating long enough to have deep feelings for each other, but I knew that there was more to this than just a little crush.

I sucked in a breath and held it as I typed a quick text, asking her what her plans were for the day. I pressed send and let it out, wondering whether she would bother to reply.

I set my phone down and tried to force myself to walk away and not obsess about it. There were plenty of things that I should be doing, but none of them were high on my priorities right now. Talking to Everly overrode everything, including the basics like feeding myself as my stomach growled in protest.

A few minutes later, I heard my phone chime and ran over to check it like the desperate loser I was.

Everly: I'm at work. Not sure how long I'll be here.

It was quick and kind of cold, but I tried not to read too much into it.

Me: Anything I can help with?

I smacked my palm against my forehead after I pressed send. What in the world would I possibly help with? I knew nothing about investments or what she did with them.

Everly: No, but thank you.

I sucked in a deep breath and held it. At this rate, I would pass out from holding my breath so much, but I didn't care.

Me: Okay. Let me know if you need anything.

I set my phone down and pushed it across the table to keep from typing anything else. I sounded desperate and pathetic enough already as it was.

Forcing myself to focus on anything other than her, I left my phone where it was and went to start a load of laundry. There was plenty of house cleaning that I could get done to kill some time.

Thirty minutes later, I was sitting on the couch, folding

a load of towels that I had forgotten in the dryer. They weren't soft and fluffy like they were when they first came out of the dryer, but I didn't have the energy to worry about that. It wasn't like Everly was rushing right over to come take a shower and let me wrap her in my warm towels.

I shook my head and tried to clear any thoughts of her, but it didn't work. She was on my mind constantly, and I hated that I couldn't think about anything else. I finished folding the towels and put them away. The other load of laundry wouldn't be ready for twenty minutes, and then I would still have to wait for it to dry.

I gathered the trash in the house, collecting it in one bag before running it out to the trash can. The snow was falling hard again, and the news had predicted that we would get another two inches before dusk. I hated the thought of Everly driving in this weather, but it wasn't like we were on the best of terms right now. Then again, I cared more about her safety than I did this stupid *fight* we were having. I wasn't even sure if that's what you could call it since we weren't dating.

Convincing myself that I was doing the right thing, I grabbed my keys off of the coffee table and slid my coat on before rushing out to my truck. Then, without giving myself the chance to talk myself out of it, I headed to her work, wondering if I should tell her that I was coming.

Fifteen minutes later, I was pulling into the parking lot, relieved when I saw her car was still there. There were a few other cars parked a few spaces over, so I took the open space right beside her.

I pulled out my phone, ready to text her to let her know I was there when a woman came walking out of the door.

"Hey, you're Jared, right?" she said, smiling and holding the door open. "I'm Susan, Everly's friend from the Christmas party."

"Oh, hey," I said, smiling as I remembered how Everly had spoken so kindly about her. "It's great to see you again."

"You too. Are you here to see her?"

"Yeah, I was worried about her driving in this weather, so I came to give her a ride home."

"Well, aren't you the sweetest," she said, clutching her hand to her chest. "She's the luckiest girl in the world to have such a caring boyfriend."

"Thank you," I said shyly, feeling guilty for accepting her compliment.

"Well, she's up on the fourth floor. You'll see her desk in the middle cubicle." She stepped to the side and held the door for me.

"Thanks, I appreciate it," I said as I moved inside.

"Have a Merry Christmas," she called over her shoulder as she walked to the parking lot.

"You too," I hollered back, hoping she had heard me.

I let the door close behind me as I made my way over to the elevator and waited. Finally, the doors opened, and I climbed in, pushing the number four repeatedly until the doors closed and it started to move. I was equally anxious and excited to see her.

Once the doors started to open, I slid through and pushed my way out, scanning the floor for her. There was a light on at a desk in the middle where Susan said she would be, but

I didn't see her. So I walked around, looking in the empty offices when suddenly something caught my eye.

In the corner office, the light was on, and voices were floating through the air. I made my way over and stopped short when I saw Everly pinned against the wall with Tom on top of her.

"Tell me you want it," he said, loud enough for me to hear through the rush of blood pulsing through my ears. "Come on, Everly, tell me how bad you want this."

I couldn't hear what she was saying, but it didn't sound the same as when she was begging me to touch her. There was something in her voice that sounded off. I kept walking until I was right outside the door, staring at them.

He pressed his body against hers, holding her in place as one hand caressed her breast. She flinched at his touch, and I watched her body stiffen.

"Stop it," she said sternly but not loud enough to get his attention.

Everything around me turned red as my anger ignited quicker than a match. Within seconds, I was on him, grabbing him by the shirt and flinging him off of her.

He stumbled back, shocked as he tried to focus on what had just happened. Then, before he could fully register who I was, I pulled my arm back and swung as hard as I could, feeling the crack of his nose against my hand.

"You son of a bitch," he yelled, reaching up to touch it.

I swung again, this time hitting him in the jaw. I could feel the adrenaline coursing through me as I tried to swing again, this time, my arm was held back by Everly.

"Jared! Stop it!" she screamed. "It's not what it looks like!"

Her words stopped me in my tracks. I lowered my arm and turned to look at her. Her face was red and flushed as she reached down and adjusted her shirt.

"What exactly do you think it looks like?" I asked. "Because to me, it looks like you were saying no, and he wasn't listening."

"You don't know what the fuck you're talking about," Tom hissed, grabbing a tissue out of the box on his desk.

"I think you should go," Everly said, looking at me.

"You want me to go?"

She nodded her head and wrapped her arms around her body.

"I think it's for the best."

I shook my head and let out an exasperated breath.

"Fine. If that's what you want."

I turned and walked away, my hand starting to ache from hitting that asshole's face.

Seventeen
Everly

I was an idiot. A big, giant, stupid idiot.

After Jared left, I immediately regretted asking him to do so. I had no idea why he was there in the first place, but the last thing that I wanted was for him to stick around and have another go-round with Tom. Not because I thought that he couldn't handle Tom, but because I worried that Tom would be his typical self and press charges against him after he got his ass kicked.

"You better tell your boyfriend that he's not welcome in this office again. If I see him, I'm going to—"

"You're going to what?" I interrupted, feeling my anger bubble over. I stood in front of Tom with my hands on my hips.

"I'll get a restraining order against him," he said, jutting his jaw out.

"Why? Because you're afraid that he'll come back and finish what he started?"

I don't know if it was because Jared had been there and left some sort of magic in the air that gave me the confidence to stand up to him or what, but suddenly I felt strong enough to stand up to him.

"I could take him," he scoffed, wiping at the blood that was still dripping from his nose.

I rolled my eyes and stepped back with my arms folded across my chest.

"You couldn't take him if you tried," I corrected. "And you're not going to get a restraining order against him. In fact, if I were you, I would start looking into other job options because I will be filing a sexual harassment report with Gail as soon as I get home."

"Sexual harassment, please." He snorted and sat down in his chair, applying more pressure to try to stop the bleeding.

"Do not dismiss this as if it didn't happen," I said angrily, placing my hands on his desk and staring down at him from the other side. "You pinned me against the wall and touched me inappropriately when I told you to stop."

"You wanted it."

"You wouldn't know what I wanted if it was staring you in the face. You're too selfish to think about anyone else. But I can promise you this—that will be the *last* time that you touch me."

I pushed away from the desk and glared at him, finally seeing him for the asshole that he was.

"I'll make sure Gail gives you a copy of the report once she has it. I've also requested to be transferred from this department if I don't get the promotion."

I watched as his face reddened with anger as I turned and walked away. I didn't bother finishing the project that we were working on. He could figure out how to fix his own damn errors. I grabbed my stuff from my cubicle and stormed out, making sure he didn't follow me.

Once I was in the car, I locked the doors and pulled out my cell phone. The snow had gotten worse since I got here, and I knew that the drive home would be difficult. I found Gail's number and pressed send, knowing that if I didn't call her now that I would talk myself out of doing it later.

I turned on the speakerphone and set my phone in the cup holder, waiting for her to answer as I got the hell out of there.

A few rings later, her voicemail picked up instead. I waited for the beep and gripped the steering wheel, hoping that it would brace me for what I was about to do.

Once I heard the end of her greeting, I began speaking.

"Hi, Gail. This is Everly. I needed to talk to you regarding an incident that just happened while I was in the office with Tom. I'll give you the details in this message and then email you a written statement as soon as I get home." I paused and took a deep breath, hoping that it didn't cut me off. Then, keeping it as short and to the point as possible, I continued.

"I went into the office today to help Susan after she sent me a message about needing help with a client. I didn't expect her to meet me there, but she showed up anyway. A little while later, Tom came in as well. Susan and I finished what we needed to, and then she left. I was heading out right behind her when Tom asked for my help. I told her to go ahead and go home, so she wasn't stuck driving in the weather. When I went to Tom's office, he mentioned that he needed help with a problem that he was having. When I asked what it was, he walked across the room and pinned me against the wall. I wasn't able to move from the weight of his body against mine. I told him repeatedly to get off of me, but he didn't listen. He continued to try to kiss me and groped my breasts before my boyfriend, Jared, showed up and pulled him off of me. I confronted Tom and let him know that I would be filing a report, however, I wanted to make sure that I told you about it as soon as possible. I'll be available on my cell phone if you get this and want to talk. Bye."

I stopped at the red light and picked up my phone, ending the call. My fingers were shaking, and I couldn't believe that I had done that.

I knew that I needed to talk to Jared and explain what happened, but as a gust of snow blew past me, I realized that I was better off getting home first. I could always call him once I got there safely.

Twenty minutes later, I pulled into my driveway and climbed out of the car, struggling to open the door against the snow that had piled up in the driveway. I carefully made my way inside, making sure to avoid moving too fast and slipping on the ice beneath me. Once inside, I kicked off my boots and rushed over to turn up the heater.

It was warm in the house but not warm enough to thaw the icy cold chill that continued to run through me. I changed into a pair of fleece pajama pants and pulled on my favorite hoodie, hoping that would help. What I really wanted was to cuddle up next to Jared and let him warm me up with his skillful hands.

I sat on the couch and turned on the TV as I got situated. My phone showed a missed call from Gail with a voicemail but nothing from Jared. I listened to her message, checking to make sure I was alright. She promised that she would get the report started immediately and have me transferred to another department first thing on Monday morning. I didn't have any idea what that meant as far as my clients, but I was too tired to care.

I was disappointed that Jared hadn't called or texted me, but then again, I couldn't blame him. I had been terrible with him the last few times we had seen each other. So, why would he want to talk to me? I knew that I needed to fix whatever this was between us, but I didn't know how.

Working off some of the adrenaline that was still in my system, I picked up my phone and dialed his number. The phone rang several times before he finally answered.

"Hello."

I closed my eyes and pulled my lips together. He was still pissed.

"Hey," I said softly, hoping to ease the tension.

Silence.

"About earlier," I started, "I'm sorry about what happened."

"Sorry that you got caught?"

I whipped my head back as if I had just been slapped.

"Caught?" I asked in disbelief. "I wasn't doing anything."

"Then why are you apologizing if you didn't do anything?"

"Because I felt bad for asking you to leave."

He huffed out an irritated breath, and I started to worry that this was a mistake. Maybe I should have given him more time to cool off.

"I don't think I can do this, Everly," he said evenly.

"Do what?"

I could feel the panic rising inside of me.

"Whatever this is between us. *Was*."

My heart started racing, thudding loudly in my chest.

"Jared, I said that I was sorry," I stammered.

"And I've told you that you shouldn't say sorry if you didn't do anything."

"So then, what are you upset about? We can try to fix it," I pleaded.

He paused for a moment, keeping me on pins and needles.

"I can't be with someone who doesn't value themselves, Everly. It's too exhausting."

I closed my eyes and pinched the bridge of my nose to keep from crying.

"It was fun while it lasted, but maybe it's for the better that we end it before things get too complicated."

"Jared," I whispered. "I know that you're upset, but can't we talk about this?"

"Talk about what? I told you that I was falling for you, and you still went on a date with a guy who stood you up. Then

I walked in on your ex assaulting you, and you acted like I was the bad guy for protecting you. I can't win with you, Everly. And honestly, it's too hard trying."

"So, what are you saying?" I asked, my lip trembling.

"I'm saying that it was fun while it lasted, but I think it's best if we move on and go our separate ways."

The tears fell down my face as I cried, the line going dead a few seconds later.

Eighteen
Jared

"So, what did you get her?" Shirley asked excitedly as we shoved the bins with the costumes from the play back into the storage area behind the stage.

"Get who?" I asked, unsure of what she was talking about. I lifted another box and slid it on top of the others.

"Everly," she laughed. "It's Christmas Eve, you better have gotten her present, or you're going to have a heck of a time finding one now."

I swallowed hard before I climbed down and turned to face her.

"We're not together anymore," I said sternly before walking past her to get the other boxes.

"What?" she gasped. "Why not? You guys were the perfect couple."

"I seriously doubt that," I laughed. "It was all just a show."

"What do you mean?"

I stopped moving the boxes and wiped my hands on the

front of my jeans. I had her full attention, which meant she wasn't going to let this go.

"Everly and I weren't ever really dating. It was all fake from the start."

"Fake?" she repeated, still not buying it.

I nodded.

"I was picking up dinner a few weeks ago and overheard a conversation that she was having with her ex. He was giving her a hell of a time about being stood up, so I decided to swoop in and pretend to be her boyfriend. She needed a date to her work's Christmas party, so I offered to go. Unfortunately, her boss is the same jerk that I met that night. After the party, I asked her to help out with the play. When she ran into Staci, we had to keep the act up since she was dating Everly's ex-boyfriend."

"But you guys get along so well. So why didn't you try to date?"

"I wanted to," I laughed, sitting on one of the sturdier boxes. "But she didn't want to."

"She said that?"

"In not so many words."

Shirley narrowed her eyes and frowned.

"Nope," she said firmly. "There's more to that story. Spill it."

"There's nothing to spill. She went on a date with another guy on Saturday, and I caught her making out with her ex at work on Sunday."

"What?!" She covered her mouth with her hand. "Did you ask her about it?"

"Yeah, and she told me that she had to go on the date because her mom had set it up. Not only did her mom *force* her to go, but it was also with the same guy who had stood her up the night that I met her."

"And what about her making out with her ex?"

"Well, I guess they weren't technically *making out*," I said bitterly. "I caught him pushing her up against the wall in his office. It sounded like she was saying no. He didn't listen."

Her face fell, and I knew that she could predict where this was going.

"What did you do?"

"I pulled him off of her and then hit him a few times."

She covered her face with her hands and muttered my name a few times.

"What did she do?"

"She freaked out and made me leave."

"Have you talked to her since then?"

I rolled my head back and forth on my neck, trying to relieve some of the tension that was building with this conversation.

"She called me yesterday."

"And?"

"I told her that I thought that whatever this was between us should be over."

"Why?"

I sighed and blew out a frustrated breath as I leaned forward and rested my elbows on my knees.

"Because it's too hard. She refuses to value herself enough to say no to people and then gets mad when I try to stick up for her."

"Has she told you anything about her mom?"

"Only that she's tough on her. Everly has tried to get her approval all of her life, but nothing is ever good enough for her."

"And you don't think that's reason enough for her to feel compelled to go on this date that her mother set up for her?"

I locked eyes with her, hearing what she was saying.

"Do you think that maybe you're feeling frustrated because Everly reminds you of your mom? Especially with what happened with her ex in his office?"

I looked away, the anger starting to build again.

"She's not her, Jared," she continued. "It's okay to want to protect her, but it won't change what happened to your mother."

"But she doesn't see the harm that she could be in," I muttered, pushing my hands together as I hung my head. "All it takes is one time for her ex to decide that he wants her again. Or some creep that stood her up to think that she owes him."

"That can happen to anyone at any time. You can't let this

ruin your relationship with her."

"But she still went on that date, even after I confessed that I was falling for her and asked her not to."

"Because she didn't know how to tell her mother no. You can't blame her for not knowing how to stand up for herself with someone that has probably been doing this to her for her entire life."

 I sat up straight and looked at Shirley. I hated when she was right.

"Now go find her and fix this," she said with a smile. I got up and hugged her, holding her tight as I always did anytime I missed my mom a little more than usual. "And go buy her a present!"

"Okay, okay," I laughed. "I'm on it."

A CHRISTMAS WISH

Nineteen
Everly

I was curled up on the couch wearing the same pajamas that I put on when I got home on Sunday. So what if I hadn't changed in two days? It wasn't like anyone was rushing over to see me on Christmas anyway. My parents were cruising through the Bahamas, and Becca was out of town with her family. Jared still wasn't talking to me, and aside from him, I didn't have anyone else to hang out with.

My tabletop tree was lit up, not doing anything to add any Christmas cheer to the room. The tv had been on a channel with non-stop Hallmark movies that were supposed to make you feel warm and fuzzy but instead, they just irritated me. If I still had the rest of the costume, I would be wearing the Old Man Grumpus outfit since it seemed to fit my mood.

I got up to use the bathroom and decided I might as well feed myself while I was up. It would be a few hours before I needed to go again and since showering and getting dressed weren't on my agenda, there wasn't anything else to worry about.

I went to the kitchen, dug a popcorn bag out of the pantry,

and popped it in the microwave. It was better than nothing. There were wine bottles and empty ice cream cartons scattered along the counter by the sink, but I didn't have the energy to clean those up either.

As the kernels popped, I heard a knock on the door. I walked over and peeked through the peephole, gasping when I saw Jared on the other side.

"Open up, Everly. It's freaking cold out here," he said from the other side.

I ran a hand through my hair that hadn't been washed in days and grimaced at the thought of him seeing me like this.

"Um, I'm not feeling well," I lied. "Maybe you can come back another day?"

"Not going to happen, now please unlock the door."

I sighed, knowing that he would stay there all day if he had to.

I turned the locks and opened the door, holding my breath when a gust of wind came whipping past us.

He carried a handful of gift bags on one arm, filled with tissue paper poking out of the top of them. In the other hand, he had a brown paper bag with what smelled like food from somewhere.

"What are you doing?" I asked, stepping aside to let him in.

He walked over to the counter as I shut the door behind him.

"I came to talk to you," he said, busying himself with unpacking the food. "And, I brought dinner."

"You didn't have to do that."

I stayed standing where I was and watched him work effortlessly as he unpacked several to-go containers.

"I wanted to."

"Why?"

"Because," he said, finally turning to look at me. "I needed to say that I was sorry, and I was hoping that we could spend Christmas together."

He stepped toward me, placing his hands on my sides as I stayed frozen in place.

"Sorry for what?"

"For a lot of things," he sighed. "But most of all, for not listening when you wanted to talk about everything. I should have taken the time to hear you out, and I'm sorry that I didn't. I was angry and trying to process everything."

"I'm sorry too," I replied. "I should never have gone on that date, and I shouldn't have put myself in that position with Tom."

"I hated seeing you with him," he admitted. "It reminded me of my mom, and I lost it."

I nodded, understanding where he was coming from.

"I called Gail right after it happened and reported him. She called me back and let me know that I'll be in a new department starting Monday morning."

His eyes lit up as he squeezed me gently.

"I'm so proud of you," he said warmly.

"Thank you. And you were right about the date. It was terrible, and I should never have gone on it. I should have said no to my mother and told her that I was already seeing someone."

"Why didn't you tell her about me?" he asked, rubbing his thumb along my cheek.

"Because I was afraid that if I said it out loud that it would all end and you would just disappear. I didn't want to jinx it."

He gave me a small smile and pulled me in for a hug.

"At least you got a free meal out of it," he joked.

"Yeah, right," I snorted. "I ended up paying for the whole tab."

He pulled back and studied my face to see if I was joking. I shook my head and made a face.

"You have the worst luck with dates," he said with a laugh. "Hopefully, that's all over now?"

"Hopefully," I repeated, needing him to say it.

"If you're my girlfriend, then I would love it if you would stop dating other men and buying them dinner." I loved the way his lips turned up in the corners as he started to smile.

"Deal," I said, sticking my hand out to shake his. Instead, he grabbed it and pulled me back against his chest, holding me as if he was afraid to let go.

"Don't get too close," I warned. "I haven't showered in a day or two."

"Is that an invitation?" he asked playfully, wiggling his eyebrows.

"Maybe, but you have to feed me first," I said, ducking under his arm and rushing toward the food.

We grabbed the boxes from the counter and sat on the couch, diving right in. He had found a place serving Christmas dinner, which was something I hadn't had in a while with my parents traveling for almost every holiday.

We ate in silence, watching a love story unfold on the tv while we finished up. Finally, I set the empty container on the coffee table, ready to go take a shower.

"Wanna join me for some slippery, wet fun?" I asked, lifting the bottom of my hoodie and pulling it up my stomach.

"You bet your sweet ass I do," he growled. "But first, presents."

I let my hoodie fall back into place as I rushed into the bedroom and grabbed the gift bag I had waiting for him. When I went back into the living room, he was sitting on the couch with the bags he had brought in with him.

"Merry Christmas," I said, handing him the bag.

"Thank you, Merry Christmas to you," he replied, giving me my gift bags.

"You go first," he instructed, nodding to the two small bags in my lap.

"Does it matter which one I open first?"

He shook his head and watched me, his eyes sparkling.

I pulled the tissue paper out of the first one and dipped my fingers inside to pull out the small jewelry box. I looked

at him then back to the box before I opened it. My fingers trembled slightly with excitement as they opened the lid.

Inside was a small Super Woman pin. I lifted it from the box and admired it.

"Sometimes, I know that you feel like you don't have the strength to do things," Jared explained. "But I wanted you to know that you are one of the strongest women that I know. Sometimes you just need a little reminder." He nodded to the pin and smiled.

"Thank you, this is so beautiful." I kept looking at it for a few seconds before placing it back in its box to keep it safe. I already had a few ideas of where I wanted to put it so I could see it every single day.

"Okay, now open the second one," he said excitedly, rubbing his hands together.

I laughed, pulling the tissue paper out of the other bag, and reached inside to pull out a larger box. There was no writing on it, so I opened it and found a smaller box inside. I covered my mouth as I looked at the picture of the vibrator on the outside packaging.

"Is this what I think it is?" I asked quietly, suddenly feeling shy.

"What do you think it is?" He pulled his lower lip in between his teeth. I loved when he did that.

"A massager?" I asked playfully, pretending not to know what it was.

"Oh, it's going to massage you, alright," he laughed.

I felt my cheeks flush as I set it on the couch beside me. It was Christmas, why not use my new present as soon as possible?

"Now it's your turn," I said, nodding to the gift in his lap.

He smiled and pulled the tissue paper out, laying it gently in his lap as he unwrapped each piece inside.

"Ties," he said with a grin.

"I couldn't help myself," I admitted. "After we played that game at brunch, I couldn't stop thinking of you touching my body with one. So I got you a handful to choose from."

"Thank you for the gift," he said, his voice suddenly husky. "Now, let's go use them."

He growled as he stood up and carried me to the bedroom with the ties and vibrator included as he got ready to make my Christmas wish come true.

<u>Twenty</u>
Everly

"Oh, right there," I moaned as Jared's tongue slid inside of me, parting my folds. "That feels amazing."

I arched my back, desperate to get closer to him as my orgasm crept up on me. My spine tingled as the blood rushed through my body, my breathing growing heavy with every second that passed.

He licked me lazily as if he had all the time in the world while I felt like I was going to explode against his face.

"I'm so close," I begged, shifting beneath him.

I felt him chuckle between my legs before he reached over and grabbed the vibrator lying beside us on the bed. I would have gotten it myself, but I was currently tied to the bed with one of the new ties that I had given him for Christmas.

A few seconds later, I heard it buzzing to life as he placed it against my clit.

"Ahhh!" I cried out, bucking my hips against his face.

He leaned back and scooted up to watch me as he slid

it inside of me, lining it up, so the flower at the end was hitting my clit perfectly.

I panted heavily, pulling against the silk tie as my body hummed with electricity.

"Open your eyes," he commanded softly.

I tried to force them to open, my body unable to concentrate on anything other than what was happening between my legs.

When I opened them, I found his dark green eyes locked onto mine, studying my face as my orgasm ripped through me. My body shook against the bed as he pressed the vibrator harder, pulling every last bit out of me.

"That was amazing," I panted, letting my body fall limp as he pulled the vibrator out then untied me. "By far the best Christmas present I've ever received."

He laid on his side and rested on his elbow as he laughed.

"That's not even all of your gift," he said with a dirty grin.

"What are you talking about?" I asked, rolling to look at him. "We opened our gifts before we came in here."

"Yeah, but I have one more for you. It's a surprise."

"A surprise?" My brows shot up, wondering what he was up to.

"Yes, now go get ready."

He patted the bed beside me a few times before getting up and walking out of the bedroom into the bathroom, butt naked.

"You better hurry," he called out as he turned on the shower.

I groaned, my body angry that I was forcing it to move. I followed him into the bathroom, stopping in my tracks as I looked at him through the glass shower door. He was face forward in the water as it ran down his body. His *gorgeous* body that I still hadn't had enough of.

"Mind if I join you?" I asked seductively, sliding the door open and stepping in.

"You know I like it when you're wet," he said as he stepped back to make room for me.

I stood under the hot water, feeling the heat of his gaze as he watched the water rush over my chest and down my breasts.

"I could fuck you all day long," he admitted, his voice gruff.

"Well, then, it's a good thing I don't have any plans today." I squirted some shower gel into my hands and lathered it slowly before rubbing it on my body, focusing on my breasts. My nipples hardened, and I felt the ache start between my legs again. There was no way that I would ever have my fill of him.

"Trust me, you don't want to miss what I have planned."

"Are you going to tell me what it is?" I prodded with a cheeky grin.

"Nope." He smacked his lips together and smiled back at me, knowing that it was getting to me that I didn't know what he had planned.

Half an hour later, we were both dressed and heading out the door. When we pulled up to what looked like an abandoned building with no windows and only one entry, I started to worry that maybe he had brought me here to kill me. There were other cars in the parking lot, but aside from those, there weren't any other businesses close by and no one to hear my cries for help if needed.

He parked close to the front entrance—if that's what you wanted to call it. It was hard to tell. Aside from the sign that read *Euphoria* hanging above the door, there wasn't anything else to indicate what kind of place this was. And it seemed funny that they would call this place *Euphoria* when it was painted black and looked dark and depressing.

"It'll be fun, I promise," he assured me, reaching over to squeeze my hand before getting out to come around and help me.

Before I could obsess about it, he was opening my door and extending his hand to help me down.

"What if I'm not dressed right?" I asked, suddenly nervous.

"Trust me, you're fine," he laughed lightly, his hand resting gently on my lower back as he glided me to the door.

I pulled at the short, black dress that barely covered my ass and regretted letting him talk me into wearing it. It was freaking cold outside, and I was about to freeze my ass off before he murdered me in this dark, gloomy parking lot.

We stood in front of the door, my teeth chattering involuntarily.

"Are you ready?" he asked, his hand on the handle.

I nodded and wrapped my arms around myself, trying to keep warm and calm my nerves.

He pulled the door open and stepped to the side, gently

guiding me in with his hand on my lower back.

My jaw dropped open as I walked in, hearing the door shut behind us. The room was dark, like the outside, but dimly lit to cast a sexy glow throughout the room. We moved to the side to let a waitress past me, and I found myself turning to gawk at her.

"Is she…." I whispered, letting my voice trail off as I raised my eyebrows and nodded.

"Bodypaint," he answered, leading me to another room.

I felt in awe as I took everything in. The dark grey fabric of the chairs that were strategically arranged in the room to form a square with cocktail tables lined up in front of them, creating a smaller square. There was nothing on the table— just the clear, thin glass that allowed the perfect view of what was under the table, no matter where you were in the room.

Jared escorted me to one of the empty tables in the corner of the room, and we sat down. I looked around us, finding people scattered around—some couples and a few sitting by themselves. The lights were dim in this room as well, with music floating through the speakers above. It was loud enough to drown out the thoughts that were rushing through my head but not too loud to keep me from hearing the moans of the couple a few tables down.

I curiously peeked around Jared to see what was happening. He leaned back in his chair to give me a better view as his hand slid from my lower back to my ass.

My heart was racing as I leaned into him and tilted my head, getting a full view of the girl's legs spread wide as the guy next to her fingered her. Her lips parted as her head fell back, and she let another moan escape her lips.

I felt my breathing increase as I watched, wondering if they knew they had an audience.

"Euphoria is a club where people come to be watched or to watch others," Jared explained quietly in my ear, his hand still planted on my ass.

I turned my head slightly to look at him, not ready to take my eyes off of the other couple just yet.

"The tables are clear so you can see what they're doing underneath it. Some like you to watch them fuck, others like to masturbate. You can get pretty much whatever you're into."

I swallowed hard, watching as his fingers glistened in the light every time he pulled them back before plunging them back inside of her. I couldn't look away if I tried. I was fixated on watching this couple, who probably had no idea that I was looking at them.

Suddenly, the girl opened her eyes and locked onto mine. The seas of blue lit up beautifully in the light as a grin pulled across her face. Her lips were painted red, her tongue swiping slowly across them as she held my gaze.

She whispered something in his ear, causing him to look over at me. I felt Jared's body shift next to me, his chest hardening as he turned to watch them with me.

"They like you watching," he said low in my ear before gently nipping the lobe.

I nodded, unable to speak.

"Maybe he'll fuck her and let you watch," he suggested.

Instinctively, I reached my hand down and rubbed it across his cock. I could feel him getting hard and knew he was as turned on as I was.

The other couple continued to watch us as he fingered her for a few moments before whispering something in her ear. She bit the tip of her finger seductively and nodded. He pulled his fingers out and licked them, watching us the entire time.

She stood up, smiling at us before she turned to face him. He lifted her skirt, pushing it up to expose her bare ass before he reached down and unzipped his pants. A few seconds later, she stood with her legs parted, giving me the perfect view of his dick as it sprung free from his jeans. She smiled over her shoulder before stepping forward and straddling him.

Her heels were high enough to allow her to plant her feet on the floor as she lowered herself onto his dick, arching her back as she slid down. He looked over her shoulder, watching us as he grabbed her ass and guided her as she rode him.

With her skirt pushed out of the way, I could see his cock slipping in and out of her. I felt the wetness start to pool in my panties, knowing that I was completely turned on right now.

"Are you enjoying watching them fuck?" Jared asked as he kissed down the side of my neck.

I nodded, unable to speak as she started to fuck him faster. Her ass bounced perfectly as he held on. I panted in rhythm with them, feeling myself on the verge of needing a release. My body was ready and desperate to be touched.

"Can I get you something to drink?" a female's voice asked, startling me.

I jumped and whipped my head around. My heart raced against my chest, feeling like it was going to explode as I waited for it to get back to a normal pace.

"Sorry," she laughed, clutching her notepad to her chest as she looked sympathetically at me. "I didn't mean to startle you."

"It's her first time here," Jared explained, gently rubbing his hand on my back.

"Ahh," she said and grinned. "What do you think so far?"

"I'm not sure," I laughed nervously, feeling embarrassed that I had gotten caught.

"Trust me, you'll see and hear a lot in here. Nothing surprises us anymore." She waved dismissively as if people having sex in front of her was an everyday thing. Which, apparently, it was.

I pulled in a slow, steady breath, trying to calm myself. She was still standing in front of our table, watching as another couple started fucking on a table on the other side of the room. She frowned and shook her head.

"Give me a minute," she sighed. "I'll be right back."

She walked away, giving us a few minutes as she went to talk to them.

"You doing alright?" he asked, squeezing my hand a few times.

"Yeah," I breathed, finally calming down a little. "I wasn't expecting this at all."

"You mentioned that you might like to be watched when we had sex on the stage. So I thought this would be a good place to start. There's no pressure to do anything, and if you start to feel uncomfortable, we can leave."

"I don't want to leave," I quickly assured him. "Does that make me a pervert?"

He let his head fall back with laughter.

"You and everyone in here."

I felt the corners of my lips turn up into a smile.

A few minutes later, the waitress was heading our way again.

"Sorry about that," she apologized. "We have very few rules, but sex *on* the tables is one of them. The last thing anyone should want is a shard of glass cutting their ass when it breaks."

"Ouch," I shivered at the thought.

"Alright, so what can I get you guys to drink?"

"I'll have a glass of wine," I said. "A merlot if you have it."

She nodded and wrote it down before looking at Jared.

"Just water," he replied with a smile.

She nodded and tucked the pad under her arm before walking over to the next table to check on them.

"You didn't want anything to drink?" I asked.

He shook his head and wrapped his arm around my waist.

"I'm already fuzzy-headed from all of the blood in my body rushing to my dick, the last thing that I need right now is alcohol," he joked.

I laughed and leaned into him, feeling more relaxed being there. The couple next to us had finished while we were talking to the waitress and left. A new couple had taken the seats at the empty table next to where they had been sitting.

The room was getting fuller, but there were still plenty of empty seats around us, which allowed me to feel a little more hidden as I watched everyone else.

A few more waitresses made their way through the room, and I noticed that they all had the same body paint as the one I had seen when we first walked in.

"Are they elves?" I asked, nodding to the two that were heading our way. One was our waitress with our drinks, the other I hadn't seen before.

"They like to do themes," Jared shrugged.

"Here you go," the waitress said as she set my glass down next to his water. "If you guys need anything else, just let one of us know."

They both smiled before walking away.

"I almost had you wear the green leggings," he joked before taking a drink of water.

"I would have fit in with the theme," I agreed. "But it definitely wouldn't look as good as their body paint."

"We can make that happen. I have some paint at home."

I turned to find him grinning as he wiggled his eyebrows. I shook my head and smiled, leaning into him as we watched the people around us.

"Thank you for bringing me here," I said quietly.

"Thank you for trusting me. I knew that it was a risk, and you would either love it or hate it," he laughed. "But I thought, given the nature of our gifts earlier, it was fitting to keep with the theme.”

I let out a slow, deep breath, thankful that my heart didn’t feel like it was going to explode out of my chest anymore.

“I love it, almost as much as I love you.”

He wrapped his arm around me and pulled me closer to him before whispering, “I love you too.”

Twenty One
Jared

"That was amazing," I sighed, looking over at Everly.

"So amazing," she agreed, pulling the white sheet up to cover her body. "Do you think they'll get mad and come kick us out if we don't get dressed soon?"

"Well, it was a *one-hour* couple's massage, so probably."

"Ugh," she groaned, sitting up and throwing her legs over the side of the table. "I could've stayed there all day and fallen asleep."

"Me too," I laughed, getting up and letting the sheet fall on the table behind me. I grabbed my robe from the hook on the wall and turned around to find her standing there, watching me.

"You better be careful," I warned. "I have no problem going up front and seeing if they'll let me pay for another hour. This time *without* the masseuse."

"Well, then I guess it's a good thing that we already have a room."

"Dinner first," I growled.

While I was anxious to get back to the room and make love

to her all night, I was starving—probably from our morning sex session—and ready to eat.

"Alright, alright," she joked, pulling the robe tight against her body. "Let's go get changed, and we'll head down to the steakhouse."

I nodded in relief and ushered her out of the room before she could change her mind.

We had spent the entire week together after Christmas. The night at *Euphoria* had changed things between us, and we found that we couldn't stay away from each other if we tried. We also went back a handful of times since then. For now, she was content with watching others and getting turned on before coming home and fucking my brains out. But I could tell that she was slowly getting more and more turned on by the idea of having someone else watch us.

I knew it was something she was interested in the first time we had sex, which was why I had taken her to the club, to begin with. I was relieved when she said that she liked it there and asked to go back. Each time she let me do something more than the time before, and just last night had let me finger her under the table while the waitress took our order.

We went up to our rooms and got ready. I called to confirm our reservation and smiled when they asked if we wanted to come earlier as they just had a cancelation. I quickly agreed and rushed Everly down there, loving the sound of her giggling along the way.

I watched as she ordered, smiling at the way she chewed her bottom lip as she tried to decide on which side she wanted with her steak. There were so many things that I loved about her that I hadn't noticed with other women before. At the end of the day, it felt like there was no one else in the world, but her and that was a place I wanted to spend forever.

****

Be sure to grab the bonus epilogue here:
https://bit.ly/3Qr1uUD

A Very Merry Kissmas

Samantha Baca

Cover Design: Richard Baca
Image (s): DepositPhotos

<u>One</u>
Lucy

"Yes, Nana, I made it just fine. I'm at the cabin now."

I pressed my shoulder into the door as I held it open with my foot and struggled to free the key from the lock.

"I hate you being there all by yourself during Christmas," she said sadly.

"Don't worry about it. I'm fine, I promise. I wanted to be alone and spend it snowed in, somewhere in the middle of nowhere, with nothing to worry about and no pressing deadlines breathing down my neck. This is perfect. Thank you again for letting me come up here."

"Well, it's far from perfect." She sighed heavily on the other end. "I admit that I haven't taken care of it as well as I should have after your grandpa passed away. I'm getting too old to handle the things that I used to, and quite frankly, I have no idea how to do the things he took care of. I have someone who started doing some renovations, but unfortunately, there was too much to be done to have it ready before you got there."

"It has four walls and a fireplace. I think I'll manage just fine. I'm going to let you go so I can grab the groceries out of the car and unpack before it gets dark out." I spotted a coat hanging on the rack by the door, relieved to have something warmer to put on to go back outside. It was colder than I expected but surprisingly warm inside the cabin. Maybe I really was just frozen to the bone.

"Okay honey, enjoy your break and call me on Christmas if you can. I would love to at least hear your voice if I can't see your face."

"Will do, Nana. Love you."

"Love you too, sweetheart. Enjoy your night."

"You too," I answered as I pulled the other coat over what I already had on.

We hung up, and I grabbed the keys out of my pocket, ready to go grab my stuff when I suddenly heard running water. I stood still, tilting my head, trying to find where the noise was coming from. I knew there were a lot of things that needed to be renovated in the cabin, but she didn't say anything about a water leak. *That* was the last thing I needed to deal with right now.

I tiptoed down the hallway, scrunching my face as the wooden planks creaked beneath me.

I stopped outside of the bathroom, frowning when I found the door closed and steam billowing out underneath it.

What in the hell was going on? Why hadn't I thought to go through the house and search it for intruders the second I came in? Probably because it's on the top of a mountain, and no one in their right mind would go out of their way to come up here just to hide in the shadows, waiting to murder someone when they finally showed up.

I lifted my fist, ready to pound on the door and demand that whoever it was come out immediately, and then realized I didn't have anything to use as a weapon. I looked around and found a pool noodle that had been tossed into the spare room, likely from when my brother brought his wife and kids up over the summer to enjoy the lake at the bottom of the mountain.

I bent down, picked it up, and gripped it like a baseball bat.

I widened my feet, locked my knees, and swung a few times, ready to take on whoever was on the other side.

The sound of heavy metal drifted through the door seconds before it swung open, and I was startled by a gorgeous specimen wearing nothing but a towel around his toned waist.

"Freeze!" I yelled, raising my arms threateningly as the noodle flopped behind my head.

I narrowed my eyes and held my stance as he eyed me suspiciously, leaning casually against the doorframe. The towel started to shift and he made no effort to grab it. The outline of a one-eyed monster taunting me from beneath.

"Who are you, and what are you doing here?" I demanded, trying to make my soft voice sound intimidating.

"You must be Lucy," he answered, ignoring my question.

"How do you know my name?" I kept my eyes on him, trying to ignore the perfectly sculpted muscles that ran along his chest and abdomen, begging to be touched.

I did, however, take a few seconds to allow myself to check out the tattoos covering his skin—but that wasn't because I enjoyed them—it was a protective measure so I could give the information to the police and ID the intruder.

He was 6'1, lean build with muscles protruding everywhere—and I mean everywhere. Dark gray eyes that hid beneath wild, wet hair that had fallen across his forehead until strong hands brushed it away. Well-groomed, with a thin goatee that dotted his jawline. A cross tattoo that covered his chest with a rose in the center and a woman's name written beneath it. A few smaller tattoos that covered his biceps and one on his thigh that I couldn't see all of because the towel was covering it. Stupid towel.

He cleared his throat and pulled my attention back to him.

"You didn't answer my question—how do you know my name?"

"Your grandma told me you might stop by."

"Well, that's funny because she didn't mention anything to me."

"Is that supposed to be a weapon?" he asked, pointing to the pool noodle still being held in a death grip between my fingers.

"Maybe."

"What exactly were you planning to do with it? Whip me to death?"

He shifted his position slightly, but that didn't stop my eyes from immediately following the bulge beneath the towel, hoping for a glimpse.

"I don't have to explain myself to you," I said quietly, lowering the noodle to my side before tossing it back into the spare bedroom. "If anything, *you're* the one who needs to explain what *you're* doing here."

"Your grandma hired me to do some renovations."

She had mentioned that she had hired someone to get started on them but failed to mention that said person would still be here. Why hadn't she said anything and spared me an awkward surprise? I would have skipped the whole 'snowed in on a mountain' idea and booked myself a spa weekend at the Hilton instead.

"Okay, well, let me know when you're done, and I'll see you out."

"I'm actually done for the day. I was just getting ready to turn in for the night."

I shook my head, trying to clear the confusion so I could focus on what he was saying.

"So, what, do you like live close by or something?" I couldn't remember seeing any new houses that had been built since the last time I'd been up here.

"No," he paused as a grin spread across his devilishly handsome face. "I live here."

Two
Lucy

"Nana! You have some serious explaining to do!" I hissed into the phone, covering the mouthpiece as I hid in the bathroom.

"Did you see Dick?"

"NANA!"

How in the world was she being so nonchalant about this? It was one thing to know that he might still be up here when I got here, but it was another to just come out and ask me if I'd seen his wiener. Nana had always been a little cheeky, but even this was more direct than usual.

"What? Either you saw Dick, or you didn't. There's no need to scream about it."

I ran a hand over my face and tried to steady myself with deep breaths.

"No, Nana, I didn't see dick. He was wearing a towel, but it's not like he just whipped it off and gave me a show or anything," I said sarcastically, rolling my eyes that I was even having this conversation with her.

She burst into laughter on the other end, so loud that I had to pull my phone away from my ear because she was hurting it.

"Oh dear, sweet girl," she said with a chuckle. "His *name* is Dick. It's short for Richard."

My heart dropped in my chest as embarrassment washed over me.

"Oh. My. God. Why didn't you say something sooner?!"

"What was I supposed to say?"

"I don't know, maybe a heads up of—hey, there's this really sexy guy who's staying in the cabin doing renovations, and his name is Dick would have been helpful."

"I was sure he would be gone before you arrived. His mom said that she thought he was leaving this morning to come home for Christmas, so I figured it was pointless to tell you if he wasn't going to be there. I bet she will be disappointed that he won't make it after all. But I agree, he is quite handsome."

"Why won't he make it? I'm here now so he can leave and be on his way."

I ignored her comment about how attractive he was because I didn't need her getting any wild ideas in her head and trying to play matchmaker while I was up here.

"There's no way he would make it down the mountain now. The storm has already rolled in, so he's stuck up there until it passes."

"No," I countered in disbelief. "There has to be a way. What about the sled Grandpa used to have?"

"You're suggesting that he sled down the mountain in the middle of a blizzard?"

"I mean, it could be fun." I shrugged, judging myself in the mirror for being so petty right now. "I could give him a push just to make sure he got a good start."

"Lucy Nicole, you know better than that," she scolded. "I'm sorry that you have unexpected company, but I have to admit that it makes me feel a little better about you being up there by yourself this weekend. He really is such a wonderful man, kindhearted and caring."

"Then why did you offer to let me stay here if you were worried about me being by myself?"

"That was before I saw how bad the storm was going to get. I just caught the 5 o'clock news, and they said that Cedar Point is in for a real doozy. It's been building all day, but you were already on the road, and I didn't want to distract you while you were driving. I knew that if you could get to the cabin, you'd be fine."

"But you don't think I can take care of myself in a storm?"

"I think you can manage just fine, but you're a big city girl, Lucy. If the power goes out in the city, it's usually back on after a few hours. If you lose power in the cabin, it could be days or weeks before it comes back on again. Dick grew up here. He's used to the weather and knows how to improvise when needed. I know that he'll keep you safe and make sure that both of you have what you need to ride out the blizzard."

"Fine. I guess I don't have a choice since he's stuck here now. I can stay in the guest room since I'm guessing he's already claimed the master bedroom."

"Ummm," she hesitated. "About that."

"What?" Panic was spreading through me again. I hated the unexpected.

"There is no guestroom. After your brother stayed there this summer, we decided everything needed a major re-haul. Dick just discarded the rickety mattress and tossed the frame since the kids broke it while they were there. That thing was old and had seen better days."

I let my head fall forward and closed my eyes.

"Okay, so then, what are my options? Sleep on the couch? Use the recliner?"

"I wouldn't do that either," she laughed. "Nelly broke the springs in the couch while they were there. Your brother tried to fix it, but it was so old that he couldn't. I ordered new furniture last week, but it won't arrive until early January. Everyone is backed up right now, so we're at the mercy of when they can get it up the mountain and delivered."

"Lovely. Maybe this wasn't a good idea," I mumbled, instantly regretting my decision to come up here to *get away*. I'd left corporate hell in Phoenix to deal with small-town-stuck-on-a-mountain-with-a-stranger hell.

"I'm sorry, honey. I'm sure you'll find a way to make the best of it. But I've got to get going. Earl is dressed up as Santa at the senior center this year, and I'm next to sit on his lap and tell him what I want—if you know what I mean."

Before I could say anything, she hung up. I leaned against the door and counted to ten. Whether I was ready or not, I needed to face the sexy hunk that I would now be spending Christmas with.

A VERY MERRY KISSMAS

Three
Rich

When my grandma warned me that Millie's granddaughter might come up to the cabin for Christmas, I wasn't sure what to expect. It had been years since my grandma had seen her, and all she could tell me was that Lucy was a fireball bigshot VP of a cosmetics company from Phoenix.

I had planned to get back down the mountain this morning, but a pipe burst in the bathroom, which required me to stay and deal with it. When I went into town to grab some supplies, I got one look at the clouds rolling in and knew I wouldn't be able to get out before the storm hit. I grabbed some necessities, making sure that I had plenty of food and water to get me through until I could get back to town again.

By the time Lucy came out of the bathroom, I was already dressed in a pair of gray sweatpants that hung low on my hips and a Cedar Point Bulldogs t-shirt. I wasn't huge on sports, but I wore their name proudly, given that my brother was their pitcher. They weren't too bad for a minor-league team that could fill the seats of every game.

When I walked in, Lucy was pacing the living room, looking for something.

"Everything alright?" I asked, trying to keep any hints of humor out of my voice, but it was hard with how adorable she looked.

Her straight brown hair was now piled on top of her head beneath a beanie, and her small frame was being eaten up by the oversized jacket she had on.

"Yeah. I need to go get stuff out of my car before it gets too late."

I glanced past her to the floor-to-ceiling window and arched an eyebrow. It was already pitch-black outside, and I could hear the wind howling as it whipped past.

"I think you missed that window about an hour ago. Tell me what you need, and I'll go get it."

"It's fine," she said, shaking her head. "You don't need to do that. I'll go."

She patted her pockets and then rolled her eyes, pulling a set of keys out.

"I would lose my head if it weren't attached," she murmured.

"My grandma would never forgive me if I allowed you to go out in this. Just give me the keys and tell me what you need."

"Don't worry, I won't tell. But I'm not going to have you run out in the storm to fetch my stuff. I'm a grown, independent woman and can get it myself."

"Would you stop being stubborn and just give me the keys?"

I sighed impatiently.

"You're not dressed to go out in that storm—you don't even have a jacket on."

"That's because you're wearing it."

She looked down and her face flushed with embarrassment again.

"Oh. I'm sorry. I saw it hanging by the door and just assumed…"

"That it was your grandma's? She's even shorter than you. She would trip over it." I laughed.

"No," she scoffed, narrowing her eyes at me. "I was going to say that I thought it was my brother's. And come to think of it, he's even bigger than you are. It probably wouldn't have fit him anyway."

I rubbed the back of my neck and shook my head, unsure what to do with her.

"While I would love to stand here and compare who is bigger, we don't have time for it. If I don't get the stuff from your car now, you're not getting it for a few days."

She scrunched her face and folded her arms over her chest.

"And why is that?"

"Because the snow is coming down faster than I can clear it. Give it another thirty minutes, and you won't even be able to find your car. Now give me the keys and tell me what you need."

She chewed her lower lip and then gave in, seeming to know she needed my help more than she wanted to admit. She shrugged off my jacket, gave me the keys, and followed me to the door to tell me what to grab and where it was.

Four
Lucy

Dick was right that the snow would completely devour my car, only it happened in twenty minutes, not thirty. I wondered why I didn't see his truck when I arrived, but he informed me that he had parked back by the shed. There was a clearing and the sun would melt the snow quicker once it came out again.

He grabbed the suitcases from the backseat and brought them to me before groaning when I told him there were boxes of stuff I needed from the trunk.

He moved quickly, and I tried to ignore the way he handled everything as if it weighed nothing. It took me almost an hour to get everything packed into my car before I left Phoenix and less than fifteen minutes for him to unpack all of it. To say that I was impressed was an understatement.

Once everything was inside, we stacked it in the living room since there was nowhere else to store it.

"How long were you planning on staying?" he asked, hanging his jacket on the coat rack behind the door as a smile snaked across his handsome face.

"I'm leaving the day after Christmas."

I grabbed a few of the food bags and headed to the kitchen to unpack.

"This is what you need for a *few days*?"

"Yes. This is what I need for a few days, and I didn't expect to have to justify myself to anyone, *Dick*."

I felt childish for mocking his name, but I was still on edge and nervous about the sudden change in plans that now included me being stuck here with a complete stranger. He watched me from across the island while I lined up the frozen meals that needed to go in the freezer.

"Can you please stop calling me Dick?"

I looked up and found dark gray eyes watching me.

"Why? That's your name, isn't it?" This time I was serious, and the mocking tone was completely gone from my voice. That was what Nana had called him, and she wouldn't lie to me or try to embarrass me by calling him that if it wasn't really his name.

"Technically, my name is Richard, but I go by Rich. Only my grandma and yours call me Dick. It's an old family name that my grandma insisted on keeping in the family when my mom had me."

"Oh, sorry. I didn't know. I won't call you that anymore."

"Thank you."

I lowered my head and avoided looking at him as I kept working.

"What's with all the frozen food?" he asked, nodding to the piles in front of me, effectively changing the topic for us.

I folded the tote bags and set them to the side before grabbing another one, desperate to keep myself busy so I could avoid looking at him.

"That's what I eat." I shrugged, not seeing what the problem was.

"You don't like real food?"

"It is real food," I countered. "It's just been preserved and frozen, so I can enjoy it whenever I want."

"You know as well as I do that those things don't taste nearly as good as a freshly cooked meal."

"Maybe. But some of us don't have the time to spend hours in the kitchen making meals for ourselves. I've been eating these for so long that I don't think about them anymore."

I hadn't realized until now just how long I had been in the mundane routine of getting home late every night and popping a frozen meal into the microwave, not even bothering to look at what it was first. When was the last time I had cooked? Better yet, when was the last time I'd sat down and enjoyed a freshly cooked meal?

He leaned against the counter behind him and studied me.

"You're a VP of a cosmetics company, right?"

"Yeah. How did you know?" I raised an eyebrow as I glanced up briefly while unpacking the last bag.

"Your grandma told me. She talks about you a lot."

I felt the heat prickle my cheeks as the embarrassment of what she might have been saying to him entered my mind. *Was she sitting around telling him embarrassing stories about me from when I was little? Had she told him about the time I lost control of the sled and hit a telephone pole straight on? Oh my GOD—had she shown him any of my baby photos?*

"Hopefully, all good things," I said, laughing nervously. "I feel bad that I don't call and check in with her as often as I'd like to."

The guilt started to eat at me the same way it always did anytime I thought about Nana. I was used to being busy and always on the go. It never bothered me because growing up, my parents were the same way. They both had busy, demanding jobs that required them to work long hours. My brother and I had spent a lot of time with my grandparents growing up, but once I finished high school, I was determined to get as far away from small-town Colorado as I could.

"I'm sure she understands," he said softly. "She's proud of you and everything you've accomplished. To be a VP by the time you're 25. Wow." He whistled through his teeth and tapped the counter with his knuckles before pushing off it.

"Thank you." I tucked my chin to my chest and avoided looking at him as I tried to absorb his compliments. I wasn't used to getting *this* kind of male attention, and my body reacted to it in a way that would leave me in an uncomfortable bind, given that there was only one bed, and we would both have to share it.

Five
Rich

The night went by faster than I had expected. I also hadn't expected to have company or to be figuring out how to share a full-sized bed with a beautiful stranger. When I met Millie up here a few weeks ago to talk about the demo work, she agreed that the beds in both the master and guest bedroom needed to be replaced. I'd taken the liberty of bringing over a blow-up mattress since I would be living here for a few months while I worked. It made more sense than driving an hour up and an hour back down the mountain every day to get to my home in Cedar Point.

"I can sleep on the floor," she said, looking nervously at the mattress as we stood in front of it.

"I don't think so. There's no way in hell that I'm letting you sleep on the floor. I'll sleep there if it makes you that uncomfortable to share the bed."

"I'm not going to let you sleep on the floor either," she scoffed. "I'm not kicking you out of your bed."

"Then it looks like we're sharing it." I placed my hands on my hips and smiled.

The wind was howling outside, so I knew it was only a matter of time before we lost power, which meant we would also lose heat. There was a fireplace in the living room, but tonight we would be more comfortable in the bedroom, where we could close the door and trap some of the heat in there until the morning.

"Okay, fine." She sighed heavily and looked around. "Which side do you want?"

"Take whichever one makes you more comfortable."

She eyed me for a moment before pointing to the right.

"I'm a side sleeper and sleep more on my left side. I'll take the right side so I don't startle you if you wake up and my face is next to yours."

"I think I'll be fine," I replied with a laugh.

"I wouldn't count on it," she said under her breath, climbing onto the mattress and pulling the blanket over her. She was smart and brought some thick sweats to sleep in, which would help fight off the cold once we lost power.

"Why do you say that?" I asked, waiting until she was settled before climbing in beside her.

"Because I'm an active mover in my sleep. I go to sleep in one spot and wake up in another. I also talk in my sleep when I'm stressed out, and sometimes, I get up and do things."

"Okay, maybe this was a bad idea," I teased, pulling the blankets back as I pretended to get out.

"You laugh now, but I'm serious. One time, I slapped my brother while he was in the sleeping bag beside me. It happened in this very cabin, out in the living room. He still gives me crap about it."

"What?" I laughed harder. "He still gives you shit over something you did as a kid?"

"No, it was last year." She winked at me over her shoulder before pulling the blankets under her chin. "Good night."

I laid down and shook my head, wondering what kind of night we had in store for us.

A few hours later, I was woken up by the sound of someone talking.

I rolled over and found Lucy twirling her hair around her finger while saying something to the wall across from her. Thankfully, she had warned me about talking in her sleep, otherwise, this might have freaked me out.

I couldn't remember what you were supposed to do with people who sleep talked or sleepwalked. I didn't want to startle her since she was still asleep, but she was also getting so loud that I couldn't sleep.

"Hey, Lucy," I said softly, trying to get her attention.

She didn't respond, simply just kept on with what she was doing.

I tried again, a little louder this time.

"Lucy, wake up."

Nothing.

I reached over and gently removed her finger from her hair and lowered her hand to her side. She curled it up into the blankets and shifted again. I thought for sure she was going back to sleep, but she just kept talking this time. Something about the tide going above the rocks, and if they didn't get out soon, the trolls were going to find them and eat them. Part of me wanted to stay up and listen to her stories because they were hilarious, but the other part of me was exhausted and needed sleep.

I gripped her shoulder and shook gently but with enough force to get her to turn over. Her eyes were open, but they didn't seem to focus on anything.

"Lucy?" I questioned, unsure of whether she was still asleep. It was dark in the room, so it was hard to tell for sure.

I shook her again, this time a little harder until she rolled over on her back. Her eyelashes fluttered as she blinked rapidly, trying to clear the sleep.

"What's wrong?" she whispered, looking around cautiously.

"Nothing, you were talking a lot, and it was getting louder, so I tried to wake you up."

"Oh, I'm sorry." She pulled her lips into a thin line and pulled the blankets up higher. "I told you I do that often when I'm stressed.

"I know, it's okay."

"If I do it again, just wake me up. I'll do my best not to, but I really can't control it."

"Okay."

We got situated, and she was back asleep before I knew it. It took me longer, but thankfully my body was tired enough to give in without much of a fight.

<u>Six</u>
Lucy

I woke up the next morning tired and sore from sleeping on the air mattress. I missed my comfortable bed and the expensive pillows I had in Phoenix that helped wick the heat away from my head as I slept. I looked over and wasn't surprised to find Rich was already out of bed—if you could even call it that.

I stretched and got up, reminding myself I needed to take some time today for yoga and maybe a long, hot bath if the tub was still standing. I didn't look in the master bathroom last night to see what—if anything—had been done with renovations yet, but prayed that the large soaking tub my Nana had insisted on years before my grandpa died was still there.

The smell of coffee and bacon floated down the hallway, making me full on alert as my stomach growled. I had brought some granola bars and a handful of frozen breakfast sandwiches up with me, but I couldn't deny that the food Rich was cooking smelled heavenly.

I walked into the kitchen and cleared my throat, alerting him to my presence as he stood at the stove, flipping an egg in the pan.

"Good morning," I said, wringing my hands together anxiously in front of him.

"Morning."

He smiled over his shoulder before turning his attention back to the stove, but not before I caught a glimpse of a subtle bruise under his eye that wasn't there before.

"What happened to your eye?" I asked, walking over to get a better look.

He winced as he glanced at me, not letting me see it.

"Rich, what happened? Are you okay?"

"I'm fine," he insisted, transferring the fried egg to a plate. "Do you want eggs?"

I shook my head, trying to clear some of the morning fog still lingering around me.

"I have frozen breakfast sandwiches, but thank you. What happened to your eye?" I asked for what felt like the fortieth time.

He set the spatula down and turned to face me.

"You punched me in your sleep."

I gasped and covered my mouth with my hands.

"What? When? Oh my God, I am so sorry!"

"About an hour after I woke you up the first time. It's okay," he said, lifting his hands to keep me from reaching forward to touch it. "I'm fine. Really."

I stepped away, covering my face with my hands to hide my embarrassment.

"It's not fine. I can't believe I did that."

"It's not like it was on purpose. Was it?" His brows pulled together as he asked, his lips threatening to curl up into a smile at any minute.

"No," I laughed nervously. "It definitely wasn't on purpose. I am mortified."

"Don't be. It happens." He shrugged and cracked a few eggs into the pan before sprinkling salt and pepper over them.

"Does it, though? Because I can bet that if you polled 100 random people, you would be the only one who was accidentally punched in your sleep by a random girl sleeping beside you."

"Well, when you put it like that." He chuckled and gave me another delicious wink, his gray eyes inviting me to get lost in their depths.

I looked away, trying to spare myself from any further embarrassment.

"What can I do to make it up to you? Just say the word," I offered. The cabin was clean aside from where renovations were happening, so it wasn't like I could do much there, but I could try to help with something else. Anything else if it meant that I didn't continue to be eaten alive by the guilt that was consuming me.

"Have breakfast with me," he suggested, a flirty tone in his voice.

"Okay, sure. Let me grab one of my sandwiches, and I'll heat it real quick."

I went to open the freezer door beside me when he reached over and grabbed my arm, stopping me.

"What are you doing?"

"That's not breakfast. Have a *real* meal with me."

I chewed my lower lip, unsure how to answer him.

"I didn't bring anything other than the freezer stuff."

"So." He shrugged, flipping the eggs.

"I already took half your bed and beat you up while you slept. I don't want to take your food too."

He stopped and turned to face me again after moving the eggs to a plate and turning off the burner.

"You make it sound like I got attacked by some madman in the streets."

"Well…" I squinted my eyes and shrugged my shoulders. It wasn't a complete stretch of the truth.

"It's fine. I just need to know what you want. There's bacon, hash browns, and fried eggs. Tell me if you don't want something; otherwise, I'll fix you a plate."

"It all sounds delicious, thank you. Is there anything I can help with?"

He turned back to the stove and began serving the rest of the food onto plates.

"I've got it, thanks. I made a pot of coffee that you're welcome to, or there's juice in the fridge. Grab a drink, and breakfast will be ready in a minute."

I did as he asked and fixed myself a cup of coffee before joining him at the table in the kitchen. Everything smelled delicious, and I couldn't remember the last time that I stopped and sat down to enjoy a meal, and that thought made me sad.

We ate and made small talk, filling the awkward silence of two people forced to stay together who didn't know each other. Once we were done, I insisted on cleaning up since he'd done all the cooking. He went out to gather some wood from the screened-in porch, expecting that the power would go out soon.

It was surprising that it hadn't gone out already, but I was also thankful because I could use a nice, hot shower and didn't want to get stuck taking one in the dark. There was a small frosted window in the bathroom and a skylight that didn't bring in much light because of the thick tree branches that hung over it.

While Rich gathered the wood, I excused myself to go clean up. But really, it was just because I needed to get away from watching his toned body move the way it was every time he hauled wood in and tossed it into the bins beside the fireplace. He was strong and muscular in all the right places, with calloused hands that promised me a good time.

A VERY MERRY KISSMAS

Seven
Rich

As expected, the power went out around two in the afternoon as the wind speed increased, and the snow fell in a blanket around us. We couldn't see anything outside through the windows; everything completely covered in white.

I had brought the last few loads of wood in before it really came down and set them in the living room corner while Lucy finished her shower. I didn't want to risk leaving them out on the porch, knowing that the snow would come in through the screen and get them all wet. Wet wood was the worst kind of wood unless a woman was involved.

I could hear the moment the power went out because she cursed loudly as if she had forgotten that I might be there. When she joined me in the living room wearing a Cedar Point Bulldog hoodie, I couldn't help but grin and wonder where she had gotten it and why she decided to bring it.

"What's with the grin?" she asked with a smile, pulling her legs under her as she sat in the oversized, worn-out recliner. "Did you hear me cussing in the shower and were worried that I was going to come attack you again?"

"No, I only worry about that when you're sleeping." I ran a hand smoothly across my face, trailing over the bruise she gave me. "Nice hoodie. Where did you get it?"

She pulled it away from her body and looked down as if she didn't remember what she was wearing.

"Oh, this? I got it from my Nana last year for Christmas. She goes on and on about the *best minor league baseball team of all time*." She used air quotes and an old lady voice to mimic her grandma. "Not only that, but I hear all about how the starting pitcher has the *cutest* little tooshie she's ever seen."

"I'll be sure to tell my brother," I said, my grin spreading wider as she gave me a curious glance.

"Why would your brother care?"

"Because it's his cute little tooshie she's talking about."

Her eyes bulged as she leaned forward and stared at me.

"Your brother is the starting pitcher for the Cedar Point Bulldogs?" she asked, gripping the armrests tightly.

"He's one of them. But definitely the most popular. Probably because he has the best butt. It runs in the family." I winked.

"Oh my God," she said with a giggle. "I can't believe my Nana is checking your brother out."

"Eh, he's used to it. All the women of Cedar Point do it. Hell, half of them have posters of him taped to their bedroom walls."

She scrunched her face and pretended to shiver.

I finished organizing the firewood in the built-ins next to the fireplace, admiring her grandpa for his design. It was beautiful and functional to have it off the floor and sitting right beside the fireplace so you could toss it in when needed. I also filled the extra baskets I'd found when looking for stuff in the shed the other day, just in case we ran low and required more before the storm passed.

"So, what do you do for the holiday?" I asked, looking over my shoulder as I finished up, noticing the way her eyes trailed over my ass.

Was she checking me out?

It wasn't the first time I thought she might have been, but the way she licked her lips as I leaned forward confirmed it.

I cleared my throat, startling her as her eyes quickly darted up and locked on mine.

I stood up, folded my arms, and watched her.

"I'm sorry, what?"

"I asked what you do for Christmas, but you were a little distracted, checking out my ass."

Her jaw dropped open as a flush of color kissed her cheeks. Her hair was pulled up into a messy bun on her head again, giving me the perfect view of it happening.

"What? I was not!"

"Hey, I know it's not as cute as my brother's, but I'd like to think it's still impressive. I do squats, you know."

"I swear, I wasn't checking you out," she whispered, her eyes widening again as I walked over and stood in front of her.

"Oh yeah? Then why are you blushing? It's because you got caught checking my ass out, and now you're trying to deny it." I lifted her chin with my finger, bringing her eyes up to mine. "Don't worry. I've been checking yours out, too."

<u>Eight</u>
Lucy

I couldn't believe that Rich had caught me checking out his ass. I was trying to be discreet, but I couldn't focus on anything other than how tight it was. Oh, and how I wanted to run my hands all over it before gripping it as he plowed into me. Not that he had offered or anything.

We sat in awkward silence for a few minutes until he got up and went outside for something, letting a rush of cold air in before he closed the door. I took a few minutes to gather myself and to try to quell the aching that was building between my thighs. Sure, it had been a dry spell of a few weeks, but that didn't mean I needed to jump his bones right now.

Okay, it was more than a few weeks. More like months. Twelve of them, to be exact. Twelve painfully dry months with nothing but my trusty vibrator to get me off when I needed it. Which, with the stress I faced constantly at work— was all the time. I was so impressed with its durability that I debated writing to Dark Vibes and complimenting them on such an incredible product. But how did one really write a raving review in an email about how much she loved their Dark Vibes G-Shocker without sounding a bit like a pervert?

I shifted in the recliner, trying to get comfortable, when I heard the door fling open, getting caught in a gust of wind. I turned around to find Rich stumbling in with boxes piled in his arms as he struggled to kick the door shut.

"Do you need some help?" I offered, getting up and rushing over.

"If you can get the door, that would be great."

He stepped out of the way while I pushed my weight into it, fighting against the wind until it finally closed and the lock latched into place.

"That wind is ridiculous," I muttered, following him into the living room, where he set the boxes down in front of the coffee table. "What's all that?"

"Well, I hope you don't mind, but I called your grandma and got the okay to bring the Christmas stuff out of the shed."

"You called my grandma?" I asked as my mind struggled to process the rest of his sentence. "What Christmas stuff?"

He bent down and lifted the lid to one of the boxes, revealing the decorations we used to put on the tree when I was a little girl. I covered my mouth with my hands when he lifted the angel tree topper and handed her to me.

It was always my favorite decoration, and I hadn't seen it in almost ten years. Once my grandpa got sick, we stopped coming to the cabin for Christmas and spent the holiday at their farmhouse in Cedar Point since it was too much on my grandparents to come up here.

"You didn't answer me earlier about what you do for

Christmas, but I could tell you seemed sad when I mentioned it. I came across these boxes a few weeks ago while cleaning the shed with your grandma. I thought maybe we could decorate since it is Christmas Eve." He shrugged and planted his hands on his hips while waiting for me to respond.

"I can't believe you did this," I whispered, clutching the angel to my chest.

His face fell, worry etched across his features.

"No," I assured him, crossing the room to where he stood. "This is amazing, thank you."

"Whew. I thought you were going to punch me again," he teased.

I shook my head and laughed.

"I'm not asleep. You're safe for now."

He winked and then began unpacking the artificial tree from the box while I sorted through the ornaments.

It felt like I had been transported back to my childhood, and memories washed over me in waves, pulling at my heartstrings and knotting them deep in my stomach. There were so many wonderful trips spent up here that I grew sad trying to remember the last time we had all been up here as a family.

The cabin was my grandpa's pride and joy. It was small and cozy, but he somehow worked magic to fit everyone in it when we all came up. It was always elaborately decorated on the inside and out, with warm lights creating the perfect ambiance to go with the apple cinnamon scent that was always softly permeating the air.

Once he got sick, everyone stopped coming up to the cabin, and I remembered how disappointed he looked. The fights he had with my grandma when he tried to reassure her he was fine and could make the trip up, even though we all knew how risky it was to get stuck up there without access to his medical supplies if he ran out.

Tears stung my eyes as I tried to blink them away. I had been so busy with work and starting my life that I hadn't even been there much for the end of his. I didn't come during the final trip when my brother brought my grandpa up for the day to hang out in the cabin while my grandma and mother packed up their belongings. I had tried to convince myself back then that it was fine and that they didn't need my help, but now I realized it wasn't that at all. I had avoided coming because I didn't want to deal with the pain I knew I would see on my grandpa's face as he said goodbye for the last time.

I clutched the angel to my chest and cried, not bothering to hold back the tears. Sadness enveloped me as I trembled, overwhelmed by the emotions racing through me.

"Hey," Rich said, pulling me into his arms and holding me tightly. "What's wrong?"

"I wasn't here," I cried, sobbing against his hoodie, still clutching the angel. "My grandpa died, and I wasn't here for him when he needed me to be."

"Shhh," he whispered, rubbing my back. "It's okay, Lucy."

We stayed like that for a few minutes as I fell apart in his arms, years of regret eating away at me.

<u>Nine</u>
Rich

"I'm sorry about earlier," Lucy said, barely peeking up to look at me as she continued to wrap the string of lights around the tree, handing the strand to me so I could continue on my side before passing it to her. It was getting late into the evening, so we were doing our best to work with what light we had from the candles and lanterns I'd set up earlier.

"Don't be. It's okay to feel whatever you're feeling. I'm sorry for bringing the stuff out without asking first."

"No, it's perfect. I didn't plan to decorate at all, but now that we have everything and we're actually doing it, it feels really nice. Kinda puts me in the holiday spirit, I guess."

"Good, I'm glad."

I took the last of the strand and wrapped it around the base, leaving the plug next to the outlet. We stepped back and took it all in, though I could imagine it would look even better once the power was on and we could see it lit up. It was still pretty with the decorations and made it feel a little more like the holiday.

"It's beautiful," Lucy whispered, wrapping her arms

around herself as she stared at it. "It brings back so many memories."

I smiled and then went back to the box, pulling out a bag of fake snow. I looked at Lucy, watching as she leaned over to see what it was. Her eyebrow immediately raised in warning as I tore it open and grabbed a handful.

"What are you doing with that?" she asked, stepping back.

"Decorating."

"That's going to make a mess," she warned, moving away as I advanced closer.

"I'm not afraid of a little mess."

She took another step back, this time bumping into the couch that needed to be hauled out and taken to the dump. I had her just where I wanted her.

Without warning, I brought my hand back and threw the fake snow at her like I would a real snowball if I had one.

Tiny bits of white plastic floated in the air around her, green eyes dancing wildly as they watched the pieces fall, coating her hair before they did.

"You didn't!" she exclaimed, staring at me in disbelief.

"Oh, I did. Whatcha gonna do about it?"

I grabbed another handful from the bag and tucked it under my arm before launching another attack on her. She moved quickly, careful not to trip over the coffee table before making her way over to the box and grabbing the other bag.

"It's on," she warned, ripping it open so hard that a cloud of white exploded in front of her.

"Is it? Because I think you should be more worried about me getting you again before you even have a chance to get your bag opened right."

I grabbed another handful and wound my arm up like I'd seen my brother do a million times during practice.

"You can run, but you can't hide," I warned, following her into the kitchen as she ducked down behind the island. I walked slowly, creeping up on her, when suddenly she whipped around it and came out of nowhere, smacking me upside the head with fake snow.

"You sure about that?" she teased, licking her lips. She reached into her bag and grabbed another handful, lifting it above my head before slowly releasing her fingers and allowing it to rain down over my head.

There was something in her eyes at that moment that made me forget all about the competition. I wanted to get lost in the depths of her green eyes and follow the light that had suddenly appeared, making her entire face look angelic.

We were standing close to each other, nearly toe to toe, our breathing heavy as we locked eyes and refused to look away. There was a powerful pull that I could tell she felt too, because her body kept leaning closer to mine.

"Fuck," I growled, pulling her into me as our mouths crashed down on each other.

She whimpered and deepened the kiss, her hands going up into my hair and gripping it tightly. I lifted her to my hips, grabbing her ass as she rubbed herself against my groin.

"Should we stop?" I asked, barely pulling my mouth away for a split second to talk.

"No," she panted, grinding harder against me. "I don't want to stop. I want this. I want it so bad."

I carried her down the hall to the bedroom and groaned when I remembered all we had was an air mattress. I felt like a college kid all over again, trying to get it on without even having a decent bed to offer her.

"I'm sorry," I muttered against her lips.

"For what?"

"Not having an actual bed."

"I don't need one. Now take off your pants."

"So demanding."

"If you only knew."

I lowered her from my waist, making sure she was good on her feet before I let go.

"Strip," I said, nodding to her as I pulled my hoodie over my head and tossed it to the floor. Her green eyes studied me intently, watching every move as I undid my buckle and worked the zipper down on my jeans, giving her a show.

"Now, Lucy," I growled, my voice snapping her out of her trance.

Her eyes snapped up to mine as my jeans fell to the floor before I stepped out of them. She slowly lifted her hoodie, bringing it up over her head, but taking forever. I crossed the space between us, wearing nothing but a t-shirt and boxer briefs that barely contained my erection.

I grabbed the hoodie and freed her of it before tossing it across the room. She stood before me, wearing a black lace bra and tight yoga pants.

"Fuck me," I whispered, thinking about all the things I wanted to do to her.

"I was kinda hoping you would," she teased with a giggle.

"How much do you like these pants?" I asked, slipping my fingers into the waistband and pulling her closer to me.

"They're my favorite."

"Then I suggest you take them off before I rip them off you," I warned, giving her a minute to do as I asked.

 She moved quickly, keeping her eyes on me as she stripped down, showing off her bra and a matching thong.

I closed my eyes and bit my lip to keep from losing control and coming right then and there. I hadn't even touched her yet, and I was already losing it.

"You're so beautiful," I said, pulling her against my body again. My hands wandered over her smooth skin while my lips soaked up the taste of her skin, leaving goosebumps in their wake.

"Thank you," she replied softly, tipping her head back so I could kiss her neck while I rolled a pebbled nipple between my fingers through the thin lace of her bra.

"There are so many things that I want to do to you," I groaned. "But I don't think I can wait to be inside of you."

"I can't wait either."

I kissed her deeply, lifting her to my hips again as I walked us over to the dresser. I sat her on top of it, thankful that it wasn't too tall and looked sturdy enough for us to use. She spread her legs invitingly as I hooked my thumbs into the waistband of my boxer briefs and slid them down my legs. My erection sprung free, a drop of pre-cum glistening on top.

She licked her lips, watching as I stroked it slowly, teasing her as I stepped closer. I pinned her in as I reached to the side, grabbed my wallet from the top of the dresser, and retrieved a condom. I tried to steady my breathing as she leaned back on one hand and used the other to push her panties to the side, exposing her bare pussy to me. She licked her finger and then reached down and rubbed it down the middle of her slit, playing with herself as I locked every single movement into my memory and sheathed myself.

I stepped back slightly, mesmerized by how her features changed as she let her legs fall open wider, sliding a finger inside before pulling it out, coated with her wetness. She circled her clit, rubbing the moisture in a figure-eight pattern as her eyes pinched shut and her breathing grew rapid.

"Make yourself come," I urged, stroking my cock as she rubbed faster, already on the brink of an orgasm. "I want to see you come on your fingers."

She moaned and let her head fall back, holding herself up as her other hand came up and pulled the lace cup of her bra down. Her nipples were hard, begging to be sucked.

She rolled it between her fingers as her legs started to shake.

I wanted desperately to watch her as she fell apart, but I also couldn't keep myself from enjoying her tits that hung heavily above her stomach. I lowered my head and wrapped my lips around her nipple, sucking hard enough for her to hiss in response.

"Oh my gosh," she whimpered, rubbing herself faster. "I'm so close."

"Let me," I offered, letting go of my cock and pushing her hand away.

I replaced her finger with mine, my balls aching when I felt how fucking wet she was. I rubbed her in the same motion she had been rubbing herself, increasing the speed and pressure as her body reacted beneath me.

Within seconds, I felt the first spasm as her pussy locked against my finger, wrapping so tightly around it as she came. I continued to suck while I kept rubbing her clit, making sure she got every bit of that orgasm.

"Holy shit," she breathed, her dark lashes fluttering as she opened her eyes. "That was amazing."

I grinned and pulled my hand away long enough to grab my cock and line it up at her entrance.

"Good. Because we're just getting started."

Ten

Lucy

I tried to keep my eyes open so I could watch Rich's face as he plowed deep inside me, but it felt so good that I let my head fall back and just enjoyed every second. I couldn't remember the last time I'd been with someone, let alone the last time I had enjoyed sex. Usually, my mind was busy thinking about the laundry list of things I needed to do. Orgasms were never on those lists, given how infrequently they happened and how hard they were to come by.

I didn't date often, mainly because I never had the time, but when I did, I didn't bother waiting around to see if the guy knew how to get me off. I could usually tell within the first three minutes, and that was when they were usually finishing and pulling out with a condom filled with their release, not worrying about whether I had mine.

But Rich wasn't like that. There was something different about him, and that worried me. I was so quick to fall for his touch that I worried about what would happen if I never experienced this with anyone else. I knew that whatever this thing was that was happening between us was only temporary. A fling, for lack of a better word, and it would be over once I left and returned to Phoenix.

I could feel his butt cheeks clenching as he drove in deeper, my nails scratching his skin with need. His mouth lowered to find my nipple again, driving me wild. I could tell that he was getting close to coming, but instead of just pounding into me and getting off, he slowed his thrusts and began rubbing his thumb over my clit again.

"Come with me," he whispered, nipping my ear before returning his mouth to my other nipple. "Now."

I pinched my eyes shut harder, allowing my nails to dig deeper into his plump ass cheeks. I could feel the tease of another orgasm and desperately wanted it. He seemed to sense my frustration when I couldn't come easily this time and pulled his finger away.

I was about to tell him not to worry about it since I'd already had two, but before I could say anything, he pulled out and lowered himself between my legs. His tongue was hot against my sensitive flesh, lapping at the wetness before clamping down on my clit and sucking.

I almost bucked off the dresser, my nerve endings skyrocketing out of control as he continued his torture, bringing me even closer to climax.

"Oh, fuck!" I panted, reaching down to grab a handful of his hair.

He continued sucking, his tongue mercilessly working over me as I tightened around him seconds before allowing it to wash over and consume me. I knew he could feel it happening by his chuckle as I spasmed and clenched.

I cried out, my moans captured by his mouth as he crawled back up my body and sank inside me again. It didn't take long before he came, his body jerking violently with his release. Once he was done, he pulled out and helped me down as we tried to catch our breath.

"That was amazing," I breathed.

"It was," he agreed, still panting. "But next time, you come when I say so."

"Next time?" I questioned, laying down on the air mattress and smiling when he joined me.

"We're stuck here for a while until the storm passes. The power is out, and I don't know about you, but I think this is a fun way to pass the time."

I chewed my lower lip, trying to keep from giggling. He was right, and I couldn't say I minded having mind-blowing sex with a handsome stranger until the weather cleared.

"What about when we run out of condoms?" I asked, knowing that was highly likely, given that he was just staying up here to work on the renovations and probably didn't need a ton of condoms.

"We won't. Lucky for us, I stopped by Costco to stock up on supplies while I was in town. They happened to have a bulk box of condoms, so I grabbed them as a gag gift for my brother."

"Well, that's convenient, isn't it?" I teased, allowing him to pull me closer and wrap his body around mine. Cuddling with a gorgeous man in a room lit solely by candlelight wasn't a bad way to spend Christmas Eve.

Eleven
Rich

It was nothing short of a Christmas miracle to wake up with the power back on, given the storm that had rolled through. With the lights on, it gave me the perfect view of Lucy's amazing body as she slept sprawled out on the air mattress. The thin sheet barely covered her heavy breasts, the hardened nipples peeking over the top, begging to be sucked.

I felt my cock stiffen and shifted beside her to adjust myself. We had sex three times last night, and I still felt like I couldn't get enough of her. While I'd had my fair share of women, no one had ever come close to Lucy. She was a breath of fresh air, and I wanted to inhale and never let it out.

Last night was better than the night before in that she didn't assault me. She did roll over, and the next thing I knew, she was sitting on my cock, grinding over it until I woke up enough to put a condom on so she could fuck me. She wasn't sleeping, and I definitely wasn't going to complain about missing some sleep if it meant I got to be inside her.

Wanting to let her rest some more, I quietly rolled off the air mattress and went to the kitchen to start breakfast. Half an hour later, I heard her footsteps coming down the hall and felt a grin spreading across my cheeks.

"Good morning," I greeted, feeling her hand as it gently tickled my skin beneath the t-shirt I had thrown on. "The power is back on, so I'm making breakfast. Anything special you'd like?"

She leaned up and placed a kiss on my cheek.

"Good morning to you, too. Whatever you're making is fine with me. Can I help with anything?"

I turned my head and raised an eyebrow.

"Do you know how to make toast?"

She pulled her head back as if she were truly offended.

"It's toast! How hard can it be?"

I grinned and nodded to the counter where the toaster was tucked into the corner beside a fresh loaf of bread I had picked up at the store before the storm hit.

She worked on making toast while I finished up the omelets. They weren't anything fancy, but it sounded better than scrambled eggs. Part of me hated that it was Christmas morning and I didn't have a gift to give her. Then I had to remind myself that I hadn't planned to spend Christmas up here in the first place and that even if I had, I definitely hadn't expected to have company.

I flipped the omelet one last time before transferring it to a plate with sausage and hash browns. She brought a few slices of toast over a few minutes later and set them down while I cooked the next omelet. It was different cooking with her in the kitchen, especially with how little time we'd spent together. But it was fun to move around each other, grabbing what we needed and setting it on the table to enjoy another meal together.

When I turned to join her at the table, I stopped and felt my heart skip a beat to see it covered in a red tablecloth with some decorations we'd found in the box last night. There was a small vase filled with artificial poinsettias and two pine-scented green candles beside it. The table was beautiful, but it was dull compared to the girl sitting at it, shining like the brightest fucking star in the universe.

"Merry Christmas," she said cheerfully, extending her arms to show me what she had done.

"Merry Christmas. It looks beautiful."

But not as beautiful as you.

I wanted to spit out the constant compliments floating through my head, but I knew it would be better if I didn't. Lucy was only here for a few days, and then she would be heading back to Phoenix, back to a demanding job that would leave her little to no time for a relationship. Not that she had ever said she was interested in one, but I also wasn't the kind of guy who did the whole casual hookup thing aside from this.

It wasn't like I could expect this thing between us to work once she was gone. Lucy even admitted herself that she hadn't been back to Cedar Point in a while. Aside from a quick weekend trip with her brother and his family last year, it had been a few years since she'd been back. Why would I think that that would change for me? It wouldn't, and I needed to keep reminding myself of that.

"I didn't have a gift to give you, so I thought I could at least make it *feel* like Christmas," she explained when an awkward silence fell between us.

"I woke up feeling the same way," I said with a chuckle as I took my seat across from her. "Didn't have a gift for you either, and I don't think I've ever had a single Christmas where I've spent it with someone and didn't have something to give them."

"Me too. Though I usually stay in Phoenix for Christmas because work is insanely busy with holiday specials. My family and I mail our gifts to each other, and then I try to find time in the evening to FaceTime them so we can thank each other for the gifts."

"Isn't that lonely?" I asked, taking a bite of sausage.

She swallowed hard and looked down at her plate.

"Honestly? Yeah, I guess it is. I didn't realize how much I missed celebrating Christmas until last night when we decorated the tree together. It used to be my favorite holiday when I was a little girl."

"What changed?"

"Life." She shrugged. "My parents have always been workaholics, so it didn't faze me when we stopped spending the holidays together. I always knew that our family Christmas celebrations would stop once my grandpa passed. I guess I never realized how much I missed them until now."

"I'm sorry."

I wanted to reach across the table and hug the sadness until it lifted and the beautiful green returned to her eyes.

"It is what it is."

"Why don't you talk to your family and see if they want to start spending the holidays together again? I know your grandma would absolutely love it."

"It's not that easy," she sighed heavily. "My parents are so stuck in their ways that they won't change. My brother has his family, and they always have plans with his wife's side of the family, so it would be hard getting them together. I know my Nana is by herself, and I think the only thing that keeps me sane is knowing that she has her friends at the community center that keep her company. She always talks about how much fun she has there and how they do so much stuff for the holidays."

"She would leave all of that behind in a heartbeat if you told her you wanted to spend it with her," I said softly. "I know she misses the family holidays too, Lucy."

She studied her food, not bothering to eat it as she lowered her head and refused to look at me. I hated overstepping, but I felt she needed to know she wasn't the only one who missed it.

"A lot has changed since we lost my grandpa," she said sadly, her eyelashes lifting as she looked at me. "I thought I had to find a job that I loved and throw everything that I had at it, but I didn't even take the time to make sure that I *loved* this one before throwing everything I had at it. And do you know what the worst part is?"

She laughed, but I could tell it wasn't a happy one—it was the kind of laugh you have right before you lose your shit.

"What is the worst part?"

She leaned back in her chair and inhaled heavily before releasing it in one heavy breath.

"I fucking hate my job."

My eyebrows shot up, caught off guard by her statement.

"What?"

"It's true, I fucking hate my job," she laughed, covering her mouth.

"Then quit. Find something else."

"I can't do that."

"Why not?" I leaned back in the chair and wiped my mouth with a napkin. "If you hate your job, find something you love and quit."

"It's easier said than done. I have no idea what I even want to do. What I would be good at. I've spent so long working my way up the corporate ladder that I didn't bother to look around and make sure this was where I wanted to be. I make great money, but work my ass off and work so many hours that I don't have a life outside of work."

"Do you have any hobbies?" I asked, hoping that maybe that would give me some insight into what she liked to do so I could offer some ideas for new job opportunities.

"I haven't had time for anything in so long, I can't even remember. All I know is work, work, work."

"Well then, I guess it's a good thing you got stranded here."

"Why?" A grin pulled across her face, matching the mischievous one on mine. "What does that mean?"

"It means that you're in for a real treat because I'm buckets of fun." I gave her a playful wink as the wheels in my mind started spinning.

A VERY MERRY KISSMAS

Twelve
Lucy

"You owe me big," I said, lifting the card to see how much.

"Ugh," he groaned, covering his face. "How much is it this time?"

"Well, with a hotel, you're looking at $1275. You'd think you would learn to stay away from Pacific Avenue, my friend."

He looked through his small stash of cash, both of us knowing he didn't have enough to pay what he owed for landing on my property.

"I'm a bit short," he said with a lopsided grin. "Would you, by chance, be willing to settle this with sexual favors?"

I ignored the spark that ignited between my thighs and shook my head no. I had been a total shark in this game, beating him three times in a row. It was like he was a glutton for punishment because he refused to back down and kept demanding a rematch. But that was probably because he was able to pay with sexual favors in the first match—not that I was complaining after my fourth orgasm.

"Fine," he sighed, looking over the board to see if he had anything else left to sell.

I grinned smugly, knowing that I had won another round.

"I can feel you watching me with those judgmental eyes," he teased, briefly glancing at me before returning his focus to the game.

"Hey, I'm just waiting for you to give up and admit you lost again."

"I let you win."

"Oh, really?" I arched an eyebrow and folded my arms over my chest.

"Yeah, you know, *anything* to cheer you up."

The dimple in his cheek was even more prominent the deeper his grin spread as he leaped across the floor and tackled me, tickling my sides as I struggled to contain my laughter.

"That's cheating!" I squealed, loving the way his body felt on top of mine.

"No way." He dug his fingers into my side, pressing harder against me as I laughed and struggled to get free. "The only cheater in this room is the one who won four games of Monopoly in a row. There's no way you're just that good."

"What can I say?" I said breathlessly, giving in and allowing him to pin my arms over my head as he laid on me. "I've always loved the game. I've been the reigning champion in my family since I was seven."

"Really?"

I nodded and felt my body start to relax again.

"I've always loved real estate, and playing Monopoly was always intriguing because I loved its strategy. I think that taught me a lot about what I needed to know in my current job. It's the same strategies I find myself using at work, and that's the only thing I love about my job."

He rolled off me and sat up, giving me a puzzled look.

"Why don't you do that?"

"Do what?" I frowned, sitting up beside him.

"Why don't you quit your job and go into real estate instead?"

"Ha!" I snorted. "There's no way I can just quit my job and move into a different field. Plus, I would have to study and pass an exam to be a licensed realtor. Where would I find the time to do that?"

"You'd have plenty of time if you quit," he said with a shrug of his shoulder.

"Okay, but how am I supposed to pay my bills without a job? I know I beat you four times in Monopoly, but even you have to admit that it wouldn't be a sound financial decision to give up a steady stream of income for something unknown. Phoenix is brutal; there's no way I could afford to live there without the income I currently have."

He nodded, but I could tell there was something he wanted to say but wouldn't.

"I appreciate the suggestion, really. It's just not as easy to make that big of a change. My life is too busy, too complicated."

"And you hate it," he blurted out.

I pulled my head back, slightly offended.

"I'm sorry, but you do. You've admitted it yourself."

"I said there were things I didn't like about it, but I never said that I *hated* it."

"You said you hate your job," he said sharply. "And that you missed spending the holidays with your family. Come on, Lucy, is there anything you actually love about your life? You don't have to lie to me, and you definitely shouldn't keep lying to yourself."

I paused momentarily and thought about it, frustration mounting when I couldn't think of a single thing I loved about my life right now.

"No," I sighed, hating the way I felt right now. "There's nothing I love about it."

He leaned forward and held my chin between his fingers.

"Then why not start over and make it something you love?"

"How?" I asked, not pulling away from his touch.

"Move back to Cedar Point. Live with your grandma for a bit or stay up here with me. You know as well as I do that things aren't as expensive up here, and your grandma isn't going to let you pay rent regardless of who you stay with. You can find your happiness again, Lucy. You just have to try."

Thirteen
Rich

Lucy didn't say much after I asked her to move back to Cedar Point. I couldn't blame her, though, given that I'd sprung the idea on her and asked her to move in with me to a house I didn't even own.

What the hell was wrong with me?

She was what was wrong with me. She'd gotten under my skin in a matter of days, and now I couldn't imagine not having her with me. I wanted to spend every day with her, watching her laugh and every night making love to her.

By lunchtime, we'd both sat down to eat, though we didn't say much other than some small talk about the storm outside. The power had stayed on for a while, so I felt confident that it wouldn't go out again. That also meant that the worst part of the storm was over, and Lucy would be able to leave and go back to Phoenix sooner than I wanted her to.

Needing some space to clear my head, I went and took a long, hot shower after cleaning up the mess from lunch. When I went back to the living room, I found Lucy on the floor in front of the entertainment center, searching for something in one of the cabinets.

"What are you doing?" I asked, sitting on the arm of the couch so I didn't crowd her.

"Looking for something," she said quietly, picking up an old photo album and looking at the cover before putting it back. "There it is!" She got up and took it to the kitchen table, inviting me to join her.

"This was the first Christmas up here that I remember. I was five and so disappointed that Santa wouldn't come to our house if we weren't there. My parents tried desperately to convince me otherwise, but I wouldn't listen and was in a complete meltdown when we arrived. My grandpa pulled me up onto his knee and asked what was wrong. When I explained it to him, he simply nodded and said he understood.

"We sat down for dinner, and I thought it was odd how quickly he ate before he excused himself from the table. Once we were done cleaning up, we sat in the living room, watching a movie on the TV while keeping warm by the fire. Suddenly, there was a heavy thud outside and then a loud knock on the door. When my dad opened it, Santa was there with a heavy bag filled with presents."

My cheeks split as I listened to the story, knowing exactly where she was going with the story.

"I waited my turn and sat on Santa's lap, doubting that he was the real thing. When I told him that, he tipped his head back and laughed. I told him that Santa was supposed to come down the chimney, not the front door. Do you know what he said to that?"

"What?"

"You're the one who lit the fire. I wasn't going to burn my ass off to get these gifts to you!"

We both burst into laughter, Lucy blotting the corners of her eyes as tears formed.

"My grandma scolded him, then realized she was about to blow his cover and stopped. I hadn't noticed that it was him because I was so stunned that Santa had said *ass*."

"That was nice of him to do that for you."

"He was the nicest guy I've ever known. He'd give the shirt off his back to someone if they needed it."

"Was he already planning to dress up as Santa?"

"No," she laughed even harder. "No one had even given it any thought because my parents usually took us to the mall on Christmas Eve to see Santa before he left to deliver gifts. Since we didn't go to the mall, they completely forgot about it. My grandpa used to dress up as the Santa down in Cedar Point, so he already had a suit."

"Where did he get the gifts from then?"

"That's the hilarious part," she giggled. "He took them from the stash my grandma had hidden for Christmas morning. She chewed him out for messing up her piles and not asking beforehand."

"Sounds like it was a fun time, though."

"It really was. That was when my parents seemed happy and weren't constantly on their phones, checking in for work. Most of my memories of Christmases after that are of my grandparents and brother. I know my parents were there, but I don't remember much about them being there."

"I'm sorry. That sucks."

She shrugged and flipped the page, smiling as memories came through with the pictures.

"I used to love coming up here."

Her voice had so much sadness that it pulled at my heart and made it ache for her.

"Life was so much easier, and I used to tell myself it was because it was a vacation. Life is always better when you're on vacation and not stuck in the daily rut you need a break from. But part of me wonders if life really is just easier up here. Away from the masses of people. The chaos. The unfulfilled void that lingers around you."

I shifted in the seat beside her, folding my hands in front of me as I tried to figure out how to say what I wanted.

"I love my life in Cedar Point. It's calm and predictable, but that's what I love about it. I take breaks and go fishing at the lake during the summer, or sometimes I take a few days to go skiing in the winter. But other than that, there's nothing else that I crave or feel like I'm missing."

Other than you now that I've met you.

"That must be nice," she teased, bumping her elbow with mine.

"It is. And I wasn't lying when I said that you could have all of that too. Move back to Cedar Point, Lucy. Start over and give yourself a second chance. Give *us* a chance."

Her fingers trembled as I reached over and covered her hand with mine.

"That's a lot to ask for, Rich."

My stomach sank, along with my hopes and dreams of having her with me.

A VERY MERRY KISSMAS

Fourteen
Lucy

Things felt off and strained between Rich and me after I declined his invitation to stay with him. It wasn't that I didn't want to say yes and jump on the opportunity of a lifetime. I was scared, and I didn't want him to see me fail if things didn't work out how I needed them to.

We kept our distance for a few days while I stayed stuck on my phone, dealing with emails and taking calls while I worked remotely. The roads were still being cleared, so I had to wait for them to get all the way to the top of the mountain. But my work didn't care about any of that since my holiday vacation was technically over on their end. Every night I was drained from the overwhelming amount of things piled up on my plate, and I hated that I had become the same grumpy person I was back in Arizona.

Rich was nice enough to give me space and keep his distance while he worked on some of the renovations. We both kept an eye on the weather—me so I could leave and get back to Phoenix, and him so he could leave and celebrate the missed holiday with his family.

I tried not to dwell on the fact that mine hadn't even seemed to realize that they'd missed talking to me on Christmas. Aside from Nana, no one even texted to wish me a Merry Christmas. I FaceTimed her as she'd asked, and she was pleasantly surprised to see Rich and me together as we both wished her a Merry Christmas.

Something pulled tightly in my chest, making me miss the holidays I'd spent at the cabin when I was little. Looking through the photo albums had been wonderful, but they did nothing to replace the emptiness I felt when I thought about returning to Phoenix.

I sat in the recliner, responding to another email that had just come in and was marked urgent. It was after ten o'clock and I should have turned my phone off hours ago. My fingers flew across the keypad, typing a response as a call interrupted me.

"Hello, Jacinda," I said, trying to keep the annoyance out of my tone as I greeted the president of Clutch Cosmetics.

"Lucy, yes, there is an urgent matter that requires your immediate attention. I've sent an email and outlined the portions of the upcoming—"

"It's ten o'clock at night," I blurted out, interrupting her. The tone in my voice grabbed Rich's attention as he put his tape measure away and watched me.

"I'm well aware of the time," she snapped. "But pressing matters call for attention. As the VP, it is your responsibility to—"

"No," I said firmly, standing up and taking a deep breath. "I quit."

I heard a low gasp on the other end.

"Excuse me?"

"I said I quit, Jacinda. You heard me. I quit. I quit you. I quit Clutch Cosmetics. I quit everything."

"You can't just quit," she scoffed. "You need to provide a two-week notice, and you can start that by responding to the email I—"

"No," I interrupted again. "I will not respond to anything. Arizona is an at-will employment state, meaning I have no obligation to provide any notice of my resignation. Which, by the way, is effective immediately."

My fingers trembled as I struggled to hold on to the phone.

"I'm sorry. Let's take a step back and calm down before we make any rash decisions."

"I'm good with my decision. It's final. I'll be in to collect my things in a few weeks once the roads have cleared and I can safely make it back to Phoenix. Until then, do not call, text, or email me unless it's regarding my unpaid PTO and final check. I'll copy you on the email I send to HR, confirming my resignation and the hours of leave I'm entitled to take."

Before she could object, I hung up the phone and tossed it into the chair behind me. Rich rushed over, studying my face as he cupped it in his hands.

"Are you okay?" he asked.

I covered my mouth with trembling fingers.

"I don't know what happened," I laughed nervously. "I've

never quit a job before, but she made me so mad. I just snapped."

"I don't blame you. Enough is enough."

"What am I going to do now?" I could feel the panic coursing through me as I refrained from picking up my phone and calling her to beg for my job back.

"Move in here with me. Take some time to get on your feet again, and then decide what you want to do from there."

"I can't just move in with you," I said with a laugh.

"Why not?"

"Because it's crazy! We don't even know each other, and what if we get tired of being around each other? Plus, I need a real bed soon—no offense."

"None taken. And a *real bed* is being delivered as soon as the rest of the road clears. I got an email from the delivery company tonight, and they think they can get the beds for the guest room and the master bedroom here in two to three days. If you can handle the air mattress for a little longer…"

I worried my lip between my teeth while I considered it. Everything in my life had always been so rigid and perfectly regimented that it felt weird to be so reckless and liberated. But maybe that was *exactly* what I needed. Maybe that was the thing that was holding me back from the happiness I was desperately searching for.

"Okay," I sighed, giving him my biggest smile. "But before we commit to anything, I do have one question to ask you."

"Sure. What is it?"

"Since your name is Richard but your nickname is Dick, does that mean if you take a dick pic, it's really a selfie?"

I tried to keep my face straight to keep the laughter from bursting out of me.

His cheeks split into the most beautiful smile I had ever seen before his head tipped back in laughter. He leaned down and pulled me up from my seat, tickling my sides as he wrapped his arms around me.

"You think you're cute, don't you?" he teased, his mouth nipping at my ear.

"The cutest."

"Indeed." He stepped back for a second and studied my face. "You sure you want to do this?"

"Yes," I replied confidently. "Let's do this!"

<u>Epilogue</u>
Lucy
Six Months Later

"Do we have everything ready?" I asked, rechecking the tote bags.

"Yes. We have everything we need, and if we don't, I can drive back up to get stuff."

"Okay. Sorry, I'm just nervous."

"Don't be. It's going to be fun, you'll see."

I took a deep breath and slowly released it, trying to remind myself that planning a family reunion wasn't a terrible idea.

Instead of having everyone come stay up at the cabin like we used to do, I rented out a few of the cottages that Rich and I were currently managing. It turned out that it wasn't real estate that I loved as much as it was property management.

Shortly after I quit my job as VP of Clutch Cosmetics, Rich went with me to Phoenix to collect my things and terminate the lease on my apartment. It was exhilarating and freeing to walk away from everything, knowing that I was heading down a path that had already made me happy.

I moved in with Rich and helped him with the cabin renovations, surprised by how much I enjoyed the physical side of it. Not only that, but I had a great view of watching him work as well.

Things had been running smoothly, and once the cabin was done, Nana came up to check it out, handing me the keys to my very first house. Rich was renting his house in Cedar Point to a new family in town, which felt like another piece of the puzzle falling into place.

We packed the Jeep full and then headed down to meet everyone at the lake. I'd invited my family, and Rich invited his. It was fun and exciting but also super nerve-wracking, given that I had never met the parents of anyone I was dating, nor had my family ever met any of the guys I dated.

When we pulled up, my brother's truck was already there, and his wife was busy setting up the food under the pop-up tent with Rich's parents. He had a pile of rafts he was working on blowing up while the kids took the time to lather themselves with sunscreen. We were a few minutes late, but I was thankful that everyone had apparently taken the time to introduce themselves, and there didn't seem to be any awkwardness about it. I glanced around, not spotting my parents, even though they had assured me they would be there.

We parked and got out, the humid air wrapping around us. I helped Rich unpack the food stuff before taking it over to the tent while he handled the rest. The energy around us was fun and exciting as everyone prepared for a day at the lake. I loved these trips when I was little, and I had hoped that I could recreate that feeling by calling everyone together for a family reunion.

Nana came over with Rich's grandma, the two constantly looking like they were up to no good. They made it a point to brag about how they succeeded in setting us up and joked that they should start a Cedar Point dating service. They joined us for a few minutes making small talk before heading over to see what kind of trouble the kids were getting into. I opened a bottle of water and took a sip, nearly choking when I spotted my parents' Lexus pull up.

The doors opened, and my mom got out, lifting her hand to shield her eyes as she looked around before spotting me. She gave me a quick wave before pulling her sundress over her head and tossing it into the car.

My dad came around, and I burst into laughter when I spotted the swimsuits they were wearing as they walked toward us, holding hands.

When I sent out the invites to the reunion, I'd included one of my favorite family photos that had been taken at this very lake almost twenty years ago. In the picture, my mom wore a one-piece swimsuit with a giant pineapple stretched across the front, while my dad wore neon pink swim trunks.

It was as if we were reliving that moment as they paraded over, showing off the lookalike swimsuits from the photo.

"Oh, my gosh!" I squealed, pulling them both in for a hug. "Where did you guys find these?"

"Amazon," my mom replied with a laugh. "It turns out you can find almost anything on there."

"I'm so glad you guys could make it. Thank you for coming."

We hadn't talked much about me quitting my job,

mainly because I felt like they must have thought I was a disappointment for not being as dedicated to work as they were. Maybe that was why I felt the need to include Rich's family today, sort of a buffer to keep the attention off of me that I didn't want right now. I just wanted to get back to spending time with my family.

"Thank you for putting this together. Sometimes, it's nice to take a step back and remember where you came from." My mom squeezed my hands while my dad took off running to the dock that everyone loved jumping into the lake from.

"Cannonball!" he yelled before diving in.

"Just like old times," my mom said wistfully before walking around and saying hi to the rest of the family and introducing herself to Rich's.

I stood there grinning like a fool when Rich came up and wrapped his arms around me. I tilted my head to the side to give him access as he planted kisses down my neck.

"You better knock it off, Dick," Nana warned, shaking her finger. "This here is a family establishment, and we won't be having no hankey-pankey business going on."

She turned and pointed her finger at my mom, who shrugged and then winked at us. Nana and Rich's grandma linked arms and snickered like school girls before walking off to grab a beer from the ice chest.

"Be thankful for that, or you wouldn't be here." My mom winked, and I heard a low chuckle deep in Rich's throat behind me.

I felt my cheeks burn as I blushed. My mom turned away, giving us a moment to ourselves.

I lifted my head back and leaned into him.

"Tell me again how you get Dick out of Richard?"

"You ask nicely," he growled, nipping my ear.

"Or maybe I could just tell you how much I love you and that even though your brother may be known as the pitcher with the cutest ass, I still think yours is ten times better."

"I love you too." He leaned in and gently kissed the tip of my nose.

"My ass is *the best,* and people literally spend money to come see it in action," his brother teased as he passed by, eavesdropping at the perfect time, given that I hadn't seen him walk up on us. He grabbed a beer and headed to the dock to join everyone else.

"People would pay to see mine if I asked," Rich called out, earning a middle finger in the air from his brother as he kept walking and didn't look back.

"And if anyone has the best ass—it's you. Now let's leave so I can take you home and ravish it." He wiggled his eyebrows playfully.

I giggled as his fingers tickled my sides, making everything inside me feel alive again. I thought I had everything I wanted out of life until I met Rich and he taught me how to live again.

＊＊＊＊＊＊＊＊＊＊＊＊＊＊＊＊＊＊

Looking for more steamy holiday novellas?

Be sure to check these out!

Sugarplum Falls Series:

Blame It On The Mistletoe

https://books2read.com/u/bw1rqe

Blame It On The Eggnog

https://books2read.com/u/38PPY6

Blame It On The Candy Canes

https://books2read.com/u/31DNo7

Blame It On The Blizzard

https://books2read.com/u/b6z6XE

Want to hang out and chat about books?

Come find me in my reader group on Facebook!

https://www.facebook.com/groups/2945710968775398/

Other Books By Samantha Baca
Romantic Suspense

The Haven Brook Series (small-town romantic suspense):
'Til Death Do Us Part (Haven Brook Book 1)
The Cradle Will Fall (Haven Brook Book 2)
The Ties That Bind (Haven Brook Book 3)
A Very Haven Christmas (Haven Brook Book 4- Novella)
Three Strikes, You're Gone (Haven Brook Book 5)

The Dark Shadows Trilogy (romantic suspense):
Five Steps Ahead (Dark Shadows Book 1)
Ten Seconds Too Late (Dark Shadows Book 2)
Against The Clock (Dark Shadows Book 3)

Broken (Standalone)

Romantic Comedy

Beaumont Creek Series
Just One Time | Second Chances | Third Time's The Charm | Four-ever Single | Fifth Wheel

Whiskey Mountain Series
Something To Talk About | Something To Think About | Something To Believe In | Something To Live For

Holiday Novellas

Sugarplum Falls Series
Blame It On The Mistletoe | Blame It On The Eggnog | Blame It On The Candy Canes | Blame It On The Blizzard | Blame It On The Reindeer | Blame It On The Carols | Blame It On The Lattes Blame It On The Secret Santa |
Blame It On The Holidays: A collection of bonus epilogues

The Stone Creek Series
Chocolate Covered Mistletoe (Stone Creek Book 1) | Candy Coated Promises (Stone Creek Book 2) | Pumpkin Spiced Possibilities (Stone Creek Book 3)

Standalone Holiday Novellas
Snow Place To Go | A Very Merry Kissmas | A Christmas Wish | Holiday Hijinks

Standalone Holiday Full Length
Wild Winter

Standalone Books
One Last Wish | Finding Love In Apartment 2C (novella) | Breaking All The Rules (Previously published as: Cocky Counsel: A Hero Club Novel) | All Is Fair In Food And War (novella)

About the Author

Samantha lives in the southwest with her husband and two children, where she enjoys writing, drinking iced coffee, and watching the greatest show of all time—Friends. With over 30 books published, Samantha enjoys writing across several different genres, from steamy romantic suspense to laugh-out-loud spicy romantic comedies. She also has a sweet spot for holiday stories, so grab a blanket and get ready to binge some of the sweetest—yet spicy—holiday romance your heart can handle!

Samantha loves connecting with her readers, so here's a list of where you can find her:

Facebook Reader Group:

https://www.facebook.com/groups/2945710968775398/

Facebook:

https://www.facebook.com/AuthorSamanthaBaca

Instagram:

https://instagram.com/author_samantha_baca

Webpage:

www.samanthabaca.com

Goodreads:

http://www.goodreads.com/authorsamanthabaca

Books2Read:

https://books2read.com/ap/RQAYK9/Samantha-Baca